Chakra

Chakra

A Novel

Richard Bulliet

Chakra
A Novel

iUniverse books may be ordered through booksellers or by contacting:

iUniverse LLC
1663 Liberty Drive
Bloomington, IN 47403
www.iuniverse.com
1-800-Authors (1-800-288-4677)

ISBN: 978-1-4620-4955-4 (sc)
ISBN: 978-1-4620-4956-1 (e)

Printed in the United States of America

iUniverse rev. date: 06/27/2014

In memory of
Lucy Bulliet
1939-2011

Prologue

At the airport, waiting for her helicopter, Christine Sens pans her camera across the Nukus skyline outlined by the first dim glow of dawn: Stalinist concrete apartment blocks and the domes of half-collapsed mosques. The run-down capital of this impoverished post-Soviet republic will have a part to play in her photo-essay about environmental catastrophe in the heart of Central Asia. But only if the helicopter pilot she's hired for an exorbitant fee gets her to the Aral Sea wasteland in time to see those same dawn rays create bizarre shadows as they pick up the wrecks of grounded fishing boats on the salt-encrusted plain that was once the floor of the sea.

The Uzbek pilot gives her the once over as she climbs aboard. The close-cropped blonde hair, svelte figure, and prominent cheekbones say model, but the work boots and khaki vest bulging with camera equipment overrule the image. She sits behind him and snaps pictures from either side as they approach. The black expanse of the water contrasts sharply with the gray luminosity of the surrounding salt crusted plain as the sun's first rays rake the landscape. As Christine had hoped, the grounded fishing boats listing on their sides cast strangely elongated shadows.

"Down." The pilot follows her instruction.

"Now turn right." The helicopter banks to give her an angle on a ship with a bizarrely canted crane.

"What's that long thin line?" The pilot does not respond. "What's that line on the ground?"

"No line. Just salt."

"Yes, there was a line. A long faint curve. It flashed for a second when we were turning, but I'm sure I saw it. You didn't see it?"

"No line on ground."

"Go up and take the curve again." The pilot earns his fee. As they come around, "There! See it? The sun makes it glint. Very thin, curves up all the way . . . well, all the way as far as I can see." Her camera clicks repeatedly.

"There is line," says the pilot.

"Go around again and follow it up. I want more pictures." *Pictures that will make me famous*, thinks Christine.

Chapter One

Rejep Muratbey let his jowly face sag onto his more than ample chest. "Is my fault. My fault all of this." Sunk in puffy sockets, his porcine eyes made their halting way down a column of the international edition of TIME magazine. Its cover featured the photo that had shocked the world: a perfect circle against an irregular whitish background with what looked to be cross-hairs disappearing into the irregular dark area of the Aral Sea. The headline in garish red: CENTRAL ASIAN MYSTERY: "THE GREAT ARRAY"

Lee Ingalls, in her reluctant role as English tutor of the first and thus far only president of the Ferghana Republic, poured tea into small, slender glasses and held her tongue. During twelve months in Kokand, Ferghana's ramshackle capital in the eastern reaches of the old Uzbekistan SSR, she had learned to flavor her tea with fresh blackberry leaves. She had also learned from her husband Donald, who fancied himself a diplomat, that silence was the strategy of choice when high officials waxed stupid or vented their spleen. This had been a hard lesson for someone who prided herself on speaking her mind regardless of circumstances.

As Lee concentrated on the tea ritual, President Muratbey furtively shifted his eyes to her elegant fingers and perfectly manicured but unlacquered nails. And from there, with unmistakably lecherous purpose, to the pale skin of her forearms below the sleeves of her blue shirtwaist dress. The burly politician touched one thick hand theatrically to his broad forehead while receiving his tea with the other. "I am the fault. I am cause of my country's fall-down."

"Downfall, Mr. President. You must remember. We worked on that word. Also, you can say 'I am at fault,' but you can't say 'I am the fault.'"

"Lee, you are so wonderful," moaned Muratbey, "but I cannot concentrate on the English, Lee, on a day when that . . . that . . . *tavshan boku* . . . what is the English word?"

"Politely, *tavshan boku* means 'rabbit dropping.' If you really want to be rude, however, the more coarse translation would be 'rabbit shit,'. But no one would call someone this in English." Though punctilious in her own speech, Lee took perverse pleasure in instructing the President in rude and even obscene English expressions. She felt she was helping him find his proper level.

"Thank you. I remember. On a day when rabbit shit Vahidoglu, may his mother be . . ."

Lee straightened her already erect posture and caught the president's attention with a prim clearing of her throat. At thirty-eight, with her naturally curly brown hair drawn back from her angular face, she channeled both the look and the manners of her Connecticut patrician mother. She had more than once relied on this not entirely genuine surface gentility to keep the President on task. "Mr. President, I told you I disapprove of the expression you were about to use, and of any expression suggesting rudeness to women or referring to their personal parts. I'm under no obligation to teach you English, and . . ."

"I am million times sorry, Lee." Remorse fairly oozed from the president's tiny eyes. "I will remember. You are so kind let me practice my English. But on day when rabbit shit Vahidoglu receive half billion dollars from big American capitalist I must be permitted. In Soviet time, I was in government in Tashkent. Vahidoglu was janitor. Emptied ashtrays. Now he calls himself President."

The agreement between the Carpenter-Beckenbaugh Corporation, America's largest dealer in farm commodities, and President Ahmet Vahidoglu's Karakalpak Republic had headlined the noon news on CNN. Rebuffing American, Russian, and UN proposals for scientific missions to study the sensational Great Array on the floor of the Aral Sea situated in the republic that had been carved out of the western reaches of the old Uzbekistan SSR, President Vahidoglu had sold exclusive exploration rights to Carpenter-Beckenbaugh Corp.

for half a billion dollars. The videoclip contrasting the portliness and expansive personality of the billionaire-sportsman Hayes Carpenter with the cadaverous physique and sunken gray eyes of the Karakalpak president had visually reinforced the headline of mega-rich American capitalism coming to the rescue of post-Soviet Central Asian poverty.

For Lee Ingalls, the news report, like the initial discovery of the Great Array by a French woman photographer three weeks earlier, was a matter of no interest. In her scholarly moments, which she deemed her real life, nothing more recent than 1000 BC counted for much. So while His Excellency the President of Ferghana performed his ritual of outrage and self-mortification, she sat calmly, savoring the subtle fruity flavor of her tea and the geometrical patterns of the Turkmen carpets on the bungalow walls. Cut his rant short, or give in to his obvious desire to detail his professed guilt? Which option would get him out the door faster?

When husband Donald had exultantly told her that the president of the republic wanted to practice English with her, Lee's take had gone the other direction. Anyone with eyes, she explained, could see that President Muratbey, whom she had met twice at U.S. embassy receptions, was an overweight, ego-centered nitwit. "But he's the president of the republic," Donald had argued. "He's important."

"Not to me," said Lee. And in truth, a first-name acquaintanceship with the ruler of a destitute mountain republic in the middle of nowhere had afforded her little pleasure.

Donald had only made things worse with his, "You are developing a closer relationship with the President than any other American."

Not as close as the pig desires, thought Lee as she wondered at Donald's obtuseness in failing to perceive Muratbey's flirtatious designs.

"And just what good does that closeness do, Donald? Muratbey is so desperate for American money, he'd order the Star-Spangled Banner sung at soccer matches if Ambassador Bane asked him to."

"Lee, we are diplomats. This is what we do."

"Donald, we are not diplomats. Donald. You are a Commerce Department small business advisor. You once had a career selling the world's best toilet valves. Then you decided to share your business acumen with the underdeveloped world. That makes you part of Kokand's embassy community, but it does not make you a foreign service officer. As for me, it goes without saying that I am not a diplomat. I have never been diplomatic in my life. What I was before coming to this God forsaken backwater was a lady scholar of leisure."

Lee's female chums found her tartness of speech and manner utterly charming. So did Donald . . . some of the time. At six-foot-three he towered over Lee's slight, five-foot-five frame so he had accustomed himself to feeling in charge even when he ended up, as he usually did, on the losing end of their verbal fencing matches.

"What you were before we came here, my love, was an unemployed Ph.D. One of about a zillion in the United States. But what you are now, and will be as long as I am assigned to this embassy with the charge of spreading the gospel of free enterprise among the heathen, is an official American personage who is expected to behave exactly like diplomatic personnel."

President Muratbey's raspy voice penetrated Lee's reverie. He had finished his tea and resumed his litany of self-accusation—"Is really all my fault"—in a tone so plaintive that Lee decided to take pity on him.

She looked into his eyes with detached curiosity as she would a lemur in a zoo. "Mr. President, you keep saying that. Do you want me to ask you in what way it is your fault?"

"I held back the water."

"The water?"

"Yes. The river water. The Confederation have agreement . . ."

" . . . has an agreement . . ."

" . . . has agreement for so many cubic meters each month. Water goes into Aral Sea. Rabbit shit Vahidoglu insults me. I hold back one-third the water. Aral Sea in Karakalpakstan dry up. So-called Great Array is found in sea. Rabbit shit get half billion dollars. If I give more water, no Great Array."

Lee Ingalls' lack of patience with tedious mental processes had served her poorly in the dog-eat-dog academic job market, but she ascribed her failure to secure a professorship to the obscurity of her field of study. Demand for instruction in Sanskrit, India's ancient religious and literary language, barely existed in a post-Cold War intellectual climate that saw little point in studying foreign areas. Of the handful of scholars who, like Lee, devoted their efforts to Vedic, the ancestral form of Sanskrit used in the ancient hymns to the Indic gods, scarcely a one held a full-time teaching post. Rather than being discouraged, however, Lee took pride in belonging to a tiny band of pure but unemployable scholars.

"Forgive me, Mr. President, but what you are saying makes no sense."

"I should say, 'If I . . . had given? . . . more water.'"

"No, it's not the English this time, though 'had given' would have been better. What I mean is that your holding back the water did not cause the Great Array to be found. It only caused it to be found now. The Aral Sea started to dry up in Soviet times and would have continued drying up no matter what you did. The water was squandered on irrigating cotton fields. Therefore the Great Array would surely have been discovered sooner or later. Only a fool would blame himself." She thought of adding, "and you are no fool," but her conscience rebelled.

Muratbey gazed at Lee enigmatically, his saggy eyes somehow expectant. Lee recognized the look. It signaled the end of each tutorial session. It was also the look her father's overweight basset hound had worn at every mealtime, and most times in between. The tutorial pattern never varied: Muratbey would make a dramatic entrance; he and Lee would exchange friendly greetings; they would drink tea and talk about a topic of Muratbey's choosing; Lee would correct his English; and then he would abruptly become melancholy, stare mournfully, and fall silent as if the conversation had somehow failed of its intended conclusion.

As always, his driver was holding the door of the black presidential Volvo as Lee saw the President off from the porch steps. She watched the car back down the driveway and then wandered for a few minutes among the luxuriant rose bushes and fruiting trees that more than made up for the bungalow's decayed state. Meanwhile, on the back seat of his car, President Muratbey shut his eyes and brought her willowy form and intelligent facial expression to mind, resolving, as he did after every lesson, that the next time he would offer to elevate Lee to the status of his mistress.

She was still in her garden pinching wilted blossoms from a rose bush when Donald drove into the driveway.

"Muratbey come today?" he asked after a ritual welcome home kiss.

"Of course. He's very regular. In fact, he seems to like me very much. Perhaps there's not enough for him to do as president now that he's finished restoring the Presidential Palace."

"What did you talk about?"

"I talked about the use of participles. But he insisted on sharing with me his feeling of guilt about impounding river water and thus speeding the discovery of the Great Array. You can imagine my gratitude for his confidence."

Donald's attention had suddenly intensified. "Withholding water? Withholding water is a violation of the 2005 Treaty of Tashkent. Did he say how much he had withheld?" Donald nursed a secret dream that he would one day astound Ambassador Darla Bane with secret intelligence gleaned by his clever wife from her sessions with Muratbey.

"Yes he did say, but I wasn't paying attention." In truth, Lee remembered everything Muratbey had said, but she deplored her husband's transparent effort to turn her into an intelligence source, and even more his presuming that he could keep this intention a secret from her. "Would you like rice with mutton kabobs tonight? . . . or just rice? . . . or just kabobs?"

Chapter Two

As the sound man fixed mikes on his guests and guided the wires under neckties and lapels, Paul Henning clipped on his own microphone and adjusted his earbud. He scanned the opening lines on the teleprompter. "Dotty, are we going with Great Array?" He nodded at his producer's response in his ear. "What happened to Mystery Circle?" He nodded again.

The director, wearing a full headset, spoke to the guests. "You'll all be looking at Paul at the opening when we have a profile shot of the group, and then look at Paul or one another as you speak." He looked abstracted as he listened to something on his headset. "We're ready," he announced. He counted down the last four seconds silently with his fingers.

Paul Henning brightened and leaned slightly into the camera. "Good morning and welcome to Sunday Special. I'm Paul Henning, and today we'll be talking about what is being called 'The Great Array,' the giant circle discovered just one month ago under the Aral Sea in Central Asia. Joining me this morning are Christine Sens, a photographer for Agence France Presse; Margie Hicks of the Reuters News Agency; Shanelle Whittaker, Communications Director for the Carpenter-Beckenbaugh Corporation, and Dr. Abraham Stein of the Council on Foreign Relations. As everyone in the world knows, portions of a giant circle fourteen miles across were spotted one month ago on the floor of an evaporating sea in the Karakalpak Republic, way out in Central Asia. You are looking at the first pictures of that circle as they were shot from a helicopter flying at an altitude of four hundred feet. Christine Sens was on that helicopter. Christine can you tell us what it was like to make this discovery? You were the first to spot the Great Array, weren't you?"

Looking more the model today than the news photographer, Christine Sens smiled at the word "discovery." "Yes, the first. It was the angle of the sun made it visible. At first just a flash, but once the pilot and I had gotten a fix on it, we were able to trace it."

"Tell us what it was like?"

"We fly over the sea in the helicopter to see the environmental damage. The Aral Sea is big environmental disaster, yes? Then, very suddenly, I see it. The Array was very hard to make out in my original picture. But once I found the right filter, it became clear. Just a thin circle with the crosshairs, like aiming a rifle."

"It must have been very exciting."

"Very exciting."

"Now this part we're showing on the monitor, tell us what we're looking at, Christine."

"That is where the north-south crossbar joins the circle. You see very faint dark lines going out at the angle of ninety degrees. And then you see the top one meeting the circle."

"Now we're switching to a satellite photo that's been enhanced to show both the exposed and what everyone assumes to be the still underwater parts of the Array."

"Yes. We were flying over portion where most of the sea has dried up. Very white from the salt. One third of Array is still under water, including the middle where the straight lines cross. But it is a perfect circle."

"Very exciting discovery, Christine. Thank you."

Paul pivoted smoothly to his other side. "Margie Hicks, you've been covering Central Asia for Reuters News Agency since the '04 Uzbek crisis. Tell us about the Aral Sea and the Karakalpak Republic. These are places most of us don't know anything about."

Weathered and tired looking even with camera makeup, Margie Hicks had no use for television journalism's obsession with combining news and good looks. "As you know, Paul, when the Soviet Union broke up in 1991, five republics became independent in its southern area between the Caspian Sea and the Chinese frontier."

"The Stans."

"That's right. Kazakhstan, Uzbekistan, Kyrgyzstan, and so forth. To make a long story short, when I first went to the area in '04, Uzbekistan was breaking up, and the UN was actively trying to head off a civil war. In the end, Uzbekistan was split into three smaller states by the Treaty of Tashkent in 2005."

"They would be the Karakalpak Republic in the west, the Tashkent Republic in the middle, and the Ferghana Republic in the east."

"Right, Paul. Each one seemingly poorer and more economically desperate then the other."

"So why is this political background important for the Great Array, Margie?"

"Because the bone of contention that broke up Uzbekistan was water and investment. The country depended on two river systems, both of which empty into the Aral Sea. The sea had been drying up for years because the Soviets diverted river water to irrigate cotton fields. Already by 1997 it was no longer a single body of water because a ridge across its northern portion had become dry land. Then came the '05 treaty, and things got worse, primarily because President Rejep Muratbey of the Ferghana Republic cheated on the treaty and illegally withheld water."

"And why did he do that, Margie?"

"The best guess is that he personally despises Ahmet Vahidoglu, the president of the Karakalpak Republic. They are old Communist Party rivals from the Soviet era, and they almost went to war against each other in 2004. Withholding water was a form of economic warfare designed to damage the Karakalpak cotton crop, on which the Karakalpaks rely for foreign exchange."

"Let me just break away there, Margie." Paul looked squarely into the camera. "This past week President Ahmet Vahidoglu has been the man of the hour announcing on Tuesday a spectacular deal with American businessman Hayes Carpenter. The Carpenter-Beckenbaugh Corporation, which Mr. Carpenter founded and still heads, will donate a half billion dollars to the treasury of the Karakalpak Republic in return for exclusive rights to explore the Great Array and exploit any discoveries that might be made. Never before in history have exploration rights been sold in such a manner.

To find out more about Mr. Carpenter and the deal he has made we have with us Shanelle Whittaker, Communications Director for the Carpenter-Beckenbaugh Corporation." Paul pivoted in his seat and fixed the attractive, brown-skinned woman on his right with a gleaming white smile. "Shanelle, welcome to Sunday Special."

"I'm delighted to be here, Paul," she replied with a smile that made his look slightly dingy.

"You are Communications Director for the Carpenter-Beckenbaugh Corporation. Your boss has just handed over a huge sum of money for exploration rights in Central Asia. This isn't what people expect of Hayes Carpenter, is it."

Shanelle laughed. "No, I guess it's not, Paul. But Mr. Carpenter has done a lot of different things in his life, and he's not the sort of man who avoids publicity. As you know, besides being CEO and Board Chairman of the Carpenter-Beckenbaugh Corporation, this country's largest dealer in agricultural commodities, Mr. Carpenter is the country's primary private supporter of sport parachuting and sky diving and the publisher of *Freefall* magazine."

"And he parachutes himself."

"As often as he can fit it into his schedule."

"At the age of . . . ?

"Sixty-one last month. He's been jumping for forty years, Paul, ever since he volunteered for paratroop training during the Vietnam War."

"Amazing. Now, what can you tell us about the half billion dollar deal he has negotiated with President Vahidoglu."

"It's going to amount to a lot more than half a billion dollars, Paul. That amount goes directly to the Karakalpak treasury to help support the country's economy and give a boost to its industrialization program. Economic diversification is the only way to overcome dependence on cotton, with all its terrible environmental consequences in terms of pesticide polluted ground water, salt storms blowing off the exposed bed of the Aral Sea, and rampant lung and intestinal disorders. But of course Mr. Carpenter will also be paying the expenses of the expedition itself, which will be quite considerable."

"Are there other terms in the contract that we might be interested in?"

"Not really." Shanelle had learned to lie with disarming ease when it was in Carpenter-Beckenbaugh's interest, and candor about the half billion dollars paid into various out-of-country bank accounts accessible solely to President Vahidoglu was clearly not in Carpenter-Beckenbaugh's interest.

"How was Mr. Carpenter able to pull off this deal. Everyone wanted to explore the Array. But the U.N. failed, Russia failed, the United States failed. President Vahidoglu seemed determined to keep everyone out. Then, suddenly, Hayes Carpenter flies to Nukus, and a deal is announced."

"That's easy to answer, Paul. First, Carpenter-Beckenbaugh is a private corporation, and after three dismal generations of government-dominated enterprise under Soviet rule, President Vahidoglu has developed the deepest respect for private enterprise. His goals are safeguarding national independence, exploring the Great Array quickly and efficiently, and turning a profit for his people. And second, the Carpenter-Beckenbaugh Corporation has been buying Karakalpak cotton for years. President Vahidoglu already knew Mr. Carpenter as a man he could trust."

"They make quite a pair. How about the mission itself?"

"It's pretty straightforward, Paul. Build a circular dike around the center of the Great Array where the crossbars are believed to cross, pump out the water to expose the seafloor, examine any surface features, and then drill down to find out what's underneath."

"How much water has to be pumped out?"

"That's the deepest part of the sea, about fifty feet or sixteen meters deep. And the area to be pumped is a hundred meters across. So that means roughly a hundred and twenty-six thousand cubic meters of water."

"A hole in the sea."

"You've got it, Paul. A hole in the sea." Shanelle liked the sound of the phrase she had dreamed up and fed to Paul before the show.

Paul swiveled to the camera. "We'll be back with more about the hole in the sea on Sunday Special after this."

"You're off," called the director.

Henning turned to his guests with a beaming smile. "That was great. Christine, Margie, Shanelle excellent. Lets continue to keep things short and simple. This is a complicated story, but we only have eight minutes in this next segment."

* * *

The television set in the spacious but barren dining room of the Mehmansaray Hotel in Almaty, Kazakhstan shifted to a commercial for the Hyundai Corporation. At nine-thirty in the evening only three of twenty-eight tables were occupied, testimony to mediocre cooking and worse service dating back to the Soviet era. People who cared about eating well went to one of the city's newer, mafia controlled restaurants. At one table four middle-aged waitresses had been conversing in Russian for hours, stirring themselves only rarely and reluctantly to attend to customer business. At another a German couple dressed in hiking books and rugged camping clothes were discussing their itinerary over an unfolded map.

At the third a man who looked to be some forty years of age sat looking at the CNN broadcast and caressing a liter bottle of vodka, his second of the evening. His beard was reddish, full, and bushy, making it evident that he was not a local Kazakh; but his clothes were of the plainest sort, quite different from the pegged pants and Georgian tunics of the local mafia, the roughing-it look that the German couple shared with most other tourists, or the blocky, Soviet-style, double-breasted suits still popular in Kazakh officialdom. But for his hair color, angry facial features, and protruding belly, the man looked like a Kazakh sheepherder from one of the collective farms turned ranches that reached into the foothills of the mountains. It was known among the waitresses that when he left the hotel every Sunday night, he half limped, half staggered to the edge of the city and disappeared into the dark countryside, but beyond that he was a man of mystery.

"Vodka?" called out Olga, the senior waitress with stringy hair dyed jet black. The man's gaze was fixed on the television set waiting for the end of the commercials. "Nadir!" she shouted. "Vodka?"

Nadir lifted his bottle and wiggled it to indicate he was okay.

* * *

"Back in four," said the director in New York. He counted down with his fingers.

"Welcome back. I'm Paul Henning and on Sunday Special we're discussing last week's announcement of an agreement between the Karakalpak Republic and the Carpenter-Beckenbaugh Corporation for the exploration of what is being called 'The Great Array' underneath the Aral Sea in Central Asia. With me on this portion of our show, Dr. Abraham Stein of the Council on Foreign Relations and Doctor Yasuo Takahashi of Columbia University's Earth Institute." He pivoted to his left. "Dr. Stein, what can you tell us about the political aspect of the pact between Hayes Carpenter and President Vahidoglu?"

Balding and bespectacled in a black suit and red-striped tie, Dr. Stein was the very model of a faceless policy wonk. "Well, that's still a bit of a mystery. It has been suggested, of course, that the Great Array is the remnant of some Soviet effort to deal with the environmental crisis in the Aral Sea area. But the truth is that the Soviet Union never showed the least concern for environmental disasters. It's much more likely, therefore, that the Array has, or had, a military purpose."

"Which the Russian government is now denying."

"Yes. Denying so strongly it almost seems to confirm it."

"Can you suggest for us what military advantages the floor of a landlocked sea in the middle of Central Asia might have?"

"Secrecy would be one obvious advantage, Paul. Totally invisible to satellite or overflight surveillance. The Array is possibly a communications or detection system. Very low frequency waves traveling through the earth, for example, can be used to communicate with submarines, and we know that the Soviets were very interested in tracking U.S. nuclear submarines at sea."

"Fascinating. Tell us a bit now about President Vahidoglu and his unusual reaction to a discovery made on Karakalpak soil."

"Vahidoglu is an old Communist Party official from Soviet days, and he rules with a pretty strong hand. His speeches are a bit on the bombastic side, but at base he consistently follows a shrewd strategy of protecting his country's independence against his rivals within the Uzbek Confederation and against any effort by Russia to reestablish its domination. This is a pretty tough job given that apart from cotton he doesn't have much of an economy. Nevertheless, if the Array *is* a Soviet military project, he surely isn't going to let the Russians in to cover it up unless he gets something in return. But by the same token, he doesn't want the U.S. or the U.N. coming onto his soil and learning things that he might be able to take advantage of if he learns them first. So that makes a deal with a private corporation an unusual but logical undertaking."

"Dr. Stein, is Hayes Carpenter a stalking house for the U.S. government?"

Dr. Stein ventured a scholarly chuckle. "Hardly, Paul. Hayes Carpenter has spoken out against almost everything President Boone Rankin stands for, and he donated heavily to the other side in the last campaign. If the President were ever to go hunting for a tycoon to do a job for him, the last doorbell he's ring would be Hayes Carpenter's."

"Thank you, Dr. Stein. Fascinating."

"Now finally," pivoting right, "I want to ask Doctor Yasuo Takahashi of Columbia University's Earth Institute about the possible scientific implications of the Great Array."

Dr. Takahashi had sounded like a middle-aged man on the telephone during producer Dotty Bennett's pre-interview, but in person he looked disconcertingly like a recent college graduate, complete with long black hair, parted in the middle above almost shaven sides, and baggy casual clothes.

"Thank you, Mr. Henning. To start with, I want to make it very clear what the Great Array is. The circle is made up of very slightly discolored soil. The ring portion and crossbars are only three feet in width. That's why normal air traffic didn't see them when they first began to emerge. Airliners fly too high. And it's also why satellites didn't pick it up. They can see it when they look only at the red end of the spectrum, but otherwise it's too faint. The soil of the ring and crossbars looks slightly dark in photographs because it absorbs red wavelengths. The soil is actually transparent to red light. It absorbs what hits it and presumably could flash red if there were a light source somewhere underground."

"Transparent? You mean red light shines through it? Like glass?"

"Yes, but not in such a way that you could see an image on the other side. The soil is actually almost a powder, and the samples we have available show a crystalline structure that is completely unknown in naturally occurring rock anywhere on Earth."

Paul sensed his audience reaching for their remotes to switch to another channel. "Is it a weapon, as Dr. Stein suggests?"

Dr. Takahashi crooked his head in wonderment at where the question had come from. "Is a toaster a weapon? Mr. Henning, if you don't mind my saying so, the suggestion that the Great Array is a weapon is scientifically ridiculous."

"And why is that Dr. Takahashi?" Henning liked dispute on his show.

"The core samples the Karakalpak Academy of Sciences took in the outer ring and crossbars showed the same crystalline powder down as far as four thousand feet. No known technology is capable of inserting a special soil underground in this way. It is much more likely that the powder built up or was generated gradually from below."

"That makes no sense at all," interrupted Dr. Stein. "Sediments at four thousand feet were deposited hundreds of thousands of years ago. Anything artificial that far down . . ."

"Must have been placed there by aliens from outside our solar system," concluded Takahashi vehemently.

Paul Henning involuntarily rolled his eyes up and wondered how Dotty Bennet could have failed to screen out an obvious space nut. He turned quickly to Shanelle Whittaker. "Shanelle, is Hayes Carpenter searching for a spaceship from prehistoric times under the Aral Sea?"

Shanelle's laugh was artfully light and engaging. "I'm afraid we don't base Carpenter-Beckenbaugh policies on *National Enquirer* stories, Paul. Mr. Carpenter has no assumptions about the expedition beyond looking to see what he can find. But we're not expecting little green men."

Takahashi was visibly agitated. "But scientifically there's no other explanation! The formation isn't natural! The Russians couldn't have done it!"

"Dr. Stein?" said Paul.

"We had a long history during the Cold War of underestimating the Russians. Just because they embarked on some project that we still can't understand, and one that they're still trying to keep secret, doesn't mean we should let our imaginations run away with us."

"We're not talking about runaway imaginations, Mr. Henning," persisted Takahashi. "Whatever is down there has been there for hundreds of thousands if not millions of years. People just feel uncomfortable admitting it."

"Shanelle, any last words?"

"If Hayes Carpenter were here now, Paul, he'd say it doesn't make any difference to him whether the Array was built by Russians or Martians. It's a mystery to be investigated, and let the chips fall where they may."

"And on that note, we conclude another edition of Sunday Special. I'm Paul Henning. Thank you for watching."

The host and guests sat still until the director's hand showed them they were off.

"Dotty!" called Henning as he strode off the set.

The diminutive Sunday Special producer rushed to Paul Henning's side. "He didn't say anything about space aliens on the pre-interview, Paul. Not a word. Just good hard science. He's from Columbia University, for Christ's sake."

"There are more and more of them, Dotty. They're nuts! You have to be more careful. I never want that guy on the show again. Understood?"

"Understood."

Paul caught up with Shanelle removing pancake in the makeup room. "When are we going to have the big man himself on the show, Shanelle."

"You wish."

"Come on. Don't be like that."

"You put as much company money on the line as Hayes has, you have to look at where you're going to get it back."

"So Carpenter's going to market the project?"

"TV, movie, electronic—sewing up everything. I'm just the trailer."

"Think he'll make his money back?"

Shanelle smiled. "He already has," she lied.

Chapter Three

Minister of Defense Pyotr Kalenin gazed out at the salmon pink Moscow Metro station in Arbatskaya Square as he listened to the report. "Your informants are trustworthy, Colonel?"

"Completely. Each of them has many years of flawless service and excellent English. Neither Hayes Carpenter nor President Vahidoglu had any objection to their being assigned as the personal translators of the four Americans, though Vahidoglu is too experienced not to know that they will report to us everything they report to him. I suspect that neither of them cares about keeping secrets."

"Not keeping secrets is a form of publicity, and Mr. Carpenter hungers for publicity. Knowing that his exploration deal has closed us out of any discoveries he might make must give him great pleasure. He is what? Sixty-one years old? Old enough to remember us as the enemies of American big business. What about his three assistants?"

"Pumping the water out of the sea and drilling into the Great Array are being supervised by a black American named Wilson Woodrow."

The minister smiled. "Same as the American president a hundred years ago."

"That, Sir, was the other way around: Woodrow Wilson. Our informant says that Mr. Woodrow's father hated that president and gave his son the name Wilson as a joke. He is technically very competent and has been working at a high level for Chevron in Kazakhstan. He learned to be a diver in the American navy and then worked on oil rigs in Louisiana. A self-made man as the Americans say. More important, he has known Hayes Carpenter since they were young men together traveling through the center of America harvesting grain."

"So he's old."

"Sixty-two."

"And the others?"

"His press advisor is Margie Hicks."

"I've heard of her."

"Her whole career has been reporting on Soviet and post-Soviet matters. Carpenter hired her away from the Reuters News Agency. She knows as much about the Karakalpak Republic and the other members of the Uzbek Confederation as any Russian, including our best intelligence people. The other woman is also African-American, but quite young. Her name is Shanelle Whittaker. She does publicity and is said to be skilled in satellite communications."

"So tell me, Colonel, which of them works for the CIA?"

"Maybe none of them, Sir. Our American sources say the government is dismayed that Mr. Carpenter hasn't agreed to share information with them."

The minister smiled. "So perhaps we know more than our American friends."

"We either do, or people believe that we do. Sources tell us that the Americans assume we built the Array."

"So we let them assume. What about the other members of the project?"

"President Vahidoglu insisted that priority be given to specialists from Turkic-speaking countries who could talk understandably on Karakalpak television. It is a question of national pride. Carpenter's Karakalpak counterpart is Colonel Muhammet Muhammedov, Vahidoglu's chief of security. The others are Uzbek-speaking Karakalpaks in the low level jobs, oilfield experts from the Azerbaijan, and earth scientists from the Middle East Technical University in Ankara. There's also an Azeri-speaking Iranian television team."

"Why Iranians?"

"Apparently Mr. Carpenter has seen some good Iranian films and has hired a famous director."

"As I told you, Mr. Carpenter hungers for publicity. It's an American disease."

* * *

Hayes Carpenter had not only the bearded bulky looks of Ernest Hemingway in old age but a deep longing to make a final splash in the world before his prostate got any more troublesome. Buying and selling billions of tons of corn, wheat, rice, cotton, and soybeans no longer thrilled him, nor did the prospect of the hole-in-the-sea project coming up with a major scientific discovery. The Turkish scientists would be the ones to make their reputation from that. What Hayes wanted was public attention, and he conspired regularly with Margie Hicks and Shanelle Whittaker on ways to pump up interest in his project.

Margie had informed him early on that the translators assigned to all of them by President Vahidoglu were Russian spies, but that had simply amused him. The more supposedly confidential information about the project leaked out, the greater the worldwide interest; the greater the worldwide interest, the more he could demand for news and entertainment rights. Carpenter-Beckenbaugh stockholders were assured that the company's financial commitment to the project was strictly limited and that the scientific discoveries that would inevitably come from the project would be shared fifty-fifty with the Karakalpak government. Nevertheless, rumors circulated that the hole-in-the-sea was quickly becoming the hole-in-Hayes-Carpenter's-pocket; and canny financial wizards were beginning to wonder whether Hayes Carpenter's personal fortune could stand the strain, particularly if there turned out to be nothing interesting on the floor of the Aral Sea. Time would tell.

On the ground on the salt-white, smelly southern shore of the Aral Sea there was nothing to see but racks of pipe and piles of supplies. For more, journalists, tourists, and scientific visitors had to spring for an exorbitantly priced—Hayes Carpenter raked off half—two-hour helicopter ride from Nukus. The pilots flew low over the water so that the steadily deepening hole in the sea came into view suddenly and spectacularly.

Spectacle there had been from the very beginning: A hundred cylindrical steel caissons being floated into position, flooded with seawater, and sunk with utmost precision so they almost touched one another in a ring a hundred meters in diameter. Steel plates being welded with cascades of sparks between the caissons to make them into a watertight, pressure resistant dike; and in the middle, anchored near the presumed center of the Great Array, three barges, two for pumping seawater over the caisson barrier, and one carrying drilling equipment capable of taking core samples down to 10,000 feet. The roaring pumps had been operating twenty-four hours a day ever since the caisson wall had been declared watertight. Slowly the water level at the center of the sea sank, and it became more and more evident that the Aral Sea was developing a hole in its center.

Dredging equipment having been deemed too imprecise, divers regularly descended to the seafloor to scoop bottom samples from the murky depths. Though they could discern no soil discoloration underwater and had difficulty hitting the right spots, their samples confirmed the convergence of the crossbars. The center of the Array seemed to be a circular area some four meters in diameter at the geometrical center of the search area—the bull's-eye. The Turkish scientists in the laboratory the Carpenter-Beckenbaugh Corporation had thrown up quickly in Nukus reported that the bull's-eye soil differed somewhat from that in the outer ring and crossbars and eagerly awaited purer samples.

On the sixth of November, four months after the Array's discovery, the first chilly winds sweeping out of Siberia were blowing icy salt spray into the faces of the television crew scanning the sky. Precisely on schedule, a light plane appeared over the lip of the caisson ring and circled the barges below. Then Hayes Carpenter appeared in the airplane door and jumped, free-falling until the last moment when he opened his parachute and made a perfect landing on the deck of the drilling barge, a feat that was telecast live via satellite uplink to millions of viewers around the world.

World interest in the hole-in-the sea, coordinated by Margie Hicks and Shanelle Whittaker, was intensifying. Hard news was carefully spaced out, but the sensationalist end of the journalistic spectrum increasingly focused on one or another space visitor theory. Margie and Shanelle made no effort to stem the bizarre speculation and made footage from helicopter and barge-mounted cameras showing eerie shots of the now fifty-foot deep hole-in-the-sea available, for a fee, to whoever wanted to broadcast them.

Shadows created by floodlights mounted on the barges and caissons criss-crossed the entire area. Shallower areas were dramatically lit to heighten the spectacle of a dry—actually soggy—seafloor amidst a frightening wall of water artificially held back by the caisson wall. It looked as though it would take but one small shrug of the earth's shoulders to sweep away the entire enterprise in a crushing, cataclysmic flood.

The barges had long since given up their anchors and secured their positions by sinking legs into the seafloor. The two pumpers stood on stilts in the deepest remaining water just south of the bull's-eye and were connected with each other and with the drilling barge by steel grating walkways. Having made his parachute entrance so he could be present when the bull's-eye of the Great Array was finally uncovered, Hayes Carpenter kept vigil at a viewing post halfway along the walkway between the drill barge and pump barge #1. He had chosen his spot to be as far away as possible from the roar of the pumps and the almost equally deafening hammering and clanging of roustabouts assembling the drilling tower from steel pipes and beams. But it also provided photographers with dramatic views of the master overseeing his domain.

As the moment neared for uncovering the bull's-eye, Margie Hicks gathered the Turkish scientists aboard pump barge #2 so that she could have them all ready for on-camera interviews as soon as the last foot or so of water was pumped away.

"How long will it be?" she asked the pumping chief in Uzbek.

"Perhaps two hours," he replied in Azeri.

A television cameraman climbed atop a pump to shoot Margie staring intently into the few inches of water remaining, though the roiling murk stirred up by the pumping made it quite impossible to see anything.

The drill barge rested on two-meter in diameter tubular steel legs directly on top of the bull's-eye. Beneath its deck the Iranian television crew had rigged banks of floodlights in different colors and at different angles to illuminate the area where the bull's-eye would appear. The lights could be lit in whatever combination might be needed to highlight any sort of pattern on the floor of the sea.

Suddenly a Turkish geologist's high-pitched voice could be heard yelling "*Sijak su*! *Chok sijak*!" over the roar of the pumps. The other scientists made their way to where he was examining a digital thermometer and began to converse excitedly.

Wilson Woodrow, as always the picture of calm amidst the fury, turned to Margie and shouted in her ear, "What's going on?"

"He says, 'hot water, very hot.'"

"Damn, I wish these boys spoke English," said the rangy Texan. "This whole operation go 'bout twice as fast."

Margie screamed across the metal deck to her interpreter. "Shukru! Get over here!"

The Karakalpak translator broke away from the cluster of scientists and ran over.

"Hot water," he said excitedly.

"That's what I heard. What do they mean hot water? What water?"

"The sea. The water is very hot."

"How hot?" shouted Wilson.

"Thirty-four Celsius."

"Almost a hundred degrees Fahrenheit, Wilson," yelled Margie. "What do you think?"

"The soil in the Array channels infrared. Makes me think the heat's coming out of the Array itself, and that can't be good. In an oil field this is the feel you get just before a well blows." Wilson turned to the control cabin and cupped his hands around his mouth. "STOP THE PUMPS! SHUT IT DOWN!" Steam was beginning to rise from the shallow water all around. "Damn. Can't hear or don't understand. Shukru!"—the round-faced, middle aged interpreter looked terrified—"run tell the pump chief to shut everything down and radio the same to #2. Git! I want those pumps off now!"

Shukru scurried away.

"We pump real slow from here on, Margie. Hope it don't spoil your TV show."

The roar of the pumps stopped abruptly, followed a few seconds later by the pumps on the other barge. The sudden silence after weeks of constant din made Margie feel she had gone deaf. "A little tension never spoiled a news story, Wilson," she said, almost surprised to actually hear her own voice.

The sudden stoppage of the incessant noise and vibration sent a thrill of apprehension and anticipation through Hayes Carpenter standing on the catwalk between barge #1 and the drill barge. Almost like standing in the door of an airplane a moment before jumping. "Why have the pumps stopped, Abdolla?" said Hayes Carpenter to his interpreter. "Have they reached the bottom already?"

Abdolla didn't answer but instead looked toward the bull's-eye underneath the drill barge. Hayes followed his gaze and saw a cloud of steam and a brightening red glow chaotically illuminated by the television lights rigged beneath the barge's deck. "Oh my god."

As the words left his mouth the bull's-eye erupted in a brilliant deep red flash followed in the next instant by the wrenching screech of twisting steel culminating in a series of explosive cracks as the massive legs of the barge broke and the entire superstructure soared into the air in a blizzard of disintegrating pieces. Hurling the seemingly flimsy obstacle of the barge aside, the intense red ray, thick as a giant sequoia, shot into the atmosphere to form a taut crimson thread that appeared to be suspending the entire earth.

Hayes and Abdolla felt the catwalk give way beneath them as the end that had been connected with the drill barge jolted upward and then dropped to the seafloor. Thrown to the metal surface, Hayes thrust his fingers through the diamond-shaped holes in the grating as his heavy body slipped down the eighty-degree slope. With his cheek pressed flat to the rough metal surface, he glanced down just in time to see Abdolla skid down the catwalk, arms flailing, into several inches of boiling water. Through the crashes of debris falling all about him, he heard Abdolla scream as his entire body was instantly scalded. Still screaming, the translator tried momentarily to stand only to fall again face down. Then his screaming stopped.

On pump barge #2, a few of the scientists and crew had rushed to the rail along with Margie Hicks and Wilson Woodrow to gaze at the disintegrating drill barge riding the eruption of the colossal red beam into the sky. The rest had taken cover. The Iranian television team calmly stuck to their task recording the column of red light shooting into the heavens, the explosive destruction of the drill barge and of everyone on board it, and the surrounding vista of boiling seawater, dangling catwalks, and debris showering down from the sky into the hole-in-the-sea.

Being farther from the bull's-eye, barge #2 took numerous small hits, but the larger pieces of the drill barge didn't carry so far as they plummeted back to earth. The Barge #1 fared worse. Sections of drilling pipe, scaffolding, deck, tower girders, and all manner of smaller items pelted down heavily as workmen ducked for cover or were struck down where they stood.

"Where's Hayes?" yelled Margie.

Wilson Woodrow looked toward the demolished catwalk. "He was watching from over yonder." He looked around for someone to give an order to, but everything was in turmoil. "I'll go find him."

Like everyone else, Margie was unable to remove her eyes for more than a few seconds at a time from the mesmerizing red beam splitting the sky. One by one those who had ducked for cover, miraculously mostly uninjured, returned to the rail to gaze at the bull's-eye and trace the path of the silent beam upward and out of sight.

When Wilson got to barge #1, he found devastation. Dead and seriously injured men sprawled on the deck, some of them impaled by sections of pipe or torn pieces of twisted steel. Seeing that the remaining crew were already turning to rescue duties and needed no direction from him, he muscled aside a thirty foot pipe section and climbed across the tangle of wreckage to reach the catwalk on the far side.

Barge #1 was half destroyed. Holes gaped where major pieces of the drilling equipment had crashed through the deck to the seafloor. Wilson heard moans but saw no one moving. He looked across for the catwalk leading to the drill barge. It was gone. Through the holes ripped in the deck he spied a dozen bodies boiling in the few remaining inches of seawater. Heedless of the cracking and twisting sounds threatening further collapse, he clambered across rubble and around yawning holes to the place where the catwalk had been. Its remains were hanging almost straight down from the cables that attached it to the barge's edge. Peering over he saw the unmistakable figure of Hayes Carpenter clinging with both hands to the grating.

"Hayes!" he shouted.

The billionaire craned his neck upward awkwardly. “Wilson, I can’t climb up. The grate’s too fine to get a toehold.”

“Hang on, Hayes.”

“What in the hell do you think I’m doing?”

“I’ll get a rope.”

Wilson looked around. The nearest rope was tangled together with a coil of electrical conduit that had fallen in a chaotic spiral from the sky. Quickly judging his needs, he drew a sheath knife from his belt, cut a section of the rope free, expertly threw a bowline on one end, and dropped the loop over a sturdy upright welded to the deck. He lowered the free end over the edge so that it fell just to Hayes’ right. The heavy man agilely snagged the rope with his foot and drew it toward him, managing to wrap it twice around his leg as he did. Grabbing first with one hand and then the other, he transferred his weight from the catwalk to the rope.

“Can you pull me up?” he yelled.

Instead of a reply he felt a sudden burning on his shoulders and the top of his head, and the water and steam beneath him reflected a red glow that made it look like the gate of hell. Peripherally he saw the entire area around and below him bathed in bright red light.

Wilson instinctively looked up when the incoming beam hit. The intense red light was stunningly bright. Suddenly he felt a sharp pain in his eyes and threw himself sideways facedown on the deck. A burning sensation on his back lasted for less than a minute and then subsided. Wilson opened his eyes, but the darkness did not go away. Controlling his fear, he blindly reached about to orient himself. The upright he had tied the rope to was just to his right. He ran his hand upward until it encountered the still taut line.

He stood up uneasily, knowing he was only inches from the side of the barge and a drop to the boiling water below.

“Still there, Hayes?” he called out.

“Not going anywhere,” came the answer. “What was that?”

“Incoming light. Got me in the eyes. I can’t see.”

“Oh my god!”

“I’ve got the rope, though.”

The sinews of his long brown arms standing out like cables, the blinded oil driller began hand over hand to haul on the rope. Hayes doubled his knees, pushed off from the catwalk, and straightened his legs so that they gained purchase on the grating. With his weight divided between the rope and his legs, he walked up the catwalk as Wilson hauled him in.

On barge #2 the incoming beam had struck as both the crew and the scientists were gazing into the sky, rapt at the spectacle of the outgoing red beam. Margie Hicks' younger years as a war correspondent served her in good stead. She reflexively dove for the deck at the first flash. When the heat subsided a minute later, she felt the pain of a serious contusion where her cheek had hit the metal. Then she realized she was blind. Lying still and trying to control her racing heart, she called out to locate who was near her. Others were doing the same, or just moaning or screaming. Margie heard a shout, a splash, and a scream of agony as someone went over the edge. She tried to remember how close to the brink she was herself.

Minutes passed. She felt the vibrations of a few people moving on the deck, but no one came to her aid. Feeling about to make sure she was safe, she sat up. A thought came unbidden to her mind: I hope they got it on videotape. She reflected that that was a pretty strange thought for a person who had just lost her eyesight.

*　　*　　*

A day later, at the overcrowded military hospital in Nukus, Hayes visited her.

"Margie, it's Hayes." He took her weathered hand awkwardly between his own heavily bandaged palms. "How are you doing?"

"I'm okay. How are you doing?"

"Lacerated hands and some superficial burns. Otherwise, not a scratch on me. My face was flat against the catwalk when the laser hit. The doctor says you're going to get your eyesight back."

"He told me. When they took the bandage off a couple of hours ago, I could see colors and moving shapes." Her voice was steady but tired. "But tell me, Hayes, what happened? I'm so damn mad for missing the biggest news story of my career."

"You're one of the lucky ones, Margie. We lost everyone on the drill barge and about a third of the crew on the number one pump barge. Of the rest, all but three were looking up and had their retinas burnt out."

"Wilson?"

Hayes' voice choked. "Wilson's blind. The catwalk collapsed, and I was hanging on. He found me, but he looked up at the beam. After that he couldn't see a thing, but he pulled me up anyway." There was a long pause; Margie sensed he was fighting back tears.

"Nothing you could have done, Hayes."

A long sigh. "I know it. I know it. But damn . . . I've known Wilson for more than forty years. We used to work on harvesting teams together when we were teen-agers."

"Don't think about it Hayes. Tell me how big the beam was."

"The incoming beam covered the whole Array, fourteen miles in diameter. All sorts of people got blinded out in the dry areas. Poor souls."

Margie was quiet for a while. "How did I get rescued? I don't remember a thing except that I was lying on the deck hearing people moaning and afraid to move?"

"Shanelle was on her way to Nukus for the satellite uplink. She saw the beam and personally kicked every helicopter pilot we had into the air and got Vahidoglu to do the same with his army pilots. You probably got a shot of morphine before they moved you."

"But Shanelle's okay? You say she looked at the beam."

"But from over a hundred miles away. Besides, it was apparently a laser. Look into it directly for a couple of seconds, and your eyesight's a goner. But it's different from the side. Laser light doesn't diffuse when it goes through the air. You shouldn't even be able to see a perfect laser beam from the side. This one did diffuse some, but it had too much power for it to make a difference. What Shanelle saw was just a pretty light, but she figured that if she could see it from a hundred miles away, it must be devastating at ground zero."

"Hayes, you know, don't you, that this means we're dealing with outer space stuff just like the kooks have been saying. I've been lying here thinking about it. Thinking back over the last twenty-five years that I've been in the news business. I can't imagine the Soviets could have put up a satellite that powerful and kept it a secret for all these years, and I know the U.S. couldn't have kept it a secret. It would have cost billions, and to send it up without crowing about it, or even testing it operationally once it was in space, goes against everything I know about government and the military. So something extraterrestrial is the only alternative. Who would have thought it? UFOs, aliens, all that tabloid stuff?"

"I guess it's the story of the year."

"Of the year? Of the century. And you know what, Hayes?" Margie managed a weak smile.

"What?"

"You own that story. You own it, Hayes."

The bone weary billionaire nodded his heavy head slowly. "I can't tell you how ashamed I am to admit it, Margie . . . everything so tragic and all . . . so many people dead or blind . . . but that very thought has crossed my mind . . . the thought has crossed my mind. It's ironic, too, because even though Shanelle's been telling everyone I'm making my money back with television rights and charging journalists an arm and a leg to fly out to the site, the truth is, this whole operation's just a money pit. Only reason I did this in the first place was because I'm getting old and I was bored. And of course I had the money . . . got fucking money to burn. You know, there's only so much satisfaction a man can get out of buying wheat, rice, and cotton. I just decided to make a splash and have some fun. But now that's all changed."

"How's it changed, Hayes?"

"Well, first of all, if it is UFO stuff and I get my hands on alien technology, I'll probably make more money on this than I can possibly count. But leaving that aside, one way or another I'm going to get my revenge on the . . . on whoever they are that did this."

"Even if you just stumbled on something put on Earth a million years ago? Tough to take revenge against an act of God."

"If this was an act of God, Margie, then some god is going to get his butt kicked once I figure out how to do it. You can bank on that."

Chapter Four

"How do you say in English *esholeshek*?" The Turkish words President Muratbey used with Lee were always in the Istanbul dialect of Turkish she had studied in Washington rather than in his native Uzbek. Lee noted that once again he liked testing her knowledge of vulgar and sexual expressions, most of which she had actually picked up from a Turkish boyfriend in college.

"You are a donkey, the son of a donkey," she replied primly.

"So many words?"

"Very long and awkward. Besides, we wouldn't actually use that expression in English, Mr. President. Telling an American he is the son of a donkey won't make him feel very insulted. But you can say, 'you are a jackass.' That is rather insulting and has something of the same meaning. Jackass means male donkey."

"Jackass . . . jackass . . ."

"Then again, if you want to be more coarse . . ."

"Coarse is strong? Strong insult?"

" . . . you can say, 'you are an asshole,' or, if speaking to someone directly, just say 'asshole!' in a loud and very firm voice." Lee looked the president in the eye and demonstrated. "ASSHOLE!" It felt very satisfying.

"ASSHOLE!" mimicked the president.

"Very good. You seem to have a natural talent for insult."

"What does it mean, 'asshole'?"

"It actually has the same general meaning as *eshek* or 'jackass': stupid, insensitive, obstructive, insignificant." Muratbey nodded and smiled with each term. "Literally, however, it means the opening you excrete through."

Muratbey was uncomprehending.

"Defecate? Eliminate?" Lee was groping. "Shit?"

Muratbey's eyes widened. "*Bok*? Shit? Very coarse! You Americans say such?"

Lee laughed wryly. "Calling someone an asshole is very American these days, I'm afraid."

"Very American. I use it. ASSHOLE Vahidoglu . . . . It sounds good!"

"You only shout if you are talking to him directly. Otherwise, you use your normal voice."

"Okay. Asshole Vahidoglu, may his . . ." Lee raised her eyebrows. " . . . *father* roast in hellfire." Muratbey grinned slyly. "I make joke with you, Lee." Only momentarily illuminated by the grin, his face quickly returned to its usual jowly sag. "Asshole Vahidoglu make speech yesterday to say Karakalpak Republic is original home of mankind. This is why people from space build Great Array. It is insult to all Turkic people."

"An insult?" ventured Lee skeptically. "Why would that be an insult?"

"Insult because in old days all Turkic peoples—Uzbek, Kazakh, Turkmen, even Kyrgyz—live with horses and sheep and go from one place to another. No one own the land. It is land of all great Turkic people. Now asshole Vahidoglu makes it Karakalpak land, his land. It is my land too. He steals our land, our heritage. Space people choose to visit all Turkic peoples."

"Actually, Mr. President, what you have said is quite silly." Lee could sense a distant shudder pass through the ambassador's wife in Washington who had taught the course on protocol for embassy spouses. "Even assuming the Great Array was made by space aliens, which is still to be proven, they would have come here long before there were any Turkic peoples. According to CNN, the hole in the sea expedition has drilled cores down to 2500 meters without hitting anything hard. They say this probably means that the machine that sent out the laser beam was installed at least two million years ago. Modern human beings don't even appear on earth until half a million years ago. And your people, the Turkic people, didn't appear in this part of Central Asia until about fifteen hundred years ago. We've talked about this, Mr. President. This is what I work on. Before the Turkic peoples, the people who lived here spoke old Indo-Iranian languages like Vedic."

"Vedic?"

"The language I study."

"Ah! I remember. You study old, old language. Then why does Vahidoglu say space people picked Karakalpak people to visit?"

"Because, as you so eloquently explained, President Vahidoglu is an asshole." Muratbey again grinned broadly. "In my opinion, the Aral Sea chakra properly belongs to no one at all because it dates from before humanity."

"You say 'chakra' in English? On CNN I hear Great Array"

"Great Array is indeed what they say on CNN. But it is a stupid term. I prefer chakra. I don't insist that anyone else use the word, but it's the one I use. Chakra means wheel in Sanskrit, but it also means the shape of a cross within a circle. It's a design that was sacred to the ancient Indo-Iranian people. A chakra looks exactly like the Great Array, and this is the part of the world where that image has a historical meaning. So I say chakra."

"How you know about chakra?"

Lee sensed the pleasant warmth of a lecture welling up inside her. "We know this, Mr. President, because the ancient Indo-Iranians carved hundreds of chakra designs into rocks—circles with crosses in them. In fact, one of the reasons I came with Donald to Ferghana was to see these ancient rock carvings in person. Aside from the hymns of the Vedas, the rock carvings are one of the few surviving expressions of the mentality of the people who lived here five thousand years ago."

"There are chakras here in Ferghana?"

"My dear President, you wouldn't believe how many. In the mountains. Hundreds of them. And other sorts of carvings, too: chariots, giant serpents, men with battleaxes."

"And there are chakra carvings also in Karakalpak Republic?"

Lee thought. "Mmmm, no. I don't believe so. At least none survive. You need big rock surfaces to carve on, and you only find them in the mountains—here in Ferghana, or in Kyrgyzstan. There are even some in Sweden, for that matter. But Karakalpakstan is all desert or cotton field, perfectly flat, no rocks."

"No rocks, no chakras."

"No rocks, no chakras—except on the floor of the Aral Sea."

A look of shrewd cunning pursed Muratbey's mouth and brow. "Then space people came here to Ferghana and carved chakras."

"No, no, no," laughed Lee lightly. "Not possible. The Aral Sea chakra is two million years old. The chakras in Ferghana are perhaps five thousand years old. Quite a difference."

"Then Ferghana people . . . Ferghana scientists . . . saw Great Array chakra and drew pictures of it."

"It was under water."

"Perhaps not five thousand years ago. Perhaps no water then. Rivers run other place. Scientists from Ferghana study big chakra, come home, carve pictures."

"A remote possibility, perhaps," replied Lee, belatedly rediscovering a sense of diplomacy. The president actually had a point. The Aral Sea was such a shallow body of water that it might indeed have been dry in some earlier era.

"Remote possibility is enough for attacking asshole Vahidoglu!" Muratbey's face suddenly brightened in a crafty porcine smile. "Lee . . . we like each other, don't we . . . I like you . . . very much . . . you like me . . . you like people of Ferghana. Now you help me and help people of Ferghana. You help Ferghana pride against asshole Karakalpaks. We make propaganda about chakra, tell world about ancient science of Ferghana. Tourists and scientists and reporters come to Ferghana to see chakras. Just like they go to Aral Sea. They bring in money for the country. Make jobs for Ferghana people. So you make this publicity to help all Ferghana people."

An internal alarm whooped in Lee's brain. "Actually, Mr. President, though I do, of course, admire you and would love to help the wonderful people of Ferghana, you know I must ask Ambassador Bane before I do anything at all of an official sort. I even had to ask her for permission to hold our conversation classes."

"Of course, your name not be used. Story of Ferghana chakras will be told by Ferghana scientists. You just help. Tell them how to do it."

"But I don't know how. You would have to hire a public relations firm."

"You are American. You find way. I read about Benjamin Franklin."

Lee wondered what Benjamin Franklin had to do with anything. "Of course I will gladly bring the matter up with the ambassador."

"No. Don't speak to Ambassador Bane. Chakras are Ferghana secret. Don't worry. I understand your position. I take care of everything." Muratbey stood up suddenly and extended his hand. "I leave now."

Startled by the unaccustomed abruptness of his leave-taking, Lee stumbled getting to her feet and upset an empty tea glass that tinkled without breaking on its glass saucer. Muratbey's warm pudgy hand grabbed hers briefly and gave it a single quick pump. "Lee, thank you for lesson." As if late for another engagement, he turned on his heel and was out the door without a further word of goodbye.

Lee puzzled for a few minutes over Muratbey's behavior and then reminded herself that since she despised the man, trying to understand him would be a waste of time. She forced him from her mind with difficulty and repaired to her study. Her beloved laptop was sitting with its top raised between Grassmann's German-Vedic dictionary and Geldner's German translation of the Rig Veda. She slipped into her carpet-draped desk chair and immediately lost herself in contemplation of verbal roots, metrical anomalies, sacrificial rituals, and the enigmatic grandeur of the ancient Indian gods.

The sound of a car in the driveway stirred her. She was astonished to think that she had worked without stop through the entire afternoon. But a glance at the time on her computer screen told her that the sound was simply Donald coming home unusually early. *Forgot his key*, she thought, as she got up to answer the knock on the door.

"Good afternoon, Mrs. Ingalls," said the uniformed officer standing on her doorstep with his gold-braided hat under his arm. "I am Major Dimitri Park." His accent was British and formal.

"I know who you are, Major Park," replied Lee stiffly. "We were introduced at Ambassador Bane's reception."

"I remember the occasion with great pleasure. It is cold. May I come in?"

Lee stepped aside to admit the much feared and much whispered about chief of the Ferghana Republic's internal security police. Major Park surveyed the comfortable living room, still furnished in the unpretentious sofa and chairs and the lacquered wood cabinets of the family Lee and Donald were renting from. "You have added some lovely Turkmen carpets to the walls, Mrs. Ingalls."

"Thank you, Major. You have a keen eye for what is new here. May I make you a cup of tea?"

"As you do for my president? I would not presume upon such a favor. I will accept an invitation to sit down, however."

Lee seated herself tensely on a straight wooden chair. The major chose the middle of the overstuffed, plum-upholstered sofa, placing his gold-braided hat beside him.

"Am I correct, Major Park, in gathering from your remark that you have been . . . following? . . . is that the right word? . . . my English lessons with President Muratbey."

"My dear president. Unfortunately, not a particularly gifted linguist."

"Not so gifted as his intelligence chief, it would seem. Perhaps he would be better advised to spend his time practicing English with you, Major. Combine business with learning, as it were."

"Thank you for the compliment. Many years ago I majored in American Literature at Moscow State University. I was an apt pupil and a voracious reader. Alas, however, Mrs. Ingalls, my president seldom seeks my company unless he needs to know something. And even then I think he keeps his hands in his pockets for fear I will cut off his fingers. As I am sure you are aware, Mrs. Ingalls, I have the misfortune of being feared and distrusted, even in these democratic times when the only mission remaining for our shrunken Internal Security Ministry is to protect our Republic from outside intruders. Not from its own citizens, as in the bad old days."

Lee felt torn between protocol and curiosity. "Rumor has it, Major, that you rather enjoyed the bad old days."

"Perhaps. But I am Korean by family origin, and the Koreans of Central Asia have always been given the unpleasant jobs. We're the Jews of Central Asia: hard workers, diligent students, good at business, attentive to detail, but, alas, everywhere mistrusted. Before independence, Russians and Ukrainians ran everything. Now

Uzbeks and Tajiks run everything. Either way, we Koreans end up with the dirty jobs."

"A sad fate indeed, Major."

"You are mocking me, Mrs. Ingalls. But I am not offended. It is . . . what should I say . . . part of your charm. I'm sure your style is very much appreciated in New York City. But here in Kokand everything is so primitive. Only a few of us understand and appreciate the undiplomatic diplomat. For the rest, one's manner does not always serve one's best interest."

"And what, pray tell, is my 'best interest'? Since I have diplomatic immunity and would not regret for one instant being expelled from this delightful country, I actually feel quite free to speak my mind."

"Free. Of course. We would have it no other way. Ferghana is a land of complete freedom. But don't you find that sometimes your attitude gets in the way of your understanding other people?" Major Park leaned forward earnestly.

"You look as though you are prepared to offer an example of my misunderstanding people."

"Consider my dear president, Mrs. Ingalls, the honorable Rejep Muratbey He has been coming to you for English conversation for five months. He finds you most charming. Turks historically have a strong liking for determined, forceful women. It challenges them. But you don't always seem to understand what the president is saying."

"I don't?" replied Lee suspiciously.

"No."

"He reports my lack of understanding to you? But keeps his hands in his pockets?"

"He doesn't report anything knowingly, but I learn what is said."

Lee looked around the room trying to guess where the unsuspected bugs were hidden.

"Mrs. Ingalls, I am not an amateur," said the Major gently. "Don't trouble yourself to search. I told you it was my job to keep track of . . ."

"Outside intruders." Lee felt both frightened and angry. "You have a lot of nerve, Major Park. Do you realize that my husband took leave from a job that paid him more than the president of the United States in order to help jump-start your ghastly economy? Without outside intruders like Donald you would be chopping down the sycamores in the palace park to keep warm this winter."

"No need to become upset, Mrs. Ingalls. It is just as you say. Believe me, my eavesdropping has been more concerned with my president's welfare, his safety, than with your husband's business activities. Don't you think the American Secret Service pays close attention to the people their president visits socially?"

"Am I a danger to President Muratbey, then?" asked Lee. "Just what is it about my conversations with him that you find insensitive. Perhaps I can improve my attitude."

Major Park picked up his hat and looked down at it as he adjusted its gold braid. "When I was as Moscow State University, I read Longfellow's poem *The Courtship of Miles Standish*. You are familiar with it?"

"I read it in high school. But what does that have to do with anything?"

The Major sighed. "I thought perhaps you might guess." He didn't look up. "Well, anyway, at the risk of seeming blunt, Mrs. Ingalls, you seem not to have grasped that President Muratbey has been seeking to seduce you."

Lee sat up straight as if prodded in the posterior with a pin. "Seduce me?"

"Exactly." The Major seemed relieved that his awkward message had finally been delivered. "Like John Alden, I have been sent here to tell you that."

"Major Park, leaving aside the fact that I am married to an American diplomat and therefore could not possibly entertain a relationship of the sort you tell me your president has in mind—and I must confess that your report makes certain aspects of his behavior more understandable—I must tell you that President Muratbey is grossly, I repeat, grossly unappealing in both his person and his intellect and that he hasn't the slightest notion how to make a proper pass at a woman."

"Precisely so! Very well put. His problem exactly. Every time he comes for a lesson, he tries to drop hints with the idea of turning to romance at the end of the lesson. But he ends up fading into silence because he can't think how to do it. If he had any attractive features at all, it would really be quite sad. He confided in me in hopes that my better English skills would enable me to speak effectively on his behalf. Needless to say, I told him that my studies did not instruct me on such matters, but he insisted that I come. You must believe me when I tell you that he is abjectly despondent at his inability to express his affection."

Lee suddenly started to laugh. "So that's why *The Courtship of Miles Standish*?"

"I thought it might give me an idea so I reread it before coming here. Let me remind you of how Longfellow describes Standish: 'Short of stature he was, but strongly built and athletic,/Broad in the shoulders, deep-chested, with muscles and sinews of iron.' Fits our president quite well, don't you think?"

Lee laughed again. "And a belly as large as a watermelon, and a face that looks like a pig. President Miles Standish Muratbey to a tee."

Major Park was smiling. "Then you are not offended?"

"Oh, I suppose not. But I can't say I'm flattered either. I can't believe he actually sent you to ask me to go to bed with him. Now it will be impossible for us to continue our conversations. He should have been satisfied with his adolescent mooning. This was also an odd day to do it since just before he left, he was trying to get me to work on some sort of tourist promotion project for him."

"Perhaps not a coincidence. He called me about an hour and a half ago. I, too, was surprised at his abrupt change of tactic, though I knew of course of his admiration for you, so I took the time to collect and review today's tape. If I understood correctly, he wants you to help him use what you call the chakra carvings to embarrass and steal tourist dollars away from the great Karakalpak Rabbit Dropping. From this I surmised that he asked me to relay his confession of affection for you as a means of persuasion. So I called him back and confirmed that this was indeed his idea."

Lee was still bemused. "He thinks that if I am his lover, I can refuse him nothing? I will be so intoxicated with passion that I will help him in his project without informing my ambassador? What a grand opinion he has of himself. And what a low opinion of me."

"He is a man formed in the Soviet era, Mrs. Ingalls. In those times, many women found it convenient and rewarding to sleep with men with big bellies and pig faces. I must tell you, he has had great romantic success in his time. Unfortunately, this is one of the many ways in which he has not adjusted his attitude since independence."

"Well, you can tell him that my bond to my husband is too sacred for me to sacrifice, even for his intoxicating embrace."

"Then you still will not help him with his project?"

"I will not."

Lee sensed a tightening of the sleek brown skin over Major Park's cheekbones. "You will not?"

"Why do I think you are going to persuade me that I will, Major Park? Your reputation?"

"You are an intelligent woman, Mrs. Ingalls. I'm sure you will figure it out." The compact, smooth-featured Korean officer drew a small tape recorder from his coat pocket and placed it on the coffee table. "Would you excuse me for a few minutes. I must go out and speak to my driver." He turned the small device on and stepped to the door.

When Park returned ten minutes later, Lee was still sitting in the straight chair. The tape recorder had been turned off. The streaks of tears lined her stunned face.

"I suppose it was considerate of you to leave the room," she said in a shaky voice. "You must have much practice in these matters."

"None at all, actually," replied the Major standing before her. "Normally I remain in the room. It has a stronger impact. I made a special exception for you."

"Who is the woman on the tape?"

"A political officer at the Cuban embassy."

Lee eyes began again to leak tears. Through a strangled sob she managed a sorrowful laugh. "It's funny. The toughest part is that even though he sold toilet valves in South America for four years, Donald never admitted knowing a word of Spanish beyond *si* and *cerveza*. Why couldn't he have used with me some of those words he used with her?" She hid her face in her hands, her shoulders shaking with quiet sobs. Recovering her composure, she looked at the Major. "I suppose you know we don't have a perfect marriage."

"Yes, I know."

"Of course you do. I'm sure you've bugged our bedroom on the off-chance your president might get lucky." Lee looked at the Turkmen carpets she and Donald had enjoyed picking out in the bazaar. "Going back to what we were talking about before," she said at length, "having refused to work for President Muratbey in the capacity of his mistress, I gather I am now supposed to work for him to protect my philandering husband. Since my country still considers Cuba a hostile regime, my cooperation with your presidential pig will keep you from telling Ambassador Bane that her evangelist of the almighty dollar is sleeping with the enemy."

"He only wants help on the chakra. You don't have to have physical contact with him."

"So his tourist project is more important than his alleged passion for me. Isn't it an awfully petty matter to blackmail a woman about?"

"So it might seem to a reasonable person. But you should never underestimate Rejep Muratbey's hatred for his Karakalpak counterpart Ahmet Vahidoglu. What you call a tourist project is for him a major act of psychological warfare. Moreover—and I don't mean this facetiously—I believe he still hopes to win you by charm now that you know the truth about his affectionate . . ."

Lee interrupted curtly. "Tell that pig that if he puts a single finger on me, I'll throw dear husband Donald to the wolves. He shouldn't rely too heavily on my sense of wifely loyalty. It's a little fragile at the moment, and it's not likely to get much stronger."

"No sex. No more English tutoring. Just chakras. I'll tell him." Major Park walked to the door and placed his hat on his head. Lee remained seated, gazing at the Turkmen carpets. With his hand on the door handle, he turned and looked back at her sympathetically. "I promise you he will not trouble you on such matters, Mrs. Ingalls." There was a long pause as if the Major were pondering what to say next. Lee turned her head toward him and saw what seemed at a distance to be a blush on his sallow cheeks. "After all," he said awkwardly, "the reason I brought up Longfellow's poem was not just to explain that I was here to speak on the president's behalf." He paused, uncertain how to proceed. "The poem is also about John Alden. As Longfellow puts it: 'Archly the maiden smiled, and, with eyes running with laughter,/Said, in a tremulous voice, "Why don't you speak for yourself, John?"' Permit me to say that I would love to see your eyes running with laughter for that reason, Mrs. Ingalls." With that he bowed slightly and exited swiftly through the front door.

"Oh my god," whispered Lee as the door closed. "They're both crazy. Stark raving mad."

Chapter Five

Putting together the NIE, the National Intelligence Estimate, bore a close resemblance to sausage making: a little bit of this, a little bit of that, a few ingredients that were better left unlisted. Every intelligence agency was eager to have its views dominate, every agency equally eager to cover its backside in case its views proved wrong. National Security Advisor and presidential intimate George Artunian rode herd on the operation with unwavering sensitivity to the painfully slow presidential reading speed and limited attention span. As usual, each of the agency reps had a sheaf of paper in hand, but Artunian insisted on brief oral presentations to get to the pith of the analysis and did not shy away from cutting people off with a bushy-browed scowl.

"Steph, DIA can start today."

"Again today. What a surprise," whispered CIA's Anthony Stone to the newcomer from NASA sitting beside him.

Naval captain Stephanie Low of the Defense Intelligence Agency was President Boone Rankin's, and therefore George Artunian's, personal favorite. Not just because she was female or, in a buxom and round-faced way, comely, but because she was the only person in the room other than George himself who could make an appointment and talk personally to the President. George mused from time to time at what formidable talents she must have displayed, given her no-holds-barred personality, to get repeated fast-track promotions even before Rankin's election.

"Two words, George," she said in an echo of the president's Appalachian twang, "top dog. Whoever gets that laser technology is top dog. And we think the Russians are goin' for it."

"Going for it?"

"They'll lean on Vahidoglu hard as possible, and if that don't work, they'll just go and take it. Since January 10 we got armor and mechanized infantry build-up on the Kazakh-Russian border, three divisions of the first, two of the second. There's also been a call-up of paratroop officers let go in last year's force cuts."

"How would the Russians get to Nukus, Steph?"

"Gettin' there's most of the trip. Karakalpaks couldn't defense a squad of cheerleaders. Best bet be drop in paratroopers, take Nukus airport, kill Vahidoglu, find a local boy to take his place. Same as they did in Afghanistan in '79, but without a bunch of tribes in a position to cause them trouble."

"That means overflying Kazakh airspace, doesn't it?"

"You bet."

"Kazakhs going to let them?"

"Hell, no. They want the laser too. And they got a land border with Vahidoglu. Russians don't. Russian paratroopers'd probably face Kazakh land forces comin' 'cross that border. Russians are stronger, but they'd have a problem with reinforcement and resupply."

"If the Kazakhs moved south against the Karakalpaks, couldn't the Russians invade Kazakhstan from the north? The Kazakhs surely can't fight two wars."

"Can't fight one against anyone other than the Karakalpaks. Problem is, Russians attackin' Kazakhstan in the north still don't protect those paratroops in Nukus, 'less they take out Kazakh air defense on day one so's they can reinforce by air. But then, of course, you got your Uzbeks and Turkmen waitin' to jump in if they see a chance. And behind them the Iranians probably willin' to mix it up. Big prize—big fight."

"I get the picture. Recommendation?"

"First off, you gotta realize that we can't do a goddam thing ourselves that far from open seas and friendly soil. 'Cept drop bombs, of course. Hell, we can drop bombs anywhere. But what good's that gonna do us? Best way to keep things from gettin' real messy is to put some NATO pressure on the Russians to keep their boys at home."

"That an Agency view, Steph?"

"You know me better'n that, George. That's my view. Agency doesn't make your strategic recommendations. Manual says its mission is to collect and analyze military intelligence. So after collectin' and analyzin' and collectin' and analyzin', Agency view is that Russia is gettin' ready to move."

The NASA astrophysicist, attending the NIE only since the catastrophic exchange of laser beams in the Aral Sea, leaned and whispered in the CIA man's ear. "How can she say things like that? She's only a captain."

Anthony Stone whispered back, "Stephanie Low can say anything she likes. She's from West Virginia and dated the president in high school. Rumor has it that's what made her decide to become a lesbian."

Dr. Gilmartin sensed that his mouth was gaping open and closed it quickly. He cast a quick look at the captain's lush form and then turned his attention to the representative from INR, the State Department's Intelligence and Research arm, who had already begun speaking.

" . . . so we concur with DIA that Russia is making preparations to take over the Karakalpak Republic. The Kazakh president flew from Almaty to Moscow on January second—that's a holiday so not a usual time for a diplomatic visit—and flew back the next day. On the fourth, he made a speech saying that as co-sharer of the Aral Sea—but, of course, the Great Array is entirely in Karakalpak territorial waters—Kazakhstan would not permit any single country to monopolize the Array's possible scientific benefits. President Vahidoglu responded on the fifth with a press conference in which he said the Karakalpak Republic would defend to the death any effort to compromise its national sovereignty or infringe its borders. This was in direct response to what the Kazakh president had said, of course, but it was obviously intended as a warning to Moscow as well. The same day, IRNA, the official Iranian news agency, distributed a statement by Iran's Revolutionary Guide defending Karakalpak sovereignty and calling on the five Caspian Sea littoral states to enter into an consortium to extend technical assistance to the Karakalpaks. Then, on the seventh . . ."

"Have we got a wind-up here, Will? Or is this a dissertation on diplomatic history?" William Stevens, the INR rep, looked up from his text and then glanced down at it again with a furrowed brow. He riffled through several pages. "You can stuff the details in later, Will. The question is what do you want the President to keep in his mind—along with how to fund next year's congressional elections, how to keep the fundamentalists and gays from bashing him, how to respond to fifty editorials a day saying he's wishy-washy, and how to keep his goddam brother out of the casino business?"

The stiff and embarrassed diplomat opened his mouth searching for a reply. "There's a complicated balancing process underway, and we can't predict the outcome."

"Thank you. Can we influence it? And if so, how?"

"No one has approached us for diplomatic help so far. Everyone knows we're too far away and have too few usable assets to be a front-line player. Besides, these weak new countries are just as afraid of us as they are of the Russians."

"So we have nothing. That it? The president of the most powerful nation on earth should just twiddle his thumbs and watch on CNN as the Russians take control of very possibly extraterrestrial laser technology that could be as important as the atomic bomb?"

"There's the Carpenter-Beckenbaugh Corporation," said Stevens tentatively.

"Last I heard, Hayes Carpenter was a Republican and President Rankin a Democrat. You know something I don't, Mr. Stevens?"

"Mr. Carpenter is an American, sir."

"Thank you for that thought, Mr. Stevens. Tony? What have you got from CIA?"

"Reports from intelligence assets with Carpenter's team at the Array."

"Our assets?"

"Azerbaijanis. They're sharing with us in return for future favors. Since the expedition got restaffed and back on track, four holes have been drilled, two on the perimeter ring and two on the crossbars, diagnostic soil runs out at 7500 meters in all of them. Echo locaters confirm a big solid mass under the bull's-eye at that level.

Presumably it's the laser emitter and some sort of power source. Now they can't drill straight down through the bull's-eye because no one knows when the laser's going to blow again. So Carpenter's drilling at an angle from a point just inside the caisson circle aiming to intersect the side of the underground mass. Then he's going to force down a solvent to dissolve some of the surrounding rock, pump out the slurry, and take a look with a remote camera."

"What's the estimate on digging the thing up?"

"Carpenter-Beckenbaugh's a big, rich corporation. They can probably do it, given a couple of years. But the Russians? It would take roughly their whole gross national product for five years. 7500 meters is a hell of a deep hole, and there's no place to put the Aral Sea in the meantime except to build a pipeline to the Caspian and drain it. Forty-eight inch pipe, highly saline water—it's a big job."

"Doesn't the hole-in-the-sea take care of that problem?"

"For purposes of working on the exposed surface of the seafloor or drilling a hole there, yes. But once you start a major excavation, you're going to get too much seepage. Anyway, to cut it short, we don't think there's a chance in a million that Russia will go in. Even if they avoid a war, they don't have the resources to excavate the thing. We think the military build-up is designed to scare us into offering a deal: they go in with our blessing and support, and we furnish the capital and expertise to dig up the laser. Share the rewards. If we don't accept the deal, we risk getting shut out. In other words, what we've got here is a bluff."

"What about the other end, Tony? The space option?"

"Won't know anything until we locate the satellite the laser in the Great Array communicates with."

Artunian turned to Dr. Michael Gilmartin. "NASA? How are we going on finding where the laser from the sky came from?"

"Hubble is still working on it, sir," began the scientist nervously. "The time and the angle of the first exchange between the Array and what we presume is a satellite, combined with the two subsequent emissions from the Array on December 16th and 24th, have given us a good sense of where to look, assuming that the satellite is in geosynchronous orbit. And we know from the time gap between the first emission and the return signal a likely maximum distance, somewhere around the average orbit of Mars—although the idea of a geosynchronous orbit that far out is, of course, scientifically absurd. Our essential problem is that assuming the laser transponder in space is dark and roughly the size of the Array's bull's-eye, even though Hubble is optically powerful enough to resolve it, there's a lot of space to search. If it would transmit to Earth again, of course, we'd have a better chance of nailing it. But unfortunately no instruments were correctly placed to pinpoint the incoming beam during the first exchange."

"And supposing we do locate it, Dr. Gilmartin," said Artunian.

"It would be fairly easy, as these things go, to design a probe to intercept and photograph it. But if it's as far out as Mars, or even half that distance, a manned inspection flight would require a big commitment."

"How about bringing it back?"

The astrophysicist shrugged. "Depends on how big it is. Something small might be towed and released in a near Earth orbit. If it's as big as the whole Array, we might have to attach some sort of propulsion unit."

"What's our time horizon?"

"After we find it—I'm talking Mars distance now for the sake of argument—a couple of years for the probe. Anything manned after that, minimum another five years."

And another administration, thought George Artunian. "Thank you, Dr. Gilmartin, and thank you again for coming. Tony? Something else from CIA?"

"Just that I don't think we should rule out Hayes Carpenter." William Stevens looked relieved and surprised at support for his earlier suggestion coming from an unexpected quarter. "He's sunk a billion dollars into this already—a billion and a half if stories about a personal bribe to President Vahidoglu are true. And of course he's buddy-buddy with Vahidoglu. It goes with getting a half billion dollar gift. The two of them drink vodka together."

"Tony, I drink vodka with the Chairman of the Republican Party when the occasion calls for it. But that doesn't mean I'd let him babysit my dog."

"Point taken. George, I know Carpenter supported the Republicans handsomely in the last campaign and has said some harsh things about the President, but I think his motivations here might go beyond politics."

"How so?"

"Carpenter thought the world of a man named Wilson Woodrow. His kind of man. Carpenter started out as an itinerant harvesting hand in the Dakotas, and he likes the Marlboro type. That's what Woodrow is. Pure Texas. Now Woodrow's blind for life. We got a transcript of a conversation Margie Hicks, Carpenter's news aide, had with an old friend. Hicks says that Carpenter almost went crazy at the thought he caused Woodrow's blindness. Says he swore a vendetta against whoever the bad guys might turn out to be. Sounds weird, of course, when you think about the Array maybe being millions of years old, but that is apparently his frame of mind. In other words, he's engaged a lot more than money in this, and he's not going to be very happy with anyone taking over from him. Doesn't matter whether they're Russian or American. The point is, if Carpenter continues to run things, which he probably will as long as Vahidoglu is in power, he has the financial and technical resources to do the job, and in the end, Carpenter-Beckenbaugh Corp. will have a claim on whatever technology they uncover."

"What about Vahidoglu?"

"Well, he gets his half share. But the Karakalpaks aren't equipped to develop anything. They'll have to depend on Carpenter. He'll probably pay Vahidoglu a personal licensing fee, or royalty, or something like that for the Karakalpak half. But even so, the basic technology ends up in American hands without the government having to spend a dime. All we have to do is lay back, keep the flies shooed away, and wait for capitalism to work its mighty magic."

"Steph?"

"Mr. Stone, with all due respect for CIA wisdom, what if that technology is as militarily significant as it appears to be? That there laser blew away a two hundred ton drilling platform in less than ten seconds. And we got a report says it could do the same thing to any one of our satellites. Now, do we want Mr. Hayes Carpenter to have that as his private plaything?"

"I don't think we have to worry about that. What would he do with it? Rule the world? Realistically, he'll get plenty of return on the technology without building weapons. He's already set up a lab to work with that funny soil, the stuff from the bull's-eye. Our information is that they think that under the heat and pressure of the laser the stuff sinters into a red-transparent solid and then reverts to particle form when the laser turns off."

"What's 'sinter' mean?"

"I'm not a metallurgist, George, but apparently some metallic powders go directly into a solid form under heat and pressure without melting first. The process is called sintering. The powder in the Array apparently does the same thing, but only temporarily. It seems to have to do with the particle size and shape, and possibly some other sort of emission from the laser."

"Excites me," said Artunian drily. "Probably put the President off his feed for a day. Okay. National Security Agency. You got anything for us this time?"

NSA Deputy Director Tom Thayer was representing his agency. "Nothing important to add, sir," he said succinctly.

"That's it? Anyone else? Good." Artunian looked at his watch. "It's ten-thirty. I'll fill in the President over lunch and expect the printed version on my desk by four. Work hard folks."

The real struggle for priority of analytical judgment began the moment George Artunian departed the room and continued for hours. The only loser from the very start was NSA, the nation's premier agency for code breaking and interception of electronic communications. They had had nothing of importance to contribute during the entire six months since the Great Array's discovery.

* * *

Next morning Tom Thayer burst out of the NSA Director's office with afterburners flaring. "Everyone!" he shouted to his secretary. "Division heads, my office. Now!"

It took five minutes for the dozen heads to assemble, two-thirds of them looking more like out-at-the-elbow college professors than top intelligence and counter-intelligence experts.

"Chief says we're embarrassing ourselves and jeopardizing our funding. President, Congress, and everyone else want to know something about the Great Array, and we're not players."

"We are working night and day on those signals that seem to have been included in the laser emissions," put in Wolfgang Zuckermann mildly.

"And so are MIT, Caltech, Columbia Earth Institute and everyone else in the world. That's public domain. If we decipher it, we win. But we haven't deciphered it yet, and it's even money that someone else will beat us to it. Remember, we get funded for reading the mail of other humans, not of space aliens. Chief wants new ideas, and he wants them yesterday. We're not going back into the NIE to sit on our thumbs."

"We could put a broader blanket over the Karakalpaks," suggested Suzanne Eastwick.

"Good. And not just the Karakalpaks. Lets focus down on signal traffic from Turkmenistan, Kazakhstan, and Uzbekistan as well. Particularly military. What about Carpenter-Beckenbaugh Corporation?"

"We're monitoring," replied Eastwick, "but they've got damn good encryption."

"Break it! I can tolerate ET holding out on us, but not Hayes Carpenter."

The heads of the three decryption divisions made in-your-lifetime-if-you're-lucky eyes at each other.

"We could surf the Internet for something," contributed programming chief Dwight Badger with a chuckle that others joined in on.

Thayer fixed him with a ferocious, no-levity gaze. "Do it, Dwight. Search the Internet. Anything else?"

"I didn't really mean . . ." started Badger only to trail off after a glance at Thayer's face.

Suzanne Eastwick stuck her head into Dwight Badger's office an hour later. The bald and bespectacled agency wise guy was staring out the window with a clouded look that belied the bright green and yellow cheeriness of his bow tie. "Surfing the Internet yet, Dwight?"

"Crawl under a rock and die, Suzanne."

"What a charming idea. Who's the chump who gets to do it?"

"Who can I spare?"

"Mmmmm, in your section? Just about everyone so far as I can see." Suzanne had all the intercept software she required and did not always see the purpose of Badger's programming division.

"Are you kidding? We're up to our ears writing signal analysis programs for the laser emissions."

"Then use your youngest. That's my principle. Works great for getting the coffee made." With that, she disappeared down the corridor.

Badger thought for a moment, then picked up his telephone and punched in four numbers.

Responding to his boss's summons, Joseph Engineer knocked and entered and took a proffered seat to the left of Badger's desk. "Joseph, are you ready for a special job?"

"Yes, Dr. Badger?"

"This one's straight from the Chief."

Joe felt that the mention of the Agency's Director called for straighter posture.

"We're going all out on the Great Array. New ideas. New approaches. Things CIA hasn't even dreamed about."

Joe wondered if he was expected to have such an idea.

"Somewhere in the world, Joseph, someone knows something we need to know. And if they don't, we need to know that too. Could be anyone. Could be anywhere. That's what national security is all about. Never satisfy yourself with the obvious. Go out, find the back door, the hidden key, the note thrown in the wastebasket. Never underestimate the enemy."

"The enemy, sir?"

"I'm speaking figuratively, Joseph. Now supposing you were to look for that back door, that hidden key. Where would you look, Joseph?"

"Dr. Badger, I've only been working here for a year. And I'm a programmer. I think you're asking the wrong person."

"Fair enough, fair enough. Then I'll tell you, and you tell me how you would go about searching, as a programmer. What about the Internet?"

"What about it?"

"I mean, as a place to look."

"Why would you look there?"

"To find out if anyone knows anything we should know."

"And posts it to a newsgroup? Or sets up a website? I don't get it. Everybody says the Array was built by space aliens two million years ago. I don't think they're likely to log onto a chat room."

Dwight Badger looked sympathetically at the twenty-five year old programmer. A bright young Ph.D. fresh from Carnegie-Mellon University, good-looking fellow from an immigrant Indian family, personable, diligent, and even-tempered—Badger felt like a movie general sending a young hero on a suicide mission. "Fact of the matter is, Joseph, on the off-chance that they do log onto a chat room, the Chief wants us to listen in on what they say."

"You're kidding."

"Surf the Internet. His words."

"You mean sift the digital sewage of the entire planet? Dr. Badger, I know I don't need to tell you what the ratio is of signal to noise on the Internet."

"No you don't."

"And wouldn't you agree that the probability of there being anything on the Internet of value to find is approximately zero?"

"To at least a dozen decimal places."

"How long am I supposed to do this?"

"For as long as it takes to get results."

"But there are no results to get. And in the meantime there's probably going to be a Nobel Prize for whoever gets to first base deciphering the laser signal."

"No need to get heated, Joseph."

"Sir, have I done something wrong?"

Badger looked at him with what he hoped was paternal kindness. "Yes, Joseph, you have. You have committed the sin of being too young."

Chapter Six

"Dotty, why are we having that bore Stein on? All he does is harp on Russian plots. Guy doesn't know when the game's over."

The Sunday Special producer looked up from the telephone cradled between her shoulder and her chin. "Sorry, Paul. Shanelle Whittaker cancelled out. I had to find an emergency replacement."

"What the fuck she cancel for?"

"She apologized. Said it was a judgment call whether appearing would help or hurt the launch of their 'Hole-in-the-Sea' movie on Tuesday."

"God, I hate it when the news is commercialized!"

Paul Henning walked into the studio and shook hands with his guests. "Dr. Stein, good to have you with us again. Dr. Takahashi, same to you. And Reverend Smith, it's an honor." The director pointed out the guests' assigned seats, and the sound woman attached their mikes.

The director's fingers counted down. Paul leaned into the camera. "Good morning and welcome to Sunday Special. I'm Paul Henning, and today we're going to look into some of the theories concerning the Great Array, or, as some people are calling it, the cosmic light show. My guests are Dr. Yasuo Takahashi of Columbia University's Earth Institute, Reverend Silvester Smith of Riverside Church, and Dr. Abraham Stein of the Council on Foreign Relations."

He pivoted smoothly to face Takahashi, who still looked more like a character from a Japanese action cartoon than an earth scientist. "Dr. Takahashi, you were one of the first important scientists to become convinced of the extraterrestrial origin of the Great Array. Tell us what we know now that we didn't know a month ago."

"That would take all day, Paul, but I can pick out some highlights. First, the core sample analyses coming out of Ankara confirm that the Array's overburden, the layers of sedimentary rock lying on top of it, are undisturbed except in the discoloration area of the Array itself. Given the depth of the laser, this means that it must have been placed there approximately two million years ago."

"But it's still working."

"That's the second important point. It has a power source, and a very strong one, and it's still operative after two million years. If it were our technology, that would mean a nuclear power plant using radioactive isotopes with very long half lives." Paul furrowed his brow for the camera but decided not to interrupt. "We'll know more when the angular probe into the bull's-eye reaches the proper level because then we should be able to detect any radiation that is now being absorbed by the rock layers. But that also means the probe must proceed slowly and carefully so that it doesn't accidentally damage the reactor or release radiation into the atmosphere."

"Dr. Takahashi, lets turn to the purpose that might have been served by this Array. There have been a lot of theories."

"Mostly bad. None of the so-called military experts quoted in the press, for example, has presented a plausible case for the Array itself being a weapon. Who, after all, would have been the enemy two million years ago? The most important thing to realize about the Array is that both the outgoing and incoming laser beams contained what appear to be digitized messages. In other words, the Array is most likely a communication device. But whether it is a communication device that has long outlived its purpose, or whether for some reason it was designed only to communicate when the Aral Sea was dry, we don't know. Given the many cycles of ice ages since the Array was installed, the Aral Sea has been dry a number of times. Just not during recorded history. What is puzzling is that whoever built the Array, presumably when the seafloor was dry, must have realized that it was in a depression. A more sensible location for continuous communication would have been on high ground. That suggests that builders probably planned to use the Array for a fairly limited period of time."

"But doesn't the return beam from space indicate that two-way communication is still going on?"

"Well, yes, of course. At least in a sense. The beam exchange that killed and blinded so many people was probably what computer people call a handshake protocol. The beam shoots up from the bull's-eye and says, 'I'm here. Is anybody listening?' Somewhere on a satellite or asteroid, a receiver responds with a beam that says, 'I hear you. What have you got to say?' The point to keep in mind, however, is that both the Array and the satellite could have been designed to long outlast their mission, just the way some of our own early space probes are still broadcasting even though they've gone much too far from Earth for us to pick up the signal. Unless there are some very, very old beings out there, this system is probably a relic that stopped being useful to its builders long before the evolution of humans."

"Makes you wonder what they thought of Earth when they came here."

"It's hard to imagine. Science fiction writers usually have people on hand to welcome visitors from space, and they usually land near big cities or remote rural towns, depending on the size of the movie budget. But since there's nothing to coordinate the evolution of life on one planet with that on another, it's actually much more probable that real space visitors would have arrived eons ago. Humans have only been around for a tiny, tiny fraction of the planet's lifetime. So while it might seem ironic that our visitors arrived when our early mammal ancestors had brains the size of marbles and were hiding in trees, and that they managed to install their communication device in what is today one of the most remote places on the globe, it's an alien contact scenario that is actually much more probable than what you see in the movies."

"Remarkable. You continue to fascinate us, Dr. Takahashi. When we come back, some religious and political views on the Great Array."

"You're off," called the director.

"That was terrific, Dr. Takahashi. Make sure Dotty has your number so we can get you down here if there's breaking news." A makeup man stepped onto the set and combed a portion of Paul Henning's pomaded hairdo back into place. Appearance repaired,

Paul smiled at the grey-suited minister to his left. "It's great to have you here, Reverend. You're up next."

"Back on four!" called the director.

A red light went on atop the camera with the teleprompter. "We are back with Sunday Special. My next guest is Reverend Silvester Smith of Riverside Church. You're no stranger to television, are you, Reverend."

The generously proportioned grey-haired man of the cloth looked perfectly relaxed. "Not after having my own show for thirteen years, Paul. It actually feels good to be back."

"Tell us, what are the religious implications of this prehistoric visitation from outer space?"

"Of course, Paul, every one of the world's great religions has its own understanding of this phenomenon, just as every religion has its own beliefs and traditions concerning the heavens and who might live there. The one thing almost everyone agrees on, however, is that there is now proof that humans are not the only intelligent beings in the universe."

"You say almost."

"That's right. That's because some fundamentalists are saying that the Array, like the fossils of dinosaurs, was placed under the Aral Sea by God during the six days of creation, and that it's activation now is a sign of the Apocalypse. And some New Age sects are saying that time becomes bent and that future humans went back in time and put the Array there for some reason we won't be able to discern until some future time."

"What do you believe, Reverend?"

"Paul, I'm an old man, and I remember well the novels of celestial theology by C.S. Lewis, and then the early efforts, some of them still ongoing, to listen for coherent messages from other planets. I've always found the arguments for life on faraway planets logically convincing. But that thought has never swayed me from my belief that we humans are on this planet for some divine purpose. We may not be able to understand that purpose, because it is unfolding over centuries at divine command. But each one of us has a very special role to play in the divine scheme of things. Paul, when I think about that Great Array, and the inadvertent tragedy it brought upon the people who were seeking to understand it, I am convinced that whoever or whatever placed it here had foreknowledge that humans would someday evolve and discover it."

"Do you believe it is a relic, as Dr. Takahashi suggests, or an active communicator?"

"Paul, deep in my heart I believe it is talking to God."

"That's beautiful, Reverend, beautiful. But now we must turn to the political side of things. Dr. Abraham Stein of the Council on Foreign Relations, bring us up to date."

"I'm tempted to talk about Ezekiel's chariot, Paul, but I'll stick to what I know. There is a good deal of speculation that Russia or Kazakhstan might try to take over the Karakalpak Republic by force since President Vahidoglu is absolutely rejecting every offer of international cooperation. But even though the Karakalpak army is very weak, it is hard to see how one country could make a military move without setting off a general war. The Russian army is the strongest in the area, of course, but it is only a shadow of what it was during the Cold War."

"How is President Rankin responding to this?"

"In his latest press conference, he continued to maintain the interested but politically aloof posture that was obviously decided on as administration policy months ago. The President has declared that the scientific knowledge represented by the Array should be the heritage of all mankind, but he has also affirmed the inviolability of international boundaries, which essentially supports President Vahidoglu. On the other hand, needless to say, he's not unaware that it's an American corporation that is undertaking the exploration."

"Is that being wishy-washy, Dr. Stein?"

The policy analyst laughed and his bald head gleamed in the lights. "You're not the first to suggest that, Paul. Some people even use the word hypocritical. But in this case, he's more wishy than washy. By that I mean I think he was a wish list of things he would like to see happen. For example, there are indications that behind the scenes the U.S. is pressuring NATO to support a policy of warning Russia off from any military adventure. Neither we nor the Europeans will stand for Russia gaining sole control of the Array."

"War a possibility?"

"Very, very remote. Nobody wants a war. What they want is for President Vahidoglu to stop being so obstinate and let the rest of the world in on the exploration of alien technology." Paul's antsy expression warned Stein that time was running out. "One final point, Paul."

"Very quickly."

"The Russians are still keeping something secret. Even though they've denied any responsibility for the Great Array, rumor has it that their Defense Ministry has assigned a team of archivists to comb their military records. But what they're looking for we have no idea."

"Thank you, Doctor. I'm sorry we're out of time."

Chapter Seven

The dark cloud of President Muratbey's blackmail was not without a silver lining. Chakra Net, the website Lee had created with technical help from the Ferghana Academy of Sciences, turned out to be a splendid diversion, even though Lee could not forgive the obscene pressure put on her to undertake it. Donald had done the right thing by apologizing for his indiscretion with the Cuban political officer, and Lee had done the right thing by forgiving him. But both were semi-conscious that they were simply postponing a crisis until they were back in the U.S. where separation or divorce might be contemplated with fewer complications.

In the meantime, Lee enjoyed the challenge of bringing the rock art of the Tien Shan Mountains on Ferghana's border with Kyrgyzstan to a broader audience. The idea that a low-budget public relations project could in any way discomfit the president of the Karakalpak Republic remained ludicrous, but Lee had taken to heart Major Park's warning never to underestimate the depth of Muratbey's hatred for Ahmet Vahidoglu.

The work had been fun: designing the site, choosing photographs of rock carvings to scan into its database, writing sometimes scholarly, sometimes speculative essays on the ancient folk who had carved and scratched the Ferghana chakras, and on the possible connections that might be drawn to the Great Array. Lee's only regret was that she couldn't attach her name to anything, both because of Muratbey's insistence that the project be "all Ferghanan" and because, other than Donald, no Americans—least of all Ambassador Bane—knew she was working for the president.

Since she connected to the Academy of Sciences server via her laptop, Lee did most of her work at home. Anytime she wished to take a break from translating Vedic hymns, she could log on and read whatever had been posted by visitors to Chakra Net. Though the posts were not numerous, they were usually amusing, and sometimes genuinely valuable, as when a Swedish professor uploaded fifty-three rock pictures of chakras from Scandinavia. More typical were New Agers proposing mystic meanings for the circle-and-cross or UFOers maintaining the chakras were ancient evidence of flying saucers. Lee took pleasure in doling out scornful responses to those who deserved them and entering into academic discussion with the occasional visitor with something worthwhile to say.

To her relief, there were no more tutorial sessions with Muratbey, and Major Park did not reappear or make any way attempt to renew his awkward John Alden-esque advance. Nevertheless, knowledge that their bungalow was bugged, and that any other place they might move to would surely be bugged as well, added additional coolness to the Ingalls' marital bed. Only in the car could they engage in frank talks about their situation, and neither of them felt inclined, or for that matter young or agile enough, to attempt sexual congress in a Honda compact.

To the degree that Lee was capable of finding an amusing side to their marital predicament, she discovered it in thinking about Donald still longing, she assumed, for his hot, but now off-limits, Cuban bombshell—Lee had never actually laid eyes on the woman—while she had been the recipient of the unsought and never to be requited attentions of two men: President Muratbey and, if she had interpreted his remarks correctly, Major Park. She decided not to share with Donald the part of Park's visit that did not involve him and the Cuban. Surprisingly, however, whenever she thought back over her visit from Major Park, as she frequently did, it passed through her mind that, despite his callousness and the cruelty of what he had done to her, he was not at all an unattractive man.

* * *

On Marmot Day, as Lee had dubbed February second in honor of Central Asia's ubiquitous burrowing rodent, she read the first posting from a new Chakra Net visitor:

From: Nadir@1Day2Day.com
To: Webmaster@Chakra_Net.com

THE TALE OF CHAKRA. FIRST POSTING.

Long gone the age of Gods; gone too the Giant age.
Remains the chakra great, the Giants' foul machine.
How base the Giants' plan the Gods did fight to stop.
As last surviving God, I tell to you my tale so when the Giant foe returns to build again, the ones who heed my words will join with me to fight.

Though Giants' lives are long, the Gods can never age.
They only die of wounds, though tough they are to harm.
Or else they kill themselves, as my companions have.
The Giants yearned to be as deathless as the Gods, but well they knew price that each immortal pays.
In all the universe, one root of life is found, the intertwining gyre that you call DNA.
All beings strive for life, but death cannot avoid.
To reproduce ones kind, the old must pass away or else the species dies from running out of food.
All creatures bear a gene that codes for age and death, a gene that's closely linked to that which codes for sex.
To all who've learned the art of engineering genes this fact has been quite clear: you cannot disengage the codes for age and sex. Though cells can be transformed so that they do not age beyond a certain point, this sort of deathless life wilts all desire for sex and cannot be passed on. If intercourse takes place, no egg is fertilized. The Gods, though thus endowed with lives that

never end, do not comprise a race, but rather were the spawn of scientific zeal.

How else could life survive? If beings do not age, yet still do reproduce, they soon become extinct for want of food or space. Fond sex and end of life, new birth then age and death—all forever linked, by double helix bound.

These facts are not surmise. On planets far and wide the double helix reigns. And known it is, though rare, that random flukes of change anomalies do cause.
A fragmenting between the codes for sex and death can leave within a gene a kind of dormant seed, a seed of endless life still able to give birth.
A species with this gene lives life as others do.
It ages and it dies, until another fluke, or scientific plan, turns off the proper gene that carries sex and death and activates instead its freakish dormant twin. A species formed this way, experiment has shown, is like a normal fish, or plant, or beast, or bird. But never does it age beyond maturity; its life goes endless on unless by force cut short. Yet since its sex is strong, it strives to reproduce, and thus it soon attains extinction of its kind.

Such was the riddle deep the Giants' would unwind.
Great builders, strong of mind, long-lived as they could be and still yet reproduce, they longed for even more.
They longed for endless life with sexual drive intact.
With that their kind could spread to galaxies afar, instead of being bound to planets fit for life within a travel range of several thousand years.
With scientific skill they laid genetic plans.
They tested all the genes from planets that they knew until by chance they found a tiny, furry beast that hid among the trees from massive lizard beings.
Their tests revealed they'd found what they so long had sought: a creature bearing genes with duplicated codes, one active and

as usual cross-linking sex with death, the other not expressed, but freeing age from birth.

Long time the Giants thought, then hit upon a plan.
They sought to make the beast more like unto themselves, to help it to evolve toward what you Earthlings call the genus humankind. Their plan was not too hard, at least for Giant skills. They moved off course a rock and crashed it into Earth. It killed the dinosaurs and freed the little beast to move outside its niche and grow in size and mind. Then waited they an age in hopes the beast would change, evolve into a breed with which they then could mate.
They even made attempts to guide genetic change.
But all their efforts failed. It seemed genetic change could not be thus controlled. Their interventions worked, when work at all they did, only when some plague brought species to the point where most of them would die and just a few adapt.
When such events befell, the Giants sought to pick a few surviving beasts to change genetic codes.
From time to time it worked. The few with altered genes engendered species new. And so the Giants schemed to engineer such change, to cause by their machines catastrophes immense so they could intervene in evolution's course.

Now come I to the thing that's called the Great Array, and also to the war of Giants and of Gods.
To speed the pace of change, as hominids emerged, the Giants caused a flux from ice to heat to ice.
Extinctions were their goal, and birth of species new
Each time the climate swung, they picked among the group they thought might best survive a few, whose genes they changed, implanting Giant traits. Thus slowly humans formed, became with every change a little closer to the species that produced both God and Giant kind.

This chakra, thus you see, earth's climate regulates.
Another one lies deep beneath the Greenland ice.

When icecaps grow so large that shallow seas run dry, this chakra sends to space a signal of this fact.
The listening Giants note that time of change is nigh.
And buried deep in Earth their climate change machines do vent a certain gas that turns the cycle round, increasing warmth of air, and melting polar ice.
Then later when the heat has caused the ice to melt, the Greenland Great Array, exposed now to the sky, beams word to Giant ears that now's a time for ice.
Earth cools, the ice reforms. And as the cycle goes, so many species go, extinct or near extinct through meddlesome intent of Giant engineers.
But with each change do Giants gain another chance to alter and improve the species most like theirs with hopes to interbreed when humankind is ripe and gain thereby the gene that humans do not use, the gene of endless life combined with sex and birth, the gene by which to spread from star to star to star.

The chakras thus control the warmth and cold of Earth, and signal they each change to monitors in space.
The sequence in the past of ice, then heat, then ice is relic of this plan to breed for Giants mates.
But now the end is near. There's but one cycle left, one melting of the ice, one last genetic step, amidst chaotic times with many millions dead.
Though humans will survive, their numbers will be few.
The Giants then will act, will alter one last gene, the gene that lets a mind engage another mind without the need of speech. This trait the Giants have, as also do the Gods, and with it humankind will be so like them both that breeding will become a simple task indeed. Some chosen human males with telepathic gifts will be the source of sperm, but never will they live to see what is produced by union of their seed with female Giant eggs.
The offspring will not die, but will be Giants still, never to be told the source of father's seed.

And as for humankind, like rats when ends the test, discarded they will be and wiped from off the earth.
The Giants, after all, care only for themselves.
Though shaping human fate, they care not if they live.

Nadir

"How clever," said Lee to herself as the last sentences lilted past her eyes. "But how terribly annoying." She looked at the name and decided it could be either Turkish or Tajik, or possibly even Arab, unless it was some sort of astronomical pseudonym. "Why in the world would someone write in meter?" She thought for a few minutes and then applied herself to the keyboard:

From: Webmaster@Chakra_Net.com
To: Nadir@1Day2Day.com

RE: THE TALE OF THE CHAKRA. FIRST POSTING.

Nadir, you seem to have mistaken Chakra Net for an online poetry journal. Congratulations on your feel for meter, but this is a scientific board that does not resonate to iambic phrases. Kindly reserve your further entries for a more appropriate site. Or, as a god, perhaps you should consider opening your own site for your worshippers. Please do not make further postings here.

Webmaster

Her right pinky poised over the key that would post her message, Lee reread what she had written and decided it was too harsh. Granting Nadir a second chance, she read back over his message ignoring its irritating rhythm and focusing on content. The seed of the idea, she reflected, was not so bad. Once you set aside the genetic mumbo-jumbo and the fairy tale about gods and giants, you were left with the notion that the Aral Sea chakra, as a communications device, was placed on the seabed, or in a depression where a sea would form, because it was only intended to operate during ice ages when the water would be bound up in glaciers. If there were, then, a twin of the Great Array beneath a glacier, there could, logically, be a balance between the two, alternately signaling one extreme or the other of the Earth's climate.

Lee made herself a fresh cup of tea and mulled over Nadir's scenario. It was actually quite clever. And if there had once been space beings capable of implanting the Array, did it in any way strain credulity to think that they could have redirected an asteroid to hit the Earth and destroy the dinosaurs? She took down her one-volume *Columbia Encyclopedia* and began to browse. The dinosaurs, she discovered went extinct at the end of the Cretaceous, 65 million years ago, while the Ice Ages were part of the Pleistocene, between two million and eleven thousand years ago. The latter was about right for the Great Array, but the idea of the so-called Giants waiting 63 million years to think up Plan B strained credulity. After a period of further mulling, she returned to her laptop and substituted a new message for the one she had just written.

From: Webmaster@Chakra_Net.com
To: Nadir@1Day2Day.com

RE: THE TALE OF THE CHAKRA. FIRST POSTING.

Thank you, Nadir, thanks sincerely, for your interesting posting.
Questions have I, questions puzzling, which will task you much to answer.
If the chakra tunes the climate, causing icecaps forming, melting,
What contains the laser signal? What's the source of warmth or coldness?

Warmth that turns the ice to water, cold that dries up seas and oceans.
What of Giants, how big are they? Will we humans gain their stature
Once the seas increase in volume, causing havoc to our cities,
Killing off our old and young ones, threatening complete extinction.
And of Gods, the Gods immortal, how come you're the last remaining?
Did the rest by inadvertence step before a charging rhino?
Did they instead leave you behind when headed back to their own planet?
Are you stuck among us earthlings, doomed to live with mortal humans?
Please excuse my questions petty, questions far beneath your notice.
Answer only if your choose to, choose to grant a godly favor,
Send to me another chapter, chapter of the Tale of Chakra.
But send it not in rhyme or meter, send it please in normal writing.
If once more you post iambics, sing-song words in measure triple,
Force upon me silly meter, irritate me near to screaming,
It will be your final posting. Banned you'll be from net of chakra.
Catch my drift, oh God immortal? Prose submit or live in silence.

Webmaster

Lee reviewed what she had written, fine tuned the meter, and with a grin hit the ENTER key. Now lets see what we get, she thought.

Chapter Eight

From: Nadir@1Day2Day.com
To: Webmaster@Chakra_Net.com

THE TALE OF CHAKRA. SECOND POSTING.

I have an old machine that goes by name of Ann.
She puts my thoughts in words with rhythm as you read.
This started at a time when first among my friends
I counted one old man who sang the songs of Troy.
I argued then with Ann about iambic form and ordered her to couch my words in metric pace.
Now this is what she does though styles of speech have changed.
If this prevents my words from being understood, it's not my fault but Ann's. She says she will not change.

So try to understand the limits that I face in warning humankind that Giants will return.
And when indeed they come, they'll like not what they find.
When last they fought with Gods, Earth's only Giants died.
And with the battle done, I dealt with their machine.
I used my weapon strong to interrupt the link that bound the Great Array to underground machines.
No more would icecaps form, no more would icecaps melt responding to machines installed by Giant hands.

Forever would they wait the signals from the Earth, for seas would not run dry nor Greenland show its soil.
My mission at an end, I rested and I watched, watched humankind increase, become a mighty race.
But now my work's undone because some human beings have dried the Aral Sea so signal could be sent.
And now the Giants know their underground machines have not begun to work. This has the laser said.
So certain now it is that soon a Giant ship will come again to Earth. An engineer will come to find what has gone wrong, discover what I wrought, repair the damage done.

This story have I told in several different ways, but no one heeds my words, no listening ear believes.
How sad the fall of Gods, who once were praised of men, who taught them how to build, who raised them from the dirt.
I think of my old friends, who fell to Giants' blows:
Twashtar, Dyaus, the Ashwins, all like me intent on saving humankind from cruel, callous fate designed by Giant schemes.

But now I am alone, my years grown very long.
Though youthful still and strong, one leg I lost in war.
The others of my kind who fought the Giant foe have ended their own lives, too bored to carry on.
But I do not complain. I do, however, hope that someday all will know what Gods for humans did, what sacrifice we made.
I sometimes get annoyed that people have forgot the honor they once paid to me and to my friends, the rites of sacrifice that amplified our strength. I long again to feel their worship as of old, but now the times are hard, the end is coming near.

Nadir

Lee still felt puzzled and angry several hours after reading Nadir's second message. Eventually she put on her hooded winter coat and went for a walk. The air was cold but the sky bright and the sidewalks clear of snow. She walked past several small bungalows like hers and then past several blocks of drab storefronts until she came to the park by the Presidential Palace. The old sycamore trees lining the streets stretched their naked limbs high into the sky. A vendor of roasted chestnuts sat huddled by his brazier of charcoal waiting for the occasional passer-by. Lee bought a quarter kilo of the sweet, hot nuts nestled in an envelope folded from newspaper. She took a seat on a park bench beside a waterless fountain. Several small children were playing noisily nearby in some remnant snow piles while a grandmother, bundled heavily against the chill, sat and watched them.

Try as she might to concentrate on the peaceful scene around her and the brilliance of the winter's day, four words of Nadir's posting returned again and again to her mind: "Twashtar, Dyaus, the Ashwins." In all of her years devoted to studying the most ancient religion and language of India, she had never chanced, in conversation or in print, upon the names of such obscure Vedic gods, except, of course, in exchanges with fellow Vedists.

Not Agni, the divinization of fire, who occasionally showed up in the *New York Times* crossword. Not the goddess Saraswati, who enjoyed a certain currency in feminist writings. Not the divine Soma, the secret intoxicating beverage drunk by the Vedic priests and made famous in Aldous Huxley's *Brave New World.* But Twashtar, Dyaus, and the Ashwins. Twashtar, the blacksmith god, equivalent to Hephaestus in Greek and Vulcan in Latin. Dyaus the god of the sky—Odin in Norse mythology, father Zeus for the Greeks, and Jupiter—Father Ju, Ju-pater—for the Romans. And the chariot-driving Ashwins, the twin gods of the dawn, the Vedic version of the Greeks' Castor and Pollux. But where was Indra, the hurler of thunderbolts, the Vedic version of the Norse god Thor?

Lee stood up with a start as a thought hit her. Her chestnuts fell into the dirty snow beneath the bench. An anagram: Nadir=Indra. Indra=Nadir. How clever, she thought, but what a nasty thing to do. She scurried back to her house not quite sure what she would do once she got there. Seating herself at her laptop, she printed out both of Nadir's messages and read them over again with care.

"Someone's tricking me," she said aloud. "Some bastard . . . ." She began to turn over in her mind the names of the Vedists she had been in contact with since arriving in Kokand, already contemplating a dreadful revenge. Which of them, she wondered, could have found out about her secret connection with Chakra Net? Had one of them really thought she was going to believe that the god Indra was alive and communicating with her under the name Nadir? Was her former boyfriend John Russell, for example, sitting back in his office at Penn waiting for her to address a return message "Dear Indra" so he could tell everyone that Lee really believed in her Vedic gods? *I would have been a laughing stock*, she thought. *They all know I study the Indra hymns. Maybe they're all in it together.*

Lee was still mulling over the situation, occasionally casting curses or threats at the unidentified trickster, when she heard the snow crunch under the wheels of the Honda.

"Whoa! Who are you going to kill?" said Donald at his first sight of his wife's face.

"Don't worry. Not you," she replied curtly, "though you may deserve it. One of my friends has been jerking me around."

Donald hazarded a peck on her cheek. "You're pretty when you're mad at someone else," he said lightly. "Which friend? And what did he do?"

"I don't know which friend. That's what I have to find out. Remember that bizarre posting I got last week on Chakra Net? The one in iambic meter?"

"Space aliens controlling Earth's temperature."

"That's the one. Jerk calls himself Nadir. You know why? Because it's an anagram for Indra, the thundergod. Today he posted another message saying he was the last survivor of a group of gods, including Twashtar, Dyaus, and the Ashwins."

"Dyaus is Zeus?"

"Very good."

"I haven't heard of the other ones."

"That's because they're totally obscure to people who don't read the Vedas. That's what was so tricky, using god names only a few people have ever heard of."

"People like you."

"Exactly."

Donald looked down at his furious wife. "Lee, you didn't . . ." She glared up at him ferociously.

"Didn't what?"

"You did, didn't you! You believed you got a message from a genuine Vedic god!" He burst into hearty laughter.

"Not for one instant. Not for a millisecond. And if you ever tell anyone I did, I'll kill you," said Lee grimly.

Donald's laughter was out of control. "You really believed," he said breathlessly, "I can see it in your eyes. Old Indra getting in touch with his lady friend on the Internet?"

"The tiniest, tiniest fraction of a millisecond. No, less than that."

"Oh, let me sit down. My side hurts. You poor thing. Come and sit on my lap."

"I'm not feeling lappish, thanks. I'm feeling vengeful."

"Who do you think did it?"

"I've made up a list. But I can't believe any of them would have done such a thing. Unless they all are in it together. I figure it has to be someone I've been in e-mail contact with so they know where I am. And it has to be someone who knows I study the Indra hymns."

Donald was still chuckling. "So you got this on e-mail?"

"No. It was on Chakra Net."

Donald frowned. "I thought you hadn't put your name on Chakra Net. You promised me you wouldn't. And you promised President Muratbey. You know Ambassador Bane would be pissed to learn about this second hand. You're not allowed to do things like this without her permission."

"Don't worry. I never put my name on Chakra Net. I sign my messages 'Webmaster'."

"Well, you must have slipped."

"No, I didn't slip."

"Then how did your friend associate you with Chakra Net?"

Lee thought for a bit. "Maybe they . . . ." she trailed off when no answer came. "You must have told someone, Donald. Or maybe Muratbey."

"Me? Absolutely not. It's bad enough having . . . you know, the Cuba thing . . . hanging over my head, never knowing if the

Ambassador is going to find out. The last thing I want is for people to know my wife is working on a private project for the President. And why would Muratbey talk about it? He wants this thing to be pure Ferghanan."

"Then the guys at the Academy of Sciences must have leaked it. I shouldn't have trusted Olga and Reshat."

"Wasn't everyone told this was Muratbey's project? Why would they tell anyone who's running it? And how would they know who your friends are?"

Lee considered Donald's questions. "They could have mentioned my name to colleagues in one of the Russian universities. Maybe some friend of mind happened to be around. I don't know. It's hard to explain." She went to the kitchen and sampled the soup that had been simmering gently all afternoon. "Did you bring home the bread?" she called into the living room.

"Yup," came the answer.

Dinner was a quiet affair as Lee sullenly pondered her dilemma. Her anger at being the butt of a practical joke was compounded by her inability to figure out how the joke had been perpetrated. Donald tried to distract her. "Radio report today about an earthquake under the big reservoir at Andijan over on the Kyrgyz border. Lucky it didn't hurt the dam." Lee was uninterested. Her mind had begun to formulate a strategy.

At her laptop after dinner, she typed in a new posting:

From: Webmaster@Chakra_Net.com
To: Nadir@1Day2Day.com

RE: THE TALE OF THE CHAKRA. SECOND POSTING.

Nadir

If you insist in writing in meter, so be it. I shall no longer reciprocate. You say you are the last of the gods, and the gods you list are named in the Rig Veda. If you are indeed a god, you should know certain things. So if you want to be believed, you must answer my questions:

1) What was the demon Vrtra whom you killed?
2) What was the vajra you used to kill Vrtra with?
3) What was the name of your wife Indrani's ape?
4) Who were the dasas?
5) Why were pictures of chakras carved in the mountains?

I am eager to learn your answers to these questions.
Be convincing or be gone.

Webmaster

Lee dispatched the message with a sharp snap of a key and sat back with a smile of satisfaction. *If this is a game*, she thought, *I'm willing to play*. The telephone rang in the living room, and she heard Donald pick it up. "Lee," he called. "For you."

She walked to the living room and took the phone from his hand. He silently mouthed the words "Major Park." She stiffened.

"Hello, this is Lee Ingalls."

"Mrs. Ingalls, this is Major Park. I am sorry to disturb you."

"That's quite all right," she said sourly. "Your bugs disturb me every time I open my mouth in my own house. What can I do for you?"

"I have a question. Have you told anyone that you are the operator of Chakra Net?"

She felt a thrill of apprehension. "Of course not, Major. The agreement was that Chakra Net would be seen as a purely Ferghanan enterprise. Just today, however, as you will discover when you review your tapes, I had reason to suspect that one of my colleagues in Vedic studies has figured out what I am doing and posted a message as a joke."

"Which colleague?"

"I have no idea. Could you tell me why you are asking?"

"Because someone has been trying to find out who is operating Chakra Net."

"Who?"

"Someone at the National Security Agency in Washington. Do any of your colleagues in Vedic studies work there by chance?"

"Not that I know of, Major."

"You are absolutely sure of that?"

"Not absolutely, but Vedists don't usually go into spying as a trade. If you tell me the person's name, however, I can tell you if it's someone I know."

"His name is Joseph Engineer. He made an inquiry to the Academy of Sciences."

"I'm afraid I've never heard of him."

"Nor has he heard of you, Mrs. Ingalls. The information we provided to him was that the sign-on you use at the Academy of Sciences—which he had already found out—is an unassigned address. Your identity is therefore as much a mystery to us as to him."

"Did he believe that?"

"I assume he did not. But please be vigilant, Mrs. Ingalls. Please be vigilant."

"Thank you for that advice, Major Park."

"Good-bye then, Mrs. Ingalls."

"Good-bye."

"What was that all about?" said Donald.

"Someone in the National Security Agency is trying to find out who's running Chakra Net."

"NSA? You're kidding." An anxious frown clouded Donald's face. "You're sure it's not your jokester friend?"

"Apparently not. Some guy with a funny name. Joseph Engineer. It's all very puzzling."

Chapter Nine

Tom Thayer was in shirtsleeves and yellow suspenders, his desk littered with paper; but the appearance of informality was belied by his taut body language and the piercing eyes behind his gold-rimmed glasses. He was Deputy Director of NSA not because of technical expertise, but because he got things done. And he was notoriously impatient with the head-in-the-clouds linguists and jargon-spouting techs who populated so many of the agency's departments.

Thayer had never met Joseph Engineer, nor when the young, bronze-skinned Indian timidly entered the office could he recall even seeing him in the corridor. "You're Joseph?" He reached out a hand across the desk. "I'm Tom Thayer. Have a seat." He picked up the ten-page report Joseph had submitted two days earlier to Dr. Badger. "This is an interesting report, Joseph. More interesting than most. Tell me where it comes from. I can't read all that technical crap you have at the beginning."

"It's from the Internet, Mr. Thayer. Dr. Badger assigned me to surf the Internet for possibly important information on the Great Array."

"Right. I figured that much out. Tell me what you did and how you came up with this report."

"Well, first I programmed a software robot called a spider or crawler to cull out what I thought might be significant keywords. That was a total failure. I don't know whether you know this, sir, but there are upwards of ten thousand websites now devoted wholly or partly to the Great Array. So I wasted a lot of time on that. But then

I thought: If I knew something significant, why in the world would I put it on the Internet instead of going to some authority? And it occurred to me that such a person might already be working for an authority but have it in mind to be a kind of leaker or whistle-blower. Like, maybe the information he possessed was secret but he thought it should be in the public domain. Given the weapons potential of the Great Array laser, this seemed not out of the question. Or maybe he thought his information or his ideas were being ignored in-house, but he couldn't afford to make his view public and go against his boss. That kind of thing. So I decided to take my ten-thousand-plus sites and match postings with our list of remailers."

"What's a remailer?"

"Remailers are for anonymous postings. You pay a fee to a company to provide an untraceable electronic address."

"We keep a list of these remailers?"

"Yes we do. Mostly they're used for pornography, but you never know."

"So you decided to check whether pornographers were posting things about the Great Array."

"I already knew that, sir. There's a ton of stuff about sex with aliens, about the President having sex with aliens, about TV sitcom stars having sex with aliens, about comic book characters having sex with aliens. It's all over the place. But to get rid of that, I fed a list of bad words into my crawler and told it to disregard postings that contained them."

"And that cut the list down?"

"Cut it down to under a hundred posters. Of those, I eliminated another bunch who had made up their own words for alien sex and some more whose language was too soft-core to make my naughty list. The long and the short of it was that I came up with eleven postings from one person directed to ten different sites."

"If the postings are anonymous, how do you know it's the same person?"

"Same name, same remailer: Nadir@1Day2Day.com in Dayton, Ohio. But more important, the guy writes in iambic hexameter."

Tom Thayer's eyes bored into the twenty-five year old programmer. "Is that in this report?" He shook the sheaf of paper.

"No, sir. I left it out. I didn't think Dr. Badger would read it if I put it in. I never dreamed it would get to you, sir."

"So this report is based on the writings of a fucking poet!?"

Joseph fought to keep the tremor he felt in his chest out of his voice. "No, not really a poet. There's no rhyme, and he doesn't have what I would call a poetic sensibility. It's just rhythmic, sort of lilting. You wouldn't necessarily think it was poetry, unless maybe doggerel."

"So a nutcase."

"I don't think so. That's why I submitted the report. He posted one message each to nine websites of all different sorts starting the day after the first laser emission. Postings to technical sites were technical. Ones to UFO sites were science fictiony. But they all said the same basic thing: the Great Array and a twin array under the Greenland icecap are communication devices connected to machinery capable of causing global climatic oscillations. He says they are responsible for the ice ages. But no one responded to any of these postings. He was totally ignored, presumably because of his way of writing, until he posted on a really obscure site in the Ferghana Republic. The webmaster hates his poetry but otherwise seems to be taking him seriously. So now they've got an exchange going."

"All right. Good for him. He's found a pen pal. My question to you is why I should be spending my time talking to you about one of ten million cranks trying to sell their science fiction plot instead of doing something more useful, like relieving my bowels."

"Please, Mr. Thayer, let me go on for just another two minutes. I tried to find out who the poster was by getting onto the remailer in Dayton."

"Aren't they supposed to keep clients' names secret?"

"Yes, sir, unless you have a court order. But they have to keep a master list so they can bill them. 1Day2Day is a very small outfit so I gambled that their master list was on the same computer they used for remailing. Then I hacked into it."

"You what? Don't you know that's against the law?" said Thayer explosively.

"I didn't think we had grounds for a court order, sir. And I figured I could do it without getting caught . . . and it was needed to carry out my mission . . . sir."

Tom Thayer sat back in his leather desk chair and smiled. "Good work. You might have the makings of a spy after all, you know that? But don't tell me more than I need to know. Just tell me who the guy is."

"I don't know. The hack worked, but it turned out Nadir was using two remailers. The only address 1Day2Day had was a remailer in Denmark that rotates a series of addresses in a complicated way to prevent anyone from identifying their clients."

Thayer lifted his eyebrows expectantly. "I hope you hacked the fucker. No one hides from the NSA. And if this guy is using a double blind drop, what he has to say just might be important."

"That's exactly what I thought, sir. But Danish laws are different from ours. They permit greater electronic secrecy. Nevertheless, I had a German friend when I was in grad school at Carnegie-Mellon. We had both hacked around when we were teenagers, and we compared techniques a lot. Since I didn't think I could get permission to use Agency personnel, I called Gerhard and asked him what he could do. I told him it was important."

"That was enterprising. Go on."

"He found out."

"Hacked in?"

"I don't think so. I think he broke into the office. Gerhard . . . uh . . . doesn't do things the way I would. Anyway, he didn't get caught. So at last I had an address, and it turned out to be at the Kazakh State University in Almaty." Thayer leaned forward, entirely focused on Joseph. "The guy is right there in Central Asia, but writing in English like he wants to be a poet. Very strange."

"So. Who is he?"

"I still don't know. Kazakh State University says the address he's using is unassigned."

"And you believe that?"

"I didn't at first, but they opened up their log for me and they were right. No action at all from that address except the eleven messages I had found, and no address assignment to any personnel. Moreover, no record of those eleven coming through their land lines.

I have no idea how he's routing his messages through their system without their knowing it, and they don't either."

"So. End of the line?"

"No, sir. As I told you, the last site he posted to he got a response and posted again. I decided, if I can't find him directly, maybe I can track him down through where he's posting. The sysop . . . the system operator . . . might know who he is. So that board was easy to locate. It's called Chakra Net, and it's hosted by the Ferghana Academy of Sciences in Kokand. Almaty and Kokand are practically next to each other, just a three hundred mile hop over the mountains. So things seemed to be looking up, except that—this may be hard to believe, sir—the Ferghana Academy of Sciences says they don't know who their own sysop is, and the address the sysop is using is unassigned, just like in Almaty."

"You're kidding."

"No, sir. Two dead ends."

"Do you believe the Academy of Sciences?"

"No, Mr. Thayer, I don't. They show no interest in helping me at all. Whoever I talk to refers me to the office of the President."

"The President of the Ferghana Republic?"

"Correct."

"And what do they tell you?"

"They say Chakra Net is a scientific board devoted to publicizing the relationship between the Great Array and the history of the Ferghana Republic and that its operator is not available to talk to except on-line. And, of course, on-line the sysop just uses 'Webmaster.' It's common jargon."

"Well isn't that the damnedest thing. Isn't that just the damnedest thing. What in the world is everyone covering up?"

"That's why I thought it was important enough to write up for Dr. Badger, Mr. Thayer. It's not just what is being said, but that it's being said with such apparently pointless secrecy."

"Absolutely fascinating," mused Thayer under his breath. "Where do you propose to go from here?"

"Uh, nowhere sir. I've hit dead ends. All I can think of is asking CIA to put people onto finding Nadir in Almaty and Webmaster in Kokand. I can't imagine it would be very hard to do, especially for Webmaster."

Tom Thayer was suddenly leaning across his desk again, his face grimly serious. "Joseph, don't you ever again mention giving a job to the CIA in this office. This is an NSA lead. It is NSA's and no one else's."

"Except that we only work electronically, sir," said Joseph defensively.

"I don't want to hear that, Joseph. We are spies, and we have to learn to act like spies or face the consequences." Joseph wondered what the consequences might be. "Let me think about this. And keep your report to yourself. I'll tell Badger to button up. Who knows? If need be, we may send you to Central Asia." He stood up and offered Joseph his hand across the desk. "Now get out of here and let me work."

Out in the corridor, Joseph took several deep breaths. He could feel his accelerated heart rate. *I should have mentioned the gods and giants*, he thought. *But then no one would have read the report at all.* His mental debate continued as he headed for his office on automatic pilot. *But still, without the gods and giants Nadir's postings do sound reasonable. So now I've got the Deputy Director all heated up about a fantasy. But I had to show something. I couldn't just read crap on the Internet all day forever. But now I have to face the consequences.* He again wondered what the consequences might be.

Chapter Ten

Like others of his kind, Bix reveled in using equipment. All the more thrilling was the prospect of wowing a local species. On his other two planetary assignments, the most developed organisms had still been swimming around in seawater digesting and multiplying, digesting and multiplying, digesting and multiplying: hardly appreciative audiences for his state of the art technology. But here he had already witnessed a terrifically gratifying shock reaction from the boatload of the dominant species that witnessed his little flyer break the surface of the Andijan Reservoir and zoom off into the sky. For an added thrill, Bix had swooped around and buzzed them only six feet above the water. This was going to be a fun repair job. If only the dominant species didn't look so much like disgusting *pramodzi*.

On his shoulder, Frak, his biocybernetic interface, silently communicated navigation information downloaded at the satellite where they had stopped first to get an overview of the situation. Bix's hands on the flyer's controls responded with effortless speed and dexterity, trimming its suspensors to the atmospheric density and keeping it just above obstacle level. Snow-capped mountains towered on three sides, but the flat plain of the river valley presented no problems. His infrared display showed a group of animals clustered near a tall, spindly structure with a rotor at the top and a water tank at the bottom. Frak informed him that they were called "sheep" and were not of the dominant species. Bix touched a control and watched them combust colorfully on the screen.

Whoo-ee, good to be back at work! he communicated.

Just here to get a job done, Frak reminded him.

Bix cocked his head and communicated humorously to an imaginary audience, *That's Frak for you.*

Settling the flyer into the courtyard surrounding the historic brick and tile citadel restored as the Presidential Palace required delicacy. Sizable objects, ranging from primitive hydrocarbon propelled vehicles to tubes for projecting metal objects by chemical explosion, filled most of the space. As Bix guided the flyer's descent, the infrared showed a scattering of beings scampering into apertures in the courtyard walls. After completing a landing check, Bix attended impatiently to Frak's required readout of the protocols for contacting intelligent aliens.

Like I don't know this already, communicated Bix. He looked at the infrared screen. A being of the dominant species, looking suspiciously like a *pramodzi*, was standing alone beside the flyer. According to the protocols, a group of beings holding pointed things usually meant you would have to kill most of them to get your message across. A single being not holding a pointed object was a good sign. It signaled either idle, pre-rational curiosity, which seemed to Bix an option he could rule out, or a more advanced rationality that wished to communicate. The proper protocol in the latter situation was to open the door.

Major Dimitri Park mused as he waited in the icy courtyard for something to happen. Floodlights on the crenellated walls and corner towers cast brilliant light on the spherical ship. *Pick the Korean*, he thought. The litany had been a part of his interior reflections since early childhood. *Something dirty or dangerous? Pick the Korean. Well, who, in fact, better to pick? If somebody has to be the first human to talk to an extraterrestrial, it damn well should be a Korean*, thought the Major proudly. *More likely to get things right that way and not go all hysterical.*

The dark-hued machine hovering half a meter off the ground next to President Muratbey's Volvo was essentially a sphere ten meters in diameter, but its surface was marked by numerous grooves and irregularities. At top and bottom, well away from its center, pairs of cylindrical meter-wide holes bored all the way through the ship. Park surmised that these somehow must provide its propulsion. The door that glided upward in the machine's side was surprisingly large.

Made for big guys, thought Park. As it opened, a stairway extended down to the paving stones. The stairs reassured Park that whatever was inside probably walked rather than slithered. Park straightened his posture and strode forward.

The dim corridor inside was tall and wide, its walls fitted with a variety of objects and devices Park could not begin to identify. Park counted three full steps forward before the corridor opened onto a larger space on his right. The larger space proved to be a sphere within a sphere, approximately six meters in diameter with a grating providing a floor about two thirds of the way down. The light level was as dim as in the corridor, but not to the point where Park had to strain to see. The being in front of him was clearly a man, a strongly built man with a long torso and very short legs. Park looked again and corrected himself: the man was sitting down on a chair so skeletal that it hadn't been evident at first. Park added the probable length of his thighs to the rest of him and realized with a start that he must be almost as tall as a basketball hoop.

An object moved on the man's shoulder by his cheek. What Park had taken for a shock of long hair was an animal; in fact, an animal that looked exactly like a marmot. The marmot spoke. "Hello," it said in English in a surprisingly mellow feminine voice, "I have come here from another star system to repair some equipment." The man smiled confidently and radiantly while the marmot spoke. "I hope the language I have chosen is satisfactory. It is the one most abundantly available to outside recorders. My translator has a capacity in a dozen others, but its vocabulary and command of idiom is fullest in this one."

"I speak English," replied Park. "Who is your translator? Are you yourself present?"

"I am present." The marmot spoke, but the man bowed his head deeply in evident greeting. His face was young, but there was a lassitude in his posture that did not seem quite youthful. "I am named Bix. My translator I call Frak. My race communicates without speech so we use translators when we must speak. Since some species—ones much more primitive than yours, of course—find it easier to grasp a speaking being than a speaking machine, we clothe our translators with an animate shell suitable to the surroundings. It also puts on them the burden of hanging on."

"Then I am to understand that what looks like a marmot on your shoulder is a kind of computer? And when it speaks, it is on behalf of the person in the chair? And that person is you?"

"Exactly. My name is Bix."

Marjor Park nodded deeply as Bix had done earlier and replied, "I am Major Dimitri Park, Director of the Internal Security Service of the Republic of Ferghana."

"Excellent! You are an official! We are making superior progress. We will be friends." Bix mentally consulted the protocols. "In our experience, we have found that species at your level of development usually initiate official contact through an individual whose death is acceptable." Bix noticed his small interlocutor grow suddenly tense. He interrogated the protocols and found he had mixed up an explanatory passage with one of the dialog suggestions. Why hadn't he studied them more closely? "Do not be alarmed, Major Dimitri Park. The reference to death was a mistake. We never speak of death. I meant to observe that you are probably not very important yourself, but possibly sent by someone who is important."

Park relaxed slightly. "That is correct."

Weapons have been assembled around the courtyard and in a flying device circling over us, communicated Frak in Bix's mind.

Protocols seem to be right on that one, responded Bix with an added feeling of confidence. If he was going to demo his destructors, it was nice to have targets like weapons and flying devices to demo them on.

"Major Park," said the marmot, "my need is to arrange a contract with the person in authority so that I can get about my repairs. Who would that be?"

"That would depend on where you need to go to make your repairs," replied Park shrewdly. "If the laser device under the sea is yours, then it is located in a different jurisdiction."

"Oh yes, the beam belongs to us. But the beam is working perfectly. The repair problem is here, not over there."

"Nevertheless, you would have to show me exactly where the device you need to repair is on a map for me to answer your question."

Bix smiled his amusement. "You are a clever as a well as a brave person, Major Dimitri Park. I will record your response in our protocols for dealing with aliens. You want me to reveal where my broken equipment is so that you will gain valuable knowledge. I will play along. My broken equipment is within a hundred mile radius of this place."

"If that is the case, Mr. Bix . . ."

"Just Bix. Only people who need titles use them."

"Then I am just Park."

"Excellent reply, Park!" Bix had never realized what fun it could be communicating with a more or less thinking species. His training program had made the process seem so much more sterile.

"The man you must make the contract with, Bix, is President Rejep Muratbey. He has authority over the territory you describe."

"Will you bring me Muratbey?"

"With him, you must always say President Muratbey."

"Thank you. That is important to know. Will you bring him now?"

"I will speak with him. But I am certain he will not come right now. He will need time to reflect on his situation."

"What will you tell him?"

Park thought for a spell before replying. "President Muratbey is not a learned man, but he is a man who understands and wields power."

"Say more."

"If I tell him a man from space three meters tall, with a marmot on his shoulder that speaks for him in a soft female voice, wants to negotiate a contract, he is likely to respond in an undesirable way . . . undesirable from your point of view."

I told you we should have used the deep voice, Bix communicated to Frak. *The high voice is more peaceful*, Frak responded. *Nevertheless, it's confusing him*, communicated Bix.

The marmot replied in a deep, resonant baritone voice. "Would it be helpful if I destroyed the weapons you have surrounded my flyer with? My protocols say that that may be appropriate as a way of getting my message across, but I would appreciate your opinion."

Park found the change in voice disconcerting and possibly ominous. "Am I to assume you could do that if you wished?"

"Why would you want to test me with a question like that, Park? Isn't trust better than fear?"

"All right. I'll take your word for it. However, even if you did destroy the weapons, it would not necessarily persuade President Muratbey to meet you. Men of power use the bravery of others more often than they display it themselves."

"That is a sour sort of philosophy, Park."

"It is not a philosophy, merely an observation. My point is that a display of force is not needed to make President Muratbey meet with you."

"What is needed?"

"You need to give him something."

"Give him what?"

"What do your protocols say?"

Frak and Bix consulted silently. "Trinkets!" said Bix brightly. He swung a control board across his lap and let his large hands scurry deftly over its keys. "This will just take a moment." He rolled his chair to his left and opened what looked like a bin beneath where the control board had been situated. "Give him these," he said, holding out his hand.

Park stepped forward and looked into the immense palm. A dozen objects that looked like cut diamonds, each a half inch in diameter, glistened up at him. He scooped them up with both hands and dropped them into his overcoat pocket.

"I hope President Muratbey will be pleased," boomed the marmot.

"I hope so as well," responded Park.

"If not, maybe I should try destroying the weapons."

"I shall try to convince him to meet you. When would be best?"

"The protocols specify during a dark period. Fewer people see things during dark periods."

"Tomorrow night, then. At this time."

Bix stood up. He was fully three meters in height, a veritable giant. "We are friends, Park?"

"We are friends. I will do my best."

Bix nodded his head deeply in apparent polite dismissal. Park responded with a similar nod and backed out of the room.

President Muratbey had taken the opportunity of Park's confrontation with the flying sphere to leave the palace and set up a makeshift command post in the more easily defended Internal Security Ministry. By the time Park arrived, the sphere had departed as silently and effortlessly as it had arrived. A phone link with the Kokand air base reported continuous radar tracking in the direction of the Andijan Reservoir on the border with Kyrgyzstan.

Meeting privately, though in a room containing four of Park's bugs, Park described what he had seen and heard in exhaustive detail. At the end he pulled from his pocket six large diamonds. "He called these trinkets?" said Muratbey, his small eyes squinting as he examined the stones. "We must summon a jeweler. These were intended, I assume, as a personal gift to me."

"Without question, Mr. President. If you wish, I shall not speak of them outside this room."

"It will avoid misunderstanding. Tell me, did he say anything about Rabbit Shit Vahidoglu? Will he visit him, or is he just interested in negotiating with me?"

"He gave the impression that it was just you, Mr. President."

Muratbey slapped the flat of his hand on the top of the desk with a resounding crack. "I have decided, Park. I shall meet with him. It will be a historic moment for the great Ferghana people."

* * *

Bix and Frak idled away the time in desultory communication while playing a game of algorithms. Frak was programmed to win, but Bix enjoyed the challenge. He had a flair for obliquely quoting famous algorithms that Frak appreciated.

Local electromagnetic transmissions report that a device has burrowed down to the level of the beam emitter, communicated Frak.

They can't hurt it, Bix responded.

They plan to bring it to the surface.

Can they do that?

Their plan is clever. They will force a hot solvent into the shaft to dissolve the rock just above the emitter. Then they will force down a heavy liquid that will seep beneath the emitter and float it upward. If they repeat this often enough, they may succeed in floating it to the surface. But if they dislodge it at all, it will destroy its alignment, and it will have to be repaired.

Should I think of a way to stop the plan?

Fix it now, or fix it later.

* * *

From his post in the Ministry building Muratbey maintained close contact with all command centers. Radar had followed the flying sphere to the Andijan Reservoir and then suddenly lost track of it. However, a border outpost reported that fishermen had seen a dark flying machine rise out of the water earlier in the night. As they had struggled to keep from overturning in the waves it threw up, it had swooped down to within a few feet of them and then soared off.

Ingenious of the giant to place his machine underwater on the Kyrgyz side of the border, mused Muratbey. He obviously fears what I might do if he were to land on this side.

"Karim!" he called to his army chief of staff. General Karim Chengizoglu looked up from a large table where he and a group of officers were examining detailed maps of the Andijan area. "Karim, what are we doing?"

"We are moving artillery and anti-aircraft battalions into position along our part of the reservoir."

"But not in sight of the border?"

"They are well hidden, Mr. President."

"And radio silence?"

"Radio silence, Mr. President."

"Make sure. I don't want that dog who calls himself President of Kyrgyzstan to know that my visitor is resting on his side of the border. Are there any signs the Kyrgyz know he's there?"

"None so far. But they may be keeping their military units out of sight and be observing radio silence."

Muratbey picked up a flimsy white telephone made in Hungary. He dialed five numbers, waited, and then yelled into the mouthpiece. "Hasan! Tell me there have been no newspaper or radio reports of the spaceship." He nodded. "Good. If any materialize, total denial."

He slammed the phone down. “Karim!” The general looked wearily in the President’s direction. “Have the fishermen been detained?”

“I’ve told you yes, Mr. President. Why don’t you let me get on with my job?”

“Anyone on the street who talks about flying saucers must be put in jail.”

“Speak to Internal Security, Mr. President.”

* * *

The courtyard of the Presidential Palace had been emptied of vehicles and swept clean. While a crew of painters slathered whitewash on walls that still contained pockmarks from bullets fired in the last tribal uprising against the pre-Soviet ruler in 1917, workers unrolled strips of red carpet and placed them closely side by side to cover the oil drips and potholes of the flagstone parking area. Under instruction from a television director, electricians mounted new floodlights on the walls and in the courtyard’s corners. Cables snaked through doorways and climbed walls like tropical vines. A security perimeter had been established fifty meters outside the walls on all sides of the palace. Barricades blocked major thoroughfares, and ropes from tree to tree bisected the palace park.

Small groups of onlookers huddled for a while in the cold, exchanged guesses as to what was happening, and then moved on. Among the older people, the talk was mostly of coups or political infighting. But the absence of tanks and armored cars belied their suspicions. Some younger people, more attuned to an American movie that had recently played, speculated about a medical emergency, a rare deadly virus perhaps. This idea was pooh-poohed by people whose sons or husbands had been called into the palace to paint or do electrical work. Their reports led speculation in the direction of some sort of gala celebration, but no one had any idea what there might be to celebrate. One man said he had seen a flying saucer over the palace in the middle of the night. He was quietly escorted away by two police officers.

Ambassador Darla Bane waited impatiently in her embassy office for someone to find out what was going on. An energetic, large-eyed woman of forty-five, the American ambassador was known publicly for her volubility and disarming smile. Within the embassy, however, any rumors of charm were quickly dispelled by stories of authoritarian procedures and coruscating tongue-lashings. As her country's first envoy to a small state in the remote heart of Central Asia, Darla felt that her first duty was absolute command of her post. Representing her country's interests before the Ferghana government placed a distinct second.

The embassy's political officer was Miguel Espinosa. "Mike," roared Darla into the phone, "get in here and tell me what's going on!"

Looking slim and stylish in a three-piece suit he had bought when he thought he was going to be posted to Caracas, the black-haired young diplomat entered quietly and calmly. He looked at his boss and fancied that her tawny mane was looking more leonine than usual. "It's a celebration. I spoke personally with Major Park."

"What's being celebrated? Did Muratbey get an erection?" Darla reserved her vulgarity for a select few.

"Major Park said he could not be specific. But he did say there would be a ceremony in the courtyard that had to be kept secret for reasons of state."

"Well what in the hell is that supposed to mean?"

"My words to the Major exactly," murmured Miguel.

* * *

Ferghanan spotter planes picked up Bix's flyer a few moments after it rose from the surface of the reservoir. They also noted the presence of two Kyrgyz helicopters hovering over the reservoir on the far side of the border. As he had the night before, Bix made no effort to escape detection on his way to Kokand. *Let them get used to you,* he quoted to himself from the alien contact protocols.

As he began to descend toward the Presidential Palace, he observed with satisfaction that the courtyard was empty and well lit with a sizable patch of red fabric covering its center portion. Everything indicated that ceremonies were about to take place. So perhaps he would not have to use his destructors.

Picked men from the army and internal security forces snapped to attention along the sides of the courtyard. They brought their weapons to present arms position, a formal salute not usually performed with loaded magazines. President Muratbey waited patiently at the edge of the carpet in a greatcoat and fur hat, reminding himself of bygone days when he had twice joined the Soviet Politburo members atop Lenin's tomb to review a parade. *The spaceman did not come to see Lenin*, he thought as the condensation from his breath rose like a cloud in the chill night air. *But he comes to see Muratbey*. Major Park stood behind and to the side of Muratbey, just off the red carpet.

When the sphere came to a halt and its door opened, Muratbey stepped solemnly forward, proud in the thought that he was representing the Republic of Ferghana and the whole human race. Major Park could not help admiring the president's firmness of step as he fell into place behind him.

Bix was momentarily confused when President Muratbey and Major Park entered the flyer's compartment because he thought the President was wearing a translator on his head. He was reassured when the President identified himself in his own voice.

"I am Rejep Muratbey, President of the Republic of Ferghana. I am honored that you choose to visit land of great Ferghana people."

"My name is Bix," said the marmot. Bix bowed his head deeply. President Muratbey and Major Park responded in kind.

"I am man of direct speech," said Muratbey. "Major Park tell me you want to negotiate contract. What you want? What you give?"

What do you want, corrected Frak silently for Bix's benefit. *I must be careful not to misunderstand. This man does not speak this language well.*

Bix reflected a moment before communicating his thoughts to Frak. "I will make this as simple as possible," said Frak. "I am a repairman. I am here to repair equipment in the mountains. I need some assistance."

"What is equipment?" asked Muratbey.

"It is a machine for controlling the weather on this planet. It should be emitting carbon dioxide and methane to make the planet warmer, but it is not operating. I must fix it. Then I will leave."

"Why you want to change weather?" asked Muratbey with a touch of belligerence in his voice. "We like weather."

"Warming the planet will melt the ice at its poles. Then another machine will cool the planet, and the ice will form again. The machines have been doing this for a very long time, measured in your species' lifespans."

Muratbey thought. "You're talking about ice ages," he said at length. "You want me to help you start ice age."

I don't think he got it, communicated Frak.

Bix tried again. "No, it is just the opposite, President Rejep Muratbey. I want you to help me to make it warm. And then later will come the ice age."

Major Park stepped forward and whispered in Muratbey's ear. "Why don't you ask what he is going to give you as part of the contract?"

Muratbey nodded. "Comrade Bix, what you give me as part of contract to help you?"

"Did you like the trinkets?"

"Yes, but they are not suitable for contract. You are from space. You must give technology to Republic of Ferghana."

"Ahhhh! Technology! Mister President Rejep Muratbey, I have plenty of technology I can give you. Plenty of technology. I have a machine that makes trinkets like the ones I gave you, and other kinds as well. I will leave behind with you this flyer, and Frak will instruct someone on how to use it."

"Frak?"

"The marmot," whispered Major Park.

"Yes, flyer," said Muratbey, waiting for more.

"I will be using a plasma boring machine for cutting into the mountain. I have two with me. I can leave one behind."

"Maybe technology not work without proper energy source," said Muratbey craftily.

The marmot laughed; Bix smiled broadly. "If our laser beam emitter is still working after two million of your years, do you think I would leave you something that breaks down? President Rejep Muratbey, I guarantee that the technology I leave you will make you and your people the most important members of your species."

"You also leave weapons so we can protect technology?"

Once again the protocols proved absolutely correct. "We are so close to a deal, Mister President Rejep Muratbey, and you mention weapons. There I must say no. Weapons might endanger me and members of my race. No weapons. I have weapons. I can use weapons against your enemies, if that is called for. But I cannot give you any weapons."

Muratbey nodded ruminatively. He turned to the Major. "Park, step outside. I will join you."

Major Park hesitated and then left the compartment. As soon as he was out of sight in the corridor, he paused and listened. He could barely make out Muratbey's whispered demanding sentences. Frak's eventual reply was fully audible, however. "I think you have yourself a deal, Mister President Rejep Muratbey. I had business to take care of there anyway so it will just be killing two birds with one stone, so to speak." Park heard the president begin to take his leave and stepped quickly out of the sphere. Moments later President Muratbey walked past him to a well-lit portion of the red carpet where the television director had marked a stopping point with gaffer's tape. He threw his arms wide as if to embrace his unseen audience and delivered in Russian a speech about friendship in the universe and friendship around the planet. Just in case he might someday want to broadcast it.

Chapter Eleven

Dawn broke dull red over the drab concrete buildings of Nukus. It was six-twenty AM on February 18th. In Los Angeles, it was evening news time of the previous day. Margie Hicks paced the Carpenter-Beckenbaugh Corp. television studio in Nukus awaiting the start of a live remote hookup between an Iranian camera crew on the seafloor recording the effort to drill down to the laser emitter and the gala Hollywood premier of Hayes Carpenter's second hole-in-the-sea documentary. She was happy to be closer to the shiny reflecting glasses and aluminized coveralls issued to the seafloor workers against a possibility of another laser beam from space than to the crowd of gowned and tuxedoed glitterati fawning over her boss in Hollywood.

Resplendent in a tieless ruffled shirt and tuxedo beautifully tailored to his stout torso, Hayes Carpenter glided like a Hollywood star through the not-to-be-missed premier party at the Beverly Hills Hotel. While telling himself that he could do without the sex goddesses and action heroes lining up to exchange words with him, he had paid special attention to trimming his short salt-and-pepper beard and had a nagging fear that the tiny orchid in his lapel would wilt or be crushed in the hubbub. Knowing that with Margie in charge the remote hookup would run perfectly, he was nevertheless nervous. He wondered whether Shanelle Whittaker was out of bed yet in Nukus, decided she was, and slipped out to the patio around the pool to call her on his cell phone. Her sleepy voice was cystal clear despite being relayed half way around the world.

"Shanelle, this is Hayes. Sorry to get you out of bed."

"I was up. What's the problem?"

"No problem. I'm just nervous. Thought I'd share that with you."

"Mmmmm, thanks. What are you nervous about?"

"I don't know. Just nervous."

"When you get here on Wednesday, do you want to see Vahidoglu right away? Or rest first?"

"I'd better see him right away. Hell, he may even show up at the VIP lounge or send his car."

"I can head him off if you like."

Hayes considered. "Okay. Do that. Set me up to see him on Thursday. Lay on something fancy for dinner: me, you, Vahidoglu, and whoever else he wants. That Georgian restaurant can cater it. Vahidoglu loves their seventy-five varieties of preserved fish. Make it late evening. My body should be feeling awake by then."

Meanwhile, at the Blue House, the wall-enclosed dacha that served as the official residence of President Ahmet Vahidoglu, the weary and bleary-eyed dictator sat on the side of his bed and leaned his bony elbows on his bony knees. His penis was chafed and red. Past the rumpled satin sheets and through the open bathroom door he watched the stunningly beautiful Russian economics student who had kept him from getting enough sleep dry her lush breasts and gleaming thighs and then tie up her wet golden hair in a towel turban. He was torn between making love to her yet one more time, getting some more sleep, and relieving his bladder.

Elsewhere in the city, an elderly pensioner in a threadbare overcoat swept a deserted street with a long-handled besom. Nearby, one policeman dozed while his partner drank tea in a parked Moskva waiting for a mafia bag-man to come to the back door of a nightclub and pay them their weekly salary supplement. Within the club, the last drunks were being coaxed out the front door, all except for the Karakalpak Minister of Culture, who was still in a back room with a bored but compliant stripper.

At the brand-new American embassy on the city's outskirts, Marine guard Rupert Johnson came on duty and took his seat behind the bullet-proof glass in the lobby. He checked the duty roster to see who was supposed to be in the building and then screwed in place a prohibited earphone: classic rap by Staten Island's Wu Tang Clan. Two miles further on, in a brown and barren-looking field belonging to the Karakalpak Cotton Cooperative, a team of Israeli irrigation specialists was up early with a crew of wool-hatted, high-booted farmers to continue laying out a pipe system that would result in major water economies.

At six-twenty-six, pajama-clad Shanelle Whittaker said good-by to Hayes Carpenter and closed her phone. At the same instant, two hundred meters away, in a parking lot where it had chanced to land after being dropped from Bix's flyer, a sphere of plutonium imploded into a critical mass triggering a chain reaction that cascaded into an explosion equivalent to a hundred thousand tons of TNT. Shanelle's body, the room she was in, the hotel, the policemen, mafia bag-man, bored stripper, pensioner with his besom, Marine guard, Israelis and farmers, and everything and everyone else within a five mile radius of the bomb vaporized or flew into pieces under the impact of the explosion's blinding flash, volcanic heat, and pulverizing shock.

In an instant of hell Shanelle's retinas conveyed the flash to her brain, but she was dead before her ears could register the bomb's awesome thunder. Death overtook Ahmet Vahidoglu's gangly body just as it was twining itself with the soft, naked limbs of the Russian economics student. Margie Hicks and her smiling, energized director died just as she raised her hand to give him a go signal.

At the hole-in-the-sea, one hundred and twenty miles away, drilling operations had been proceeding night and day irrespective of the comings and goings of dignitaries, well-heeled tourists, and especially television broadcasters, who had turned the immense ring of steel caissons holding back the sea into a worldwide icon of the scientific quest to understand the universe. The most recent headline news had been the scientific determination, based on radiation readings and deep core drilling, that the laser's power source was almost certainly a small thermonuclear reactor. Speculation about the dawn of an era of cheap, clean energy had briefly displaced UFO stories.

At six-twenty-six, an Azerbaijani roustabout named Murat Alpay was belted securely to the girders at the top of the drilling tower muscling a chain into place around a defective pipe section preparatory to its being lowered to the deck. Stunned by a brilliant flash on the southern horizon, he gazed in astonishment as the top of a mushroom cloud began to loom over the lip of the caisson wall. He watched the cloud rise and expand for several minutes before feeling a vibration in the girder he was clinging to. He clutched the girder harder as the vibration mounted into a powerful shaking. Then he heard the sound of steel rending under great pressure. He looked again to the south in time to see the caisson wall crack open from lip to seafloor with an ear-splitting screech. "Praise be to God . . . God is great . . . Glory be to God . . . Praise be to God . . ." he intoned as his horrified eyes watched two caissons buckle completely and the sea crash thunderously through the gap.

On the seafloor the flash had only brightened the sky overhead. Those who were on the deck of the drilling platform thought a new kind of laser event was occurring and immediately looked down and turned their backs as they had been instructed. But nothing happened. Some were already returning to their tasks when they felt a rumble underfoot, followed by a jolting earth tremor, and then the chilling sound of ripping steel as the caisson wall succumbed to the nuclear shock wave propagating with crushing force through earth and seawater. Caught like Pharaoh's army on the floor of the sea, the drillers, television crew, and scientists watched in horror as a fifty-foot wall of water came crashing toward them. Buoyant escape pods had been placed in strategic locations on deck, but only four men managed to seal themselves inside before the wall of water overtook the massive platform. The only other survivor was Murat Alpay, found many hours later still strapped to the top of the tower projecting five feet above the level of the lapping water. Otherwise the sea seemed at peace, its hole erased.

In the sky the crisp wind bent the mushroom cloud toward the southwest where it deposited its lethal burden of radioactive fallout on the barren deserts of Turkmenistan and further downwind on the Caspian Sea.

* * *

President Boone Rankin was line dancing in the White House to a country music band after a sumptuous dinner of Carolina-style barbecue, hushpuppies, coleslaw, and apple cobbler. As he saw it, he was bringing the simple pleasures of life to the conduct of the people's business. As the nation's cultural guardians in Cambridge, New York, and D.C. itself saw it, he consistently and willfully demeaned his high office and lowered the dignity of the presidency. Nevertheless, as Rankin took pains to point out, no guest ever came away hungry from dinner and line dancing at the White House, or complained that they hadn't had a helluva good time.

George Artunian squeezed himself in between the jovial President, his adopted daughter Sarah, and his pixie-like press secretary, Katherine Kourek, and picked up the beat.

"Two forward, George," called the President. "Arm swing . . . clap . . . back . . . turn around . . ."

"There's been an atomic explosion in Nukus," said Artunian under his breath.

"Two forward . . . arm swing . . . you're gettin' it, George."

"Mr. President . . ."

"I heard you, George," murmured Rankin. "Now just keep on smilin' and dancin' for another minute, and then we go talk."

Five minutes later, a beaming and seemingly out of breath President excused himself to get some air with his National Security Advisor. Katherine Kourek picked up a familiar surreptitious wink and followed them out of the room a few seconds later.

"George," said Boone Rankin, grabbing his friend's arm, "the National Security Advisor can't come into a party, whisper something to the President, and then me go all over serious and stalk outta the room. Francis Scott Key Bridge would be full of people tryin' to evacuate D.C. before we got our ties off." They went down a flight of stairs. A guard saluted and opened the door to the situation room. "All right, now. Give me the details."

"Nukus is totally destroyed, probably two hundred thousand dead or dying. Six-twenty-six in the morning, local time. Apparently no warning of any kind."

Uniformed technicians were quietly entering the room and taking seats at electronics consoles.

"Missile?"

"Air Force says no. Satellites picked up the flash and heat of the detonation, but no preceding flash of a missile launch. It was either dropped by air or delivered on the ground."

"Terrorists?"

"It's what we've always been afraid of. Could have been trucked in and triggered by remote control or a timer."

The door opened and Air Force general Henry Royce, Chairman of the Joint Chiefs of Staff, strode in. "Henry? What's the latest?" said the President.

"Satellite reconnaissance indicates the yield was around a hundred kilotons. Not huge, but the explosion had a ground effect that collapsed the hole-in-the-sea."

"That could have been the target, Mr. President."

"Why do you say that, George?"

The National Security Advisor knitted his bushy brows. "Because . . . actually, I'm not sure I have a very good reason. It's just that I can't think of any reason at all to blow up Nukus. We don't know of any active anti-regime movements. The Karakalpak economy is riding a boom on Hayes Carpenter's money. Vahidoglu's got envious neighbors, but what they covet is the Great Array, and it wouldn't make any sense for them to destroy access to it."

"Vahidoglu is a real jerk, though," mused the Rankin.

"You don't destroy a city of a couple of hundred thousand people because you think their president is a jerk."

"Well, maybe you don't, and maybe I don't . . ."

"Mr. President?"

"Oh, yes, Kathy, almost forgot you were here."

"I should get to the briefing room. What do you want me to say?"

Artunian replied. "Say that Nukus has been destroyed by an unexplained nuclear explosion, and that we are sending aid and decontamination equipment to help the Karakalpak government cope with the tragic situation."

She looked uncertainly at Rankin. "That okay, Mr. President?"

"That's okay, Kathy. And say my prayers and the prayers of my family and of all Americans are with all those innocent people killed in the explosion, including the heroic Americans serving in the U.S. embassy or elsewhere. Say we're compiling a list of Americans believed to have been in Nukus and will release it as soon as it's ready."

"What should I say about the source of the explosion?"

"Just say it's undetermined at this time, but that it probably was not a terrorist attack."

"Are you sure, Mr. President?" interjected Artunian.

"Last thing we want is for people to think about nukes in terrorist hands, even if that's what it was." He turned to the General, "Henry, are there still any Soviet nukes on Karakalpak soil?"

"There never were any. Nearest ones were in Kazakhstan, and the last of those were decommissioned and shipped back to Russia almost ten years ago."

"Then where did this one come from?"

Kathy Kourek slipped from the room just as a blue telephone rang. George Artunian took the receiver from a technician and said curtly, "Artunian." He listened for two minutes and then replaced it in its cradle. "That was the NSA duty officer. They've had the Karakalpaks and their neighbors under special communications surveillance. They just monitored an exchange between an airbase at Tashkent and the Karakalpak airbase at Urgench, which is southeast of Nukus. Urgench reported a blip moving toward Nukus from the east very fast at 70,000 feet before the explosion. Tashkent confirmed and said it first appeared on their screen over Andijan on the Kyrgyz-Ferghana border. After the explosion, electrical interference jammed the Urgench radar, and Tashkent didn't pick it up again either."

"Mr. President," interjected General Royce, "No operational bombers fly at 70,000 feet. That's up where our U-2s and SR-70s, and the Russians' Mandrake fly."

"A low satellite firing from orbit?"

"No. Too low for that, unless the orbit was decaying and the satellite was dying. Besides, we're pretty sure the Soviets never got to the point of putting missiles in orbit."

"Where's . . . what's that place the blip came from?"

"Andijan," said Artunian.

An army electronics specialist busied herself with a mouse and keyboard. Within a few seconds a fifty-inch video screen lit up with a map centered on the town of Andijan.

"That's less than a hundred miles from the Chinese border," said General Royce with a puzzled tone. "But that might not mean anything. Must be at about the limit for Tashkent radar. We should check with Kokand." As everyone gazed at the map several more uniformed people entered the room, and two telephones began to ring. The General turned to the newcomers and began a quiet consultation.

Rankin's mind drifted back to the party, and he hummed a favorite Garth Brooks melody. He had never had a feel for foreign crises, and his administration had been blessed by having few of them to face.

"Mr. President," said the General, interrupting his reverie, "we have reports from our seismic stations that the ground wave from the explosion was much larger than the apparent size of the bomb."

"What does that mean, Henry?"

"It means the bomb was probably designed to collapse the hole-in-the-sea. Sort of an earthquake bomb."

"Earthquake bomb? Never heard of such a thing."

"Neither have we, sir."

"What would the Chinese want an earthquake bomb for?"

"I can't imagine, sir. But there's another possibility." President Rankin's clear blue eyes looked expectant. "It could be we're not dealing with a . . . umh . . . with a human-type bomber."

There was a long silence as the implications of the General's remarks sank in. "Shit on a stick," said the President at long last, his voice laden with exasperation. "We'd be better off if they was terrorists."

* * *

In his spacious private office in the Presidential Palace, President Rejep Muratbey consulted some loose pages of instructions and then carefully punched a thirteen-character sequence into the control keyboard of the machine on his desk. Small squares of paper bearing Cyrillic characters had been pasted over the keys. He squeezed close to the machine and pressed his ear against it. He thought he detected a high-pitched whine. Straightening up he stared at his watch as the stipulated number of seconds ticked by. Then he pulled a handle that caused a small bin to tip open toward him. He reached inside and pulled out an emerald almost an inch in diameter. He held it up to his desk light and marveled at the stone's deep green internal reflections as he turned it over and over again between his pudgy fingers. Then he placed it carefully on a piece of black velvet that already held an assortment of diamonds, rubies, and emeralds.

To the side of his desk a television set was tuned to CNN with the sound muted. President Muratbey looked over at an aerial shot of smoking ruins and turned up the sound.

"As these pictures from the Russian news crew that flew in with the first rescue teams show, the city of Nukus is no more. A burning, smoking ruin, totally destroyed by a massive nuclear explosion whose ground shock was clearly felt over four hundred miles away in Tashkent."

Muratbey muted the sound but continued looking at the picture. "Esholeshek Vahidoglu," he muttered under his breath. Eventually he returned his attention to the instruction manual of his trinket machine.

Five miles away, Kazakh Air's Flight 0017 was landing at Kokand airport. Though uninformed about the bombing of Nukus, Joseph Engineer was edgy and exhausted after a full day in Moscow's crowded, uncomfortable domestic service airport waiting for a flight to Kokand that had been reported to be indefinitely delayed because of a lack of jet fuel. This had been followed by a similar day-long wait in the Kazakh city of Almaty before he began the final leg of his trip. The on-board meal of greasy chicken parts had been inedible and the flight over the towering Tien Shan mountains frighteningly bumpy. But the primary source of his edginess was what was to come next. Mr. Thayer's instructions had been to act as though his sole reason for coming was to install and calibrate new NSA coding equipment at the American embassy, and then to use his imagination to identify the Chakra Net webmaster and through him the elusive Nadir. Unfortunately, Joseph's imagination had never extended much beyond the realm of computers and telecommunications technology.

* * *

By midnight, Hayes Carpenter had watched enough news reports, made and received enough telephone calls, and spoken with enough company specialists. His driver dropped him off at Santa

Monica beach. He walked down to the upper limit of the incoming waves and sat down in the sand in his tuxedo trousers and ruffled shirt. From childhood, he had always been able to fix his mind firmly on one thing regardless of other distractions. It had been the secret of his rise from poverty. Looking out at the dark, murmuring sea, he now fixed his mind on going to war. Mingled feelings of anger, excitement, fear, eagerness, pride, determination, and willingness to sacrifice coursed through his mind and came to bear on the enemy, the enemy that had twice attacked the Carpenter-Beckenbaugh empire, the enemy that had killed and blinded his friends, the enemy that could not be identified, the enemy that he now pledged himself to defeat.

* * *

War was also on the mind of the Russian Minister of Defense, Pyotr Kalenin, as he looked at the piles of intelligence reports and technical analyses stacked on his desk. During the four decades of the Cold War no city had ever been nuked. But now it had happened, and the target was a city that had not so very long ago been part of the Soviet Union. An estimated twenty-six percent of the casualties were ethnic Russians, including an entire visiting football team from Saint Petersburg.

The reports told him everything . . . and nothing. There was no obvious enemy. No one in the Soviet nuclear establishment had ever even broached the idea of developing a bomb specialized for seismic destruction. The radar tracking of an aircraft at 70,000 feet pointed toward China, but the Chinese denials of involvement were credible since they had no aircraft capable of flying at that altitude. Plus the radar tracking had stopped over Andijan on the Ferghana-Krygyz border and never reached the Chinese frontier.

Kalenin mulled over a brief report forwarded to him from the commander of the Russian land forces, General Repin. The source was a retired colonel and veteran of the war in Afghanistan, Ilya Kramskoy. He also happened to be the uncle of the second-in-command of the Ferghanan army. Though his record was far from spotless, he was a man whose loyalty to Soviet-era Red Army traditions took priority over his feelings as a citizen of the Ferghana Republic.

According to Kramskoy's report, four days before the attack on Nukus the Presidential Palace in Kokand had been sealed off for eighteen hours. During that time a spherical aircraft had risen from beneath the waters of the Andijan reservoir, flown to Kokand, and landed in the palace courtyard. The president of the republic and his chief of internal security had entered the craft and exited again about an hour later. The craft had then flown back to its point of origin. News reports of the incident were banned, and security agents were silencing gossipers on the street. Such was the information the colonel had learned from his nephew.

War between Ferghana and Karakalpakstan, perfectly understandable, thought Kalenin. *Vahidoglu and Muratbey hate each other. So Muratbey lets the spaceship help him fight. But why did the spaceship go to Kokand rather than Nukus? Maybe the Aral Sea array isn't the only space secret in Central Asia. The Americans beat us to Nukus, but maybe we can steal a march on them in Kokand.*

Kalenin picked up his phone and dialed the extension of Dr. Nikita Yurenev, the Chief Historian of the Russian army. "Yurenev," he said when the phone was picked up, "this is Kalenin. You need to do some research on General Frunze's expedition to the Tien Shan."

"Not the legendary lost secret, I hope."

"You have a keen mind, Yurenev. If there is a lost secret, I want it found. The legend wouldn't exist if there weren't some truth to it. This is a top priority. Do you understand?"

"Yes, Mr. Minister. I will put my best researcher on it." *And she will find nothing, just like her predecessors*, thought the historian as he hung up the phone.

Chapter Twelve

From: Nadir@1Day2Day.com
To: Webmaster@Chakra_Net.com

THE TALE OF THE CHAKRA. THIRD POSTING

So now you've learned the truth of what the Giants do.
No care have they for lives of lowly human folk.
Perhaps it is too late to stop their evil plan, but still I'll tell the tale of how ere now we fought, of how with vajra strong I slew the Giant host.

But first you ask of me some foolish little things:
What name Indrani's ape? And who the dasas dark?
I'll take them one by one, the things that you have asked; but you must realize that time and times have passed, eleven thousand years. There's nothing I forget, but very much had changed between the time of Gods and time of writing hymns. What now you call your myths are based on mighty deeds, deeds wrought by Gods like me,
Gods splendid in their wrath. But much has been confused; the myths are full of holes. So do not waste my time by asking questions more. The evil is at hand; a Giant's come to Earth. He's bombed a city's heart as you would crush an ant without a second thought.

So question number one: Who's Vrtra whom I killed?
In myth a snake is he, who holds the waters back.
Twas this we told the men who helped us in our fight.
They knew not how to think of things of metal made, or using unseen force, or life in outer space.
They fought with sticks and stones and knew not plow or grain.
The way they helped us fight was not by might and main.
They let us join their tribe. We dressed in furs and skins.
Our hair grew long in plaits. We looked like Earthly men.
And thus we sallied forth to set upon the foe, the Giants from the skies, who never realized the danger they were in because they could not tell a human from a God. To make our trick succeed, we told our men a tale about a demon grim, a snake on mountains high. We pointed to the peaks that rose then fell then rose, the profile of a snake stretched out on summits four. We said we had to kill the snake upon the heights because it water held in form of ice and snow.
The reason for this tale is simple to unfold.
The place we had to go was high upon the peaks, where holes the Giants bored reach down to their machines providing entry points at which to make attack.
The tribe we journeyed with into the mountains high, that now are called Tien Shan, were hunters from the lake, the lake called Issyk Kul. Twas there we came to Earth.
Twas there we hid our ship, beneath the water deep, the deep of Issyk Kul. And so to hunters brave we told the Vrtra tale, of how we'd stalk a snake and kill him in his lair upon the lofty heights where hunters did not go.

So now to question two: The vajra that was mine, what was it's nature true? The hunters heard its sound, a boom so loud it hurt. They saw its flashing beam go coursing through the sky. To some it thunder was and lightning seemed its beam.
But others saw a club, a stick with bulbous end, and thought its flash a spark like those they struck with flint to make themselves a fire. When later tales were told of

Gods who demons killed, the lightning bolt was used my vajra to describe, or else a hammer great that sparked and smashed and slew. But myths like these you know.
Learn now the truth you seek. A plasma tube it was like those the Giants used to bore the mountain holes.
I stole it from their ship, like ours at Issyk Kul, and learned to use it well to work the Giants woe.
But when I undertook to spike their great machine and stop the climate's change, I used its final charge.
My vajra is no more.

Now on to lesser things. That Indra is my name your question shows you've guessed. I had no wife Indrani.
Immortal Gods don't wed, nor do they reproduce as I explained before. But humans think of sex an hour at least per day so when they wrote their myths, they gave to us our mates, invented tales of love, adultery and rape. They gave us lives like theirs.
But though I had no mate, the story of the ape reflects a true event. There still existed then a few primeval men. Neanderthal they're called in recent books I've read. We had one as a guide, a man of sloping brow. The hunters called him ape and wanted him to slay as was their practice fell whenever they did find another of his breed.
But him did I protect. He knew the mountains high, knew pathways to the peaks, to caverns deep within.
He did not speak the tongue that you would Vedic call, the language of the tribe that helped us in our quest.
But Dyaus, who led the gods, possessed a good device, like vajra, giant-built. Upon his shoulder sat what looked to be a bird, a raven black as night; but never did it fly, for under beak and wing was placed a small machine designed to learn to speak whatever tongue it heard and translate from that tongue into the speech of Gods. (My own machine named Ann
I stole in later times.) So though we Gods did learn the language of the tribe, the ape and raven spoke a very different tongue. What name the man was called by others of his kind I do not now recall.
It sounded strange and wild. But to the hunting band

Vrshakapi his name. "Bull ape" it meant to them, a term that honor bore, but humbling was its sense as when you give a dog a name like Duke or Rex.

You ask who dasas were, your question number four.
The term was not in use at time I'm speaking of.
Much later did it come to mean the common foe encountered by the tribes who spoke the Vedic tongue upon their venture south across the Hindu Kush, into the Indus vale, a land of cities strong.
By then the Vedic tribes had learned what we had taught.
They drove in chariots swift and fashioned spears of bronze.
But on the Indus plain another people dwelt, a people great in arts, but small and dark of skin.
The hunters from the north descended on their fields; they seized their stocks of grain, confined them to their towns.
By dasa did they mean both enemy and slave.
I was not with them then, but still I heard it told that through the ruined towns the hunters drove their cows to pasture in the fields that once were green with grain but now were sparse and sere.

The chakra last of all the questions that you posed, its explanation lacks nobility of mind.
When victory was ours and all the Giants dead, their underground device disabled once for all, the few of us who lived got very, very drunk.
We drank the soma dear, a nectar we had brought, unlike all Earthly quaffs, a truly godly high.
And drunken we remained as generations passed, as hunters aged and died, and then their children too.
And though at first we tried to guide the hunters' ways, to teach them what we knew and elevate their lives, our teachings somehow fell into a pattern set.
We boasted of our deeds, our battle with the foe, of how we slew the snake upon the mighty peaks.
We told each crop of youth the tale of chakra wheel, explaining where it was and how it beamed the skies, explaining how it

linked unto the mountain snake controlling ice and snow by puffing smoky breath.
In time the youth grew bored; long dead our hunter friends.
No chakra could be seen beneath the water deep, no Vrtra high above, no Giants here below.

You must appreciate how greatly this annoyed.
We'd come from planet far, a tiny band of Gods, knowing that our path could never be retraced.
We'd saved the planet Earth, and humankind as well.
And this we'd done with one, and only one desire, to right the ghastly wrong the Giants had imposed upon a helpless Earth, upon its beasts and birds.
So now we wanted thanks, unending gratitude, and all we got were yawns from surly, restless youth.
Twas then we by design decreed the godly rites, demanded holy hymns be chanted in our names, demanded cows be killed and burned on altars high, demanded signs be carved upon the stony cliffs to ever tell the tale I've told on Chakra Net.
We went a little mad; we killed a lot of men.
The rest bowed down in praise and slaughtered cows as bid.

In time we sobered up; our soma all was drunk.
By then it was too late to change the godly tales or stop the sacrifice of cows on altars high.
Intent we never had to make ourselves divine, but what was done was done, and Gods we had become.
One hope, you see, we'd had to save the human race, to give immortal life and teach it wisdom deep so if and when the Giants spread throughout the stars, then might a species brave take issue with their plans and blunt their science great with force of moral will.
Instead we forged a cult among a simple folk and lost our grand design in drunkenness and rage.
My friends could not endure the failure of their dreams, and one by one they chose to terminate their lives.
Now I alone am left, the one they called a sot, insensitive and dull, a glutton and a beast.

The smart ones all are dead, the sensitive of soul.
I guess eternal life demands a thicker skin.

Nadir

Major Dimitri Park blew cigarette smoke into the air above his computer screen. He saw in its reflection the medals of his uniform tunic and thought how twenty-five years of service had eaten the best part of his life. To be feared? To be hated? Why should people hate and fear a man who felt so tired, whose zest for spying and interrogating and arresting had long evaporated? In the days of Mikhail Gorbachev, when he had joined the KGB after university graduation, he had believed ferociously in what he was doing, convinced that a better society could not be achieved without the elimination of wreckers and plotters. Shortly thereafter had come Uzbek independence and years of trying to convince himself that its rulers were honorable men. He had longed to be in Moscow, but fate had assigned him to Tashkent just before the Soviet Union's collapse.

Then Uzbekistan, too, fell apart. Seniority and rank had given him an option, and he had chosen Ferghana—Ferghana and Persident Rejep Muratbey. He had chosen Ferghana not because of Muratbey, who was no better than those he had already worked for, but because of the mountains. Riding a horse in the high pastures of the Tien Shan he would sometimes imagine himself in northern Korea, the homeland he had never seen, where his square face, lank black hair, and high cheekbones would not mark him as a foreigner. It was in the high mountain meadows too that he learned to know and respect the Kyrgyz and Uzbek sheep and horse herders, the free and forthright men of the summer pastures who had fought a guerrilla war against Soviet rule for thirteen years.

How unlike the free Turks of the mountains was the president he now worked for, a man who had just committed a crime so vast that it could never be forgiven. Park hadn't the slightest doubt that Bix had bombed Nukus at Muratbey's request: "two birds with one stone," he had said. And beyond that horror was the seeming fact that

Muratbey was now collaborating with Bix to commit a still greater crime that would someday flood much of the inhabited world.

Park blew some more smoke at the Chakra Net message on his computer screen. Somewhere there was a man, or perhaps not a man, who understood everything and wanted to act. He reread Nadir's posting. Lake Issyk Kul was next door in Kyrgyzstan, a hundred miles from its capital, Bishkek, and not much farther away from Almaty, both places with computer access to the Internet. If Nadir would only come to the mountains, thought Park, I could help him.

* * *

Joseph Engineer was feeling positively jubilant. Not forty-eight hours since his arrival and he had already almost certainly identified the Chakra Net sysop. It had taken, first, a visit to the Ferghana Academy of Sciences, where he had heard nothing but praise and admiration for the American Dr. Lee Ingalls through whose influence with President Muratbey the Academy's budget had been suddenly increased along with the pay of its chief researchers. Then he had asked the embassy staff about the selfsame Dr. Ingalls. They had described a trim, proper, sharp-tongued woman obsessed with the study of some ancient language . . . Vedic, they thought . . . or perhaps Sanskrit . . . or maybe Vedic Sanskrit.

And now came Nadir's third posting, the icing on the cake. He wasn't far away, somewhere within easy reach of Lake Issyk Kul. All that was left was to reel him in, and Joseph felt quite confident that Dr. Lee Ingalls was just the person to do it.

* * *

Donald found his wife in her study huddled, as usual, over her laptop. "I have a gift for you," he announced when she looked up. "Put out your hand and shut your eyes." He placed in her outstretched palm a radiant blue sapphire three-quarters of an inch in diameter. "Ta-DAH!"

"My lord, Donald! Where in the world did you get this?" Lee loved sapphires.

"A new business enterprise."

"This isn't mine to keep, then?"

"Yes it is. It's sort of a signing bonus from my partner."

"Who is . . . ?"

"Get this, Lee. I am in business with President Muratbey himself!"

Lee looked askance. "The man who's blackmailing you?"

"In return for my going into business with him, he has destroyed the evidence . . . that tape."

Lee felt unconvinced. "How do you know?"

"Because he wouldn't have given me a hundred and fifty gemstones to market for him if he was still intending to do me some harm. He actually gave me the stones. I have them."

"So what about me and Chakra Net? I thought the whole point of his blackmail was to make me run it."

"He has decided to close it down. He thinks it's brought enough attention to Ferghana, and besides he doesn't need to compete with the Karakalpaks anymore. The hated President Vahidoglu."

Lee gave her husband a puzzled look. Was he seeing the upside of a nuclear attack? "Donald, doesn't this all seem a little fishy to you? Where do the stones come from? Why call on you to sell them? You don't know anything about gems."

"Ah, but I know about marketing. President Muratbey has a private business he keeps very quiet. He owns mines in the mountains. He recently struck a great find, but he can't let it be known because of his official position. So he needs someone he can trust, namely me, to handle the marketing for him."

"How are the stones being cut? This one is absolutely stunning."

"He didn't mention that. I suppose he has gem cutters working for him."

"How are you being paid?"

"Twenty-five percent. I'll set up a bank account somewhere in Muratbey's name, and the money will be paid into that. Then I'll take my share. And, of course, there's the sapphire just for you."

It crossed Lee's mind that Muratbey's gift just for her might not be entirely innocent, but she saw no point in saying anything since Donald was still unaware of the president's pathetic attempt at seduction. "I'll have to get it set. There are some good inexpensive jewelers here in Kokand. I think I'll have a pin made with the sapphire as the big round stomach of a pig."

"A pig?"

"Just a whim. Maybe a couple of tiny rubies for its tiny little eyes. By the way, Nadir posted another message to Chakra Net."

"Did he give himself away? Are you able to tell who he is?"

"Not really. He knows his Rig Veda well enough to look up the name of Indrani's ape, Vrshakapi, but then he said Indrani was only a myth. Vrshakapi, according to Nadir, was a Neanderthal man who served the gods as a guide. That's pretty clever, but it rules out my friend Dolores. She wrote her dissertation on Indrani and the other Rig Vedic goddesses, and she would never say they didn't exist. She would have gone on and on about Indrani and Vrshakapi. And then on the dasas Nadir came down on the side of the Vedic speakers as invaders from the north, so that rules out Edmund, who is so enamored of the thesis that the Vedic people were native to India. Now on the vajra . . ."

Donald leaned down and gave her a husbandly kiss on the forehead. "You know I don't understand a word you're saying, don't you. Is the upshot that you've ruled out all the possible perpetrators?"

"Not all, but the most obvious ones. And the funny thing is, the story Nadir tells is pretty good. I mean, for science fiction. Makes me sort of sorry Muratbey is giving up on Chakra Net. I wonder if I can make another posting." Donald by this time had departed the study, and Lee was talking to herself. She looked down at her keyboard and thought for a few moments before starting to write.

From: Webmaster@Chakra_Net.com
To: Nadir@1Day2Day.com

RE: THE TALE OF CHAKRA. THIRD POSTING

Nadir, your latest posting was full of matters of mutual interest. It also indicates that you are not too far from Kokand, where I am located. Since Chakra Net will soon terminate its service, might it be possible for us to meet in real time? If you were to come to Kokand, I would be delighted to serve you a cup of tea.

Webmaster

Donald poked his head back into the study as she consigned her message to the net. "By the way, there's someone new at the embassy who's dying to meet you. Young NSA guy named Joseph Engineer. He's here installing new code machines. But isn't that the name you mentioned to me? Someone who was looking for you? Funny name. I invited him to come by for a drink at six."

* * *

Eight thousand miles away, in Washington, D.C., Boone Rankin greeted Hayes Carpenter as he was ushered into the oval office. "Mr. Carpenter, pleasure to meet you. You know George, I think." He gestured toward a sofa and two easy chairs where George Artunian was waiting to shake his hand.

"The pleasure is all mine, Mr. President."

"Didn't seem that way during the last campaign. But then it's been all of a week since your people were blown up in Nukus, and durin' that time you've written checks to every charity, public interest group, educational institution, and party fund-raising operation I've ever so much as given a friendly nod to. And you've made it a point to tell George what you were doing. So am I right in feelin' that you've changed your allegiance all of a sudden? Or were you just tryin' to get an appointment to see me?"

"It seemed like the most efficient way. Money opens doors."

"Indeed it does, Mr. Carpenter. Indeed it does. But it doesn't determine what happens once you get inside the door. So what is it that you want?"

"Only one thing. The name and address of whoever bombed Nukus."

"So you can take revenge?"

"So I can take revenge."

George Artunian stepped into the discussion. "As I'm sure you know from the news, Mr. Carpenter, there's no evidence as of yet as to who did the bombing. All possibilities are being considered: terrorists, covert action by a foreign government, some sort of accident . . ."

"Mr. Artunian, I'm a farm boy. I know when I'm standing up to my neck in bullshit. I can smell it. If after forty-five years of a goddam Cold War we never figured out how to trace an atomic explosion, then a whole lot of my taxes got wasted. So if you're telling me we don't have any idea who blew up my hole-in-the-sea, then I don't believe you. Now I can understand that maybe we're not able to do anything about it in such a goddam faraway place. And I can understand that maybe we're even friends with the bad guys. Wouldn't be the first time. But don't feed me this line that we're completely in the dark."

"Mr. Carpenter, there are certain technical specifications about the blast that I can't divulge. But I can say that they don't point to any weapon we've ever seen before."

"George," interrupted the President, "no point tellin' Mr. Carpenter what we don't know. He wants a name and address. Do we have one?"

"No, sir."

"Then that's your answer, Mr. Carpenter." The President stood up and put a friendly hand on Carpenter's elbow as he guided him toward the door. "I'm sorry we couldn't be more helpful, but don't let that stop you givin' more money to the Democratic Party and other good causes." He put his hand on the doorknob, gave Carpenter's elbow a squeeze, and said very softly, "We don't have a name and address, Hayes, but if I were looking for one, I'd look in Kokand." Boone Rankin winked and gave the businessman's hand a final shake as he left the office.

"What did you say that for?" queried Artunian as soon as the door closed.

"Well, George, we'd look like damn fools if we said or did anything traceable to follow up the space invader theory. But it don't hurt none for Hayes Carpenter to look like a damn fool. What do you suppose the probability is that NSA is right about that Internet source, that Chakra Net? Fraction of one percent? Well, let ole Hayes check it out for us. Doesn't cost a red cent and can't lose us any votes."

* * *

From: Nadir@1Day2Day.com
To: Webmaster@Chakra_Net.com

THE TALE OF CHAKRA. FOURTH POSTING

To Osh I'll come in March.

Nadir

* * *

Wilson Woodrow felt the sun on his face, heard the creak of his rocker, and smelled a hint of Texas spring. But his eyes saw nothing. He heard a car coming up his gravel driveway. The door opened and shut. The boot-heels of a heavy man clunked on the porch steps.

"How are you doing, Wilson?"

"Pretty good, Hayes. Pretty good." Wilson heard his friend lower his bulky body onto the wicker armchair facing him.

"Nice out here on the porch."

"Yep."

"You know all about . . ."

"The bomb? Yep. Heard it on the news. You've had tough luck, Hayes."

"Not as tough as you."

"Oh, I'm getting around. I should thank you for fixin' me up with money."

Hayes fiddled with his cowboy hat and looked at the black man staring sightlessly into his front yard. He seemed drier and more leathery than he had six months earlier. The lines of his skull stood out starkly under his skin. Hayes wondered what was going on inside. "Something I want to talk to you about, Wilson" he said at last.

"I got nothing else to do."

"I suppose you wouldn't take me for being a poetry reading man, would you, Wilson?"

"Nope. You didn't read none back in the old days. But you've done a lot of other dumb things since then."

"Well, I wouldn't take me for a poetry reading man either. But there's this one poem about growing old that I can never seem to get out of my mind."

"You really need some poem to tell you 'bout that, Hayes?"

"No," replied Hayes thoughtfully, "I guess I don't. Truth to tell, there are days when I think I'm just about wore out. I think we both probably pushed ourselves too hard when we were young."

"Speak for yourself. I'm two years younger'n you."

"Well, you're acting like a fucking retiree sitting here on your porch. You ought to try and do more. I'm the one who needs the rest. I take medicine for blood pressure and cholesterol. I'm overweight. Doctor tells me I've got about six more parachute jumps before my knees give out. And I've got an enlarged prostrate that makes it hurt like hell to sit for very long. Yet I don't want to have it out because . . . well, you know."

"Speakin' of which, you ever get in the pants of that colored gal? Shanelle?"

"Nope. I kept thinking she'd look at me one day and say to herself, 'Girl, that man's old and rich and not half bad looking,' but I think all she really ever saw was old and rich and who gives a fuck?"

Wilson laughed softly. "She was a classy gal."

"Let me tell you about this poem, Wilson. That's what I came here for. You ever heard of the *Odyssey* by Homer?"

"I'm black and Texan, but I ain't ignorant."

"Then do you know a poem by Alfred Lord Tennyson called *Ulysses*? About the same guy. It's the one I read over and over again."

"You hear me say I was a college professor?"

"All right, then. I'll read it to you, or at least part of it." Hayes leaned forward with his elbows on his knees holding a blue book between his hands. "Story is that Ulysses gets home after all his travels, kills all the guys who are after his wife, and rules for a while as king. Then he gets bored. He lets his son take over as king, but his son rules in a different way. Not bad, just different. So then Ulysses, who's getting old, thinks about what to do with the rest of his life. Now this is the great part." Hayes took a pair of glasses from his shirt pocket, adjusted them on his nose, and opened the book at a paper bookmark. "You listening?"

"You just read."

"Remember now, he was a sailor. Like you." Hayes cleared his throat.

There lies the port; the vessel puffs her sail;
There gloom the dark, broad seas. My mariners,
Souls that have toiled, and wrought, and thought with me
That ever with a frolic welcome took
The thunder and the sunshine, and opposed
Free hearts, free foreheads—you and I are old;
Old age hath yet his honor and his toil.
Death closes all; but something ere the end,
Some work of noble note, may yet be done,
Not unbecoming men that strove with gods.
The lights begin to twinkle from the rocks;
The long day wanes; the slow moon climbs;

"That's right. I like that line. Read it again."

The long day wanes; the slow moon climbs; the deep
Moans round with many voices. Come, my friends,
'Tis not too late to seek a newer world.
Push off, and sitting well in order smite
The sounding furrows; for my purpose holds
To sail beyond the sunset, and the baths
Of all the western stars, until I die.
It may be that the gulfs will wash us down;
It may be we shall touch the Happy Isles,
And see the great Achilles, whom we knew.
Though much is taken, much abides; and though
We are not now that strength which in old days
Moved earth and heavens, that which we are, we are,
One equal temper of heroic hearts,

Made weak by time and fate, but strong in will
To strive, to seek, to find, and not to yield.

"That's a fine poem, Hayes. 'That which we are, we are.' 'Though much is taken, much abides.'"

"Though much is taken, much abides, friend."

"Now what you read that to me for? You sayin' you want me to go to sea with you, Hayes?"

"I'm saying I want you to go to war with me, Wilson. And you know who against. 'Death closes all; but something ere the end, Some work of noble note, may yet be done.' What do you think? Yes or no?"

"Does a bear shit in the woods?"

Chapter Thirteen

"Hello. Is this Dr. David Waldron?"

"Yes."

"My name is Dotty Bennett. I'm the producer for Paul Henning and Sunday Special on WABC. I was given your name as someone who can speak on some of the issues involved in the Nukus bombing."

David Waldron rolled his clear blue eyes at his wife Libby and mouthed the word television. "Yeah, I might be able to do that."

"Right now we're still not sure what angle we're going to go with on Sunday, but if we use you, could you be in our studio at nine in the morning? We'd send a car for you."

"I could do that."

"Good. Do you have a couple of minutes now to give me some idea of what you think?"

"Sure. Go ahead." David leaned his desk chair back and put his feet on his desk.

"First, who do you think bombed Nukus?"

"That's pretty obvious. Something or someone from somewhere other than Earth."

There was a long pause. "I'm just writing this down," said Dotty. "You say that's obvious, Dr. Waldron, but no one in any official position agrees with you. Could you tell me how you reached your judgment?"

"Certainly. I'm a political scientist, and many political scientists adhere to what's known as rational choice theory. This means that they analyze political phenomena on the basis that, when all is said and done, people normally act for rational reasons, at some level of analysis. With this in mind, if you look at Nukus, you ask yourself: for whom would it be a rational decision, on any level, to destroy the capital of an obscure Central Asian republic with an atomic weapon. The answer is no one. Not the Russians, not the Chinese, not the Kazakhs, not the Iranians . . . just no one."

"Then you discount theories about terrorist groups and nuclear accidents."

"Completely. They're nonsense. Terrorism is the weapon of weak political groups that use fear to put pressure on some government to concede their demands. If you totally wipe out the government, as happened in Nukus, there's no one left to react to your demands; and you can't take over the capital because you've blown it up. As for an accident, there's been no end of scientific comment in the newspapers showing how impossible it is to build a weapon like this from scratch, how ridiculous it would be to build one in the middle of a city of two hundred thousand people, and how many safeguards there are to prevent accidental detonation of a normal military weapon, such as a missile warhead. Besides which, the international inspection team that has been overseeing on-site Russian and American nuclear disarmament reports no missing weapons."

"But isn't it going pretty far to suggest a space . . . person on this basis?"

"Not at all. A functioning machine of extraterrestrial origin is discovered only what? A hundred miles or so from Nukus? Nobody disagrees about that. The Carpenter-Beckenbaugh Corporation sets up a huge project designed to interfere with the machine. Now that project is destroyed. Who other than the builders of the machine would want to do such a thing?"

"But if the target was the hole-in-the-sea, a bomb could have been planted somewhere other than in the middle of Nukus."

"Indeed it could. But by destroying Nukus, the perpetrator eliminated both the project that threatened its machine and the government that authorized it."

"But . . ."

"Remember, these guys might have twelve arms and three eyes and squish when they walk. There's no reason to think they have the slightest compunction about killing humans. When they built the machine, there weren't even any humans around. They may have no idea of what a human being is." There was a long pause on the other end of the phone. David forged ahead. "One more thing. An assumption has been made for generations by science fiction writers that when faced with a threat from beyond the earth, humans will rally together to repel it. Nothing could be less likely. The world is made up of nation-states that act in their own interests and no one else's. Unless there is some obvious advantage in joining forces to fight a threat from space, it's just as likely that any given state will find it to its advantage to get on the space bandwagon and help the invader. After thousands of years of collective selfishness, it's pretty hard to believe that humans will suddenly work together in the face of a great threat. There are dozens of examples in history precisely of people not working together in the face of great threats. It wouldn't surprise me a bit to learn that at this very moment some government somewhere is working with the extraterrestrials because they are convinced it is in their interest vis-à-vis other states. Maybe even helped them bomb Nukus."

"Dr. Waldron, these are very challenging ideas that I'm sure would make for an interesting show. When we've finalized the lineup, I'll call you back and tell you for sure whether we want you to come down. Thank you very much."

"I'll be here. And thank you for calling."

"So you're going to be on television?" said Libby with a big smile as soon as her husband hung up the phone.

"Not a chance."

"Why not? Sounded good to me."

"It isn't what they want to hear. Scares people too much, and makes the government seem powerless."

"But the government is powerless."

"All the more reason not to let people know."

"Oh, that's too bad. You'd look so cute on television. You could have worn the suit you got married in.

On West Sixty-Eighth Street Dotty Bennett turned to an expectant Paul Henning and shook her head sadly. "No go. Thinks it's space aliens."

Henning threw up his arms. "What's the world coming to? Nut cases all over the place. Have you talked to Dr. Stein at the Council?"

"I have, but I thought you were down on him."

"We may have to use him anyway. What's his take on the bombing?"

"He thinks it was a Muslim terrorist device intended for Israel that went off accidentally. Says the U.S. should retaliate against Iran and hit their atomic reactor at Bushire."

"Oh, that makes a lot of sense." Dotty caught Paul's expression as he jiggled his eyeballs in his patented burlesque of a demented fit. "Who else have we got?"

* * *

Joseph Engineer proved a delightful cocktail guest. Chakra Net being on the brink of shutting down, Lee readily admitted her role as sysop. In return, Joseph told her, more or less truthfully, that he had been pursuing an Internet project related to the Great Array and had stumbled on her site by accident.

"You two are peas in a pod," laughed Donald. "Your mysterious Nadir has got both your panties in an uproar."

"That's a crude expression."

"But appropriate, for at least the slightest fraction of a millisecond, wouldn't you say?"

"I don't know what you're talking about."

Joseph sensed a sudden chill in the air. "Nadir's last reply to you said he was coming to Osh. Why not here to Kokand? He must know that that's where Chakra Web is."

Lee was happy for the new turn of conversation. "I've wondered about Osh. Maybe he can't leave Kyrgyzstan. Osh is the closest Kyrgyz city to Kokand. But Donald and I couldn't go there to meet him without clearing it through the embassy."

So she doesn't know that Nadir posts from Almaty in Kazakhstan, thought Joseph.

"I can assure you there is no way I'm going to Osh to meet anyone," put in Donald.

"And I wouldn't ask you to, Dear," replied Lee icily.

Joseph looked at his watch and stood up. Whatever the hour was, it was clearly time to leave. "I really must go. I'm still all out of whack with jet lag. I want to thank you both for your wonderful hospitality."

Lee stood. "Not at all. We must have you again. In fact, would it at all interest you to see the collection of antiquities at the Ferghana Academy of Sciences? I'm going over there tomorrow and would be happy to give you a tour."

"That would be perfect," said Joseph.

They met the next morning in the Academy's foyer and ordered tea in the adjoining café. Having wrestled with his conscience throughout a largely sleepless night, Joseph had decided to come clean about the purpose of his mission to Kokand. His story of being tasked by the Deputy Director of the National Security Agency to surf the Internet and then to identify the Chakra Net webmaster elicited nothing but amusement from Lee.

"So you're not angry with me for spying on you?"

"I've been spied on by more experienced professionals than you, Joseph. I'm getting used to it. But if you're done with your tea, let's go up to my study area."

Old steel filing cabinets lined the walls of the frigid, musty smelling archive room. The tabletops and floor space in the rest of the room were strewn with chunks of inscribed stone from the mountains, sections of tile mosaic from old mosques, ancient pots glued back together, small Buddhist figurines made of bronze, and a huge green banner adorned with Arabic calligraphy that Lee had been told identified it as coming from the tomb of a Muslim saint.

Lee placed a photograph of a rock carving on a table. "I think this one is particularly important."

Joseph blew on his fingers to warm them before picking the photo up to study. "What is it? It looks like stick figure people hunting an elephant."

"I'm sure that's just what it is. But, of course, there weren't any elephants around here five thousand years ago."

"Do you think it's a mammoth?"

"I don't think it could be anything else. The tusks are too long for an Indian elephant, and the maximum known range of Indian elephants ends almost a thousand miles south of here. So this carving could well go back to the last ice age. That would date it closer to 11,000 BC than 3000 BC. Yet the stick figure style is just like the carvings with chariots and chakras. It makes one wonder whether we've misdated the whole bunch or whether rock carvings in a consistent style were made over an enormously long period of time. Now look at this one."

Joseph studied it closely and then blushed. "It's appears to be a homosexual orgy."

"Unmistakably. A little prehistoric man on man action. You can bet I'm going to ask Nadir about this image if we ever meet him. It will be a kind of test. He's proven he can answer question based on texts because he is obviously very well versed on Vedic matters. But we don't know how he would do interpreting pictures he's never seen before." Lee put down another photo. "Now here's one with Vrtra the snake. Just a wavy line with a bulge for the head. You see how you can also look at it as a range of mountains on the skyline?"

"You're right. But if the carvings really are much older than we think, maybe go back to the last ice age, what about the chariots? I thought chariots didn't appear until . . ."

"About 1800 BC. But there are carts drawn by oxen and two-humped camels back fifteen hundred years earlier. We have both pictures of them and clay models. Still, you can't prove anything by its absence, and rock art is intrinsically hard to date. Actual wheels have been excavated in Denmark from before 3000 BC and datable pictographs of carts show up in southern Iraq at almost the same time. That's a huge span of territory. For an invention to be attested more or less simultaneously all the way from Iraq to Denmark suggests that wheels might have been devised much earlier but not left any traces."

"Isn't that surprising? That they wouldn't have left traces? I mean, wheeled vehicles must have had a huge impact on economy and war and things."

Lee smiled. "Joseph, you're so clever. You're just like me. You ask all the right questions. I wish I were teaching a class so I could have you as a student. What you have to understand is that the earliest wheels, like the ones from Denmark, were carved from huge planks and rotated on a thick pole stuck through a hole bored in the center. The wheels themselves were solid oak and weighed a ton so the friction was enormous. You have to ask yourself, what good was a cart that weighed so much even unloaded and had wheels that generated so much friction? It certainly wasn't used for carrying camp goods around. And it certainly wasn't very useful in war. Those things came much, much later after they learned how to make light wheels with spokes and reduce the friction. At the beginning, particularly over rough ground, it was almost certainly easier and more efficient to put things on a sled, or on a travois made of two poles like the American Indians used."

"Then what were wheels good for?"

"That is something else I would ask Nadir if I really believed he was eleven thousand years old. After reading his postings, it's come to my mind that wheeled vehicles were invented not for practical use but as symbols of the gods traveling through the sky. Maybe based on round spaceships. I'm trying not to say flying saucers."

"Remember, Mrs. Ingalls, if we talk about space things, I'm not allowed to use the terms gods and giants."

"Oh yes, your Mr. What's-his-name?"

"Thayer."

"What again are the terms that he wants you to use?"

"Space enemies and space friends. That's what he's using in the summaries of Nadir's postings he distributes at intelligence briefings."

"But that's so silly. Anyone can just read the postings on Chakra Net . . . or could read them before the Academy closed it . . . and see that Nadir actually says gods and giants."

"But only Mr. Thayer and Dr. Badger, my direct boss, know about Chakra Net. Officially, NSA has developed a contact so secret that they are not at liberty to divulge it even to the other intelligence agencies."

"Even though it's was a public website open to anyone to read?"

"Mr. Thayer says that happens all the time in intelligence work. A lot of secrets are in the public domain, but aren't recognized."

"Well, so be it, then. I will try not to corrupt your young spy mind. My theory is that what the chariot carvings show, to go back to your question, is not vehicles used for commerce or war, but vehicles the . . . space friends . . . used to teach primitive humans about the chakra machine and how the space friends came here from some other planet. At first, they were just symbolic, I think, maybe circles with crossbars and nothing suggesting a practical vehicle. The identifiable carts and wagons would have come much later, probably long after their symbolic meanings had been buried in myth. That's why we find chakras and chariots carved at 16,000 feet on mountain passes where certainly no real chariot ever went, and why we sometimes find figurines of chariots drawn by geese or carrying a huge disk representing the sun, and why all of the Indo-European gods—whether Indian, Norse, Greek, Roman, or Celtic—are described as riding in chariots."

"So the war chariot had nothing to do with the origin of wheeled vehicles?"

"I think that's the clear implication of Nadir's throwing the rock carvings back to a much earlier era . . . assuming, just for the sake of argument, that Nadir is, in fact, very old, etc., etc., etc. It would actually make perfect sense. When earthly warrior kings wanted to seem like gods . . . . Really, Joseph, I can't always be saying space friends. It sounds ridiculous. When the kings wanted to seem like gods, they rode in chariots, and they raced chariots to honor fallen heroes in the way they imagined the gods raced through the heavens. Just read the *Iliad*. Godlike Achilles and Hector ride to battle in chariots, but they fight on foot. Or take the earliest Romans; they fought on foot, but the victorious king rode a chariot through the city painted orange like a statue of Jupiter while a slave ran beside him saying, 'Remember, thou art not a god.'"

"Wow, you really know a lot about this."

Lee sighed. "So much to know, and to so little purpose. You and some of the people here at the Academy excepted, I haven't talked to anyone in over a year who cares a hoot about the ancient people who lived in this region. My husband is an expert on marketing toilet valves."

"But what about Nadir?"

"Well, yes, of course. There's Nadir. Though I don't for a minute believe he is either a god or a space friend, or, for that matter, that he is going to show up in Osh. I still think he's probably some malicious friend of mine. And what's more, I don't know how I can get Donald to take me to Osh. It's not very far away, but there's nothing to see there, and Donald likes sight-seeing. Not to mention the fact that he would have to get authorization from Ambassador Bane to travel into Kyrgyzstan." Lee continued in a musing fashion. "Besides, I don't know how I would meet him if I did go to Osh. I have no idea what he looks like, and with Chakra Net closed, we can't communicate anymore. He doesn't even know I'm a woman."

"Don't you think that as a space friend he probably has advanced ways of communicating, Dr. Ingalls?" said Joseph confidently.

"You're such a sweet, naive boy, Joseph. You actually believe in who Nadir claims to be."

"Of course."

"Including that his own fellow space friends considered him a weak-minded drunkard?"

"That was surprising, I admit. But technically, everything he posted made perfect sense. I can't believe that you don't consider him a space friend too. Haven't you ever believed in him?"

"Not really, except on occasional moments when I've had too much tea. Caffeine seems to make me more credulous. But you have to admit that there are other possibilities. Some science fiction addict could have invented the climate change story just to explain the laser beam exchange."

"Nadir's first posting, which went to a site devoted to geology, came before the laser exchange."

"It did?"

"Yes. And your science fiction theory doesn't explain the iambic trimeter."

"Nevertheless, I looked at some lists of publications from Almaty University and the Kazakh Academy of Sciences after you told me that that is where Nadir's posts were coming from. There are at least five professors there who have sufficient scholarly backgrounds to invent what Nadir has been posting. My guess is it's probably one of their students."

"Who combines knowledge of the Vedas with a taste for science fiction and has fun writing English poetry?"

"It could happen. Why not? Some people acquire very unusual skill sets. I happen to know a torturer who has a taste for Longfellow. Quite frankly, Joseph, I'm not quite sure what to make of your own willingness to accept Nadir's story. For a spy, you are immensely gullible. It makes me worry for the future of our government that you work for the National Security Agency. You have a scientific training, but you also accept the idea of space friends and space enemies with no corroborating proof whatsoever. A scientist should demand more. Are you just trying to impress your Mr. Thayer? Or did you read too much science fiction in high school?"

Joseph blew on his fingers again and thrust his chilled hands into the pockets of his coat. "I don't think those are very fair questions, Dr. Ingalls. NSA hired me to write programs, not to go searching for the abominable snowman in the wilds of Central Asia. This isn't science. And it isn't spying either. I have no training whatsoever for what I'm supposed to be doing here, and I don't think I or anyone else from NSA would even be here if there weren't some kind of politics going on between NSA and the other agencies. The Director told Mr. Thayer to make something happen, and I turned out to be their only hope. But they're also obviously afraid I'm going to embarrass them, so they're keeping me sort of secret. But that doesn't make me credulous or gullible. I think open-minded is a better term. What Nadir wrote about the purpose of the Aral Sea chakra is plausible, and the fact that after he told his story, the Carpenter expedition confirmed that there is something millions of years old buried under the seafloor does provide come scientific corroboration. So my view is that if you accept part of Nadir's story, you have to go with the whole thing. Otherwise, how would Nadir know what he obviously knows? Climate change machinery isn't in the Vedas."

Lee had been closing the photograph folders and filing them away while Joseph talked. "We should leave. I think it's colder in here than it is outside." Their footsteps echoed on the hardwood floor of a long corridor lined with romantic paintings reimagining the nineteenth-century exploring expedition of the Russian Nikolai Przhevalsky. "You know, Joseph, your argument still doesn't convince me. You spent weeks wading through what you yourself describe as an electronic cesspool before you hit on my poor defunct Chakra Net. And there you found a whimsical writer who for some reason has a passion for anonymity. Maybe he's J.D. Salinger. I don't know who he is. You don't know who he is. But he's got a good imagination . . . as good as probably a few hundred, maybe a few thousand, science fiction writers. Even if he has actually come up with the right answer to the today's greatest riddle, that does not mean that he comes from another planet and has been living on Earth for at least eleven thousand years. I still call that just plain gullible. It's what my mother used to call a pretty idea. Nothing more."

The glare of the afternoon sun reflecting from the two inches of snow that had fallen during the morning forced them both to squint as they exited the Academy. The air was still and crisp. They turned away from the glare and proceeded toward the Kokand Hotel where they could hope to find a taxi. "You know, my family's from India," said Joseph.

"So I assumed from your skin color and that lovely wavy black hair, but you don't have an Indian name."

"Actually, I do. Some Anglo-Indians took the names of their occupations as surnames, like Merchant. My great-great-grandfather was an Englishman, one of the first engineers in the Indian railway system. He married a Christian Indian woman, and all of his family took the name Engineer. It showed they had English blood. But my own mother is Hindu; and even though she has been living in the United States for thirty years, she keeps a shrine to the Lord Shiva in her bedroom. She taught me always to invoke the god Ganesh . . . you know, the one with the elephant's head? . . . when starting out on something, or taking a test in school, whenever I wanted good fortune."

"So you are a Hindu?"

"Not in any significant way, except for being a vegetarian. But I think it's important that I grew up in a family that never lost the feeling that there are gods in the world."

"Space friends?"

Joseph laughed. "My father says that when I was little, maybe around six, I went with him to a wedding in a Christian church. I looked at a stained glass window showing Christ and the four-and-twenty elders. I asked him what it was, and he said it was a picture of God. So I asked him which god. And he said it was just God. So he says I looked again and announced, 'He's the god of popcorn,' and then walked away, very satisfied. I have no idea why I said such a thing, but the idea of a plurality of gods doesn't present any problems for me."

No taxis were in sight as Lee and Joseph jaywalked across the street to the Kokand Hotel. The one car waiting in front of the hotel was a black Toyota Land Cruiser. A small cloud of white exhaust showed that its engine was running. As they neared the vehicle, the back door opened and a man in an officer's uniform climbed out. "Dr. Ingalls, Mr. Engineer," called Major Park, "may I offer you a ride? It's very cold."

Chapter Fourteen

"I would not have accepted your offer if Joseph hadn't been with me," said Lee in a tone as icy as the air outside.

"I realize that."

"And if you had taken me home, as I requested, after dropping Joseph off, I would not have invited you in."

"That is why we are eating ice cream in a bright, sunny shop with large windows instead of drinking tea in your living room. That and to assure you that our conversation is not being recorded."

Lee gazed through the heavily steamed window beside her and wondered if she would ever be free of Kokand. Two passing schoolboys were kicking pieces of ice to one another like hockey pucks. Lee sighed and looked again at the Major sitting stiffly in his brown overcoat with red epaulets and hat rimmed with gold braid. "I can never forgive you, Major Park, for what you did to me and my husband. I am sure you can understand that. But at least the blackmail is over now. Your stupid president has closed Chakra Net so I am free of his demands even though I regret forgoing the amusement of being a webmaster. If the pig should ask, you may tell him that if he should put pressure on me again, I will go to the American embassy, apprise our ambassador of everything that has gone on, and return to the United States. Protecting Donald no longer makes much sense to me, not since I learned that he has chosen to ignore my being compromised by the president and instead gone into business with him. But I'm sure your bugs in my house have made you aware of the words that have passed between us on the matter."

"They have." Lee looked again into the street at a line of bundled up women with string shopping bags waiting for a bus. The reflection in the glass told her that the Major was studying her closely. "I hate to deepen your unhappiness," he said at length, "but I gather you are unaware that your husband has resumed his visits to Miss Ramirez."

Lee kept her face averted as tears welled in her eyes. "I suspected it, but he hasn't told me. I hope you will spare me another tape recording."

"There is no need to inflict that on you."

"None." After a pause she added bitterly, "I suppose once again there's something you want of me." *How quickly the things you most want can melt away*, she thought as she stirred the suddenly unappetizing ice cream softening in her dish.

"Your husband gave you a sapphire."

Lee thrust her hand into her handbag. A small round object the size of a large pill puzzled her, but she felt past it to a folded envelope, which she extracted and laid on the table. Opening it she slid the glittering blue stone onto the marble tabletop. "I took it to a jeweler to consult about a setting. However, I suppose you're going to tell me it's not mine to keep."

"The Jewish jeweler on Przhevalski Avenue?"

Lee struggled again to suppress tears. She leaned forward and whispered fiercely, "Why are you following me?"

Major Park likewise leaned forward and whispered to her from eight inches away. "I'm not following you, Dr. Ingalls. I just happened to see you leaving as I was going there to pick up an item he was making for me." He straightened up and reached into his overcoat pocket. He pulled out a small box, removed its lid, and laid it on the table next to the sapphire. A simple gold pin mounting a diamond as large as the sapphire sparkled in a nest of cotton. "I would like you to have this. It's a gift."

Lee looked at the diamond with her hands in her lap and said nothing while her brain rehearsed a dozen remarks and reactions from sarcastically effusive thanks to slapping his face. Eventually she said in a studiously controled voice, "I think you need to tell me more, Major Park."

The Major's stoic visage betrayed the slightest hint of a smile. "The diamond is real, just like your husband's sapphire. Even the same cut. They come from the same place. Here are some more." He reached again into his pocket and held out five more diamonds for Lee to look at.

"Not a mysterious mine owned by Mr. Muratbey?"

"There is no mine. Nor were they stolen or smuggled. They were made in a machine. The machine's owner considers them trinkets—his own word. How many the machine is capable of making I have no idea, but my president now has the machine, and just as he blackmailed you over Miss Ramirez, he is now blackmailing your husband into moving the gems out of the country by way of the diplomatic pouch."

"This is not a business partnership, then."

"Far from it. Your husband's inability to separate from Miss Ramirez has put him at President Muratbey's mercy."

Lee sighed deeply. "Oh, Donald, why wasn't I good enough for you?"

"If I may say so, Dr. Ingalls, your husband was apparently unable to recognize a great gem when he held it in his arms."

"How gallant of you to say so . . . John Alden," replied Lee without sarcasm. "Nevertheless, I cannot possibly accept the pin."

"I will save it, then, for another time." The Major closed the box and pocketed it and the unmounted diamonds. "I have no one else to give it to, and it cost me only the setting."

"The setting is very tasteful."

"I patterned it on the pin you were wearing at Ambassador Bane's reception where we were first introduced. But this is not the time to pursue such matters. The truth is, Dr. Ingalls, I need your help. Your voluntary help." Lee's look invited him to continue. "The person who gave the machine to President Muratbey is . . . is . . ." he looked at Lee's face searching for some assistance. "Do you by any chance have some sense of who he is?"

Lee concentrated on Major Park's question and felt her heart, which minutes before had heaved mightily at word of Donald's continuing infidelity, begin to race for an entirely different purpose. "Tell me how tall he is," she said slowly.

Major Park smiled in relief. "Three meters, at least."

"Oh my god. It's true then."

"It's all true. I've seen him." Major Park was leaning forward on his crossed arms and whispering. "I've been in his ship. He made a dozen diamonds for me to give to Muratbey. They were bribes to persuade him to meet."

Lee smiled. "So you helped yourself to a fifty percent commission?"

"I took them only as proof." The Major was still whispering conspiratorily. "Everyone at the Palace saw the ship. It's round, by the way. Actually spherical, but from the side it looks like a chakra."

"Or the orb of the sun or the moon, the chariots the gods rode across the heavens. In what way do you need my help?"

"To achieve justice," continued the Major intensely. "The giant calls himself Bix."

Lee giggled. "Bix? Like the trumpeter Bix Beiderbeck?"

"I don't know who that is."

"Never mind. What about Bix?"

"Bix bombed Nukus."

Lee was stunned. "Do you know this?"

"I know it, but I can't prove it. And there's no one I can tell who would believe me. Especially not my president or anyone in his government. Bix needs help of some kind; and as a condition of helping him, Muratbey demanded that he eliminate President Vahidoglu. I heard him say it. Bix just happened to eliminate him with an atomic bomb."

"But over two hundred thousand people were killed!"

"I know. It seems incredible. But I've given it a lot of thought. Consider it this way. Imagine you're stung by a bee. You tell your husband, and he sprays the hive with insecticide killing all the bees, maybe or maybe not including the one that stung you. The lives of the bees are of no consequence. To Bix, we're just like the bees. Our lives are of no consequence. He doesn't sense that killing us is wrong. I think all he wanted to do for himself was collapse the hole-in-the-sea. That's why he used a seismic bomb. Killing Vahidoglu in Nukus . . . lets say, in his hive . . . was what he called 'killing two birds with one stone.'"

"And Muratbey?"

"Did nothing," whispered Park vehemently. "The most horrible of crimes, and he just sits in his office making gems with his machine. Muratbey is the criminal. Bix is just the gardener killing bees."

"And now they're working together?"

"Whatever Bix wants, Muratbey will do."

"Just for diamonds?"

"No. Bix has promised many machines, highly advanced technology, but only after he has finished repairing the climate controller. For that he needs some sort of help."

Lee giggled again. "Then he's not the gardener; he's the air conditioner repairman."

"Dr. Ingalls, why are you laughing?"

"Major Park, why are you whispering?"

"Because I don't want people to hear me talking about an alien from space bent on destroying civilization."

"Because they'll think you're crazy and laugh at you?" whispered Lee back.

"Yes, because they'll think I'm crazy and laugh at me." The Major's exasperated whisper had become a loud hiss.

"But you've told me. Don't you think I'm laughing at you because I think you're crazy?"

Major Park sat up straight and hardened his expression. "Do you think I'm crazy? I thought . . . from Chakra Net . . ."

Lee continued to whisper. "Don't worry. I don't think you're crazy. But I do think it's funny that the most feared interrogator in Ferghana and an American Vedic scholar are sitting in probably the one ice cream parlor in Kokand you haven't bugged whispering about space invaders. For once in your life you know what it's like to be afraid of being overheard."

"Absurd . . . the situation is absurd, perhaps . . . but not funny."

"Absurd then."

"But not funny. Not all those dead people."

"All right, not funny. Absurd . . . absurd and tragic. I'm sorry I laughed." Lee recomposed her face to a serious expression.

"Then will you help me?"

"Help you what?"

"Help me find Nadir. Go to Osh with me. Without telling your husband. He would tell Muratbey."

"May I have your permission to laugh on the inside just a little bit? Surely there is something a little bit funny, at least funny peculiar, in the idea that to save civilization and bring Muratbey to justice you tell me, for a second time, that my husband is unfaithful, you offer me an exquisite diamond pin, and now you ask me to run away with you, without telling my husband, to a city across the border in another country."

An unaccustomed smile split Major Park's face causing his dry cheeks to crease in parentheses of wrinkles. "Yes, it is absurd. It is possibly even funny. But I am sure that without you I can do nothing. Nadir is willing to meet you, but he would certainly not identify himself to the most feared interrogator in Ferghana. And only Nadir knows how to deal with Bix. So you must help me."

"You're certain you're not speaking as John Alden trying to excite the interest of a woman whose husband no longer desires her?"

"I speak only as the avenger of the people of Nukus."

Lee studied Park's face and then gave a businesslike nod. "Done. You will make the arrangements?"

"Everything."

Lee replaced the sapphire in its envelope and placed it in her purse. Again her hand encountered the pill-like object. She pulled it out and studied it. "Is this yours, Major?"

Major Park took the tiny transponder and studied it even more closely. "Not mine. Yours, I think."

"Certainly not mine," protested Lee.

"I didn't mean yours personally. I meant American."

A block away, beside a news kiosk with a direct line of sight to the ice cream parlor, Joseph Engineer turned off the minirecorder concealed behind a newspaper he was reading and collapsed the antenna of a small radio receiver. *Time to be off*, he thought to himself cheerfully.

* * *

"What is this?" asked Muratbey of the marmot clinging to his shoulder. His pudgy finger was pointing at a sturdy machine with fan-like blades standing eight feet tall on a circular base.

"That is a graviton displacer. Makes heavy things light, light things heavy. Very inefficient for masses under a million tons. It is used for major rearrangements of planetary features or for changing the orbits of small moons and asteroids."

"You have two. Can I have one?"

"Of course." Frak added one graviton displacer to the growing list of machines to be left behind.

Deep beneath the Andijan reservoir Muratbey moved purposefully on to the next bay in the capacious hold of Bix's ship. He peered at the round things inside. "What are these?"

"They convert mass into energy. We call them eggs. Bix used one of them to clean up the problem in the Aral Sea. They can be adjusted into many configurations."

Muratbey's eyes gleamed in the dim light. "You have many. Can I have some?"

He wants weapons again, communicated Frak silently to Bix in the dark compartment where he was taking his rest.

According to the protocols, a desire for weapons is species and gender appropriate, responded Bix wearily. *Tell him no politely but firmly.*

You tell him. He thinks I'm a burrowing rodent and doesn't take me seriously. "Bix will come and discuss that with you," said Frak to Muratbey, "but I suspect he'll say no."

Bix untangled his long limbs from his extremely comfortable sling bed and irritably made his way aft. The protocols had correctly predicted that the leader of a rational alien species with moderately advanced technical capabilities would be so impressed by the wonders of advanced technology, and so eager to gain control of them, that he would agree to any arrangement to get possession of them. It was just unfortunate that the egg in Nukus had caused Muratbey to demand an immediate tour of the spaceship's treasures. Bix had informed Muratbey that he needed his rest, but he suspected that Muratbey's species didn't take the notion of rest very seriously: up sixteen of their little hours, down eight, up sixteen, down eight, up, down, up, down—a whole breathless cycle every planetary revolution. No wonder they didn't live very long or get very much accomplished. They never got any decent rest. Frak had calculated that seven of the solar orbits they used to count their age were the equivalent of one lifetime measurement unit at home. Bix, on the other hand, was accustomed to resting, thoroughly resting, absolutely flat out resting, with every particle of his body, throughout one of every seven of Muratbey's light and dark cycles. And resting did not mean climbing out of an extremely comfortable sling bed to enforce the word of a nickety-pickety translator.

Bix found the pair peering into a locker full of blob suits.

"You put it on over your clothes, activate it, and it expands away from your body to form a transparent protective shield. Nothing penetrates it once the fabric coalesces, but it's permeable to gases and liquids while it's expanding. This means that if you stay in it too long or try to use it under water, you suffocate. Still, for short-term protection from everything up to the level of an egg's energy release, nothing beats it."

"Can I have a dozen?"

"We'll make it a gross, a dozen dozens. We're oversupplied, and they have a shelf life of only seven planetary orbits."

"How long is that?"

"Forty-nine of your years. The ones in this locker have only about twenty years to go. Here's Bix."

It was hardly necessary to call Muratbey's attention to the giant's arrival. Muratbey noted a decidedly peevish look on Bix's normally radiant face.

"Frak said you needed me," said Bix through Frak.

"I want eggs," replied Muratbey. "People will try to take my treasures away, so I need protection."

"NO WEAPONS! NO, NO, NO, NO, NO!" Bix matched a dramatically threatening scowl to Frak's high volume expostulation.

Muratbey had served under enough party bosses to know when no meant no. Of course, that didn't mean that no could never turn into yes. "I ask again later," he said unperturbed. With that he turned to rummage in a bin of rubbery looking things.

He wants one of everything, communicated Frak.

Give it to him. Just get it over with so I can get some rest.

Also, we have pramodzi.

Bix felt sullen and looked explosive. *That's just great! Are you sure? You could have waited until I was up again to tell me. They aren't going to go away.*

Muratbey stared at Bix with shrewd beady eyes. "You have problem? You look like you have problem. Am I problem?"

"No, you're not the problem."

"Then maybe I help."

Bix eyed the portly president. "Our problem is *pramodzi*. We have a *pramodzi* infestation."

"What is *pramodzi*?"

"It's a species on my planet . . . disgusting . . . like parasites. They sneak in everywhere, steal from us, break equipment. They follow us from place to place, cause trouble."

"Like rats."

"Not like rats. Worse than rats. Smarter than rats. Also, you can't scare them away. You have to kill them. They never die on their own."

"How you know you have them?"

"They use communicators they originally stole from us. Like Frak. When a signal is broadcast using a communicator, we identify it immediately. If the signal doesn't come from us, it comes from *pramodzi*. Frak says he tracked two signals after the egg in Nukus."

"Two *pramodzi*?"

"One, two, a dozen, who knows? Ugh, they're just disgusting." Bix visibly shuddered.

"Where are *pramodzi*?"

"We know, but knowing never does any good. The signals came from a place between the cities you call Almaty and Bishkek. But *pramodzi* move around . . . sneak around."

"What do they look like?"

"Look? They look exactly like you. Like humans."

"We are *pramodzi*?" said Muratbey with rising anger.

"No. You just look like *pramodzi*. My kind are *inamadzi*. *Pramodzi* and *inamadzi* both come from a very human-like species. Both were produced by genetic engineering. That's one reason *pramodzi* are hard to eradicate." Bix was about to add, "unless you want to eradicate all the humans around," but thought better of it.

Muratbey seemed mollified. "Then you want keep *pramodzi* away. So we keep all humans from coming here. Would that help? Would that keep *pramodzi* away?"

"Possibly. Can you do that?"

Muratbey clapped his hands once and spread them wide, smiling broadly. "That, Mr. Bix, I do very good." Bix ventured a smile. Muratbey raised his spread palms in a sort of shrug. "But, unfortunately, I need weapons."

"No eggs."

"No eggs. But weapons I look at earlier, ones for people and ones for metal."

Bix considered. "Will the weapons help keep out *pramodzi*?"

"Help very much."

"All right. One type is a microwave destructor that destroys organic tissue. It will work on *pramodzi*."

"And on humans?"

"Yes, on both *pramodzi* and humans. The other type is an induction heating destructor for use on metal weapons. But you have to promise to give both of them back when I leave."

The deal concluded, Bix shambled back to his rest chamber in a state of total exhaustion. *Pramodzi fighting pramodzi, what is the universe coming to?*

Two hours later, after a speedy return from the reservoir, President Muratbey summoned his army Chief-of-Staff into his office. General Karim Chengizoglu cast a quizzical eye on the two objects sitting on the president's desk. One was red, the other green. Both had the shape of very narrow isosceles triangles approximately one meter long. "General," said Muratbey calmly, "we are facing a national emergency. I want all borders to be sealed. No one is to enter. No one is to leave. Under any circumstances or for any reason. See to it."

The graying veteran of the Afghanistan War stood his ground. "May I know the nature of the national emergency, Mr. President?"

"No. You may obey orders." The General did not move. Muratbey waited. "Are you refusing to obey orders, General?" he said at length.

"If you tell me the nature of the national emergency . . ."

Muratbey placed his finger on a depression a third of the way from the base of the green triangle. He watched with interest as within seconds the Chief-of-Staff turned red and cooked in front of his eyes. The General's body collapsed to the floor in a lifeless, steaming heap. President Muratbey picked up the telephone and summoned the general's second-in-command.

It took fifteen minutes for Colonel Maxim Sverdlov to arrive from army headquarters. He glanced only briefly at the general's body, which was still slightly steaming.

"Colonel Sverdlov, you are Russian."

"Yes, Mr. President."

"But you are a loyal Ferghanan?"

"Yes, Mr. President."

"I cannot say the same for your former superior officer. I asked him to seal the borders of Ferghana. Told him that no one was to leave or enter by land or air. Absolutely no one. He asked me what national emergency we were facing. That was not his job."

"Yes, Mr. President."

"On my desk you see two new weapons. These are weapons no other nation has or even knows about. They are treasures of Ferghana. The green one kills with microwaves. It works very well. The red one melts metal objects in some other sort of way. Learn to use them, Colonel. They are the first of many treasures that the people of Ferghana will soon receive."

"Yes, Mr. President."

"One more thing, Colonel." President Muratbey held out a pudgy fist and opened it. "I would like you to give this diamond to your wife. Or if you don't have a wife, to your girlfriend."

"Yes, Mr. President."

Chapter Fifteen

Hayes Carpenter's Learjet landed at Almaty airport at two in the morning. On hand to meet it was Dan Nielsen, the head of the Kazakhstan office of Carpenter-Beckenbaugh Corp. Awakened forty-five minutes earlier by a telephone call from the plane, Dan's sleepiness had instantly disappeared in the adrenalin rush triggered by his CEO's unscheduled arrival. Pulling on his long underwear he went over in his head again and again the figures for Kazakh winter wheat purchases trying to figure out whether or where he might have screwed up. Lurking in the back of his mind was the possibility that his boss might have something more serious on his mind.

Aside from Dan and his driver, the airport was all but deserted. Its dirty plastic benches looked forlorn without the usual crowd of travelers eating bread and cheese, reading magazines, and complaining about flight delays. Illuminated wall posters for Korean and Japanese electronic devices contrasted sharply with the seedy waiting area.

Dan could see the sleek plane's lights as it taxied toward the terminal. He looked around at a noise behind him and saw Korkut, his office manager, burst through the door and scurry his way. "What's the matter? Why is he here?" asked the nervous young Kazakh.

Dan noticed his underling's pajama bottoms sticking out below the cuffs of his trousers. "I have no idea. He just called out of the clear blue sky and told me to be here prepared to get him, his crew, and five other passengers through customs. He didn't say anything else. Do you know anything?" He eyed Korkut sharply, but his ambitious young subordinate betrayed no sign of guilt.

"Me? Nothing. I have no idea. It's two in the morning. I didn't even know the airport was open at this hour." He looked around him. "I don't think it is open. Is there even anyone available to handle passport and customs?"

"There's one officer on duty. Did you bring the potatoes?" "Potatoes" was the Carpenter-Beckenbaugh code word for bribe money. Korkut patted his briefcase. The trip to get banded bundles of American twenty-dollar bills from the office safe had almost made him late. Dan nodded toward a gaunt uniformed man with pockmarked skin standing nonchalantly by the opaque glass door to the customs hall. "Captain Scriabin. He's very grumpy about having to receive a plane after the airport has closed. Go calm him down."

Dan marveled at the ease and assurance the Kazakhs brought to the daily business of distributing bribes. Sometimes he thought that Minnesota Lutherans like himself were constitutionally incapable of such corruption, but then he would remind himself of the times he had seen similarly Protestant and similarly Midwestern Hayes Carpenter offer outrageous sums to finalize grain deals.

Korkut returned from his conversation with Captain Scriabin. "Everything is taken care of."

Another fifteen minutes passed before the hulking figure of Hayes Carpenter emerged from the customs hall. Holding his right elbow was a tall, lanky black man with very short gray hair. He was wearing dark glasses and carrying a folded white cane. Dan waved and walked to meet his boss, noticing as he did four husky, sober-faced men come through the door pushing large boxes on rollers.

"Dan, good to see you could get out here and take care of things. Saved some awkwardness." Hayes stretched out his left hand for Dan to shake. "This here's my old friend Wilson Woodrow."

"How do you do," drawled Wilson.

"Nice to meet you, Mr. Woodrow."

"My coming like this must have taken you a bit by surprise," laughed Hayes.

"Surprise is the spice of life," replied Dan in a lame attempt to match his boss's lightheartedness. "Unfortunately, I didn't have time to see to accommodations. I didn't know who was in your party or what sort of rooms you would need."

"Truth is, landing in Almaty wasn't part of my plan so there wasn't any reason to let you know in advance I was coming."

"Oh?" Dan felt a sense of relief.

"I was heading for Kokand; but as we were passing over Tashkent, we were informed that Ferghana has closed its airport and its airspace. Damnedest thing. No explanation given. You know what's going on there?"

"No, sir. There wasn't anything on the news this evening."

"Then it must have just happened. I told my pilot to nudge us over into Ferghana airspace a little to see if they were serious, and what do you know? Two jets flew up alongside us and signaled us to follow them. They led us back to the Kazakh border. So we radioed here to Almaty for permission to land. It took them a while to clear us through since the airport isn't supposed to be open, but at least we're on the ground."

Carpenter's silent companions in military haircuts and quilted black jackets clustered with their boxes at the terminal door. Soon the two pilots of the Learjet joined them. Out in the cold, Korkut was marshalling the several taxis he had summoned by cell phone.

"I think we should all go to my house," said Dan. "I don't know if we can find beds for everyone, but we can make arrangements from there."

"If you've got beds for me, Wilson, and the pilots, that's enough. These other guys are used to sleeping on the floor." Dan wondered just who the "other guys" were. "I hope you got a good map. We have to work on how to get from here to Kokand. Do you know what would be the nearest airport?"

"Tashkent and Bishkek are the nearest commercial airports." Dan paused for a moment. "But there's also sort of a rudimentary airfield at Osh, right on the Kyrgyz-Ferghana border. It's only a hundred miles from Kokand. Dirt runway, I'm told, but the Chinese can put their version of a DC-3 down there. Supposedly it's used by smugglers. I've heard reports that the police in Osh are willing to look the other way for a consideration."

"Now how would you know a thing like that, Danny boy," said Hayes jovially.

Dan's heart clutched. Surely he can't know everything, he thought to himself.

* * *

A hundred-and-fifty miles to the southwest, a solitary figure stopped beside a sign warning drivers that the road into the mountains was closed. Nadir had been walking continuously for four days. He figured it would take another six to reach Osh. But first he had to walk over the pass through the Tien Shan mountains, and that would take snowshoes. He clamped a webbed shoe securely to his artificial leg and adjusted the one for his good leg to have more flexibility. He wasn't tired. He had never been tired in over eleven thousand years. Nor was he cold. But he was thirsty. He pulled from his capacious backpack a liter bottle of vodka and drained it. He counted the bottles remaining and hoped that he could find someplace on the way to buy some more. Vodka wasn't soma, but it helped make immortality bearable.

He stood and tested the shoes in the snow by the side of the two-lane gravel road. Looking at the snowy slopes ahead of him he thought of the thousands of times he had visited them in springtime. Soon now the first wild flowers would be pushing aside the dead grass and melting snowdrifts in the high meadows, and soon after that the Kyrgyz herders would be coming on their sturdy ponies to check the state of the pasturage. *It will all be over by then*, he thought, *at least for this planet*. But elsewhere in the universe the descendants of Pramo and the descendants of Inama—the *pramodzi* and the *inamadzi*—would continue their struggle.

He gazed again at the snows ahead. He knew the best path. He had been there before. The snowshoes exaggerated his limp as he set off alongside the road.

* * *

In Moscow, an army archivist named Isabella Gryshkin pulled a pasteboard box from beneath three dusty portfolios lying on their side on the bottom shelf of a long neglected bookcase. The portfolios contained drawings, notes, and sketch maps from the

1876 expedition of the great explorer Nikolai Przhevalsky across the Tien Shan mountains to the salt lake of Lop Nor in China. It was not Przhevalsky's expedition that interested her, however. What she was looking for were the reports from a lesser known expedition sent into the same mountains by the Bolshevik hero General Mikhail Frunze in 1920. She knew what they looked like because all of the other reports from Frunze's period as commander of Bolshevik forces against the Basmachi bandits were where they should be. It was just a hunch that had made her think that maybe some earlier researcher had mistakenly put the reports with the Przhevalsky material. She opened the box, noted the hand-penned labels on the cloth-bound notebooks inside, and smiled broadly.

Two days later Dr. Andrei Bogomil burst jubilantly into the office of the Chief Historian of the Russian army, Nikita Yurenev. "I found it!" he shouted, waving a faded cloth-bound notebook in the air. The Chief Historian stubbed out his cigarette in a marble ashtray. Dr. Bogomil placed the notebook on the desk and opened it in front of his superior. "Here it is." He moved his finger along the crabbed old handwriting as he read:

> *June 26, 1920. Verethra Kuh. 5038 meters. Thirty versts west from Sary Tash, the first village on the road from Osh, along the track leading from Sary Tash to the Kyzylsu River. North of the track three versts. Below the summit on the northern face, at the top of a cliff, is a cave said by local people to be the dwelling of a dragon. Lieutenant Khinoy and Corporal Hrehorovich scaled the cliff and reported discovering inside the cave a round vertical shaft with perfectly smooth sides. They measured its diameter with their climbing ropes. It was just over ten meters. Lieutenant Khinoy extended the climbing ropes down the shaft to their maximum extent, three hundred meters, but did not contact the bottom. He is of the opinion that the shaft was artificially constructed though there were no signs of construction. Plans to test the depth of the shaft with longer ropes were interrupted by hostile fire from Basmachi bandits. Further exploration recommended.*

The Chief Historian grunted. “All these years. I’ve been working here for thirty years, and I’ve heard about Frunze’s lost secret all that time. But I never knew what it was or where it was. Or even if there was a secret.” He looked again at the notebook page. “Hmmm. A man-made vertical shaft 5,000 meters up the side of a mountain. How do you suppose it was made?”

“Perhaps it was done by whoever made the Great Array?” ventured Dr. Bogomil.

The Chief Historian thought for a few moments and then pressed a button on his intercom. “Anastasia, make an appointment for me with Minister of Defense Kalenin. Today if possible.”

* * *

“Donald will miss me as soon as he gets home tonight,” said Lee worriedly as she wedged two suitcases among the boxes on the back seat of the Toyota Land Cruiser.

“I’ve taken care of that,” said Major Park as he helped her into the front seat.

“What did you do? Kill him?” Lee was genuinely alarmed.

The Major made his way around to the other side and climbed into the driver’s seat. “I take that as a joke. No, I didn’t kill him. I told him I had discovered you were having a love affair with President Muratbey and that he had taken you off for several days of dalliance at his dacha in the country.”

“You what!? Donald would never believe such a story! He knows how much I despise that pig. How could you!?”

“Actually, he took the news very well. I intimated that you might have succumbed to the President’s entreaties to protect his position.”

Lee’s cheeks flamed with anger and embarrassment. “I can’t believe you would do such a thing. And I can’t believe that Donald would for one instant believe such an outrageous lie.”

Major Park backed the car out of the driveway. “I counted on him feeling so guilty about his own affair that he would be relieved to find out that you were doing the same. It’s a tactic I’ve employed several times in the past. Under the burden of their own guilt men will believe the most remarkable things about their wives.” Lee turned a frosty shoulder toward the Major and concentrated on the passing scene. "Perhaps you should slide down in the seat a little bit and hold onto the handle above the door. That will shield your face while we're in town."

"Do you think anyone would notice me in your car?"

"Many people notice who is in my car, Dr. Ingalls. And give thanks that it is not them. Or do you say 'is not they'?"

"To be correct you should say 'is not they.' Do you want me to give you English lessons now?"

"No. I was just wondering. Forget I mentioned it."

As the blocks of corrugated concrete fence and squalid wooden houses with metal roofs gave way to open countryside, Lee's eyes analyzed the passing scenery while a stew of emotions, contradictions, doubts, and excitement assailed her mind. There had been no commercial advertising in the Soviet Union, and since its fall there had been little commerce to advertise so the roadside was entirely free of signs. *Is it okay to abandon your husband just because he is unfaithful and disrespects you?* Nor were there many buildings. *And if you do abandon him, isn't it insane to run off on an adventure in the heart of Central Asia with a man you barely know?* Soviet collective farmers and ranchers had cultivated or grazed most of Ferghana's countryside, and much of the land was still held by large cooperatives. *What if something went wrong? What if Park raped and murdered her?* So private farms with American-style clusters of house, barn, and outbuildings were rare, along with property lines marked by fences, hedges, and rows of trees. *Who would Nadir turn out to be if they actually found him?* The resulting landscape looked almost pristine, sweeping vistas of brown grass and fallow fields leading on to the sharply rising snowcapped mountains. *Was this the turning point in her idle scholar's life?* With private cross-country car travel still uncommon, the ride was comparatively smooth, but the narrowness and uneven grading of the road kept their speed below 60 kilometers an hour. *My mother would be appalled. This is not what Hartford girls do.*

After an hour the tide of her inner debate began to subside and Lee felt her anxiety slowly give way to enjoyment of the countryside's simplicity and beauty and the relaxing hum and vibration of the tires on the asphalt.

"If I may be blunt, Major Park, I can't understand why you and your president are both so attracted to me." She hadn't wanted to bring the subject up in so blatant a way, but her curiosity was overwhelming. Her experience at home was that men were cautious around her for fear of receiving some verbal rebuke.

Park kept his eyes steadily on the road. "For Muratbey it is a matter of conquest. He finds you attractive, but it was having his first American woman that interested him most."

"But with you, I take it, it is different."

"Very different, very different. I told you I majored in American literature at the university. It was a subject a loved very much. And I particularly liked a certain type of American heroine, the type that Henry James wrote about. Daisy Miller, for example: Fresh, free, naive. The image became my ideal, but I never met anyone in Moscow or Ferghana who fit it. Or at least no one who showed the slightest interest in a Korean security officer."

"Until me, I suppose. Assuming that despite the noble cause of bringing Muratbey to justice and saving the world, my being here in the car with you is a sign of at least some slight interest in you personally."

"You're not exactly Daisy Miller, but you have many of the qualities I used to dream about."

"Right now, I think you could pick up more appropriate images from Bonnie and Clyde or Thelma and Louise."

"I don't know those books."

"They're movies. About women who run off on adventures. And die."

Park did not respond. His stiff posture and fixed expression indicated that the conversation was making him feel awkward. Lee returned her attention to the landscape and presently closed her eyes and slept.

The sound of the driver's door opening woke her. They were parked beneath the overhang of what looked like a half-finished concrete hangar abandoned to the elements. Lee got out and stretched. "Where are we?"

"Traveler services," said the Major.

Lee looked around. By the side of the overhanging half-vault of concrete a Chinese-looking man with wispy mustaches was tending a small rectangular trough set up on concrete blocks. Smoke was rising from the trough, and Lee smelled meat grilling. "Are there restrooms?"

"Behind. But they're pretty filthy. Most people go outside."

When Lee returned from a visit to a shallow ditch well beyond the reeking outhouse, Major Park was talking to the Chinese-looking man. "Would you like to eat? We're going to skirt Andijan to avoid being seen so we won't be able to stop at a restaurant."

"What does he have?" The man was fanning a handful of glowing coals beneath a grate on which he had placed spits of meat.

"Kabob and bread."

"Smells good." Lee watched the man grill two skewers of meat, place a layer of slivered onion of a piece of round flat bread, and push the meat off the skewers onto the onion. Then he ripped two pages from an open book bound in red beside the trough and used them as combination plates and napkins for serving the kabob. "What's the book?"

"Lenin's collected works. There are probably enough sets still around to serve kabob for the rest of the century."

"Can I have some too?" The cheerful American voice at her back startled Lee so much she almost dropped her food.

"Joseph! What are you doing here?"

"I'm learning how to be a spy by doing." The curly-haired computer programmer looked very pleased with himself. "While Major Park was helping you get your things from your house, I hid under the tarp in the back of the car."

Major Park seemed more amused than angry. "You surprised me, Mr. Engineer. Not many people in Ferghana can claim to have done that. But what did you do with what was under the tarpaulin?"

"The jerry cans? I put them behind the hedge in Dr. Ingalls' garden, except for the one that I put on its side and have been using as a pillow."

"That was our extra gasoline."

"I know. I've been smelling the fumes for the last two hours."

"Did you imagine we have gas stations dotted around the countryside in Ferghana?"

"I had no idea. I didn't get much of a briefing on Ferghana before I came here. But I also had no other option. If worse came to worst, I figured that someone of your rank could simply requisition gasoline."

"You mean steal it at gun point from other drivers?"

Lee broke in. "I don't care about gasoline, you two. I want to know what you're doing here, Joseph."

"He's here because he knew from monitoring our conversation in the ice cream parlor that we were going to Osh to find Nadir. Finding Nadir is his job too, isn't it, Mr. Engineer?"

Joseph took a large bite out of his kabob sandwich. "That's pretty much it," he said between chews. "If Nadir knows what's happening and what to do about it, it's my job to find out about it and inform the U.S. government. Right now, they don't really believe in Nadir. But if Nadir turns out to be real, finding him will be quite a coup."

"You sound enthusiastic," observed Park.

"Of course I'm enthusiastic! I was given the most hopeless assignment in the world, but it's all working out. Except that riding under that tarp on a metal floor really sucks. Can I ride up with you and Dr. Ingalls now?"

The Major looked amused. "You don't seem very frightened at being a captive of the most feared security officer in Ferghana. It makes me wonder whether I should be worried about my reputation."

"Major, if I've understood things correctly—and I think I have—you've betrayed your president and are now hightailing it out of the country. So I figure having an American intelligence agent on your side may be more of an asset than a liability."

"If you had put that argument to me before we started out, we would still have our spare gasoline, and you would have had a more comfortable ride."

"But would you have let me come if I had?"

"Hmmm, maybe not. Anyway, what's done is done. We should get going again. I don't think anyone will start looking for us for at least two days, but the sooner we cross the border and get to Osh, the better."

Chapter Sixteen

When Joseph Stalin drew the Central Asian boundaries of the soviet republics in 1936, he punished the town of Osh for its support of the lingering Basmachi guerrilla movement in the mountains. Instead of being joined to the fertile and productive Ferghana valley, Osh became part of mountainous Kyrgyzstan. With the mountain road linking it with the Kyrgyz capital snowbound throughout the long winter, and the road to Kashgar across the border in China closed for decades by political tensions, Osh had stagnated. Its thirty thousand souls—disgruntled Russian officials, a handful of Uighur Turk merchants plying the age-old smuggling trade with China, and a Kyrgyz sheep and horse-herding population that waxed in winter and waned in spring—took official neglect as a license to go their own way.

Kyrgyz independence after the collapse of the USSR brought few changes. The road through Osh connecting China with Ferghana was paved but still little traveled. The statues of Lenin and Marx were toppled from their pedestals in front of the concrete municipality building. And signs sprang up informing the citizenry of the wise sayings of whoever was the current Kyrgyz president. But the buildings continued to sag and crumble, the sewer and electrical systems to suffer protracted periods of crankiness.

From the guard shack and barrier that marked the Ferghana-Kyrgyz border on the town's western edge, the colorless profile of Osh at dusk presented a bleak and unwelcoming prospect. But to Lee Ingalls' eye as she and Joseph stamped the chill from their toes beside the Land Cruiser and waited for Major Park to end his powwow with the border police, it looked like the rainbow's end. She had firmly barred herself from thinking about Nadir's claim that he was the god Indra still surviving after thousands of years. It was easier to go along with Joseph's and Park's belief that he was a being from another planet. But now as the possibility of meeting her Chakra Net correspondent in the flesh approached, her mind returned to the questions she had abandoned earlier. How would her life change once she put an international frontier between herself and Donald? The urge to have an adventure while she was still in the prime of life had grown stronger as the Land Cruiser took them farther and farther from Kokand. But with Major Park as a companion? And now with Joseph Engineer as well?

Park crunched back toward them over the ice beginning to form on the pavement. "Get in the car," he said sternly.

"What's happening?" asked Lee as she fastened her seatbelt.

"The border has been closed. No one may leave; no one may enter."

"Including you?"

The Major had started the engine and was turning the Land Cruiser around. "Including me."

"What's the reason?"

"They've been told there's an outbreak of bubonic plague. But that's an excuse. I suggested it to Muratbey two years ago when he was thinking about closing the border for other reasons."

"Are we going back, then?" asked Joseph from his perch atop the luggage in the back seat.

Park's expression was grim. "No. We'd all be arrested. We'll take the first side road and then go cross-country. With luck, we won't hit a mine."

Lee and Joseph kept silent.

Once Park turned off onto a northward-trending dirt road a mile from the border, the Land Cruiser began to lurch and bounce over frozen hummocks and furrows that were barely visible in the waning light. Its three passengers strained between jolts to spot more dangerous obstacles in time to avoid them. Eventually the dirt road intersected a rutted track that Park identified as a border police patrol route parallel to the frontier. He followed it north and asked

Lee and Joseph to keep their eyes peeled for ruts heading off to the east.

After several minutes crawling slowly along the track, Joseph shouted, "There!" and pointed over Park's shoulder. Lee could not make out the ruts, but Park grunted his affirmation and turned the car again toward the east.

"Why are you looking for ruts?" she asked.

"If there are mines in this sector, the ruts should mark the path the patrols use to get to the fence safely." He paused. "Unless the path has been changed recently."

Time seemed suspended as the Land Cruiser edged forward into the dark.

"Stop!" screamed Lee.

Three feet in front of them an almost invisible three-strand barbed wire fence blocked the way. Joseph had already found the Major's wire cutters among the boxes and was quickly out the door and at work on the fence. Holding the cut wires back to keep them from getting under the wheels, he waved the vehicle forward. As soon as it was through, he jumped inside and Park gently accelerated.

"What about mines on this side?" worried Lee.

"That shouldn't be a problem. The mines are meant to keep the mountain people from smuggling Chinese goods into Ferghana. The Kyrgyz government doesn't care what gets smuggled in the other direction since the road goes to China and not to anywhere else important in Kyrgyzstan. That's why the Osh highway is an east-west conduit for buying and selling smuggled goods."

After fifteen more minutes of jolts and lurches in almost total darkness the Land Cruiser pitched abruptly into a broad ditch. Gunning his four-wheel drive, Park angled up the steep embankment on the far side. At its top was a graded dirt road. Turning south, Park switched on his headlights. In the distance a sprinkling of tiny lights signaled the northern outskirts of Osh.

"Now we just have to figure out how to get hotel rooms," said Lee, excited by the thought that she was now safely in Kyrgyzstan. "They'll ask for our passports, and we don't have entry stamps."

"We will stay with friends," replied Park. "I've made arrangements."

They drove on in silence for another fifteen minutes. Their destination proved to be on an unlit gravel road not quite within the town. A gate opened in a tall wooden fence as the Land Cruiser drove up and honked, and then closed quickly behind it. The yard was dark, but lantern light flickered in the windows of a small, metal-roofed bungalow. Several men in tall leather boots and dark coats exited the building and greeted Park in what sounded to Lee like Kyrgyz. Their leader was short and swarthy with long stringy mustaches. Park introduced him as Uli. Acting as a good host, he ushered Lee and Joseph into a sparsely furnished room from which doorways opened onto two smaller rooms and a kitchen. A kerosene heater stood beside a rickety-looking table.

"That will be your room, Dr. Ingalls," said Park gesturing to the nearer doorway. "The toilet is out the back door." Uli's men were carrying boxes and suitcases in from the Land Cruiser.

Lee peered into her room. The two narrow beds looked slept in. "Are we forcing these people out of their beds?"

"There is a yurt behind the house. They will sleep there."

Lee looked through the window and saw the dark profile of a hemispherical, felt-walled hut. She had read that such portable structures were the traditional homes of Turkic horse nomads, but she had never seen one. After the Soviets crushed the Basmachi revolt and forced the nomads to settle, she had been told, most Kyrgyz had given up their yurts.

"Shall we go?" said Park. He had exchanged his tunic and overcoat for a rough brown vest and black wool jacket. On his head was a brimless black hat of tightly curled lambskin.

"Go where?"

"To find Nadir."

"At night?"

"It is only eight-thirty. It's best to act before anyone starts looking for us."

Driving into town in Uli's beat-up, mud-spattered Fiat, Lee broached a question she had been avoiding: how they were going to find Nadir.

"You're the specialist on the Vedic gods," replied Park. "What do you suggest?"

Lee pondered the matter. "If Nadir were Indra—which I absolutely do not believe he his—and the Vedic hymns portray him accurately, he will be fat and drunk. Of course, he gets drunk on soma, but he said in his posting that they had run out of real soma. So where do people go to drink in Osh?"

"Home, at work, on the street, in the gutter, everywhere. Drunkenness is the universal legacy of Soviet rule."

"But supposing you weren't from Osh. You were a visitor like us. Probably not staying in a hotel. After all, if Nadir is a god, he probably doesn't have a passport."

"Yeah," chimed in Joseph from the back seat. "Age: eleven thousand. Birthplace: Mars. Profession: God."

"In that case you might go to a kumys shop. That's where herders in from the country go for vodka and kumys. Not a place you're likely to find a woman, however."

"Nadir doesn't know I'm a woman."

"What's kumys?" asked Joseph.

"Fermented mare's milk. It's the traditional drink of the nomads."

"Yukh."

"Oh," Lee added, "two more things. Indra is supposed to have red or blonde hair, and his posting said he had one leg."

"The blondness is promising," said Park. "It would make him look like a Russian, and you don't seem many Russians in kumys shops." He turned from the main road and presently pulled the Fiat over and turned off the engine. There was no street lighting. The buildings appeared to be garages and sheds rather than houses. "We can walk from here."

They picked their way along the ice-crusted roadside to a wooden building with a hanging leather flap for a door. Inside a dozen men were seated at small tables or on low platforms resembling bed frames. Lanterns provided a warm, yellow light. A man with an apron was busy in one corner dipping a milky fluid from a tub and pouring it into small bowls.

At the table nearest the door Nadir was sitting with a bottle of vodka in one hand and a glass in the other. Lee, Joseph, and Park surveyed the room intently but failed to see him. It wasn't difficult for Nadir to keep humans from seeing him when he chose to be alone. It took just a slight interference with their processing of visual stimuli. Though drunk enough to be hazy about the passage of time, Nadir was dimly aware of the minds around him—worn, hard-handed men thinking about women, horses, old hatreds, funny stories, and bold exploits from years long past. He had known these minds without paying attention to them for thousands of years.

The three visitors from the cold were gone before Nadir fully grasped that a mind of a different sort had entered the shop and left again. Nadir hadn't encountered such a mind in so long that he no longer quite recognized it. He reached out and felt it moving away. Yes, now he had it. He felt a sudden warmth in his heart. The mind he was sensing *believed* in the god Indra. Truly believed. It was the mind of a worshipper. Nadir could not remember when he had last been worshipped properly, or received a proper sacrifice, but he could remember the ecstasy of it—the glow, the exultation, the intoxicating sense of godliness, the rush of power into his mind and body. He clambered to his feet and hoisted his pack by one strap. He dropped some money on the table, pulled back the leather flap, and limped into the cold night.

The trio that included the worshipper was out of sight on the dark street, but Nadir sensed them not far ahead. They had entered another kumys shop and left again. Nadir made them unaware of his approach until he was walking with them as a fourth overhearing them discussing in English other kumys shops and their frustration at not being able to find him. The mind of the worshipper felt pure, and Nadir's heart gladdened in response. Confidently he allowed the worshipper to become aware of his presence.

"Webmaster?" he asked.

A look of shock, of wide-eyed wonder, a gasp, a trembling, and finally two awe-filled words prayerfully uttered: "Lord Indra."

Nadir beamed. "Lord Indra I," he said aloud for the first time in over a thousand years. "And you the one from Chakra Net."

"No. I'm Joseph Engineer." Nadir felt confused. "This is the Webmaster." He gestured toward Lee, who had failed to see that he was speaking to someone. "Dr. Lee Ingalls."

Nadir looked askance at the slight woman Joseph indicated. Her mind was not a believer's mind. Lee looked back at the bearded, pot-bellied man, well under six feet tall, and wondered how he had managed to join them without their noticing. A feeling of relief tinged with disappointment came over her. This was, perhaps, the Nadir who posted doggerel on Chakra Net. But this was decidedly not the lord of the storm, the wielder of the thunderbolt, the slayer of Vrtra, the radiant Lord God Indra.

Major Park extended his hand. "I am Dimitri Park. Is your name Nadir?"

Nadir ignored the hand. "Nadir am I."

"We have come to help you."

"Give Nadir help?"

"Help you stop the giant. His name is Bix."

"A foolish name. A foolish quest. Kill him yourself."

Lee and Park slowly became aware that Nadir was suddenly and unaccountably some distance down the road walking rapidly away from them with Joseph half walking, half jogging by his elbow like a small dog trying to keep up. How he had left their company without their noticing was a mystery. As they watched, Nadir and Joseph became swallowed by the shadows and disappeared from sight.

After a half hour of driving slowly through the dark streets, they gave up their search. "Joseph doesn't know where we are staying," said Lee worriedly.

"He's an American intelligence agent. He will be resourceful."

"Resourceful? Joseph? That boy has done nothing in his life but play with computers and telephones. Do you know why he came to Kokand?"

"To find you, I presume. And through you, Nadir. Just like me."

"He came here because his intelligence agency is trying to prove it's better than the other intelligence agencies. He was given an assignment no one else would take, and he hasn't the slightest idea what this part of the world is like or what he is supposed to do. His boss talks *about* him at high-level meetings, but he doesn't talk *to* him. He's just a . . . a nothing." Lee sniffled.

"You're not his mother," said Park.

"No." Lee sniffled again. "But if I were, I would be so frightened for him. He's a very dear boy." Tears flowed unseen down her cheeks in the dark car.

"I will call my contacts in Kyrgyz internal security in the morning. They will find him."

"Okay," squeeked Lee between sniffles.

The bungalow was abustle with activity when they arrived. A sizable tent of the sort sold in American mountaineering stores had been set up between the bungalow and the fence, and four tall muscular men were unloading boxes into it from a truck. Inside, Uli was sitting across the rickety table from a bulky American with graying hair and beard and a rangy black man of similar age but evidently blind. A Kyrgyz teenager was haltingly working to translate their conversation.

"That's Hayes Carpenter," whispered Lee in Park's ear. "What's he doing here?"

"We'll find out." Park stepped into the glow of the lantern on the table. "Mr. Hayes Carpenter, how do you do. I am Major Dimitri Park of the Internal Security Service of the Ferghana Republic."

A huge grin lightened Hayes's face. "Well doesn't that beat everything!" He stood up and shook Park's hand. "Damn! When these boys told me they'd help us get across the border, they didn't say we'd be with an official escort."

"I'm afraid I don't understand. I know nothing about your crossing the border. The border is closed."

Hayes's expression darkened. "Of course it's closed. I wouldn't be paying these smugglers to get me across if it weren't."

"Why do you want to enter Ferghana? There is an outbreak of bubonic plague."

"In a rat's ass. Who ever heard of bubonic plague in the twenty-first century?"

"Plague is endemic in this region. It can pop up any time. It's carried by fleas that live on marmots."

"What the hell's a marmot?"

"It's a small animal that lives in the ground."

"It's the local version of the groundhog," said Lee stepping out of the shadows by the door.

"I thought I smelled a nice smell," said Wilson Woodrow turning his face toward Lee's voice.

"Major Park is quite right. Plague is endemic in Central Asia. Some historians believe that this is where the Black Death of 1348 began."

"Well who are you, lady? And what the fuck do I care about historians and the goddam black death."

"I would appreciate it if you would speak more politely, Mr. Carpenter."

"May I introduce Dr. Lee Ingalls from the American Embassy in Kokand," said Park.

"American Embassy? What are you doing in this place?"

"I came here with Major Park earlier this evening." Lee tried to think of a plausible reason but nothing came to mind.

Park leapt into the awkward silence. "Dr. Ingalls is my . . . companion." He paused. "For the weekend."

Hayes suddenly laughed. "Oh, I see."

Lee's face flushed. "You don't see anything at all. We're here to . . . to . . ."

"Well, whatever it is, lady, you picked a pretty crumby motel to do it in."

"Mr. Carpenter!" said Lee indignantly.

Hayes ignored her outrage. "If the two of you just got here, how'd you cross the border? They say it's been sealed off in both directions. Tighter than a drum. No exceptions. Or are these boys just telling me that to jack the price up for getting me across?"

"There's always an exception for the Internal Security Service," replied Park as Lee strode angrily to the door and stepped out into the cold air.

"Assuming that's really who you are. You're not exactly in uniform. And even if you are secret police and not just a smuggler who speaks English, is there also an exception for Internal Security's American girlfriend?"

Instead of responding, Park turned to Uli and carried out a short conversation in Kyrgyz. Turning back to Hayes, he said, "My friend Uli tells me you have enough weapons with you to fight a war."

"My words to him exactly. Not a big war. A small, private war. My friend Wilson and I have a grievance with someone we believe to bc in Kokand, and we're going there to kill him, or die trying."

"And your companions outside?"

"Our shipmates are four of the best England's Special Air Service ever produced."

"Mercenaries."

"That's the word for it. They get through this alive and they're set financially for life, regardless of what happens to me. But I expect them to do their best to get me through, too."

"You will have trouble crossing the border. The other side is mined."

"That's why I'm giving a pile of money and a pretty substantial arsenal to these smugglers. To get us across."

"Uli will do his best, but he and his men don't know the other side very well. I do. I've spent as many years keeping Uli out as he has spent trying to get in. You should also know that these men are not smugglers. They are Basmachi. They smuggle to supply themselves with guns and money, but their struggle is that of their fathers, and their fathers before them: to create a free home for the nomads."

Hayes looked puzzled. "Does that make sense? These people have been ruling themselves now for what? Twenty-some years?"

"The rulers speak their language, but they still follow the Soviet ways. And they still rely on people like me."

"Major?"

"Park."

"Major Park, you talk like a man who's just quit his job."

"When I cross the border again, Mr. Carpenter, I'll be going to war too."

"Then it sounds like maybe we should compare enemies."

"Fair enough. My enemy is the person who dropped a nuclear bomb on two hundred thousand people in the city of Nukus."

Hayes thrust out his large hand. "Pleased to meet you, son. We got ourselves the same enemy. Only I don't know his name. All I know is that I might be able to find out in Kokand."

"The human responsible is my president, Rejep Muratbey. The person who carried out the bombing is named Bix. He comes from another planet."

"'Some work of noble note may yet be done, not unbecoming men that strove with gods,'" intoned Wilson Woodrow. "That's Alfred Lord Tennyson."

Chapter Seventeen

Lee opened her eyes. Someone was moving in the pitch-dark room. She tensed herself as she lay fully dressed under the blanket.

"Lee," came a whisper at her side.

"Joseph?" she whispered back. "How did you get back here?"

"Nadir brought me."

"Nadir's here?"

"No. He went on. But there's something important I have to find out from you."

"What's that?"

"Do you know how to do a sacrifice? The way it was done for Indra?"

"Well, yes, I guess I do. I mean, I have the hymns on my laptop, and I know how the ritual is set up. But of course I've never seen it done. I don't think there have been any sacrifices just to Indra for a couple of thousand years."

"That's why he wants one. He wants to be worshipped properly. He says it makes him strong."

"Yes, that's what the hymns say. Sacrifice gives power to the gods."

"He's telepathic. Apparently the effect of feeling the minds of worshippers is energizing. Sort of like cocaine. So can you arrange to do it? It's the only way he'll agree to tell us about Bix."

"If he cared enough about humans to post stories on Chakra Net, why doesn't he care enough to help them now?"

"Lee, he's a god. Give him a break. Gods have failings. When he posted, he was just talking. But now he's longing to be worshipped. He says if he's never going to be worshipped again, maybe what happens to the Earth won't matter to him."

"He told you all this."

"We've been talking for hours. But he's very drunk, and I couldn't understand everything he said."

"Why did he talk to you?"

"Do you remember when he spoke with us on the street?"

"Of course."

"What did you see?"

"A red-haired man, about five-nine, full beard, maybe forty years old, lame, beer belly, backpack, plain clothes. Why?"

"Do you know what I saw?"

"No."

"When he first spoke to me, I saw a huge naked man, glowing with a golden aura. His hair and beard were red and looked on fire. His body was immense—six and a half feet tall, thick hard belly, heavy muscles. He looked like one of those huge fake wrestlers on television. Then after he started talking to you, he suddenly changed and looked just like you said. I asked him about it, and he said only a worshipper can see a god."

Lee thought for a while. "If we can do the sacrifice, how do you let him know?"

"I'm going to join him now. He needs me. I'll come back tomorrow. I've got to go now."

Lee heard him leave the room and then lay on her back wide-awake. In the pitch dark Joseph's visit seemed almost like a dream, a bizarre dream in which the god Indra was real and needed her expertise. By morning she had made a list of what the sacrifice would require, who would play what roles, and how she might compensate for the things that would be lacking.

Lee joined Dimitri Park, Wilson Woodrow, and Hayes Carpenter as they were eating bread and goat cheese around the table. "Good morning, Dr. Ingalls," said Hayes with a saccharine cordiality.

"You were very rude and offensive last night, Mr. Carpenter."

"I apologize."

"I accept your apology. And why don't we call one another by our first names. Dr. Ingalls sounds like I'm teaching in a boys' school instead of hanging out with an armed gang. What are the three of you up to?"

"Making plans for going after Muratbey. I gather you know him well. Dimitri tells me that without Nadir's help we can't do anything about Bix, but Muratbey's a sitting duck. All we have to do is fight his army."

"Suppose we could get Nadir's help. Isn't Bix the main enemy?"

"Absolutely. Muratbey's stuck on this planet. He's not going anywhere. We can kill him whenever we like. But how do you intend to rope in Nadir? Dimitri said he just looked at the two of you last night like you were steaming piles of cow manure and walked away."

"Joseph came back later. He told me Nadir will deign to let us help him if he is worshipped as the god Indra."

Looks of discomfort passed over the faces of all three men. "A little kooky," ventured Hayes meditatively, "but I guess we could manage that. What do you think, Wilson?"

"If it needs to be done I guess."

"What do we have to do, bow down when he comes?"

"I'm afraid it's a little more complicated than that."

Lee placed on the table a rough diagram she had drawn of an Indo-Iranian sacrifice and a list of materials needed. Heading the list were a live goat and a gallon of clarified butter. Hayes read the list aloud for Wilson's benefit. When he had finished, Wilson gave a low whistle. "Sure lucky my Pearl's dead. Take me down to the river make me get baptized again if she ever caught me doin' shit like this."

* * *

"Am I to understand that the mountain Verethra Kuh is not within the territory you control?" Frak's tone was accusing.

Muratbey was unfazed. He had insisted on bringing a folding chair with him to Bix's ship so that he could be as comfortable as the giant. "I never say in Ferghana. You never name exact place you go. Now you tell me where we go, I tell you is not in Ferghana."

"But when I told Park that my job was within a radius of one hundred miles, he assured me that you were the ruler."

"Major Park is a good and loyal servant. He tell you something else, someone else get technology. So he lie." Muratbey wondered where Major Park was. Every time he phoned, his adjutant kept saying he was on personal emergency leave. Just like a Korean—unreliable.

Humans aren't much better than pramodzi, communicated Bix to Frak. "This complication makes my job more dangerous," said Frak aloud.

Muratbey shrugged his heavy shoulders. "Maybe little bit. My army protect as I promise. Perhaps you don't need so much protection anyway. We interrogate everyone trying to enter Ferghana. No *pramodzi*. Still we keep them all in prison."

Bix did not like complications. "I am vulnerable when I leave my ship, and I will have to leave at the bottom of the shaft on the mountain to do my repairs. An egg dropped down the shaft would kill me. If that happens, you will get no technology."

"No egg bombs on mountain. No egg bombs near mountain. My army close shaft behind you and guard it. No worry."

"I would worry less if you were with me."

Muratbey looked unperturbed. "I go if I can ride in ship."

Aliens aboard ship for other than tours to impress them was not in the protocols, but the protocols couldn't cover every eventuality. "Okay."

"And if army get more weapons."

"No."

"Then I don't go with you, and you worry about egg."

Bix furrowed his brow. "How many weapons?" said Frak.

"Ten red, ten green . . . and one egg."

"NO EGGS!"

"Then I just take reds and greens."

* * *

The Acting Commander of the Ferghanan army, Colonel Maxim Sverdlov, had driven fifty miles to the town of Namangan to visit his beloved Uncle Ilya. Surrogate father, idol, mentor, Ilya Kramskoy, his mother's brother, had done everything in his power to make up for his nephew's loss of his real father in the Afghanistan war. The brothers-in-law had both been officers in the Spetsnaz special forces. Maxim's father, Oleg, had fallen to a sniper's bullet.

"So you are in command. Congratulations. Well deserved." The old man lifted his vodka glass to toast his nephew.

Maxim's stolid face remained serious. "You don't think I should refuse?"

"Refuse? Those who refused to serve in Afghanistan deserved to be shot. A soldier fights. We were Spetsnaz. We were trained to kill. We obeyed orders. You should do the same."

"But the mission is across the border," said Maxim intently, as if trying to get his uncle to understand something difficult. "Verethra Kuh mountain is forty miles inside Kyrgyz territory, not just a few meters. We'll be invading, but for no legitimate reason. Since I must protect my withdrawal route, I will need a substantial force. Not just a commando raid."

"But you say it will take no more than four days."

"That is my plan." The two men leaned over a map spread on the kitchen table. "On day one, I cross the border. I take Kyzyl Kiya, which is the only Kyrgyz military post, send tanks to block the road coming west from Osh, and bomb the bridges on the road that goes south from Osh to Sary Tash. This will delay any Kyrgyz counter-moves by land. When my defenses are in place, I move south along this track. At this river I turn east and follow the gorge of the river into the mountain. My reconnaissance team reports I can get to within three miles of the mountain with tracked vehicles. So that means I set up a camp and defensive perimeter here." He made a pencil mark on the map near the end of the red line he had drawn earlier.

"This is where I leave the armored personnel carriers. On the second day the strike team moves up the gorge. If all goes well, we climb the mountain. It should not be a hard climb except at the end.

The cave with the shaft in it is set in a cliff about two hundred and thirty meters high. I can't use helicopters without the Kyrgyz air defense seeing them on radar, but I have fifteen good mountaineers. They will scale the cliff, secure the cave, and signal the spaceship with a flare. The rest of the force will defend the base of the cliff. Once the ship has entered the cave and descended into the shaft, we will secure the bomb-proof net over the top of the shaft and guard it until the job is finished. President Muratbey says it will take no more than five hours. Once the spaceship has left, I have two days to withdraw our forces."

Ilya was impressed. "It is a very thorough plan. I can see nothing wrong with it."

"What is wrong, Uncle Ilya, is that we're making an unprovoked incursion into a neighboring country. We are starting a war."

"So? That is our job. We go where we are told to go and complete our mission."

"I understand that, Uncle. But we must think about counterattacks from Kyrgyzstan. It would take us months to prepare for a general war, and I'm only being given days."

"Don't worry. It will take months for the Kyrgyz too if they decide to strike back. By that time you will have the new weapons President Muratbey has promised you."

"But there is also China to think of. We will be only seventy miles from the Chinese frontier, and their forces in Kashghar are strong. If they decide to help the Kyrgyz, they can destroy us."

"Don't worry. The Chinese will never fight a war on their northwest frontier. They never intervened in Afghanistan. Helping the Kyrgyz would encourage a rebellion among their own Uighurs. These different kinds of Turks may quarrel among themselves, but they all stand together against us Russians and the Chinese. I guarantee you, no Chinese forces will get involved. The Russians maybe, if Kyrgyzstan calls on them. But Kyrgyzstan has bad relations with the Russians these days. They'll think twice about asking them to intervene. Now tell me about the new weapons."

Feeling somewhat relieved, Maxim refolded the map and put it in his briefcase. He saw an excitement in Uncle Ilya's clear blue eyes that usually appeared only when reminiscing about operations in Afghanistan.

"The green weapon is anti-personnel. Hand carried, about two and a half kilos. It shoots a continuous microwave beam that cooks anything organic it hits. The farther away the target, the longer it takes. However, it killed a sheep in two seconds at half a kilometer. What is important is that you don't really have to aim. You just sweep it slowly across the field of fire, and the beam cuts down whatever living things it contacts. No noise, no smoke, no flash, no heating of the weapon. The beam itself isn't visible."

"How long does a charge last?"

"I don't know. I've timed my tests, and it's still working after four hours of firing."

"Incredible. With that we would have won in Afghanistan . . . if the politicians in Moscow hadn't tied our hands and our feet."

Maxim had heard his uncle's analysis of the Afghanistan war enough times to want to forestall another rendition. "As for the anti-armament weapon, it is just like the other, except it is red. Same size and shape, same weight. The beam is different, but we haven't yet been able to analyze it. It induces heating in metal objects. Two minutes continuous contact with the cannon barrel of a tank at 300 meters caused the barrel to bend. Contact with a hand weapon causes the ammunition inside it to explode almost instantaneously. The same thing happens if you target the fuel tank area of a vehicle."

"Amazing. How many of these weapons will you receive?"

"We will have eleven of each for the incursion. But President Muratbey has promised that if our mission is successful, as soon as the spaceman finishes whatever he needs to do in the cave, Muratbey will make him give us enough weapons to equip the entire army."

"Maxim, our president is a great man." He refilled his nephew's glass and raised his own. "Let us drink to Comrade Muratbey."

Maxim stood up and raised his glass. "To President Muratbey."

"And now I will tell you how I would have used the new weapons against the Afghan bandits, and how the politicians in Moscow tied our hands and made us lose the war."

Two hours later Maxim wearily and drunkenly took to the road to return to Kokand. As soon as he was gone, Uncle Ilya placed a telephone call to Moscow. It took some time to reach the commander of the Russian land forces, but he patiently worked his way through a series of operators and adjutants until he heard the familiar sharp voice of General Repin himself. “Colonel Kramskoy, this is Repin.”

“It is good to hear your voice, General.”

General Repin had never been enthusiastic about the brutality of the Spetsnaz in general, and he had suspected Colonel Ilya Kramskoy in particular of wanton atrocities against Afghan prisoners and civilians. Yet on occasion he had proved a reliable intelligence source for matters affecting Ferghana. “What do you have to say, Kramskoy?”

“I thought you would be interested in knowing that my nephew will soon be leading the Ferghana army on an incursion in force into Kyrgyzstan.” There was silence on the other end of the phone. “Have you ever heard of a mountain named Verethra Kuh?”

* * *

Plans for recrossing the border into Ferghana and for sacrificing to Indra proceeded simultaneously. Alf, the leader of Carpenter’s British mercenaries, supervised his men unpacking and assembling an array of weapons that even Lee’s untutored eye could see was clearly in excess of what they themselves could use. Hayes relieved her puzzlement by telling her that much of his arsenal had been brought as trade goods. He had figured he would need them to equip or buy the help of local forces; and he was pleased that Uli, the mustached Basmachi leader, had responded so enthusiastically to his offer to exchange arms—and a certain amount of cash—for aid.

“The amusing thing is,” pursued Hayes, “that the head of my office in Almaty is a gunrunner too. Kid named Dan Nielsen. He felt so guilty he was just dying to confess to genial old Uncle Hayes. I could tell he was up to something the minute I saw him. Seems he’s been working on his own account buying arms left over from the Afghanistan war and smuggling them to Uighur nationalists around Kashgar. The Uighurs are over half the population, and they hate the Chinese ruling them. They’ve been in rebellion off and on for twenty years. Dan’s made himself a pretty penny, which I don’t begrudge him since that’s the way you do things in business if you want to get ahead. But I may have to get rid of him anyway. A man who feels such a need to get things off his chest can be a liability in a business like mine."

Lee had been only half listening to Hayes rattling on about his man in Almaty, but his last remark caught her attention. She looked up from a laptop screen filled with Vedic text. "My husband is quite a successful businessman. But his inability to confess and get things off his chest has ruined our marriage. I never thought that duplicity and secrecy might be an asset in business."

Hayes raised an eyebrow in interest. "Let me guess. He was having a little something on the side and you found out."

"Major Park recorded his couplings with a Cuban woman and was crude enough to play a tape of one of them for me."

"Ouch! That's learning the hard way."

"Indeed it is."

"My wife Helen found out about me once because the girl called her up and told her I wanted a divorce."

"Did you?"

"Hell, no. But once Helen knew, she didn't give me a choice. Even then I couldn't bring myself to confess the whole thing and ask her to forgive me. Any more than I ever apologized to all those Mexican harvesters I got working for me when I came back from the army. I got rich on their backs, and they stayed poor. Course I fund schools and clinics now, but I had a lot to feel guilty about back then. Still, confession is a bad trait in a businessman."

"Aren't you confessing to me?"

"Well, now that you mention it, maybe I am. But then maybe I won't be alive a week from now, and there isn't much of anyone else around to say these things to."

"So you don't think you're going to live through this?"

Wilson Woodrow, who had been quietly listening, entered the conversation. "Hayes won't tell you this, Miz Lee, but he don't want to live through it. Great Array operation was *it* . . . the big burrito. He was gonna be so famous they'd put his face on the hundred dollar bill. But after that bomb, project don't amount to shit. All he's left with is dead friends and one blind old black man."

"So why are you here, Wilson? Are you ready to die too?"

"I ain't decided yet. Mainly I'm just here to keep Hayes company. But maybe I can help. As that poet says, 'Though much is taken, much abides.' I'll figure out what I can do when the time comes. Beats sittin' on the front porch in a rocking chair waitin' to die."

A gust of cold wind and the slam of the door interrupted the conversation. Joseph Engineer looked around the room. "Wow! Look at all the guns!"

"Where is Nadir?" said Lee.

"Is the sacrifice on?"

"I'm working on it. Everyone's agreed. Hayes will be the *yajamana*, the rich man who sponsors the sacrifice. That means he's the big man who buys the goat and sits still while the sacrifice takes place. You will be the *adhvaryu*. That's the officiating priest. Dimitri will be your assistant. We figured he would be the most comfortable killing and butchering the goat."

Park looked up from a disassembled M16 rifle. "The Korean always gets the worst job," he said with a slight smile to show he wasn't really offended. "Despite my fearsome reputation, however, I've never killed and butchered a goat."

"And I'll be the *hotar*. That's the priest who sings the Vedic hymns. Some problems, though, I'm stuck on. For instance, the priests are supposed to be Brahmins. What caste is your family, Joseph?"

"I think we're Vaishyas, but you don't have to worry about that. Nadir was telling me about the sacrifice. I can't overstate how much he loves it, by the way. He says that originally they just sacrificed the animal and sang hymns. The idea of a Brahmin caste developed later when some families specialized in memorizing the hymns."

"What about the fact that I'm a woman? That's another problem. The *hotar* is supposed to be a man. The only woman mentioned in the books is the wife of the *yajamana*."

"You can also be that, if you like," put in Hayes with a grin.

Lee ignored him. "Go on, Joseph."

"Nadir says that's okay too because once you shave your head you become a man."

"Once she shaves her head?" interjected Hayes. "That will be something to see."

"You're going to do it too, Hayes," retorted Lee. "And that scruffy beard. Every male who enters the sacred precinct has to be shaved and wrapped in a white sheet with the right shoulder bare."

"You all gonna get cold," chortled Wilson. "Believe I'll just stay indoors."

"Indoors where?" said Joseph.

"Indoors here."

"I'm planning to take down the tent and move the cars, then draw the sacred precinct and build the covering in the yard," explained Lee.

"No, no, no. You don't understand. The sacrifice isn't going to be here. Nadir is meeting us at the site. It's about thirty miles from here near a mountain called Verethra Kuh."

"Mountain of Vrtra," said Lee. "The Old Iranian pronunciation, of course."

"Well who gives a damn whose mountain it is," said Hayes, suddenly getting angry. "I came here to get revenge, not pneumonia. And thirty miles up in the mountains is thirty miles farther away from the border, which we've got to cross if we're going hunting for Muratbey and that friend of his, Bix."

Joseph looked puzzled. "Why are you crossing into Ferghana?"

"Because that's where Dimitri says Bix is, and we know damn well that's where Muratbey is. Besides that, if Lee will forgive a rude expression, I don't give a rat's ass about making a sacrifice to this Nadir. I've never even seen him. Okay, maybe he's from some other planet. That's hard enough to believe, but I've been going along with it to make everyone happy. But what if he isn't? What if he's just some hippie jerk-off who likes to pull our chains? And for that matter, why should I let myself be ordered around by some teen-aged, snot-nosed U.S. government spy bureaucrat who's probably never done a lick of real work in his whole life? Dimitri may be a fucking secret police agent who worked for the communists, but he knows how to find his way out of the woods and how to talk to these Basmachi boys. So if Dimitri says we cross the border and go get Muratbey and Bix in Ferghana, that's what me and Wilson and Alf and the boys are going to do."

Dimitri Park had been following the conversation from across the room where he was seated on the floor amid a litter of magazines, clips, and weapon parts. "Tell us what you know about the mountain, Joseph."

Joseph, who in the face of Hayes' blast had withdrawn his head turtle-like into the wide neck and hood of his coat, reemerged slightly. "It's where the machine is located that Bix has come here to fix, the one that Nadir destroyed."

"It's within a hundred miles of Kokand?"

"About eighty miles."

"One hundred miles was the distance Bix told me when he first arrived. Where on the mountain is the machine?"

"It's in a cave at the top of a cliff, near the summit. The sacrifice area is near the cliff around a shoulder of the mountain. Nadir says it was used for several thousand years when people still believed that the cave was the home of the demon Vrtra. Then they migrated southward and lost the memory. He says we must go there, do the sacrifice, and wait for Bix to arrive."

"Along with the Ferghana army, presumably. Muratbey's deal was to give Bix whatever help he needed in return for bombing Nukus and killing Vahidoglu. So now he has to invade Kyrgyzstan to keep his end of the bargain. That should stir things up."

"Christ, just what we need," said Hayes, "a full-scale military invasion."

"If we're the first to the cave, it could work to our advantage," replied Park. "Do you know how high the cliff is?"

"About seven hundred feet."

"Hayes, do Alf and his men know how to climb cliffs?"

"Hell, they're Special Air Service. They were born on cliffs. Cliffs are their home."

"Then lets do the sacrifice the way Nadir wants it. Lee?"

"Fine with me. Only chance I'll ever have to be a Vedic priest."

"But what about Muratbey?" grumbled Hayes.

"As you said earlier, he doesn't have a spaceship so he's not going anywhere. Besides, for the time being I think Joseph and I can distract him with a couple of telephone calls."

Chapter Eighteen

Donald savored the ooze and flow of Consuela Ramirez's cream-colored breasts beneath his kneading fingers, imagining them as balloons filled with the finest and most slippery sand particles, their tumid nipples derby-hat caramel appetizers poking this way and that as they teased his hungry lips.

The doorbell rang.

Consuela slipped into a terry robe, fluffed her lush black hair over the collar in back, and closed the bedroom door behind her. He could hear a conversation in Spanish . . . a man and a woman. He caught the name "Donaldo" and promptly experienced a loss in penile blood pressure comparable to the explosive decompression of a hull-holed airliner at 30,000 feet. He pulled the sheet up to his clavicle as if his main concern was inadvertent display of his vilous chest

The bedroom door opened. Embassy political officer Miguel Espinosa was the picture of elegance in his three-piece suit.

"Hi, Mike," ventured Donald.

The American diplomat nodded the most minimal of greetings. "Donald." Then he stepped aside.

Behind him, her hair standing out electrically with a sort of charge that seemed less static accumulation than voltage emanating from seething internal chemistry, Ambassador Darla Bane glared down at him balefully.

"Ambassador Bane!"

"The bane of your existence, Mr. Ingalls. Where is your wife?"

"My wife?"

"Your wife. I received a telephone call from Major Dimitri Park informing me that President Muratbey had kidnapped her and was holding her as an involuntary sex slave."

"Involuntary?"

"He also told me I could find you here with Captain Ramirez."

"Captain?"

"Cuban intelligence." Behind the ambassador Consuela looked at Donald and delivered herself of an exaggerated shrug.

Donald's spirit felt as shrunken as his penis. "I don't understand."

"Tell me, is your wife with President Muratbey?"

"I'm not sure, but I believe so. Yes."

"You believe so?"

"Major Park told me she was."

"So he warned you of what Muratbey was planning, and you did nothing? You disgust me."

"I thought it was voluntary," peeped Donald.

"Voluntary? Voluntary? You thought your wife, one of the most elegant, refined, intelligent women I have ever met, would voluntarily sleep with that revolting warthog? You're even more disgusting than I thought. You're worse than a piece of shit. Didn't Muratbey threaten to reveal your treasonous carryings-on with Captain Ramirez unless you delivered your wife to him?"

"Good heavens, no!"

"But he does know about you and Captain Ramirez."

"Yes." Donald wondered whether he should confess about the gems he had sent out of the country in the diplomatic pouch.

"Where has Muratbey taken your wife?"

"I don't know. To his dacha in the country?"

"He doesn't have a dacha in the country."

Donald was struggling to gain possession of himself. "Do you seriously think Lee has been taken against her will?"

"Yes, I seriously think that. Why do you think I'm here? Do you imagine that whenever someone from my embassy fucks up, I go personally to drag his loathsome carcass out of his lover's bed? The top cop in Ferghana tells me Muratbey's kidnapped her. Mike checks your home. She isn't there. He phones around to the other embassy women and to her friends at the Academy of Sciences. No one knows of any plans she had to be away. You're not to be found. What choice do I have but to check out Park's assertion that I might find you in bed with the chief intelligence officer of the Cuban embassy? Here I am. There you are. Presumably undressed under that sheet. If Park was right about you, why should I doubt what he said about Muratbey and your wife?"

"Have you asked President Muratbey?"

"Thank you for that excellent idea. Of course I've asked Muratbey!" bellowed the ambassador. "Guess what? He denies it. Like, duh."

Donald couldn't believe he had just heard the Ambassador of the United States of America say "Like, duh." But even as the thought passed through his mind he vaguely realized that he was not connecting what Ambassador Bane was telling him with reality. Something had been dreadfully misunderstood, but he had no idea how.

"Put your clothes on. Mike will drive you to the embassy where you'll be put under arrest for having secret relations with an intelligence agent of an unfriendly nation. But that's only until I get a full report on what else I can charge you with. You fucking slimeball!" The ambassador abruptly turned on her heel and left the bewildered commercial advisor to grope beside the bed for his clothes. The last thing she wanted was for him to realize that she was on the verge of tears for fear of what vileness Muratbey might at that very moment be perpetrating on Lee Ingalls somewhere inside the Presidential Palace. *No one kidnaps and rapes an American citizen on my watch*, she said to herself for the hundredth time.

* * *

A White House page directed Captain Stephanie Low of the Defense Intelligence Agency to the private quarters of the presidential family. Boone Rankin received her in sweatshirt and jogging shorts. As usual, he had fortified himself alcoholically for a conversation with his high school flame. "Bourbon and branch water, Steph?"

"Light on the water." The buxom naval intelligence officer seated herself on a chintz-upholstered sofa. She downed a man-sized slug of Country Doctor and shuddered. "My, my! That feels better."

Boone Rankin was anxious to get on with it. "So what do I owe the honor to, Steph?"

"To your horse's ass Secretary of State who doesn't know how to do his job."

"Damn good lawyer, though. Talk your ear off."

"Lot of males have that problem. Need a good throat surgeon take their goddam larynx out." Stephanie leaned forward and fixed the President with a no-nonsense stare. "I'll be quick. Boonie, you know I got you by the balls."

The President first nodded and then, with a sigh, shook his head despairingly. "I won't deny it. Go ahead. What do you want?"

"Boonie, you've appointed some of the best women in this country to your administration. I give you credit for that, even if I and some others had to push you sometimes. And all these women in the administration stick together. We're like the blacks and the Jews. We're in the same shitty boat, and we help each other out. Am I right?"

Rankin finished off his bourbon and wished he could pour another without it making him seem too anxious. "I'm proud of my accomplishments in the gender area," he said lamely.

"Cut the crap, Boone. Do you know who your ambassador to the Ferghana Republic is?"

The President thought for a moment. "I haven't the slightest. Must be a woman, though. Who is she? I suppose you want me to make her Secretary of State."

"Don't interrupt, Boone. This is serious. Your ambassador is Darla Bane. She's a powerhouse. She'll get to be Secretary of State all by herself. But in the meantime, she calls your present horseshit Secretary of State about an American woman being kidnapped, and she gets the run around."

"What American woman?" The subject of women under duress genuinely grabbed Rankin's attention.

"Her name is Lee Ingalls. Ph.D. from Harvard, married to first-class prick named Donald Ingalls who works for the Commerce Department in Kokand. According to Darla, the President of the fucking Ferghana Republic grabbed this woman . . . with her fucking husband's consent, no less . . . and is doing the dirty with her in some secret rendezvous as we speak."

"You're kidding."

"As I live and breathe. Her husband was screwing a Cuban spook so maybe he didn't have much choice. But it's absolutely fucking disgusting. Darla found him in bed with the senorita, and he admitted his wife was with the President."

"How did . . ."

"Darla Bane. Name to remember. Mark my words"

"How did Bane find all this out?"

"Ferghana Internal Security chief ratted the President out. Gave Darla a call. Apparently it was too disgusting even for him. Sends chills up your spine they'd do a thing like that, doesn't it Boonie."

Rankin didn't know whether she was referring to the abduction or to the betrayal by the secret police. "What did the Secretary of State do?"

"Fucking lawyer. He said he'd send a stiff letter of protest for Bane to deliver to President Muratbey. Who ever heard of sending a note to a kidnapper asking him to be nice? What the poor woman needs is the cavalry. Did you know Ferghana has closed its borders?"

"Not the sort of thing I'd know. George Artunian probably knows about it."

"Land and air. Sealed the country tight. They say there's a bubonic plague outbreak. Bullshit! Happened the same day Lee Ingalls disappeared. My opinion is she's gotten loose, and they're trying to keep her from leaving the country. Woman's life's in danger, Boone! I can feel it. And you're goin' to do something about it. Not just send a note, neither."

"Don't you think you're overre . . ."

"Don't say it, Boone. You know what I've got on you."

He reoriented his line of thought. "Maybe the marines at the embassy could . . ."

"Embassy guard doesn't have the firepower for the job. Boone, I want guys with guns. I want them there in secret. I want them there tomorrow. And I want them to get this poor woman out safely."

The President waited, saying nothing. Stephanie glared at him. He waited some more.

"Oh, all right, goddam it. Do me this one last thing, Boonie, and I'll give you your letter back."

"You got it with you?" said Rankin eagerly.

"I got it."

"And no copies."

"I promise."

Rankin smiled broadly. "Then Steph, you've got your cavalry. But when this is over, Steph, I'll expect you to put in for retirement. I won't deny you've pushed me into doin' some good things, but I just can't stand bein' blackmailed."

Captain Low pulled an old and much handled envelope from her breast pocket and handed it to the President. "I'll file my retirement papers the minute I hear Lee Ingalls is safe. And Boone?"

"Yeah?"

"You're a son of a bitch."

"So are you, Steph. Maybe we were right for each other all those years ago after all."

Rankin saw his visitor to the door with the bittersweet knowledge that he would probably never see her again. He locked the door behind her and then withdrew a single piece of paper from the worn envelope. He read it through for the last time.

Dear Stephie,

I'm so sorry about last night. I know you must have felt hurt and insulted, and I'm very sorry. Believe me, it had nothing to do with you. I could say that this sort of thing happens with me from time to time, but normally I'm okay. But I like you too much to lie to you. The truth is I simply can't do it. I don't know why. I like girls. I'm attracted to them. I'm not homosexual. But somehow I'm just not able to do it. We fool around, and then nothing happens. I went to a doctor, and he said there probably isn't anything he can do about it. I feel very ashamed, and I don't know what to do. If you don't want to go to the prom with me, I can understand. But please don't feel that it had anything to do with not liking you or finding you unattractive or anything. You're just fine. I'm the one who isn't.

Love,
Boone

Rankin carefully tore the letter and envelope into small pieces and arranged them neatly in a glass ashtray embossed with the presidential seal. As he lit the scraps and watched them burn, he felt an old weight lift from his chest. *Say good-bye to Boone Rankin, the president who can't get it up,* he thought.

A half hour later, in response to a presidential summons, George Artunian entered the Oval Office. "George, I want to send a Special Forces team into Kokand."

"What!?"

"An American woman's been kidnapped. Got an emergency call from our Ambassador. The Ferghana government won't do anything because President Muratbey is the kidnapper. Sex thing apparently. So I've decided to send the military in to get her out."

"Into Kokand? That's crazy!"

"What's wrong with Kokand?"

"Just that it's a long, long way away, and no one can go in overland because they've closed their borders."

"You sayin' we can't do it, George?"

"No, sir. If we had to, we could send in Delta Force by MC-130 from Incirlik in Turkey, refuel over Azerbaijan, and drop the team into Kokand by parachute. But it's a hell of a . . ."

The telephone rang. Rankin walked to his desk and picked up the receiver. Holding his hand over the mouthpiece, he said to Artunian, "It's Tom Thayer at NSA." Then back into the receiver, "Goin' to put you on speakerphone, Tom. George Artunian is here."

"Hello, George," came the low fidelity voice from Fort Meade.

"Hi, Tom. What's up?"

"We just decrypted a communication from our agent in Kokand. He says he's found the person we're calling the space friend, and he confirms that the space enemy bombed Nukus. As bizarre as it seems, apparently this space alien business is true. He also says the closing of the Ferghana borders is a ruse to cover planning for a military incursion into Kyrgyzstan. President Muratbey agreed to help the space enemy in return for his wiping out Nukus and for access to advanced technology. Our man says the incursion could come in the next few days. The target is a mountain called Verethra Kuh in southwest Kyrgyzstan. The place is almost inaccessible."

"Mr. Thayer, this is the President."

"Yes, Mr. President."

"How reliable is this man of yours in Kokand?"

"One of our very best, sir. If he's NSA, you can trust him."

"Did he say where he is?"

"Signal came through a long distance line at the central post office in the town of Osh in southern Kyrgyzstan—using our agreed upon code words, of course, to keep anyone who might be listening in from knowing what he's talking about. But he's heading for Verethra Kuh. I don't know whether he will be able to get back in contact from there or not."

"Who else knows about this, Mr. Thayer?"

"Only my Chief, sir."

"Keep it that way, and keep me or George informed. Any new messages from . . . what's the guy's name?"

"Joseph Engineer, sir."

"Okay. Any new messages from your engineer go directly to me. I'll tell the switchboard to put you through on priority."

"You can count on me, Mr. President."

"I'm sure I can, Mr. Thayer. Bye now."

"Goodbye, sir."

"NSA's been way out in front of those dingbats from CIA on this from the very start," said Artunian as soon as the connection terminated. "The Chief runs a tight ship over there."

"Thank heavens someone knows how to do something right in this government. But just think of it, George. Someone from another planet comes to Earth during my administration. Damn! This thing goes right, we've got four more years sewn up."

"Should I get the president of Kyrgyzstan on the phone?"

"Hell no."

"But Tom said he's about to be invaded."

"That's his lookout. We already been fucked over by that Karakalpak guy, Vahidoglu. I don't see why we should let another of these post-Soviet pip-squeaks get his hands on alien technology. What I want is enough American force on whatever mountain that is to make sure we get whatever there is to be got. Keep it small, but make it strong."

"But what excuse do we have? We can't ask to overfly three or four countries with a military plane without an explanation."

"Tell 'em we're comin' to the rescue of American womanhood. Tell 'em it's a matter of honor."

Both men suddenly fell silent and looked at one another. Artunan spoke first. "You don't suppose the kidnapped woman and the space alien are connected, do you?"

"Same thought just passed through my mind, George. You think this could be a hoax?"

"Tom Thayer said it was one of his best men."

"I know. But remember Hayes Carpenter may be out there too. We more or less sent him to Kokand to snoop around. Nothing that rich bastard would like better than to see me make a total ass of myself by sendin' the army on a wild goose chase."

"Where did the information about the kidnapped woman come from?"

"American ambassador in Kokand. Darla Bane I think her name is."

"I know her. She's good. She's very good. She wouldn't sound an alarm without proof."

Rankin rubbed his chin skeptically. "I don't know." Then he remembered his conversation with Stephanie Low and the commitment he'd made at the end of it. "Hell with it. Lets do it. Keep it as quiet as possible. Make sure nobody knows anything about the space business. Describe it as a rescue mission for an endangered American citizen. Drop a small team into Kokand for the woman, and then drop the rest on the mountain. We don't tell Delta Force the details until they're airborne, and then only the commander gets told about the space alien with orders to keep it to himself."

"You got it."

* * *

Russian Defense Minister Pyotr Kalenin, his commander of land forces General Nikolai Repin, and the army Chief Historian Dr. Nikita Yurenev had been meeting for two hours. Thick notebooks, several layers of maps, filled ashtrays, and half-drunk glasses of seltzer littered the conference table. Kalenin returned from a visit to the bathroom refreshed by a splash of cold water in the face.

Slicking back his thinning blonde hair with a pocket comb he said to the dark, Asian-looking general, "Summary. Lets go over it again. Where do we stand?"

General Repin's reputation, forged in Afghanistan, was for thoroughness and sound judgment rather than strategic brilliance or personal panache. "I think we're agreed, Pyotr," he began, "that what Mikhail Frunze found in 1920 on Verethra Kuh must have been made artificially. Not a single page in any of his reports suggests anything other than precise observation, and the two men who climbed the cliff and went into the cave were fully credible. We're also agreed, given the height of the mountain and its remoteness, that no human group could have excavated such an immense and regular shaft inside the cave. So we logically conclude that the excavator of the shaft was not human. In addition, we know for a certainty that the Great Array was built by non-humans and involved construction on a very large scale using technologies unknown on earth. From this we conclude that the Great Array and the shaft on Verethra Kuh were probably built by the same party and are very likely part of a single project. Any disagreement on any of this?"

Both men shook their heads.

"Now we come to Colonel Kramskoy's story. Ilya Kramskoy was a reliable but brutal officer in Afghanistan. His reports were never suspected of exaggeration. And in more recent years he has supplied us with useful intelligence on Ferghana, including the first report of an alien craft landing at the Presidential Palace. On the other hand, I know that he has become an excessive drinker. As for his nephew, Maxim Sverdlov, we know less because he never served under us. But he is highly trusted in Ferghana, and army sources in Kokand have confirmed that his superior, General Chengizoglu, died suddenly. Supposedly in a road accident. So do we believe the story Maxim Sverdlov told to his uncle? I think we're agreed that we have no choice but to believe it. The question is whether if we believe part of story, we have to believe it all—including the reports about the red and green weapons."

"I still think that part is a lie," put in Pyotr Kalenin. "The weapons sound preposterous. He told it to impress his uncle. Make himself big."

"Possibly. But without the weapons, why would Colonel Sverdlov have accepted President Muratbey's claim that he is collaborating with an alien from space? Sverdlov has never seen the alien or even the alien's ship. What he told his uncle about the ship came from other military sources. So he has only President Muratbey's word that the alien exists."

"That and the steaming body of General Chengizoglu," added Chief Historian Yurenev to keep from feeling completely ignored.

"Correct. General Chengizoglu with steam rising from his corpse. It doesn't sound like a story Colonel Sverdlov would be likely to make up. So let us imagine Colonel Sverdlov is skeptical at first. He thinks perhaps his president has gone insane, but he must appear to adhere to his wishes because President Muratbey has killed his superior officer and might kill him. What, then, is keeping him, as soon as he leaves Muratbey's office, from having the president arrested?"

"Muratbey gives him the weapons to test," said Kalenin.

"Precisely. Just as he told his uncle. So even though Sverdlov does think Muratbey is insane, he has the means to check the slight possibility that he is not. He tests the red and green weapons, finds out they work, and realizes both that Muratbey is telling the truth and that with such weapons, and presumably the knowledge of how to make them, Ferghana could become the greatest power in Central Asia. In other words, without the weapons, the whole episode never could have happened, and Sverdlov would never have told his story to his uncle. Instead, he would have arrested the president and let the vice president take over, or declare a military state of emergency himself."

Kalenin frowned but nodded. "All right, Nikolai. I see your logic. So the red and green weapons are real. That's crucial. The man from space may be totally invulnerable, and he may fly off taking all his technology with him, but at this moment the weapons are in human hands. Unfortunately not ours."

"But there are only twenty-two of them, and they are all in the hands of troops who will be making the incursion into Kyrgyzstan. If we are going to capture them, we will have to go to Kyrgyzstan too, directly to Verethra Kuh where Sverdlov will have only a small number of troops at the end of his supply train and far away from his armored units. If we use the 208th Paratroop Battalion at Omsk, it's seven hundred and fifty miles. Scarcely an hour and a half flight, but all of it over Kazakh or Kyrgyz territory. The most direct route would go almost directly over both Almaty and Bishkek."

"Will the Kazakh air force oppose us?"

"Without question. So will the Kyrgyz if we should be lucky enough to get past the Kazakhs. They will both think we're aiming at their capital cities. Of course, we could suppress ground fire from the air and use a fighter escort, but that would mean a general war with Kazakhstan. And NATO has been warning us against starting something with Kazakhstan."

"Hmmm, we need a pretext." The defense minister pried the top from a fresh bottle of seltzer and let it fizz into his glass. "Something that neither the Kazakhs nor the Kyrgyz can object to."

The face of the roly-poly Chief Historian brightened. "Excuse me, I have an idea." Kalenin and Repin looked at him with minimal interest. "The Ferghanans have closed their borders because of the bubonic plague."

"Not if we believe Sverdlov's story. That's just a cover."

"Exactly. But that means they cannot deny having the plague. Supposing the World Health Organization announced that in the interest of all the world's peoples it was sending a plane full of medical specialists and plague vaccine. It could ask permission to overfly Kazakhstan and Kyrgyzstan on humanitarian grounds."

"But it wouldn't be able to land at Kokand. Ferghanan airspace is closed."

"It could still try. Make a request to land to help prevent the plague epidemic from spreading. We know Ferghana will refuse the request so the airplane would have an excuse to remain in Kyrgyz airspace all the way to the Verethra Kuh, which is about as close as it can get to Kokand without entering Ferghana. There it again seeks permission to enter. Ferghana again refuses. The plane returns to Omsk . . . minus the paratroopers who are dropped on the mountain."

"Would the World Health Organization authorize such a mission?" asked General Repin.

Pyotr Kalenin eyes sparkled with excitement. "Dr. Yurenev, that is brilliant! Who cares whether the WHO would authorize the mission? It doesn't have to. The story only has to hold long enough to get the plane in and out. That's three or four hours. If we take off at six in the morning, it will be after midnight in Geneva. It should take at least three hours for the Kazakh and Kyrgyz governments to find out from WHO headquarters whether the flight is authorized. In the meantime, we telephone and tell them what's happening. They won't dare shoot the plane down."

"But how would we extract our troops?" queried Repin.

"That should be simple. Once the incursion begins, Ferghana will be at war with Kyrgyzstan. We will offer support to Kyrgyzstan. If they ask about the medical emergency flight, we tell them it was a ruse. We had secret advanced notice of the incursion and sent paratroops to try to forestall it and protect Kyrgyzstan from violation. In any case, everything will be so confused by that time that we should be able to control the situation."

General Repin was studying a detailed terrain map of the Tien Shan mountains in southern Kyrgyzstan. "The cave is on the north face. Sverdlov's plan has the Ferghana forces coming in along this little river from the west. If our troops landed above the snowline on the east slope, and were wearing white, they could work their way around to the cave without being spotted. Sverdlov's sending only fifteen men up the cliff. They're his only mountaineers. If our men are already in the cave, they can take them by surprise, seize the red and green weapons, and hold the position until relieved. If we can establish firing points on this slope to the east of the cliff, we can pin Sverdlov's troops down with enfilade fire from above. There's no way he can get around us."

"What about from the air?" said Kalenin.

"The cave will protect the men inside. The ones on the slope will have to dig in. But if Sverdlov uses his air force to cut the road from Osh, as he told his uncle he was planning to do, the air battle will develop away from the mountain. I think the Ferghanans will have their hands full in the air and won't be able to support Sverdlov."

The Defense Minister turned to the beaming Chief Historian and gathered his round body in a hug. "Dr. Yurenev, your suggestion is excellent. I commend you."

"Thank you, Your Excellency," replied the overwhelmed historian. "Perhaps you would think to mention me—in a very small way, of course—when you report to the President."

The Defense Minister looked at the Chief Historian sourly. "Report to the President? Our President? A man who was elected because he promised to improve the economy and then lowered the pensions of every veteran of the Red Army? You must be joking. The first thing he would do is telephone Washington to ask permission."

"No," interjected General Repin, "the first thing he would do is drink half a bottle of vodka and then telephone Washington."

"But . . ." began the suddenly goggle-eyed historian.

"We do this for the army, and for Mother Russia. Not for a parliament full of hoodlums and a government run by drunkards."

Chapter Nineteen

Three panel trucks, a beat-up Honda, and Major Park's Land Cruiser disguised by a haphazard coat of spray-paint traveled a circuitous route from the Basmachi safe-house on the northern outskirts of Osh to the smugglers' airstrip off the southern road to Sary Tash. Lee and Joseph, riding in the Land Cruiser, cringed at the sight of Kyrgyz police at the airstrip gate, but Hayes Carpenter assured them that their only job was to collect bribes from smugglers. This according to Dan Nielsen's confession.

Sure enough, the smiling officers offered casual salutes to Uli, the Basmachi leader riding in the lead truck, and the convoy passed through without hindrance. While the rest of the vehicles drove to a long, low shed on the far side of the runway, the Land Cruiser stopped briefly at the Carpenter-Beckenbaugh Learjet. Hayes got out of the car and disappeared inside to speak to his aircrew, who had camped out in the plane for its protection. When he returned, Park drove on to join the trucks behind the shed.

While the dozen Basmachi men and Carpenter's SAS mercenaries unloaded assorted bundles and some two-by-four lumber from the trucks, Lee and Joseph stretched their legs. The shed screened the trucks from the police post at the far gate, but to the south and west the land opened directly into mountain foothills, their lower slopes, covered with brown grass and leafless bushes, rising gently to a snowline some miles distant. Lee noted a half-dozen different wildflowers pushing out of the ground among the tufts of grass near her feet. The sun felt warm and the air spring-like though there were still scattered icy spots where standing water had refrozen during the night.

"Look," said Joseph, pointing to a crease in the hillside.

Out of a barely noticeable gully a line of ungainly brown animals was proceeding slowly in their direction. After several minutes, the two-humped, swan-necked profiles of the dark, shaggy camels became clearly distinguishable from those of the small horses being led behind them. To Lee it was a scene out of one of the old accounts by Central Asian travelers which she had read in preparation for her stay in Kokand. The absence of camels in Ferghana had disappointed her, but now here they were, a caravan of them swaying down the mountainside as if coming to rescue her from the tawdriness of everyday life.

Provisions, camp goods, and weapons had been carefully tied into balanced loads so that it was a fairly easy matter, once the camels were in couched position with their legs folded under them, to wrestle them across the natural valley between the animals' humps and tie them to the horizontal poles attached to pads that constituted their baggage saddles. The loading process proceeded slowly nevertheless since careful loading, as Dimitri Park told Lee, was the secret of a well-managed caravan. He also showed her two camels outfitted for riding with saddles and dangling stirrups nestled between the humps. Assuming one was for her, Lee wondered idly whether she would be able to lean forward and take a nap using the long shaggy hair on the front hump as a pillow.

The other prospective camel rider had a more negative view. "Hayes, if I can't ride a horse, I ain't goin'," declared Wilson sharply and definitively. "I've ridden horses since I was a baby. Put me on a horse. Won't be no problem."

"Wilson, you're blind," said Hayes with a placating tone. "The camels will all be strung together. You won't have to see where you're going."

"Horse ain't blind, is it? You don't ride with your eyes. You should know that, 'less your fat butt has gotten too used to an armchair. Ride with your hands and your legs and your back. Eyes just for seein' where you're at. Put me behind another horse and tell the rider not to go under any low branches. I'll do just fine."

"But Wilson, we don't have another horse."

"Then you got yourself an extra camel. That's all I can say."

"Mr. Carpenter," said Joseph interjecting himself into the conversation. "I'm supposed to ride a horse, but I've never been on a horse in my life. I'd be willing to ride Mr. Woodrow's camel."

"Listen to that boy," chuckled Wilson. "Takes consideration on an old blind man."

Hayes looked at Joseph critically. "It's time you learned to ride a horse, son. Spend too much time with computers and such and you never learn how to be a man."

"I've never learned to enjoy Marlboro cigarettes, either," replied Joseph. "What makes you think sitting for two days on a horse is more virile than sitting for two days on a camel? I bet these Basmachi wouldn't have such narrow view of manhood."

Lee intervened. "Hayes, let Wilson ride the horse. Let Joseph keep me company on the camels. You're not the boss here, and it's time you learned to behave better. Look at Dimitri. He's doesn't have swimming pools full of money, but a whole country is afraid of his shadow. Do you see Dimitri trying to throw his weight around? Do you? No, you do not. Without Dimitri you'd be trying to cross a minefield right now with your fancy guns and your hired assassins. But with Dimitri's help, and only with Dimitri's help, you have a chance to get the revenge you want. So Dimitri has every right to order you around. But does he do it? No. I won't have this rudeness, Hayes. I mean it. Now you just learn to behave."

"Or what?" said Hayes grandiosely.

Lee thought for a few seconds. She saw an invisible frontier—and stepped across it. "Or I'll have you shot."

A silence fell over the group of English-speakers. Hayes looked as stunned as anyone. "You'll what? You'll have me shot?"

Lee stared him coldly in the eye. "That is correct. Dimitri will shoot you if I ask him to, and Dimitri has twelve armed friends who don't even know what we're arguing about"—Uli and his team of Kyrgyz had halted their other activities to attend to the dispute—"as opposed to your four, who probably won't collect their pay if you get killed."

Hayes looked at Dimitri but could read nothing in his impassive face. He looked back at Lee. "Are you taking command of this expedition, lady?" he said slowly.

"Yes, I believe I am," replied Lee firmly. "I've run away from my husband. I've fled the country. I'm alone in the mountains with twenty men. I've gone about as far as a woman can go. But there's just too much testosterone. So the answer to your question is yes. I am taking command. It's a role that suits me."

Joseph broke the tense silence. "You have my vote, Lee."

Hayes looked around at the others.

"I support Lee," said Park firmly.

"Sounds like Judge Ingalls gonna be the law south of Osh," said Wilson. "And I'm goin' to ride a horse."

Alf was standing in front of the three other mercenaries, all of them looking poised to act. "Just give the order, Mr. Carpenter. We'll do what has to be done."

Hayes weighed the situation for several seconds before relaxing his expression. "Wilson, get on the goddam horse, and lets get out of here."

Uli led the way looking for all the world like a warrior of Genghiz Khan with his stringy mustaches, lambskin hat, and lifelong ease on horseback. Behind him, Wilson Woodrow rode with equal comfort but a lankier, looser style bred on the Texas plains. Dimitri and Hayes came next riding side by side while the rest of the Basmachi and the SAS mercenaries sorted themselves out around and behind the camel train.

"You sleeping with Lee?" asked Hayes bluntly.

"No," replied Dimitri.

"But you want to. Want to a lot." Dimitri didn't say anything. "You think Muratbey is Hitler because he let those people in Nukus die, and you could have just walked into his office and put a hole in his head. Instead you made a bee-line for a woman who hardly knows what's going on, rub her husband's philandering in her face for a second time, and then take her off to another country. Those are the actions of a man who wants a woman."

"You forget there's Bix to deal with."

"You really think we're going to do something against Bix? As I size it up, we're depending on a drunk who thinks he's god, and we don't have a clue how he plans to handle Bix. Like as not, Bix'll fix his machine or whatever, take his ass back to his own planet, and no one will be sure he was ever here."

"Maybe."

"Don't be such a hard-ass, Dimitri. Hankering after a woman is nothing to be ashamed about. I'll grant you want to get Bix and Muratbey, but you have to admit you're after Lee too."

Dimitri rode silently for a while. Then he said, "Do you think it shows to everyone?"

"Shows? Hell no! You've got a face as blank as the Great Wall of China. Not like Joseph. He's got puppy love so bad he's practically covered with saliva. Unless you've told her, she probably doesn't know herself."

"I've told her . . . in a way. At least I indicated. I tried not to be offensive."

"Well, you're a bold suitor, aren't you?"

"In my line of work, you take what you need and don't get involved emotionally. So I'm not very experienced in emotional matters."

"Never been married, then?"

"I would have been a mistake."

"So why now? You're hitting what? Maybe forty-five? A little older? I know how it is. You're tired of scaring people, you've got no kids, your boss needs killing. Feel like being secret police makes you part of the past instead of the future. I can understand all that. Classy lady comes along. American. Educated. Speaks for herself."

"Beautiful. I think she's beautiful."

"Not a teen queen, but I can go with beautiful."

"But I shamed her, and I don't think she will ever forgive me."

"Not the forgiving sort, that's for sure. Lady's got a real tongue on her. No woman's talked up to me the way she did since Helen walked out."

"Helen was your wife?"

"Yeah. God, I was in love with her. Only woman ever really understood me . . . and still liked me. And I screwed it up. Helen used to savage me just the way Lee did back there. That brought back memories."

"Then you're not angry at her for taking charge?"

"Angry? Hell no. But don't tell her I said so. Fact is, it's a good thing. Keep you and me from getting into a butting match down the road." Hayes road silently for a while. "I'll tell you something else too, just so we don't get into some misunderstanding later. You want to get in bed with her, that's fine. You saw her first. I don't go after another man's woman. But if you're right, and she can't forgive you for busting up her marriage, then I'm going to try my best to marry her myself."

"A contest between a Korean whose principal skill is interrogating people and an American billionaire isn't very balanced," observed Dimitri.

"Word of honor. I'll stay out of your way until she's decided herself about you. You also got to remember that she's already been married to one rich American businessman. The type may not appeal to her any more. What was her husband like as a man?"

"Six-three, athletic, younger than me, energetic in bed . . . at least he sounded energetic. Perhaps too energetic, not tender enough."

Hayes prodded his thick midsection with his fingers and sighed. "I've got a hunch Korea's gonna win this round." After a few moments, he added, "So you listened in on . . ."

"Their lovemaking? Yes. I bugged the bedroom. It was my job. They stopped having sex after I made Lee listen to the tape."

"And?"

"And what?"

"Well, you know. You said what he's like. What's she like?"

Dimitri's sallow cheeks flamed red. "I can't say that."

"Okay. Sorry. I understand. Forget about it."

They road together silently, climbing steadily toward the snowline. "I dream about making love to her every night," vouchsafed Dimitri eventually. Hayes grunted and kept his silence.

Back in the camel train, the mounts that Lee and Joseph were riding were tied to separate strings of six animals each. A Basmachi rider led each string. Occasionally they would pull abreast of each other, but more often they moved in a single line. Though Lee and Joseph could have walked as fast as the plodding beasts, riding was more comfortable and allowed them to admire the scenery. Well before reaching the snowline the route of the caravan turned westward, across the grain of the foothills. They dipped into and out of a seemingly endless series of shallow valleys whose lower slopes deepened into impassable gullies. Occasionally they would see a rider on a distant hillside, but they could never tell whether it was one of Uli's men scouting their flanks or a lone Kyrgyz herder.

In the more sheltered valleys wildflowers were beginning to show in profusion, and Lee could imagine the mountainsides covered with the bright green of new grass interspersed with brilliant blossoms. More often, however, the vista was bleak and brown with the occasional hawk or eagle soaring overhead.

Alf rode up beside Lee and asked how she was doing. His English accent seemed incongruously civilized. "Doing just fine, thank you," Lee responded. "Beautiful landscape, isn't it?"

"Very appealing. Reminds me of Kashmir. Did a job for the government there a few years back."

Lee wondered which government. "You and your men don't talk much, do you?"

"Catch up with us off duty with a few pints in a pub, and you'll hear us talk. Particularly Laurence. He has some wonderful stories."

"What do you talk about?"

"Lies about previous jobs mostly. Except for the parts it's not fit for a woman to hear."

"Why don't you tell truths about your jobs?"

"Too boring, actually. Ninety-five percent devoted to training, equipment maintenance, preparing plans, standing guard . . . all pretty boring to talk about. Get those bits right, though, and you probably won't get hurt. Most of the lads with real stories to tell don't live to tell them. Laurence's the exception. He's been luckier than most."

"What's your feeling about this job you're on now? You think you're going to need luck?"

"You want a frank answer?"

"Certainly."

"To tell the truth, none of us are feeling too good about it. Mr. Carpenter offered ten times the going rate on the condition that we follow any orders he gives. More usual run of client wants to be protected and follows our orders. He told us he'd provide equipment for every eventuality. But when that includes anti-tank and anti-aircraft missiles, you begin to wonder whether the eventualities he has in mind might be a wee bit too much for four men. Mind you, we'll do our job. But it's beginning to seem like an awfully big job."

Further conversation was interrupted by the trailing string of camels beginning to pull alongside Lee's string. Alf pulled his horse to the side to make way and then dropped back to ride with the rear guard.

"Hi there!" called Joseph as his camel approached Lee's.

"Hello. How are you doing?"

"Fine. I thought I was going to be sick at first with this swaying from side to side, but I'm used to it now."

"I've wanted to ask you, Joseph, what do you think made Nadir single you out when we were on the street by the kumys shop? Why did he think you were Webmaster?"

"It's like he said in one of the postings. His people are telepathic, just like the giants. He said he could see that I had the mind of a believer."

"And I didn't, I suppose. I'm insulted. I've spent years studying Indra."

"Maybe so. But apparently that hasn't changed whatever you think of him in your mind. I mean, you still don't think of him as a real god. Did I tell you I have a little statue of Lord Ganesh that my mother gave me in my suitcase? Before meeting you at the Academy of Sciences and putting the bug in your purse, I prayed to Ganesh for a good outcome. Not very spy-like, but it worked."

"It's a good thing Nadir isn't jealous of Ganesh."

"I don't know whether he can distinguish which god a believer believes in. I think it's just an attitude of mind that he perceives and draws strength from. But I don't know for sure. He's real hard to understand. Like when I asked him about the giant and how he would fight him, he talked about what sounded like Shushna's eggs. I had no idea what he meant."

"I do. In the Rig Veda there's a demon named Shushna. Shushna's like Vrtra, one of Indra's enemies. Shushna is described as having eggs. More often, however, he's described as having a fortress. *Tvam puram carisnvam fadhaih susnasya sam pinak . . .*" she chanted, "'With your weapons you smashed to pieces the moving fortress of Shushna.'"

Joseph looked awestruck. "My god, you know it all by heart?"

"The whole Rig Veda? Of course not. It's huge. But I know a lot of the hymns and verses to Indra. Shushna also has a human enemy named Kutsa who's an ally of Indra. *Cakram*—that's chakra, as in Chakra Net—*kutsaya yudhyate musay indra suryam* . . . 'You stole a wheel, Indra, from the sun for Kutsa who was fighting.' Shushna and Indra fight each other with magic, too, but I can't remember how the verse goes. Anyway, there are about forty verses dealing with Shushna, and in a couple of them he or she is described as having eggs."

"How did you learn all this?"

"Years and years of universally underappreciated study, Joseph. Though I must say that if it ever becomes publicly known that Indra is real—assuming just for the moment that Nadir is Indra—you'll probably have dozens of people doing quick and shallow studies of Vedic and writing tacky little books about him."

Joseph had attended to Lee's last expostulation while looking over his shoulder because his string of camels was advancing at a faster rate. As his camel pulled further ahead he threw back at her, "So what connection do you suppose there is between Shushna's eggs and fighting Bix?"

"I haven't the faintest idea," she called after him.

Chapter Twenty

"First day of spring tomorrow," observed Lee as she accepted a tin cup full of coffee handed to her with incongruous delicacy by Laurence, the tallest and most muscular of the SAS merceraries.

"Yes, ma'm," he replied before returning his attention to cleaning up the breakfast dishes.

Lee had flatly rejected Hayes' suggestion that she have the mountain tent all to herself. She said she had no objection to sharing, but that was before she heard his snoring, which drowned out the night noises of Joseph and Wilson, her other tentmates. How the others survived the freezing night air entirely out of doors was a mystery, but none of them seemed the worse for it as they broke camp and prepared for the short trip to the place of sacrifice.

"Nervous?" asked Joseph.

"Hardly slept a wink all night. Hayes' snoring would have attracted moose if there were any around. So all I could do was think about the sacrifice. I didn't even dare use the laptop because my battery has to last through the ceremony."

"I slept like a baby. Now I'm really excited, though."

"Did you pray to Ganesh?"

"First thing. But Lord Indra is so much greater than Lord Ganesh. It sends chills through me. I really hope you'll be able to see him the way I did."

"That would be nice, but I'm not holding out much hope. I'm comfortable, I guess, with the idea that an alien stranded on earth prompted the creation of a cult in his honor. And I suppose that in some way makes Nadir a god. But he's still a far cry from the Indra of the hymns." Lee finished her coffee and handed it back to Laurence, who was packing the last of the cooking equipment. "Time to go."

They had camped below the snowline, but now Uli directed their course upward, and soon the horses and camels were treading through a few inches of wet snow visibly melting in the strong sunshine. Uli had made it clear, when Joseph indicated the place they were to meet Nadir, that it was a locale he was familiar with. Nevertheless, Lee was anxious that there might have been some missed communication. She would need grass for the altar, and the deeper they went into the snowfield, the more apprehensive she became.

After two hours of riding, the way narrowed and the snow gave way to stony ground. Above on the caravan's left a sheer cliff rose toward a gleaming white peak. Lee's heart began to beat faster, but Dimitri rode by to report that the peak was a secondary summit of Verethra Kuh. The cliff and summit they were heading for would not be visible until they had rounded the shoulder of the mountain and could see its northern face.

Then suddenly Lee saw something that caught her eye. "Dimitri, stop the caravan. Please."

Park Sensed the excitement in her face and voice and shouted ahead to Uli in Kyrgyz. Within a few more paces, all the animals had stopped.

Lee slipped off her camel without making it couch down and picked her way over the stony scree toward the cliff. "Look," she said in a reverential voice to Dimitri and Joseph as they came up beside her. Under the raking light of the low morning sun the grooves of the shapes incised in the rock stood out as black outlines against the ocher colored stone. It was the circle and inscribed cross of a chakra that had caught Lee's eye, but now that they were close they could see hundreds of engravings stretching off to either side. "Here's Vrtra and Indra," exclaimed Lee pointing to a wavy line and a stick figure holding what looked like a club or hammer.

"There are chariots over here," said Dimitri. "They have chakra wheels just like you said."

"And here's a scene of people sitting," said Joseph, exploring a bit higher. "They might be in a house. There's a line around them."

Lee came over to look. "Oh my heavens! It's a sacrifice! See the rectangle? That's the sacred precinct. And these are the three fires: one round, one square, and one semicircular. I can't believe no one's ever explored here before. There's never been a report of graffiti showing a sacrifice. All we know is from the Shrauta Sutras and the way priests sacrifice in India today. But this shows how it must have been done in ancient times."

Uli joined their group and engaged in a conversation with Dimitri. He was smiling and pointing out specific figures.

"What's he saying?" asked Lee.

"He says this is a sacred place, and these are the pictures of gods. His people never lead anyone to this place because it would be a desecration."

Lee was dumbfounded. "You mean these Basmachi worship Indra?"

"No. He says these are the old gods. The Kyrgyz are all Muslims now, but they don't disturb the places of the old gods. He says the only reason he's led us here is because we are coming to honor the old gods. And because we don't have cameras."

"Now do you begin to believe in Nadir?" said Joseph light-heartedly.

Lee seemed lost in wonderment and instead of replying continued to move from one graffiti-marked rock face to another, tracing the incised grooves with her index finger.

At length, Hayes joined the group. "What the hell's going on?"

"Lee's looking at some ancient Indo-Iranian rock carvings," answered Joseph.

Hayes looked impatient. "I think we have more important things to do than that," he muttered. He looked toward Lee as if he were about to bellow a command, but she was already scrambling back.

"Hayes, get back on your horse," she chided as she passed. "We have to get on with the sacrifice if we're going to finish before dark. If you wanted to be a tourist, you should have joined us sooner."

Hayes grinned at her retreating back. "Yes, ma'm," he called, "whatever you say."

Under way again, the caravan soon passed the cliff and then angled downward as the terrain flattened and opened in that direction. In less than a mile, they stopped in a level, grassy area illuminated by the full force of the morning sun. The Basmachi immediately began to unload the camels. Lee dismounted and looked around for any sign of Nadir. Joseph saw her stop at the western edge of the withered meadow and went to join her.

"Wildflowers?" he said, noting the profusion of bright green points poking through the brown grass everywhere.

Lee looked meditative. "No. This is the sacrifice area. Look at these stones. They form a rectangle. This is where the sacrifice was performed. I suspect these stones haven't been moved in thousands of years."

"Then we know this is the right place," said Joseph cheerily. "Nadir should show up soon. He's probably already here. Just waiting until everything's ready."

Under Lee's direction, the Basmachi and the SAS men dug holes at intervals around the edges of the rectangle, planted two-by-four uprights, and hammered crossbeams in place to form the framework of a room. White cotton sheets were stretched across the frame and nailed in place to form a roof, and more sheeting was spread to cover the ground within the rectangle. Toward the eastern end of the precinct, Lee had the Basmachi cut out a circle in the sheet around an ancient stone circle marking the location of the household fire. Then they did the same with the square fireplace of the offering fire at the opposite end, and half way between the two with the half-moon shaped southern fire near the rectangle's edge. The post for tethering the sacrificial goat was driven into the ground at the western edge of the offering fire, and dry grass was cut and strewn next to the offering post as the altar for Lord Indra.

Leaving the others to find fuel for the fires and eat lunch, Lee, Hayes, Joseph, and Dimitri, followed Uli down the mountain slope to a rivulet flowing from the snowfields above. "Now we bathe," Lee announced bravely.

"It must be absolutely freezing," said Joseph.

"Joseph, don't be a wimp. Hayes was right. It's time you grew up. A little girl can ride a horse, but it takes a real man to strip down on a mountside and splash himself with cold water. That's why

Hayes is going to go first." Hayes glared at her but then smiled at the challenge she'd thrown down. "As for myself, I'll respect your modesty by doing my own bathing downstream around those rocks. When I come back, however, I want you all to be wearing sandals and sheets the way I showed you." With no more ado she strode off, leaving Hayes taking off his jacket and undoing his belt.

Swimming in the Atlantic during Connecticut springtimes had steeled Lee to the sensation of ice-cold water, but it was still all she could do to keep from yelling in agony as she sloshed herself with ladles of water from the icy stream. She was gratified by the sound of Hayes hooting in the distance and then by Joseph positively screaming. Not for the first time she admired Dimitri's self-control and stoicism as he apparently bathed without making a sound.

When she rejoined the group, all three men were clad in sandals and toga-like garments that left the right shoulder and chest bare. She herself had decided to depart from the stipulations of the Shrauta Sutras and drape her garment over both shoulders. A shaved head might convince Nadir she was a male, she reasoned, but it was hardly likely to do the same for her human companions.

Back at the enclosure, they all took seats outside the rectangle but near the blazing southern fire. Lee distributed bottles of milk to her fellow sacrificers. Hayes grumbled that he was hungry, but Lee told him he could have nothing but milk until the sacrifice was over and that he should be thankful she had not insisted on starting the milk-only diet the night before.

When the time came for shaving, to everyone's surprise, Laurence stepped forward and announced that between mercenary jobs he worked as a barber. Soon he had Hayes' head and face swathed in steaming towels soaked in water heated on the southern fire. Still frozen from his bath and feeling the chill breeze through his scanty garment, Hayes moaned and sighed like a man experiencing the greatest massage of his life. Within twenty minutes, wielding scissors and razor with a professionalism that was greatly enjoyed by the Basmachi onlookers, Laurence had rendered Hayes totally bald and exposed the sagging chin previously covered by his beard. Joseph went next and then Dimitri, both of them ending up looking rather like monks.

Then came Lee's turn. Her concentration on what was to come pushed baldness concerns from her mind. Laurence quickly cropped her hair down to an inch or so with scissors and then covered her scalp with the steaming towels. She wanted to shut her eyes and savor the wonderful warmth, but the expressions on the surrounding male faces were too amusing to shut out. Irrespective of language or nationality, every pair of male eyes followed the shaving ritual with rapt attention. Lee could not grasp the precise tenor of their fascination, but she realized that she had never before felt so much an object of masculine desire, nor such a total absence of sexual response in her own body. As the razor glided smoothly over her scalp, removing the last wisps of her hair, a feeling of power came over her like an adrenalin rush.

When Laurence finished, Lee stood and faced the men. "Dimitri, I need your help." Dimitri rose and stood beside her. "I'm going to recite now the hymn to Indra that I will be chanting in Vedic during the sacrifice. I want everyone to know what it means, so I want you to translate it into Kyrgyz as I go."

"All right. But where is Nadir?"

"He'll be here," she said confidently. Then, raising her voice so she could be heard by everyone, she began to address the group, pausing between sentences for Dimitri's translation. "Friends, we're about to begin a sacred ritual, a sacrifice to Lord Indra. We won't do it perfectly. In fact, none of us is truly qualified to do it at all since we are not Brahmin priests. But we will be doing it at the sacrifical site most sacred to Lord Indra, for it was on this mountain that he confronted and slew the demon Vrtra. That is why this mountain is called Verethra Kuh, the Mountain of Vrtra. When I step into the sacred area, I will become the *hotar* priest. I will chant hymns to Lord Indra in the Vedic language until the sacrifice is finished. But I want to read one hymn now in English before we start so everyone will know something about Indra. This hymn is over three thousand years old and has been passed down by priests from generation to generation."

With that, Lee took the laptop computer Joseph held out to her, looked at the screen, and began to read.

Now I will proclaim the heroic deeds of Indra,
The first ones which he, the thunderbolt-wielder, performed:
He killed the snake, he made the waters flow,
He split open the bellies of the mountains.

He killed the snake who was lying on the mountain;
Twashtar had forged the whizzing thunderbolt for him.
Like mooing cows, flowing with milk,
The waters rushed down quickly to the ocean.

Lustily he took his portion of soma,
He drank the soma-juice from the three bowls.
The Generous One grasped his thunderbolt, suitable for hurling,
Killed him, the first-born of the snakes.

When, O Indra, you killed the first-born of the snakes,
And then you outwitted the magic of the magicians,
Thereupon, producing the sun, day, and dawn,
You did not find any enemy at all.

Indra killed the encloser, the worst encloser, whose shoulders were broad,
With his great weapon, the thunderbolt.
Like the branches of a tree, hewn off by an ax,
The snake lies hugging the ground.

For, like a drunken non-combatant, he had challenged
The on-rushing warrior who had beset many enemies.
He did not survive the collision of the weapons of death,
He whose enemy was Indra, who had crushed the streams together.

Footless, handless, he fought against Indra;
Indra threw his thunderbolt at Vrtra's back.
The castrated one, who had wanted to be equal to the virile bull,
Vrtra lay broken in many pieces.

Lying in that way like a broken reed,
The waters, flowing for mankind, went over him.
The very waters whom Vrtra with his might had enclosed—
The snake was lying at their feet.

Vrtra's mother became exhausted;
Indra had thrown his thunderbolt down upon her.
The mother was above, the son was under;
Danu, Vrtra's mother, lies, like a cow with her calf.

The body lay low in the midst of the currents which do not stop, do not rest—
The waters spread over the private parts of Vrtra.
Indra's enemy lay in long darkness.

Wives of the snake, guarded by the snake, the waters stood motionless,
Shut up like cows by the rustler Pani.
Having killed Vrtra, Indra opened the hole of the waters which had been closed.

You, O Indra, the god alone
Won the cows, you won, O hero, the soma,
You set free the seven streams so that they could flow.

The lightning was of no use to him, nor the thunder,
Nor the mist and hail which he scattered.
When Indra and the snake fought,
As when they fight in the future, the Generous One was victorious.

Indra is king of that which stands still and that which moves,
He who holds the thunderbolt in his hand is king of the tame and the wild.
Just he, the king, rules over the peoples,
He surrounds them like the rim of a chakra surrounds the spokes.

When Dimitri finished the last portion of his translation, there was an awed silence. Lee stepped over the perimeter of stones and into the sacred precinct, beckoning Hayes, Joseph, and Dimitri to join her. She seated Hayes crosslegged at the southeast corner and reminded him that all he had to do, as the host of the sacrifice, was sit still and keep quiet. Joseph looked apprehensively at the male goat tethered to the post between the grass-strewn altar and the offering fire. Lee handed him a bucket of melted clarified butter and a ladle.

Then she stood in the very center of the enclosure and began to chant. At her first words a gasp went up from the onlookers. Sitting calmly on the altar grass looking approvingly at the goat and the offering fire was the squat, bearded form of Nadir, bare to the waist and wearing a white loincloth.

Lee felt her voice begin to tremble and with an effort strengthened it and raised the volume of her chanting. Joseph, enthralled at the sight of Nadir, poured a ladle of ghee on the offering fire. Yellow flame erupted with a loud crackle. As the blaze subsided, Lee fancied that Nadir looked larger than he had only moments before. As she continued chanting, Joseph poured more ghee on the fire. Each time the yellow flame shot up and subsided, Nadir changed. His skin gradually became golden, his beard and hair flame-colored. He was clearly larger than any man among the onlookers.

At Lee's prompt, Joseph untied the goat's rope from the tethering post and walked with Dimitri to the northest corner of the precinct. There he handed the rope to Dimitri who led the goat over the stone markers. Once outside the rectangle, Dimitri circled the goat's neck with a bowstring and drew the ends across one another in a smooth, powerful pull. The goat staggered and opened its mouth, but no sound came forth. Its eyes bulged. Then it lost its footing. Dimitri continued to apply pressure until the body was lifeless on the ground. Meanwhile, Joseph, with a sickened look on his face, had returned to the offering fire and resumed pouring libations of ghee. Throughout it all Lee continued to intone the Vedic hymns in a clear, resonant voice.

Dimitri pulled the goat onto its back, slit its belly, and tugged out its entrails. Setting the intestines and organs to one side, he scraped out the fatty connecting tissue that held them in their proper places in the animal's abdomen. This omentum he carefully deposited on a white sheet. Then he turned to skinning the goat and hacking it into pieces. In less than half an hour the job was done. Joseph and Dimitri carried the large chunks of goat carcass to the household fire at the west end of the rectangle and placed them on a grill.

When the meat was all arranged on the fire, and Joseph had basted it liberally with ladles of ghee, they returned to the butchering area. Joseph picked up the sheet bearing the white, fatty mass of the omentum and walked slowly to the offering fire. Glowing like a golden statue, Nadir was waiting patiently. With an awestruck look at the figure seated on the altar grass before him, Joseph slid the omentum from the sheet onto the offering fire. Amidst a loud crackling sound tongues of bright yellow flame shot through a mass of white smoke. Then the smoke, confined by the canopy above, began to spread, and the entire precinct was suffused by the powerful odor of burning fat.

Unwavering in her chanting Lee kept her gaze fixed on Nadir. He inhaled the smoke in deep breaths like a wine connoisseur savoring a rare vintage. His skin shone like polished gold through the haze of smoke. His hair and beard seemed on fire. Though still seated with his legs crossed, his stature was that of . . . . *Of a god*, thought Lee. The words Lord Indra formed naturally in her mind, and tears watered her eyes. Her laptop lay unattended at her feet. The words of her hymn came effortlessly to her lips. Her heart was filled to bursting with emotions she had never before imagined and could not put a name to.

Presently the smoke of the burning omentum began to clear. The smell of the burning fat dissipated and became mixed with the smell of the meat roasting on the opposite fire. Without a perceptible moment of change the vision of Lord Indra faded, and the figure sitting on the altar grass before the tethering post and the offering fire was again unmistakably Nadir. He turned and looked at Lee for the first time, and she saw that his face was full of joy.

"Let's eat," he said.

Lee reached the end of a verse and stopped chanting. She felt hot, her whole body was quivering. Nadir stepped forward and put his arms around her in a fraternal embrace.

In her ear he whispered, "You are my *hotar* priest. Forget I never shall."

Nadir's leaving the altar triggered a bustle of activity. Joseph and Dimitri went to tend the grilling meat while Hayes removed himself from the sacred precinct and pulled on some warmer clothes that Wilson had been keeping for him. Hayes saw tears in Wilson's sightless eyes.

"I saw him, Hayes. I saw him," he said softly.

Hayes gave his old friend a tight embrace. "I saw him, too," he said with a tremor in his voice.

As Lee watched Joseph and Dimitri distribute plates of meat to the Basmachi and the SAS men, the thought came to mind that according to the Shrauta Sutras, only Brahmins should partake of the sacrificial animal. Then she shrugged. Who cared what the Shrauta Sutras said? With Nadir present, the sacrifice was no longer hers to run. But just for a moment she allowed herself a private prideful thought: *I did it right.*

When the feasting was over, the men disassembled the enclosure and fed the wood and cloth into the fires. Nadir sat with his back to the southern hearth and talked to Lee, Joseph, Dimitri, Hayes, and Wilson. His every word was closely attended. "A world like Earth was mine, its people, called *dzi*, much like humans. The dzi explored the stars. They spoke by mind and altered code genes. Yet still they yearned for more. They yearned for endless life, escape from jaws of death. A *dzi* Inama named found path to longer life. In chromosomes of *dzi* he placed genetic code. It slowed the pace of life, but gave five hundred years. The *dzi* that he transformed were Inamadzi called. They grew to giant size, but proved a weakling breed. Their minds hold science deep; they engineer whole worlds. Their might lies in their ships, the ships they seldom leave.

"As Inamadzi foe there stands a different breed, one spawned by Pramo great, the greatest of the *dzi*. Like Inama before, so Pramo sought to free the *dzi* from mortal doom. Instead of adding years to length of life of *dzi*, good Pramo's quest took aim on immortality. Pramodzi are his spawn, and I am one of them. Good Pramo knew full well his sons would sterile be. But this seemed little cost compared with endless life. Alas he had no way to calculate just how Pramodzi would evolve in several hundred years. He never realized that centuries of life might have a bad effect and cause them to diverge from their once noble path.

"The Inamadzi scum, though having lengthy life, did envy endless life that Pramo had achieved for his Pramodzi breed. Like Pramo did his sons have but one noble goal to save the race of *dzi*. The Inamadzi breed were able still to mate while we could only add to our Pramodzi kind by harvesting both egg and seed from normal *dzi*. That's how the war began, the war between the giants and noble Pramo's race. We fought on planets far and weakling giants killed. But on the world of *dzi* the Inamadzi won, exterminating all so there could never be Pramodzi more than we. As for themselves, they searched to find a beast that had immortal genes. They hoped to shape a race endowed with endless life with whom they then could mate.

"So here I am on Earth, the last Pramodzi god. And with me twenty men, along with final priest of Indra, god of storms. One Inamadzi vile has come unto your land in hopes that one more change in climate of the earth will cause those who survive the chaos that will come to make the final leap, become like all the *dzi*. You do not know how close you have already come to speaking with your minds as *dzi*-kind all can do. But what you all just saw in course of sacrifice was sharing of my mind, a glimpse of things to come. Though such may be your fate, regardless of the plan that giants have devised, if you attain that skill as Inadmadzi gift, your fate will dismal be. The Inamadzi have no need for living humankind, except to donate seed. All others they will kill, just as they did the *dzi*.

"Pramodzi gain great strength from melding with the minds of people who believe. As Nadir, I was weak. I was no match for Bix. But now a godlike strength is coursing through my veins. Empowered by your hymns and rite of sacrifice, as Indra now I go to fight the giant foe, to end for once and all the Inamadzi threat to noble humankind. I'll catch him when he leaves the safety of his ship, goes forth to make repairs to climate change machine that with my *vajra* strong I long ago destroyed. One egg is all I need, an egg from Shushna's ship, that Shushna whom I slew, the giant last on earth. You'll find the sunken ship in lake called Issyk Kul. Like Bix did Shushna hide his vessel from the stars beneath the waters deep. From this the story grew that Vrtra waters held and did not them release 'til Indra him did slay. Go locate Shushna's egg and bring it here to me. So for this one last time can I Lord Indra be, Lord Indra strong in war, deserving to be called a savior and a god protecting with my wrath the humans whom I love."

The end of Nadir's sing-song speech took his listeners by surprise. Smiling and self-satisfied, he looked from one face to another waiting for responses. Finally, Dimitri said, "An egg is a nuclear bomb. Muratbey told me he was trying to get some from Bix for Ferghana."

"How are we supposed to get a bomb from a spaceship at the bottom of Issyk Kul?" said Joseph.

No one spoke.

"Workman ought to bring his own tools," muttered Hayes.

"Nadir, why didn't you get the bomb yourself? You knew you were going to need it."

Nadir fixed Joseph with a look normally visited on an ununderstanding child. "Because I cannot breathe when underneath the waves."

"Well, neither can we," replied Joseph.

"Yes we can," said the unexpected voice of Wilson Woodrow. "Do you know just where that ship is at? And where the egg's at inside it?"

"I'll show you where to go," replied Nadir.

"Mister, you can't show me nothin' cause I'm blind. But I'm a helluva a diver."

"I'll show you where to go. Jut put your hands in mine."

Wilson extended his hands toward Nadir's voice. Nadir grasped them in his own. Silence reigned for several minutes as everyone watched the two men. Then Wilson said quietly to Nadir, "I can do it. I'll go get it, get the egg and the other thing you want."

"Wilson?" said Hayes.

"Hayes," said the black man, his voice decisive, "you gotta make some arrangements. Get me a guide and a fast horse. I'll take the plane from the airfield. You have someone meet me with a diving rig at whatever airstrip's nearest that lake . . . Issyk Kul. I know exactly where to go and what to do. He held my hands, it was like watchin' it in a movie, only realer."

"Wilson, you can't do all that."

"Don't give me any bullshit, Hayes. Don't make me ask Lee to tell Dimitri to shoot you." He laughed. "'*To strive, to seek, to find, and not to yield.'* You taught me that. Now get off your fat ass, and let's do this."

"How will you get back with the egg?" asked Dimitri.

"Back? That's easy. Must be. Hayes does it all the time. You make a mark the pilot can see, and I'll have him push me out the door when we're over it. Hayes don't go nowhere without chutes, do you Hayes?"

Hayes looked ready to remonstrate, then changed his mind. "Okay, lets do it," he said firmly. "Lee, is it all right with you? You're the boss."

Lee took one of Wilson's hands in both of hers and kissed his weathered cheek. "Take care of yourself Wilson. Gods and heroes work together. Always have."

While Dimitri briefed Uli on what had transpired and Uli in turn gave instuctions to the horseman who would accompany Wilson, Hayes made use of the compact NSA transceiver Joseph had stowed in his gear on leaving Kokand. He contacted the pilot of the Learjet at Osh and gave instructions both for him and for him to pass along to Dan Nielsen in Almaty. " . . . and tell Daniel if he does this right, I not only won't fire him, but I'll promote him and make him a rich man." He terminated the contact and looked sheepishly at Lee. "Well, damn it, everyone wants to be rich, don't they?"

"Did I say anything?" said Lee with a smile.

She's smiling at me, thought Hayes. *Maybe I have a chance with her after all.*

The sun was setting when Wilson and his guide mounted up. Wilson had said that it didn't make any difference to him if they rode at night so long as his companion and his horse had enough moonlight to see by. They rode out at a trot, the lanky Texan looking as natural and at ease in the saddle as any sighted person ever did.

A half hour later a rider approached the camp from the west. It proved to be a scout Uli had sent out to reconnoitre the trail to the cave. Dimitri translated his report for the English-speakers. "He sighted parachutes coming down three miles west of here. Maybe as many as twenty."

Joseph looked elated. "Wow! I never thought the US could get here that fast."

"Doesn't look like they're American, Joseph. Uli's man saw the plane. It sounds from the description like it was Russian."

* * *

Seventy miles away, in the city of Kashgar, at the military headquarters of China's northwest province of Xinjiang, a radio clerk brought the transcript of a radio intercept to the chief of intelligence. The message was uncoded and in English, and the broadcast had been pinpointed to the northeast slope of a mountain named Verethra Kuh. Much of it made no sense at all, dealing apparently with plans to dive in Lake Issyk Kul. But there was one clear reference to a nuclear bomb. Colonel Yeh deliberated by himself for a while and then decided to show the transcript to the provincial commander.

Chapter Twenty-One

Wilson lost himself in the rhythm of the ride and the vision left in his head by Nadir's touch. Hours passed; the night grew cold. He swayed and lurched whenever the horse misstepped picking its way down the dark slope, but his body instinctively compensated and kept him upright and balanced. Despite the chill creeping through his down coat, he felt stronger with each passing mile. He kept the stops to water and rest the horses to a minumum, mounting up before his guide and forcing the pace. But the rhythm of the ride inspired memories.

He wondered how an old man's endurance and fortitude could be compared with the grit and hardness of his youth, teamed up with Hayes to follow the harvest. He didn't feel all that different, but what it had actually felt like to be young and strong wasn't so clear in his mind. The early 1970s, the country awash with long-haired bead-wearers. He and Hayes had grabbed their share of the free love that was going around, but their taste for hippie life stopped at disrespect for the flag.

Neither of them knew much about Vietnam, but one day in North Dakota they decided they knew enough. Hayes saw himself a hero and was hot to enlist. Wilson went along to keep him company—at least until they were standing on a sidewalk in downtown Fargo and Hayes said he intended to be a paratrooper. Some things weighed more than friendship in Wilson's mind, and jumping out of airplanes was one. In a fog of drunken argument and name-calling they parted ways, and he opted for the Navy dive school.

Thirty years later, that had all faded away. Hayes calling on him to manage the hole-in-the-sea had felt right. The job cost him his sight; but riding on a wild mountainside, the cold air chilling his bones, the click of hooves on stone the only sound, Wilson realized he was where he wanted to be. Sitting and rocking on his porch like an old geezer had been okay. He enjoyed the smell of the flowers and the breeze stroking his face. But he had just been biding his time. He remembered his grandfather, wizened and white-haired after a lifetime of farming, sitting on the same rocking chair—though in a tin-roofed shack instead of a modern house—his hands folded over the crook of his cane, nodding and exchanging a pleasant word or two with occasional passers-by. Hell, Grandpa Woodrow had been over eighty! Man of fifty-nine had no business sittin' home and rockin' his life away, able to see or not able to see. Oughta be on a horse, doin' something useful.

Distant booms intruded on his thoughts. The guide stopped, and Wilson pulled his horse up. The easterly wind that had been in their faces at the start was now falling on his right cheek so he sensed they were heading north. The booms were coming from his right, the direction of the road going south from Osh. The guide spoke to him briefly in Kyrgyz. Wilson didn't need to understand his words to know that the Ferghanan attack into Kyrgyzstan had begun. They resumed their ride at a quicker pace and within an hour came to a final halt.

Wilson wondered how to thank his guide, but they he heard him remount. "Thanks!" he yelled at the retreating sound of the horse retracing the path to Verethra Kuh. There was no reply. Instead there was the hand of the pilot on his elbow and instructions in his ear on watching his step going up a ladder. For the first time since his blinding, Wilson felt strong enough to accept help without resentment.

"Sounded like bombs about an hour ago. What's happening?"

"We're not sure. Three jets flew over, but they were too far away to identify. Sounded like they bombed the highway."

"Must be the war startin'. You ready to go?"

"All set. Just strap yourself in and hope we don't get mistaken for an enemy."

*   *   *

News that Ferghanan forces had crossed the Kyrgyz frontier reached Major Jim Brady as the MC-130 bearing his Delta Force team entered Kazakh airspace over the Caspian Sea. After being briefed by the pilot on the substance of the radio message, he rejoined his two-dozen men.

"All right, listen up. Circumstances have changed. The Ferghana Republic has just begun an incursion in strength into Kyrgyzstan south of Kokand. They have deployed armor to block the route between the city of Osh and their area of operation, and they have bombed an alternate route through the mountains. This incursion was unprovoked, and Kyrgyzstan has announced that they consider it an act of war. So we will be dropping into a war zone. Our orders cover this contingency. Lieutenant Mercer's detachment will drop as planned at Kokand. Their mission to locate Dr. Lee Ingalls and release her from detainment continues to have priority. But his detachment now has the additional mission of reinforcing the Marine guard at the U.S. Embassy. Lietuenant Mercer will report to American Ambassador Darla Bane and follow whatever orders the Ambassador may give for the protection of American lives and property.

"The main force will drop with me on the southwest slope of Verethra Kuh. Verethra Kuh is the objective of the Ferghanan incursion, but they will be coming from the north so we anticipate arriving unseen and unexpected. After landing, we will seek to make contact with an American intelligence agent operating somewhere on or near the mountain. He will brief us on the situation. If we fail to make contact, we will consider ourselves to be acting in support of the army of Kyrgyzstan, a friendly nation. We will observe Ferghana army operations and take steps to disrupt those operations to the degree compatible with protection of our own force. Is that clear?"

"Major?"

"Hardaway."

"What's on the mountain?"

"I have no idea, soldier, but we wouldn't be flying 1600 miles to get there if it weren't important."

* * *

On the ground, Colonel Maxim Sverdlov was cautiously pleased with the conduct of operations. The Kyrgyz border post had surrendered without a shot fired, and his four tanks had encountered no opposition in blockading the road from Osh ten miles east of the main column. Reports that the air force had destroyed a bridge on the road from Osh to Sary Tash had been confirmed by aerial reconnaissance. He had sent an advance unit southward to scout the track he intended to take to Verethra Kuh while the rest of his force dug trenches, laid mines, strung barbed wire, and established a defensive perimeter. When a single Kyrgyz plane appeared overhead, two MIGs swooped in from the Kokand airbase and chased it away. The colonel hoped that it would radio back a report that the Ferghanans were digging in and reinforcing at the border crossing. That was where he wanted the Kyrgyz counterattack to be directed.

Though optimistic, Colonel Sverdlov had been schooled in thoroughness of preparation and avoidance of risk-taking. Nevetheless, the advantage of surprise would only last so long, and it was important to keep to his schedule. Radio reports from Kokand informed him of the political maneuverings provoked by his attack: Kyrgyz claims that Ferghana had invaded and calls for an emergency UN Security Council meeting . . . Ferghanan denials of an invasion and declarations that the Kyrgyz were hysterically exaggerating the sending of a small party of border police to apprehend a band of smugglers that had crossed the border and thereby threatened to spread bubonic plague . . . Kyrgyz threats to meet force with force . . . Ferghanan accusations that the Kyrgyz were blowing the humanitarian border police action out of all proportion as an excuse to attack the Ferghana Republic . . . and so on. Everything was going as President Muratbey had predicted.

The only troubling report was a Kyrgyz statement that a Russian plane full of WHO doctors had flown to Kokand to determine whether or not there truly was a plague outbreak in Ferghana, or whether the border closing had been a cover for war preparations. Colonel Sverdlov knew of no Russian plane and was sure none had landed in Kokand. Where, then, had the Russians been flying to?

After assuring himself that the defense of his line of withdrawal was properly secured, the Colonel took his position in the second of the three armored personnel carriers that would push on to Verethra Kuh. With his upper body protruding from the hatch on the roof, he observed with satisfaction the absence of dust from the damp, thawing dirt of the track. With luck, the Kyrgyz airforce would not begin to counterattack for another hour or two. By that time he would be miles away to the south. If they focused on the defensive perimeter at the border and the tank blockade on the road to Osh, they wouldn't think to explore every trail and ravine leading into the mountains.

* * *

The Learjet landed at the lightly used airstrip adjoining a shuttered resort by the shore of Issyk Kul. A joint venture with a Swiss hotel chain, the Grand Hotel Przhevalsk had been one of independent Kyrgyzstan's first experiments in free enterprise. The 100-mile long lake was in a bowl rimmed with snow-capped mountains, and the resort's brochure showed partying jet-set vacationers. But Kyrgyzstan had proved too remote for the luxury trade, and the erratic airline service from Bishkek and Almaty had inconvenienced the few tourists that had ventured to come. Eight months after opening, it had closed its doors, and the town of Przhevalsk had resumed its Soviet era slumber.

Nevertheless, the hotel's airstrip was in excellent condition and was still occasionally used for smuggling goods in and out of Xinjiang. Dan Nielsen knew the airstrip well because he had begun his extracurricular gun running there before switching to Osh, which was better located and operated with less extortionate bribes. So the hop over the mountains from Almaty had been simple, and he was waiting on the runway when Wilson got off the plane.

Acquiring diving gear in the middle of the Tien Shan had been another story. While Dan had been trying without success to pry equipment loose from one of the dozen companies working the Caspian Sea oilfields in western Kazakhstan, his office manager Korkut had taken it upon himself to explore a more obscure resource: the Kazakh Coast Guard. Since Kazakhstan was landlocked, its seashores on the Caspian and Aral seas—actually salt-water lakes—notwithstanding, its seaborne military requirements were negligible. The Ministry of Petroleum rather than the Ministry of Defense paid the Coast Guard's expenses. Its mission was to police the foreign concessionaires operating Kazakhstan's off-shore Caspian oilfields. It had two cutters and five smaller craft. Included among its personnel were a handful of divers.

It was one of the divers, Yevgeny Satlov, who had responded to Korkut's promise of wealth beyond measure. "Borrowing" a diving suit, compressor, and other equipment from the Coast Guard station in Guryev, at the mouth of the Ural River, and recruiting his brother Ivan to pilot a rented plane, he had accomplished the 1100 mile flight to Przhevalsk precisely on schedule and touched down only an hour before the Learjet. Dan Nielsen had paid him $10,000 in American currency on the spot and assured the happy diver that twice the amount would be forthcoming when the job was over, regardless of success or failure.

Yevgeny was standing next to Dan when the pilot helped Wilson off the plane. "The man's blind?"

"He's blind. And we don't know exactly where we're going. Or how deep the dive will be."

"But you pay the money . . . whether he succeeds or fails."

"Correct."

"Good. Let's get to work."

The failed resort's tour boat still functioned on an occasional basis, but primarily for day travelers from Bishkek instead of rich vacationers. Since its season had yet to begin, Dan had had to locate its captain and persuade him charter it for a day. As with Yevgeny, a large quantity of American currency had done the persuading. Yevgeny having already stowed the diving gear, the boat was under way within twenty minutes of the Learjet's touchdown. Once clear of the dock, Wilson instructed the captain to head west. When Dan asked him how he knew where to go, he replied, "It's in my head."

Three quarters of an hour later Wilson told the captain to cut the engines. The boat was standing close to the lake's northern shoreline. The sun glinted brightly off the deep blue waters, and the surrounding mountains looked like a tourist post card. A lead dropped in the water indicated a depth of sixty-five meters.

Yevgeny took Dan aside while Wilson suited up. "It's too deep. Or almost too deep. He should use special gas, but we don't have any. Otherwise, he might get too much nitrogen. Also, it will be very cold. Issyk Kul is a very deep lake fed by mountain streams."

"The man doesn't have a choice," replied Dan with a shrug. "Whatever he's going for, he's only got one shot at it."

"In my village we had a blind madman," replied Yevgeny. "Crazy Paul. As kids we were all afraid of him. But the farmers would hire him to find water. I never saw it myself. They said he did it with a stick."

"We had people like that back in Minnesota, too. Called them dowsers. No one ever knew how they did it."

A shout from Wilson told them he was ready for his helmet. "Keep this position," he told the Captain sternly. "You got a satellite locator?" Dan translated into Russian. The captain nodded. "Good," said Wilson

Over the side and sinking fast, Wilson felt the cold immediately, a different cold from that of his nighttime ride . . . closer, unrelenting, no way to shift his body to fend it off. Wilson forced his body to relax and accept the cold flow through him like a subtle fluid. *I'll live*, he thought. *I'll just live cold.*

As he descended he sensed exactly his location but not his depth. He kept his legs flexed for contact with the spaceship, but his feet hit yielding mud instead of hard metal. He knelt and felt the lake bottom. Under a thick layer of soft silt he could make out a smooth curved surface that matched the image in his mind. Sweeping the silt aside with his hands, he crawled toward the ship's stern. The thought struck him that even if he could see, the silt would be making the water so murky that it would do him little good.

By the time he found the groove of the ship's hatch, and then the panel covering its lock, he was chilled to the bone. He rested a moment before placing his fingers on the lock. When he did, the feel was as familiar as the doorknob of his own front door. The hatch slid open smoothly while Wilson braced himself to avoid being dislodged by the inrush of water. When the entry compartment had flooded, he dropped inside. In accord with the vision Nadir had impressed on his mind, he felt the vibration of pumps stirring to life after a sleep of thousands of years.

Now he had to act quickly. If the hatch closed, it would sever his air hose. He had to override the pumping system to keep the hatch open. He felt for the manual control panel. It was a maze of indentations and protrusions. Opening the interior of the ship to flooding or to the vacuum of space was a possibiliy the designers had worked to avoid, not facilitate. He placed his fingers where they felt right and then stopped to check their location by counting down from the top of the panel and in from its right hand side. Suddenly he felt a new vibration, one not included in his vision. Unseen overhead the hatch began to slide.

His heart pounding, Wilson repositioned his hands, relying this time on feel instead of calculation. He pressed four indentations, waited, pressed four others, waited, then jerked hard on a stick-like protrusion. The vibration overhead stopped. Cautiously he reached up and felt along his airhose and lifeline. They had three inches of play left in the nearly closed hatch opening. It would be enough. Returning to the control panel, he pressed in another coded series and then paused before the final movement that would silence the pumps and open the airlock's inner hatchway. After untold millennia, the waters of Issyk Kul were about to claim the spaceship of a long-dead Inamadzi named Shushna. Wilson gripped one handhold tightly and located another. Then he punched in the final combination and held on for dear life.

The rush of water into the ship went on for several minutes. Only when Wilson could no longer feel the tug of the current on his airhose and lifeline did he release his grip and slowly drop into the ship's interior. What Nadir had been unable to prepare him for was the flotsam thrown into the passageway by the inrush of water. He stepped carefully and felt before him with his hands. But he was as sure of his orientation within the ship as if he would have been walking through his own living room.

The stores compartment had even more floating litter than the passageway, but Wilson knew that the eggs were too heavy to have floated away. He stopped by the bin that contained them and reached inside. Even through his gloves he could tell that their smooth, ovoid surfaces matched the feel Nadir had implanted in his mind. He lifted two eggs and put them carefully in the wire sack attached to his belt. Out of water, they would weigh a hundred pounds each, but at sixty-five meters they were easy to manage.

The medical compartment was harder to find. A large rectangular object stood where its door should be. Wilson walked back and forth several times, wondering whether nitrogen build-up was beginning to cloud his senses. Finally he thought to explore behind the rectangular object with his hand, and there he felt a door handle that matched his interior vision. Unable to muscle the object aside, he finally managed to tip it over, making the upper portion of the door accessible. Exhaustion was rapidly overtaking him. His interior vision was becoming dim.

Once inside the compartment, finding what he was looking for proved mercifully easy. He opened the round door to a tube-like cavity and extracted a smooth cylinder rounded at both ends like a two-foot long capsule of medicine. With the cylinder secured in his sack with the eggs, he clambered back through the doorway.

Puzzlingly he found that he couldn't remember the direction he had been facing when he entered, or which way to proceed along the passageway. He searched his memory for the vision that for almost twenty-four hours had been as vivid in his mind as his first ride on a horse when he was six years old. It had vanished without a trace. Nevertheless, he felt eurphoric. Giddily he started down the passageway and took a turn to his right.

Above, looking over the side of the tour boat, Yevgeny payed out and took in the air hose and lifeline with practiced hands. "He should be coming back now," he said to Dan. "He went to the farthest point, and then started back. Now he's going away again. I think something's wrong. I'm going to call him."

"No, he told us not to. It might disturb his vision."

Deep inside the ship, Wilson decided he didn't need his gloves and ripped them off. He ignored the water leaking into his suit at his wrists. He didn't know when he had felt so wonderful. Maybe he would feel even better if he took off his helmet. In his ear, a voice with a thick Russian accent came from the end of a long, long hallway. "Come up!"

Wilson pondered the words, trying to decide what they meant. Then he felt a tug on his lifeline. As far away as the voice in his ear a voice in his mind spoke the word "nitrogen." Lethargically, Wilson began to move in the direction of his lifeline. He couldn't formulate why, but he had a sense that that was the thing to do. It was hard to put one foot in front of another down the flotsam-obstructed passageway, but eventually he reached a point where his lifeline went straight up. He reached for his belt to undo the heavy wire bag and make himself buoyant, but it was too securely fastened for his ice-cold fingers. Then his hands drifted to his chest and felt the lead weights that were part of his suit. They released at a touch.

Moments later his helmet banged against the hatch above him. He could go no farther. The hatch opening was only six inches wide. Nor did he wish to go farther. He wished only to sleep. Again came a sharp tug on his lifeline, shaking him out of the idyll taking shape in his mind. He reached up along the line and put his hand through the hatch opening. It contacted something that felt vaguely familiar, something he had touched once before. Or was it a thousand times before. His fingers moved instinctively to the proper points on the exterior lock and pressed the indentations. The hatch began to open, and Wilson floated free. Free but no longer conscious.

Yevgeny intercepted him in scuba gear and a wet suit and stopped his too rapid ascent. Ignoring the penetrating cold, he brought the unconscious diver to the surface and helped hoist him aboard. Wilson's lips and fingernails were blue, but he was breathing. His wire bag contained two extremely heavy objects the size and shape of rugby balls and a frost-covered cylinder two feet long.

"What are these?" asked Yevgeny.

"I have no idea," said Dan.

When Wilson opened his eyes twenty minutes later, his lips and fingernails had regained their normal hue. Dan put Yevgeny's question to him.

"Two eggs," said Wilson weakly. "Two eggs and a birth control pill."

Yevgeny asked Dan what he had said. Instead of replying, Dan made a circular movement with his index finger at his temple and shrugged his shoulders.

* * *

In Ferghana, the American MC-130 had come in low over the drop zone east of Kokand allowing Lieutenant Mercer and four men to drop from the wind-shielded rear ramp onto a withered brown sheep pasture. There to meet them in a classic black leather jacket and motorcycle boots was Miguel Espinosa. Within moments the Delta Force team had gathered their chutes and climbed into the embassy bus. A half hour later they were at Darla Bane's walled residence on the eastern fringe of the city receiving a briefing from the Ambassador that matched in ferociousness of language and dedication to mission anything they had ever heard from their colonel.

In the meantime, the MC-130 had completed its mission and dropped the twenty other Delta Force members onto the stony slope just below the snowline on the southwest flank of Verethra Kuh. While his men fanned out and secured their perimeter, Major Jim Brady tried to contact Joseph Engineer, not realizing that the entire bulk of Verethra Kuh was between them. Getting no response, he gave orders for the unit to move cautiously northward in hopes of intersecting the route of the Ferghanan army's advance.

* * *

Wilson rested for two hours under layers of blankets before he felt warm enough for the final leg of his mission. Barely able to stand, he ordered Dan to drive him to the airplane and put him on board. The copilot cover him again with blankets, and he sank into a deep sleep as the Learjet winged its way southward. When the copilot shook him awake, he was having a dream in which the sexy brown-skinned woman his unconscious matched with the voice of Lee Ingalls was wheedling him to do one last favor for her, and he was laughing and teasing her that he wasn't quite sure he was willing to go that far.

"Beacon coming up in about five minutes, Mr. Woodrow," said the copilot.

The memory of an ancient television ad for a donut chain popped into his head. "Time to make the donuts," he murmured.

The copilot had already fastened the eggs and the frosted canister to a second parachute. It made a heavy load. "I'll push this out, and you jump after it."

"No, I want to push it out. Afterward I'll always be able to say I dropped an atomic bomb." A look of shock came over the copilot's face. "Joke," said Wilson with a weak laugh. "Don't mind me. Part that ain't frozen is half crazy. Did I tell you I don't like much jumpin' out of planes?"

"Yes, sir."

"Goin' to be easier blind. Don't have to worry about lookin' down."

"Yes, sir."

A series of metallic noises and Wilson felt a blast of icy wind on his face and hands. The copilot led him to the open door and placed his hands on either side of it. The wind tore at his coat trying to rip him out of the plane.

"There's the flare, sir. Time to go."

Wilson put a foot to the bundle in front of him and gave a hard push. Feeling it disappear through the door, he drew a deep breath and jumped after it. After the nighttime ride through the mountains and the dive in Issyk Kul, the blast of icy wind seemed almost familiar. He counted three seconds before pulling the lanyard as the copilot had instructed him and then felt the reassuring jerk of the parachute opening and arresting his freefall. *Not half bad*, he thought as he floated downward toward the unseen ground. He tried to keep his knees flexed for the impact, but when it came, it took him by surprise. His legs buckled under him, and he rolled in the snow, the wind in his billowing chute still trying to pull him into the unknown. He groped for the shroud lines and managed to collapse the chute. Then he lay on his back in the wet, melting snow and laughed through tears. Pain was shooting up his leg from his left ankle, but what was a little more pain compared with what he had already endured?

At the sound of voices, he yelled and waved his arm. Moments later he felt hands undoing his parachute harness and the voice of Dimitri Park asking if he was all right.

"Think I sprained my ankle," Wilson replied.

* * *

As the last rays of the sun withdrew from the silent mountain, ten Russian mountain troops in white uniforms completed scaling the cliff on the north face of Verethra Kuh. After a technically perfect parachute drop and careful reconnoitering, they had chosen to climb the sheer eastern edge of the cliff instead of the obvious route in the center where a hundred feet from the bottom a ledge gave access to a crevice that extended all the way to the top. When the Ferghanans arrived, they would find no fresh scars on the rock to warn them that someone had made the ascent before them.

The shaft that General Frunze's men had discovered so many years ago was toward the front of the cave and came so close to the walls on either side as to leave only narrow footpaths into the deeper interior. It was perfectly round with sides as smooth as polished granite. Safely past the sheer drop, the Russians shone their lights into the back of the cavern. Crude paintings and engraved designs covered the illuminated walls, but the soldiers ignored them. Under orders to display as little light as possible, they disposed themselves behind sheltering rocks and settled down in the dark to wait for the Ferghanan mountaineers.

At exactly the same time, eighty miles to the east, two truck-loads of Chinese soldiers pulled up to the Kyrgyz border post outside the mud-brick village of Irkeshtam. The Chinese captain informed the bewildered sergeant in command of the post that the Commander of the People's Army in the Province of Xinjiang had personally ordered him to speed to the aid of the valiant Kyrgyz people.

A telephone call from the border guards' shack to the sergeant's superior at the district headquarters of the Border Police in Sary Tash confirmed that Ferghana had, indeed, launched an attack and that the country was at war. The lieutenant in Sary Tash ordered the sergeant to tell the Chinese captain that he should wait at the border until the lieutenant could find out from the Border Police commander in Bishkek whether to allow the trucks to pass. After receiving his orders, the sergeant exited the hut and looked around for the trucks. One of the two privates that made up his unit gestured down the road. The tail lights of the rear truck were just disappearing from sight in the direction of Verethra Kuh.

Chapter Twenty-Two

The Ferghanan base camp was situated in forest two kilometers off the dirt track that flanked Verethra Kuh. Cut brush concealed Sverdlov's armored personnel carriers, and his scouts reported that the ravine leading to the base of the cliff was clear. Radio messages from the border reported airstrikes by Kyrgyz jets, as well as two of them shot down, one by a Ferghanan MIG, the other by ground fire. No mention of the Russian and American paratroopers already on the ground on the northern and southern heights of the mountain. Or of two truck-loads of Chinese troops approaching from the east.

The Colonel addressed his troops. "Today is the most important day in the history of our beloved country. We may not encounter an enemy, but we shall destroy any that we do encounter. We may not learn what happens inside the cave shaft that we are to secure, but we shall protect it from every threat. You are not many, but you are our best. And you have the honor of being the first troops ever equipped with weapons of unimagined effectiveness. When this action is completed and you are back in Kokand, you will be celerbrated as the pioneers of a new army that will make every Ferghanan proud. Today I salute you. Tomorrow the world will salute you."

At first light, the assault team moved up the brush-filled ravine. Scouts carrying green and red weapons flanked the advance. Rolls of heavy gauge steel mesh three feet in diameter slowed the progress because bushes had to be cut away. An experiment with a red weapon fired the brush almost instantly but produced smoke that might alert a passing airplane. The rate of advance slowed further when the brush gave way to a scree of boulders and loose, slippery stones and an increased angle of slope. The two rolls of mesh required four men each to haul them up the sharp incline and maneuver them over and around boulders.

Each hour that passed without a Kyrgyz spotter plane appearing in the clear blue sky buoyed Sverdlov's spirits. A radio report that two of his tanks had been knocked out on the Osh roadblock was not unexpected. Their hulks would still block the road, and they had done good service as decoys. In further good news from the border, no Kyrgyz ground forces had yet found their way to the point of the incursion, though scouts had spotted Kyrgyz helicopters near the village of Iski Naukat, only five miles beyond the destroyed tanks.

Messages from Kokand were no less encouraging. Kyrgyz planes had managed to bomb the capital, but aside from holing the runway at the Kokand airbase, their hits had been random. President Muratbey had echoed Kyrgyzstan's call for an emergency meeting of the United Nations Security Council charging Kyrgyz violations of Ferghana's sovereignty. The next step according to the plan he and Sverdlov had worked out would be for the Ferghanan ambassador to the United Nations to stall Security Council action for half a day and then agree to a ceasefire and withdrawal to the international boundary within forty-eight hours. Given the difference between New York time and Kokand time, that would give Sverdlov twelve hours to spare in making his withdrawal.

By noon the cliff was in sight. The lieutenant assigned to lead the mountaineering team studied the sheer rock face long and intently through binoculars.

"Good news, Colonel. There is a crevice after the first thirty meters that looks like it goes clear to the top. It's going to be an easy climb."

"How long do you estimate?"

"Another two hours to get to the cliff, then two hours to climb it and hoist up the mesh."

"The alien's ship will arrive at 1900 hours. He wants to work at night, though once he's in the cave and down the shaft I can't see that it makes any difference."

"We should be in place in the cave with an hour to spare, sir."

"Excellent, Lieutenant. Let's keep to that schedule."

Sverdlov checked his watch again when they reached the base of the cliff and his men took a fifteen-minute rest. It was precisely 1400 hours and still no sign that his strike team had been spotted by the Kyrgyz. *Uncle Ilya would be proud of me*, he thought. *And so would my father.*

* * *

Thoughts of Colonel Ilya Kramskoy also coursed through the mind of the Russian paratroop commander dug in with ten white-uniformed marksmen in the snowfield northwest of cliff. The Ferghanans were in plain sight far below. A handful were beginning their climb while the others set up a perimeter defense among the boulders at the foot of the cliff.

"It's happening just as Colonel Kramskoy told General Repin it would," he said to his second-in-command as he peered through binoculars. "I wish we knew if our men inside the cave are ready to receive visitors."

"They will be ready, Captain," replied his number two. "You can rely on Lieutenant Andreyev."

* * *

Another set of binoculars observed the uniformed mountaineers climbing the cliff from a rocky crag to the southeast of Colonel Sverdlov's line of approach. Major Jim Brady's Delta Force team had spotted the Ferghanan force as soon as it emerged from the ravine and set its course toward the cliff. Being on higher ground in an area strewn with rocks, the Americans had easily found cover.

"Can you tell what those big round things are that they're hauling?" he asked his second-in-command.

"Look like rolls of cyclone fence, Major."

"Well what do you suppose they're planning to do with those?"

* * *

As invisible to the concealed paratroop units as the Russians and the Americans were to each other and to the Ferghanans at the cliff, a third set of observers looked on and said nothing. Dimitri Park and the Basmachi leader Uli hugged the ground on the mountain's eastern shoulder just over the ridgeline from their camp. They knew from the scout's report that there were white-uniformed Russians somewhere above them in the snowfield, but they could detect no trace of their positions. Dimitri counted the rock-climbers as one by one they began their ascent. When the fifteenth had cleared the base of the cliff with no one following him, he nodded to Uli and the two of them slithered back over the ridgeline until they were out of sight both of the cliff below and the snowfield above.

Back at the camp where the sacrifice had been performed, Dimitri reported to Nadir. "There will be fifteen men in the cave, twenty more defending the base of the cliff. There is a smaller group, probably Russian, up in the snowfield, but they are too far away to do anything in the cave."

Nadir nodded. "To climb up to the cave and enter it unseen is but a simple task for strong Pramodzi god. The rest of you will face the risk of loss of life when joining me inside you clear and guard the shaft, protect me while I drop with Shushna's egg in hand into the giants' hole. But first the men who guard the pathway to the cliff must leave for somewhere else, or else they'll warn the men who've climbed up to the cave. So here's a vital task that needs not might but skill to lead astray the men who wait and guard below."

"I can do that," said Joseph. "I wasn't too sure I could make the climb up the cliff anyway."

Hayes looked at him skeptically. "I wasn't sure you could either, son. But how do you plan to get the guys down below away from the cliff?"

"My radio is the best the NSA can fit into a suitcase. I've been monitoring the radio reports that Dimitri says come from the force holding the border crossing. Since there's been no reply from the people we're looking at, we can assume they're keeping radio silence to avoid being detected by the Kyrgyz. Where they are now they're completely vulnerable to air attack. That means they'll be listening in on any frequencies used by the Kyrgyz army and air force to try to get advance warning of an attack. All I have to do is pretend to be the Kyrgyz army."

Hayes smiled. "Why, that's not a bad idea!"

"I just need to prepare. Before you all sneak down to the cliff, Dimitri and Uli can record some real-sounding stuff for broadcast . . . status reports, air-ground chatter, small unit exchanges, that sort of thing. I'll hike up this shoulder of the mountain with my transmitter so there will be nothing obstructing my signal. Maybe some of the Basmachi can come with me. When I get to a good position, I'll start sending . . . mix in some static, some fweeps, some fadein-fadeout, make it sound genuine. If they've got any smarts at all, they'll figure out that the Kyrgyz army is about to pop in on them and scatter."

"Then what? They're still around the cliff."

"You don't see the beauty of it, Mr. Carpenter. Let me diagram it for you." As everyone watched, Joseph knelt down and drew a triangle in the dirt. "Here are the Ferghanans," he said pointing to one apex. "And here we are." He pointed to a second apex. "Now we don't know exactly where the Russian paratroopers are, but they're somewhere around here"—he drew a circle around the third apex—"east, maybe northeast, of us and definitely northeast of the Ferghanans." Then he marked a point on an extension of the line between the Ferghanans and the Russians. "This is where I'm going to go to broadcast: above the Russians with them between me and the Ferghanans. Once the Ferghanans hear the broadcast and scatter, the Basmachi who go with me will start shooting. They won't even have to aim. All we want to do is get the Ferghanans to start up the mountain along this line. They'll be walking right into a Russian ambush, and the Russians won't dare hold their fire because they'll assume they've been spotted and are under attack."

"But they'll know the shots are coming from above and behind them," observed Dimitri.

"True. But if we quit shooting as soon as the Ferghanans start up the mountain, the Russians will have their hands full defending themselves. Even if they spot us, they probably won't come after us because the bigger danger will be in front of them."

"What if they do come after you?"

"If they do come after us, we run. Either way, it clears the base of the cliff."

"But alerts the Ferghanans in the cave."

"Doesn't make any difference. They'll be prepared for gunfire. That's why they've left the force down below, to protect them in case the Kyrgyz attack. Trust me. This will work."

*   *   *

The telephone rang on President Rejep Muratbey's desk. A glance at his wristwatch told him he had five hours to kill before Bix arrived. He picked up the receiver and was greeted by the voice of Donald Ingalls.

"Hello? Mr. President? This is Donald Ingalls. I'm so sorry to disturb you, but I have some bad news and some good news about our business."

Muratbey frowned. "Go on."

"The bad news is that gems over a certain size cannot normally be placed on the market without a certificate of provenance . . . a piece of paper saying exactly where they come from."

"So. Make paper."

"Yes, I thought of that, but gem dealers are not happy about mines they have never heard of before. They tell me that no mine in the world produces both diamonds and stones like emeralds and saphires. Did you know that?"

"You agreed to sell stones, Mr. Ingalls. You take care of details."

"Well, that's where the good news comes in. As I was looking into the market possibilities for unusual gemstones, I met two very interesting men from Odessa. They're Armenian, and they seem to know how to sell things that are not easily marketed. From what they tell me about their business, they're very strongly committed to free enterprise."

"They are mafia."

"Well now, Mr. President, I don't think so. But the way you use the term mafia over here is very different from the way it's used in the United States. Here it seems as though many of the most far-sighted and innovative businessmen get called mafia. In the United States we only use the term for criminals."

Muratbey smiled. "So you want sell gems through mafia. Go ahead."

"Actually, Mr. President, the gentlemen want to meet you personally. I don't know why, but they're not entirely convinced that you and I are working together. The reason I called was that I wondered whether you might have a few minutes free to say hello to them . . . today."

Muratbey looked again at his watch. "Good. Bring them. You know Kyrgyzstan attacks us. For this reason you stop at gate. I tell guard you come. What are names?"

"Thank you Mr. President. They just want to see you and shake hands. Their names are Mr. Hagopian and Mr. Hovannesian, but also . . ."

"Yes?"

"They have three young men with them. Employees of some sort."

"Bodyguards stay at gate. Only you and the two."

"Yes, of course. Thank you, Mr. President. Thank you very much. We'll be over in an hour."

Muratbey hung up the telephone and drew a keychain from his trouser pocket. He picked a small key and unlocked a deep drawer in his desk. Placing the trinket machine on his blotter, he set it to produce diamonds. *Something to impress the Armenian mafia,* he thought.

Back at Ambassador Bane's residence, Donald Ingalls was trembling with excitement. "I think he bought it! I think he bought it!"

"Of course he bought it," said Darla Bane. "He's an extraordinarily greedy man. And I congratulate you on sounding fawning and obsequious over the phone. You have a gift."

"Only two can go with me. The rest have to stay at the gate."

"No problem," said Lieutenant Mercer. "You get us in to see him without any guards, and Sergeant Maxwell and I can take care of everything."

"They'll search you for weapons."

Sergeant Maxwell, a short, dark man with jet-black hair, chuckled. "We don't need weapons, Mr. Ingalls."

The front door opened, and Miguel Espinosa entered with an enormous armload of clothing. "This is what I've got," he said, spreading the garments out on the furniture. "This is genuine mafia chic. I bought it at Kokand's premier boutique for mafia styles. I only hope I got the sizes right."

"Change quickly," ordered Darla. "Don't keep Muratbey waiting. We don't want him to think about this long enough to call a jeweler and ask questions about marketing gems."

Fifteen minutes later, Donald Ingalls and the five Delta Force members crowded into a black Mercedes sedan hastily borrowed by a gracious and charming Darla Bane from a wealthy neighbor widely rumored to have mafia ties. Five minutes after the car departed the ambassadorial residence, Bane and Espinosa left in Miguel's smaller Mercedes and headed for the Presidential Palace by a different route.

Donald was glad that three of the Delta Force team would have to stay at the gate. The best tailored mafia suit in Kokand couldn't disguise their University of Nebraska linebacker looks, though Donald had been prepared to try to pass them off as Ukrainian thugs. The dark, rapier-thin lieutenant and his swarthy sergeant were another story. Lieutenant Mercer spoke limited Russian, and Donald hoped that no one at the Palace would be too familiar with what an Armenian accent in Russian sounded like.

As they approached the Palace, the Lieutenant leaned out the window and announced who they were. The gate to the courtyard rose smoothly. Donald identified himself to the English-speaking young lady sent from Muratbey's office to escort them and followed her into the Palace followed by the lieutenant and the sergeant. Donald noticed the stares his companions were drawing in their dark suits, mandarin collar white shirts, and sleek Italian loafers. Two attractive female secretaries walked parallel to them on obviously invented errands to check them out more closely, whispering together as they went.

The escort ushered them into the familiar waiting room outside Muratbey's office. Donald gestured that they should sit and wait patiently. Fresh fruit and bottles of seltzer adorned the coffee table, and the walls featured paintings of heroic episodes from Ferghana's history. After a wait of five minutes, the young woman reappeared at a different door and invited them into the presidential presence.

President Muratbey greeted Donald with a Russian-style hug and shook hands with Mr. Hagopian and Mr. Hovannesian. Mr.

Hagopian greeted him formally in Russian; his shorter colleague maintained a surly silence. Beckoning them to sit in the comfortable chairs reserved for official visitors, Muratbey went to his desk before joining them. When he returned, he ceremoniously placed a double handful of exquisite diamonds on the low table before them.

"Wow!" said Sergeant Maxwell.

Muratbey looked at him acutely and then at Donald. "Wow? Wow? Donald, who these men?"

"Mr. President, where is my wife?" retorted Donald explosively.

Muratbey was taken aback by the urgency of Donald's voice. "Your wife? Lee? Why you look for Lee here?"

Donald face contorted with emotion. "Because it was reported that you . . . you took her."

Muratbey laughed merrily. "Me? Who tell you that?"

"Major Dimitri Park," replied Donald.

Muratbey laughed again. "Major Park? Mr. Ingalls, before four days, your wife and Major Park cross border illegally from Ferghana to Kyrgyzstan."

Puzzlement replaced passion in Donald's face. "Lee with Major Park? Are you sure?"

"Yes. Identified at border. Automobile seen in Osh. Major Park not return to duty."

"Then you didn't try to . . . I mean, you didn't have any intention of . . ."

Muratbey smiled and clapped a heavy hand on Donald's shoulder. "Your wife is perfect lady. I am perfect gentleman." Then he looked at the two members of the Armenian mafia who had been following the conversation with bewildered expressions. "Now tell me, who are these two men?"

"I am Arvid Hagopian," said Lieutenant Mercer in Russian, "and this is my business associate Krikor Hovannesian."

"Ah, you understand my English! Tell me, does Bolshoi ballet still perform in February in Odessa?"

No one spoke. Muratbey scooped up his diamonds and retreated to his desk. He placed the diamonds in its broad center drawer and withdrew from it a long, green triangular object that looked a bit like the broken-off handle of a plastic tennis racket. Then he picked up his telephone, gave a brief command in Uzbek, and returned it to its cradle. He looked directly at Lieutenant Mercer. “All American spies here in Kokand? Or some at Verethra Kuh?”

“Where?” said Donald in confusion. The lieutenant maintained a stony-eyed silence.

“Your spies not tell you their mission, Donald. Just use you.”

Suddenly, with astonishing speed, Mercer and Maxwell were on their feet and across the intervening space between the chairs and the desk. Just as fast Muratbey placed his finger in a depression in the side of the long green object and moved it from one to the other of the charging figures. Momentum carried Lieutenant Mercer forward so he lunged against Muratbey’s legs as he fell. Sergeant Maxwell did not quite reach him.

Donald looked down at their steaming bodies in horror.

“Dead,” said Muratbey matter-of-factly. Then he looked up at Donald. “You too,” he said as he again activated the green weapon.

Parked a block from the gate of the Presidential Palace, the first sign Darla Bane and Miguel Espinosa had that something had gone wrong was the sight of the three Delta Force men bolting from the guardhouse by the gate. Then they heard shots. Miguel gunned the engine and drove toward the fleeing men. As he skidded to a halt, they tugged the doors open and piled into the back seat. Miguel executed a screeching one-eighty and laid rubber for half a block down Palace Boulevard.

“Go to the Embassy,” ordered Darla. “It’s American territory.” She looked into the back seat. “What happened?”

“We don’t know,” answered a soldier. “We were sitting on a bench keeping our mouths shut when the phone rang. Then they put their guns on us and told us to stand and face the wall. Archie killed two of them, and we all ran.”

“Which of you is Archie?”

“I am, ma’m,” said a muscular, ham-fisted man in an incongruously meek voice. “Archie Kohler.”

“You did all right, Archie. Don’t worry about it.”

“They won’t have identified the car,” put in Miguel. “They might not come to the Embassy right away.”

“No,” said Darla, “they’ll come. As soon as we get there, tell the marines to break out the heavy weapons.”

"What do you think happened?"

"Happened? I don't know what happened with Muratbey, but I think maybe Darla has fucked up."

Meanwhile, in Muratbey's office, a squad of guards was dragging away the bodies, and a secretary with a fearful look in her eyes was rearranging the toppled furniture. Muratbey himself smiled and reassured them all. "Mafia. They think I am too tough, and they try to assassinate me. But they learn their lesson."

A guard came into the office and stood at attention just inside the door. "The others killed two guards and escaped, Mr. President," he reported. "They were picked up by a man and a woman in a red Mercedes."

"Mercedes. Mafia car. Running like cockroaches. Don't worry about them. They will tell the other mafia how strong President Muratbey is. Remember, we are under attack from the Kyrgyz. This is no time to pay attention to cockroaches. Everyone get back to work." Muratbey looked at his watch: 5:45. He had an hour to restore order and tranquility to the palace before Bix arrived.

Chapter Twenty-Three

At 14,000 feet, Joseph's heart felt near bursting and he gasped for breath as he flopped in the snow. Climbing the smooth expanse of snowfield to get to the position above the Russians that the Basmachi had scouted had looked simple. Should have been simple. The three stocky men accompanying him were barely winded and busied themselves building a snowfort to conceal them from any Russian who might think to turn around and check the slope above him. The one named Ahmet had taken over carrying Joseph's radio. Now he looked impassively at Joseph lying on his back and sucking air and waited patiently for instructions.

Joseph couldn't seem to get a complete breath. He felt sick to his stomach. It was all he could do to indicate the radio's collapsible antenna and watch Ahmet extend it to its full length. Yusuf, another Basmachi, tapped Joseph on the shoulder and handed him a pair of binoculars. Joseph looked where Yusuf pointed. Some three hundred feet below them the white-uniformed Russians were clearly visible stretched on their stomachs in the snow. Their binoculars were pointed at the Ferghanans still farther below. The last of Colonel Sverdlov's rock-climbers were nearing the top of the crevice where the first to arrive had lashed a sturdy block-and-tackle to a boulder and were lowering a rope down the cliff. As soon as one of the rolls of steel mesh was securely attached, the men at the top applied muscle to the rope and slowly, hand over hand, began to hoist the burden up the cliff.

After watching for a few minutes, Joseph resolved that his lungs and heart would simply have to do their jobs. Ignoring the sick feeling pervading his body, he opened his radio case, turned on the power, and fixed the settings of the dials. Then he removed a minirecorder from his pocket and placed it next to the microphone.

At the bottom of the cliff seven hundred feet below, Colonel Sverdlov was gazing intently at the second roll of bombproof mesh edging its way up the cliff. He looked at his watch: 1800 hours—an hour left before the alien ship's arrival. If his force could remain undetected for another ten hours, they would be back in their vehicles heading triumphantly for the border.

"Colonel Sverdlov!" called his radio operator. "Listen to this."

Sverdlov took the earphone and listened carefully to a crackling transmission. Two voices speaking Kyrgyz . . . military voices . . . on the ground, not airborne. "Can you get better reception?"

"I'll try, sir, but the mountain may be blocking the signal."

"In that case, we shouldn't be getting it at all."

"They may be just coming into range, sir. Or possibly it's a reflected signal from farther away. It's strong, but something is interfering."

"Perhaps bad equipment." Sverdlov scanned the heights to the east and west. His position was totally exposed to fire from above where any enemy would have ample concealment.

Unseen among the rocks on the hillside opposite Joseph and the Russians, Major Jim Brady watched intently. "Something's going on," he said to the sergeant behind the neighboring rock. "They're sending out more scouts."

"This way, sir?"

"Three this way, three up the slope on the other side of the cliff."

"Sounds like they haven't seen us."

"Something's spooked them, though."

A radio operator scrambled up behind the colonel in a low crouch. "It's a radio signal, sir. Kyrgyz military frequency."

"Do you know what they're saying?"

"No idea, sir. I speak Russian, but we don't have anybody who knows Kyrgyz."

"What does it sound like?"

"Interference is bad, but it sounds like two ground units. I can make out two voices."

"Can you tell where it's coming from? My god, I hope they're not behind us." Brady looked around the way they had come but could see nothing suspicious up to the snowline.

"I think we're okay, sir. I would guess that the signal is coming from the other side of the Ferghanans."

"From the northeast?" Major Brady examined a map. "There's a town called Gulcha. Could be Kyrgyz troops coming from there."

In his snowfort on the eastern shoulder of Verethra Kuh, Joseph interspersed staccato bursts of speech from the recorder with an imaginative assortment of whines, pops, and crackles. Every couple of minutes he looked through the binoculars. The Ferghanan scouts sent to the southeast had come back in with the picket stationed on that part of the perimeter, and more troops had been dispatched to shore up the defense of the northeastern flank. *All right,* he thought, *you know where we are. Now just come on up the hill.*

Yusuf touched him on the shoulder and directed his attention to the Russian position. Two of the ten soldiers in white had begun to pick their way up the snowfield toward Joseph's position.

"That's not good," said Joseph aloud. He raised his hand and signaled the Basmachi to open fire. Joseph had never heard automatic rifles fired except on television, but the sight of the Russians scrambling for cover reassured him that everyone else knew the sound well. After half a dozen three-round bursts, the Basmachi stopped firing. Through his binoculars Joseph could see a Ferghanan officer pointing to the snowfield on the northeastern shoulder of the mountain and making hand signals to the men nearest the apparent source of attack to return fire. So far, so good.

Down below, Sverdlov wondered at what seemed to be the extreme range of the gunfire. Why had the Kyrgyz tipped off their position so soon? He told his sergeant to pass the word that the fire could be a decoy and to be alert to attack from other directions. Then he instructed his two mortar teams to lob two rounds each onto the snowfield.

The four mortar shells exploded well away from Joseph's position, but one of them landed within fifty yards of the Russians. Joseph could see three of the Russians come together in a huddle. He prayed that they would decide to act as allies of the Kyrgyz mystery force above them and return fire on the Ferghanans. A minute later, the Russian mortars answered back. With full visibility and firing from a commanding height, the Russians placed their first rounds in the midst of the Ferghanans, who scattered like cockroaches for the boulder-strewn slope leading up to the snowfield. Joseph saw two Ferghanans go down. The entire Ferghanan force quickly deployed to face the attack from the northeast. Joseph could see their pickets dodging from rock to rock as they moved up the hillside.

The Russians could see the pickets too and opened fire with their rifles. Within three minutes of the first Basmachi gunshots the Russians and Ferghanans were fully engaged. The Ferghanan mortar-men traced the trajectories of the incoming fire and began to zero in on the Russian position, but the Russian mortars continued to dominate and force Sverdlov's men to stay behind rocks. Joseph shifted his binoculars to look at the mouth of the cave. Several Ferghanan soldiers were observing the exchange of fire, but they soon disappeared inside the cave.

Beyond the ridgeline and out of sight of the action, Lee and Wilson tried to divine what was happening from the rattle of the automatic rifles and the thumps of the mortar explosions. Lee stood and stared up at the snowline. Wilson lay on an air mattress with his left ankle wrapped in an elastic bandage. Three Basmachi had remained at the camp to protect them while Uli and the five others had led Hayes, Dimitri, and the SAS men down the mountain in a wide loop around the Ferghanans' flank, their aim being to approach the cliff from below and behind Sverdlov's defenses. Nadir had silently disappeared.

Though Lee's Kyrgyz was non-existent, the Turkish she had studied in Washington enabled her to communicate slightly with the Basmachi.

"I think Joseph's diversion is working, Wilson. At least if I understand correctly."

Wilson accepted the good news with a grunt. "Let them do what they have to do. You sit back down here. I've got more of Nadir's genetic stuff to tell you, and I want to get through it before it slips my mind."

Lee sat back down with a mixed feeling of fascination and dread. What Wilson was passing on to her was a part of the instantaneous enlightenment he had experienced when Nadir took his hands, a part he had not revealed to anyone else.

Meanwhile, Colonel Sverdlov coolly appraised his position from the shelter of a jagged boulder sticking out of the rocky scree. The Kyrgyz had the advantage of the high ground and near invisibility in the snowfield, but their numbers seemed suspiciously small—two mortars and possibly a half dozen riflemen. If they were sent from Gulcha or Sary Tash, why were they so few? Scarcely more than a scouting party. And why did the radio messages carry only two voices? Were they border police who didn't know how to call in airstrikes? Or perhaps the Kyrgyz airforce was too busy elsewhere to spare planes for Verethra Kuh. He had to assume that air attacks were on their way. And this meant that he would have to take out the Kyrgyz spotters as quickly as possible. He beckoned to six of his men who were sheltering near him. Three carried long triangular green weapons, and three carried red.

"We'll keep their heads down with the mortars. You work your way onto their right flank and take them out." The six nodded and slipped away.

Still breathless, Joseph looked with fascination on what his plan had set in motion. The entire Ferghanan force had scattered from the base of the cliff and taken cover on the northeastern slope. Four Ferghanan bodies lay sprawled on the ground. Though the initial plan had been simply to provoke a firefight between the Russians and the Ferghanans, Joseph decided to continue broadcasting in spurts until Hayes and Dimitri had made it up the cliff and then slip away to join Lee and Wilson. The more confused the Russians and Ferghanans were about who they were shooting at, the less likely they were to notice Nadir's team creeping toward the cliff behind their backs.

The exchange of fire was no less puzzling when viewed by the Delta Force team from the opposite slope. The party under attack was obvious, the Ferghanan troops that had shifted their position from a cluster at the foot of the cliff to a defense line strung out along their left flank. Who the attackers were was less obvious, particularly since they were almost invisible in white uniforms. Major Brady was surprised that the Kyrgyz army would just happen to have a rapid response unit at the ready prepared to fight in a snowfield. He was even more surprised that the unit had opened fire from long range instead of keeping their presence secret and acting as spotters for air strikes. But topping these surprises was the arrival of a dozen men at the top of the ravine Ferghanan strike force had used to gain access to the cliff. Rather than reinforcements, the dozen men who emerged from the brush onto the scree were moving stealthily from boulder to boulder in an obvious effort to keep the Ferghanans from seeing them. Seven looked like civilians in rugged winter clothes; the other five had on what seemed to be commando outfits.

As Brady watched, six of the men took up concealed positions below and behind the Ferghanan firing line. He guessed that they were a part of the unit in the snowfield sent to flank the Ferghanans and catch them in a crossfire. But he put his guess on hold when he saw the other six move on to the base of the cliff. Were the first half dozen, now hunkered down and holding their fire, there to protect the ones at the cliff? And if so, why? The answer to these questions became apparent when the group at the cliff, which included the five wearing commando gear, deployed ropes and began to climb.

The hand of his sergeant on his elbow attracted the Brady's attention, and he retrained his binoculars in the direction the sergeant pointed to. Beyond and beneath a huge stone outcropping on the end of the cliff farthest from the shooting, a lone figure in summer civilian clothes and a full beard was climbing a rock surface that looked as smooth and featurless as a concrete wall. Brady had never seen anyone climb in such a fashion. Without ropes or pitons, and seemingly with only minimal use of one leg, he appeared from their vantage point to be climbing with the ease and agility of a gecko walking up a vertical wall. Brady wondered how he would manage the overhang, but it proved no obstacle as he scaled it with ease. And apparently in blatant defiance of the law of gravity.

Brady looked at his sergeant, who shrugged his shoulders. "Beats me, sir. I didn't think people could do that."

"They can't, sergeant," said Brady. With the climber now out of sight somewhere near the cave mouth, Brady and the sergeant returned to observing the firefight.

* * *

Muratbey waited impatiently in the courtyard of the Presidential Palace. Bix was due. At one level, his mind was a jumble of riddles: Why had Park and Lee gone to Kyrgyzstan? Was it connected to the raid on Verethra Kuh? Why had Park told the Americans he had kidnapped Lee? Why had the Americans sent agents to his office? Why had Donald told the American officials about their jewel deal? What would happen when the three Americans he had fried failed to return from the Palace?

At another level, however, he was composed: Bix would arrive momentarily. They would fly to Verethra Kuh. Colonel Sverdlov would protect the shaft in the cave from pramodzi. Bix would fix his machine and be grateful for Muratbey's protection. And then Bix would fly away forever leaving Muratbey with the greatest treasure in the history of the world—including eggs to protect him from the Americans, Russians, and Chinese. In his mind's eye, each event led ineluctably to the next. And he could see beyond to a moment not far in the future when the world's leaders would be at his feet begging to share in the alien technology. The historical memory of great Central Asian heroes—Attila, Genghis Khan, Tamerlane—stirred his blood. But Muratbey the Great would conquer the modern way, conquer by technology and economic power, not by rivers of blood and pyramids of skulls . . . except, unfortunately, for Nukus.

Muratbey was cursing the memory of Asshole Vahidoglu, whom he saw as virtually compelling him to destroy Nukus, when Bix's spherical ship dropped lightly out of the dusk and settled in the courtyard. Muratbey entered the moment the door opened and made his way to the control room. Bix was reclining in his usual posture of relaxation with Frak clinging to his shoulder.

"Everything on schedule?" said Frak lightly.

"Of course. We have no direct report because radio silence. But plan was perfect."

"Excellent. I suggest you put on a blob suit."

"Blob suit?"

"I explained that to you before. When you activate it, it forms a protective shield around you. It's very effective." Bix was proffering a small, clear package.

Muratbey removed the blob suit from its envelope and unfolded it. It reminded him of a plastic raincoat he had bought in Moscow that had been so brittle that it cracked along a seam the first time he used it. The clear film of the blob suit proved finer and softer. Indeed, despite being designed to Inamadzi proportions, it seemed to melt into his clothes and become unnoticeable as soon as he had it on.

"It doesn't protect head."

"Yes, it does," said Frak. "When it inflates, it closes at the top."

"How I make work?"

"It works automatically. Your mind activates it when you become frightened. It's almost instantaneous. Then when you stop fearing, it contracts."

Murabey grunted. Through a window he saw the tops of mountains zipping by though he had barely perceived the ship's taking off. A few minutes later, he looked at his watch. It read exactly seven o'clock. Bix was looking intently through the window.

"There is fighting," said Frak.

Muratbey crowded next to Bix and looked out. The fading light made details difficult to discern, but the flash of explosions showed that a battle was under way. But the explosions were on the slope that flanked the approach to the cliff on the north and in the snowfield above. The cave area itself looked perfectly peaceful. According to plan, flares outlined the cliff-top ledge to guide Bix's approach, and the cave mouth was brightly lit. The few bodies lying on the ground looked to be wearing Ferghanan uniforms, but they were strewn around the bottom of the cliff.

"Plan is perfect," Muratbey announced. "Cave ready for Bix to repair machine. Army protecting Bix from pramodzi." To himself he wondered who was firing at whom.

* * *

Joseph gaped in awe at the spherical black craft that approached at high speed, then in a matter of moments slowed to an almost stationary hover at the top of the cliff. When it disappeared inside the cave, he redirected his binoculars to the bottom of the cliff.

Hayes' SAS mercenaries had begun their ascent, moving rapidly on the ropes and pitons left by the Ferghanans. It was time for another burst of decoy broadcasts to ensure that the Ferghanans did not turn around and take note of what was happening on the shadowy cliff face below and behind them.

While Joseph worked with his recorder and radio, his Basmachi companions followed the action below with concern. Finally Ahmet crawled into Joseph's snowfort and tugged his arm. Joseph poked his head out from behind the snow wall and looked down the slope. Six Ferghanan soldiers were above the snowline and moving at an angle that would give them a firing position on the Russians' flank. Though the twilight made colors difficult to distinguish, all six appeared to be carrying brightly colored red or green weapons, with their customary assault rifles slung on their backs. Unaware of their approach, the Russians were concentrating their fire on the Ferghanan troops concealed in the rocks below them.

Suddenly one of the Russian mortars exploded spectacularly, as if all of its ammunition had detonated at once. Though one soldier in the Ferghanan flanking detachment had stood up and pointed his red weapon, Joseph had seen or heard nothing to indicate he had fired it. Now the other Ferghanan flankers were standing too and walking forward, sweeping their colored weapons through narrow arcs directed toward the Russian position, from which all firing had abruptly ceased.

Fearful that the stoppage of incoming fire from the Russian position might cause the Ferghanans below to come out of hiding and look around them, Joseph returned his attention to the cliff. Alf, Laurence, and the other two SAS men were almost invisible in the crevice and had almost reached the ledge in front of the cave. Dimitri and Hayes, identifiable by their shaven heads, were still at the bottom of the cliff, apparently waiting for the mercenaries to use the block-and-tackle to help them climb. Joseph put down his binoculars and returned to the radio. With the Russians eliminated, keeping the Ferghanans' distracted by an enemy in some other direction was more important than ever. He fast-forwarded the tape to the command Dimitri had told him to save for last.

At the foot of the slope, Colonel Sverdlov was elated by the flare signal from his flanking party that the enemy in the snowfield had been eliminated. *With the red and green guns we will conquer the world*, he thought as he cautiously extended his head above the rock to take a look. Suddenly the radio on the back of the soldier beside him squawked loudly. “All units attack! All units attack!” it said in the clearest signal yet received. Sverdlov was puzzled. What units? Through the entire fight only two voices had been distinguishable on the radio, and now those who had been shooting at him were dead or captured.

“We’re breaking radio silence,” he said to the radioman. “Tell Sergeant Akbulut to take his men all the way to the ridgeline and see if there are other enemy troops. I think a small group has bluffed us.”

At the same moment, Alf pulled himself up enough to look cautiously over the lip of the cliff. Laurence was right beside him. Their two comrades only a few feet below. Guns at the ready, Alf and Laurence surveyed the smooth, flare-lit ledge. Both the ledge and the cave mouth looked unguarded. As they crept onto the ledge, they heard gunfire coming from inside the cave. Sending the other two men to flank the cave entrance, Alf and Laurence manned the block-and-tackle. Two jerks on the rope from below signalled that Hayes was ready to climb.

“Why don’t we just ‘aul ‘im up like a sacka coal?” said Laurence.

“Wants to climb the bloody cliff himself. Thinks it’ll make him feel young again. Just wants us to belay him.”

“Bloody ‘ell! What choice ‘as ‘e got now? I say ‘e’s a sacka coal.”

Alf listened to the gunfire in the cave intensifying. “Sack of coal it is. Let’s give a heave.”

Hayes was already twenty feet up the sheer part of the cliff with only eighty feet to go before the crevice . . . and then another 600 feet of climbing to get to the top. Suddenly the tension on his belaying harness tightened and he was being pulled free of the rock face. Dangling at the end of the rope, he began to rise. *Thank the lord for smart men who know when to disobey orders,* he thought. Dimitri nodded with satisfaction as Hayes disappeared into the gloom. Fat, obstinate old man had no business trying to scale a cliff at an altitude of 14,000 feet.

Up in the snowfield, the growing darkness made what was happening on the cliff invisible even though Joseph had spotted the SAS team move onto the well-lit ledge outside the cave. Hoping that he had done enough to keep Dimitri and Hayes from being detected, he packed up his radio. Closer to hand, the Basmachi, well hidden in the snow, kept their guns trained on the six Ferghanan silhouettes cautiously moving up toward the ridgeline from the Russian position. Joseph signalled he was ready to leave, but Ahmet motioned him to keep down. The Ferghanans were only thirty meters away and heading straight for them in a widely spread line. Joseph grasped that it was too late to try to run. Ahmet cocked a pistol and offered it to him. A passionate opponent of gun ownership, Joseph had never held a loaded weapon, but he quickly revised his philosophy.

He started to edge forward to what looked like a better firing position but stopped when Yusuf put a heavy hand on his shoulder. Joseph saw the grim-faced Basmachi cup a hand to his ear. He held his breath and listened. The Ferghanans were close. He could hear the chink of their equipment and the crunch of their boots. But was there another sound? From another direction?

Ahmet and Yusuf were peering back over their shoulders trying to penetrate the gloom. Joseph followed their look. He could see nothing on the shoulder of the mountain but unbroken snow and the black eastern sky beyond. Yet there seemed to be something moving in his peripheral vision. He moved his head slightly. There it was again. And again. Then he could see it all—a party of perhaps twenty men moving toward them through the snow. After a few moments he could make out that they were in uniform.

"Chin," whispered Ahmet.

Joseph wondered for a moment what he meant until an idea dawned on him. "Chinese? Chin? Chinese?"

Ahmet nodded.

The silence lasted for another half minute until the leading group of the Chinese silhouettes simultaneously slumped to the ground for no apparent reason. There was a moment's pause, and then a world of gunfire exploded in Joseph's ears. The Basmachi were crawling on their bellies out of the snowfort and beckoning Joseph to follow. When they had gone about ten yards, they helped Joseph roll himself into a ball around his radio case and began to cover him with snow. Joseph could see nothing, but he could hear the gunfire and the yells of the Chinese troops coming closer and closer. He hugged his radio to his chest and prayed ardently to Lord Ganesh, the elephant-headed guarantor of successful enterprise.

The resumption of gunfire in the snowfield took Colonel Sverdlov by surprise. He could see nothing, but apparently the radio messages had not been a bluff. Other units were attacking. He had also heard gunfire from the cave. He sent three scouts to reconnoiter his rear and began to consider the contingency of withdrawing his men under fire.

Dangling from a harness halfway up the cliff, Dimitri saw a Ferghanan scout walk directly past a Basmachi hidden among the rocks below and approach the base of the cliff. Feeling as helpless as a target in a shooting gallery, he kept his pistol trained on the man and hoped that the Basmachi was doing the same. He held his breath waiting for the scout to look up. Seconds passed. He continued to rise steadily and silently. A sudden burst of renewed firing from the cave caught the scout's attention, but Dimitri's dangling form was now lost in the dark. Then he felt strong arms grab his harness and pull him onto the ledge.

Deep inside the cave a battle was raging. The arrival of Bix's ship had gone smoothly. The huge sphere had hovered over the shaft and then sunk downward, just fitting inside its smooth walls. As soon as it disappeared below the cave's floor, Lieutenant Yeshilalp, the commander of the rock-climbers, ordered his men to stop gawking and secure the bombproof mesh. They had already pounded pitons into the rocky floor like tent pegs, so as a half dozen men manhandled the heavy mesh across the opening, four others hooked the ends of cables woven through the mesh to the pitons and tightened the slack with turnbuckles.

Stiff and chilled from an hour crouching behind a boulder in the dim recesses of the cave, Lieutenant Alexander Andreyev saw the Ferghanan actions as the answer to a tactical problem that had haunted the Russian paratroopers since they had climbed the cliff. With no place to wait in ambush at the cave mouth or on the ledge outside, the Russians had been forced to move deep into the cave and hide among the rocks beyond the shaft. This left the narrow ledges on either side of the shaft their only way out, or their pathways to plummeting over the edge. The Ferghanan plan, conveyed to General Repin by Colonel Kramskoy, had accurately put the number of Ferghanan mountaineers at fifteen. Andreyev had ten and a near certainty of taking the Ferghanans by surprise. However, once they hid among the rocks, the possibility of being trapped behind the yawning shaft became only too real. But now the Ferghanans had covered the shaft with a mesh surface strong enough to run across. There would be no better time to spring his ambush. He raised his arm and dropped it.

The first Russian fusilade cut down six Ferghanans and scattered the rest. Within moments the two sides were exchanging bursts of gunfire with the dark and boulders of the inner cave giving the Russians the tactical advantage. Bullets pinged and thwocked against the cave walls, the sounds echoing and reechoing from the high stone vault of the ceiling. Grenade explosions compounded the din.

Lieutenant Yeshilalp sprawled on the cave floor near its mouth with the six of his soldiers equipped with red and green weapons. Assigned to guard the ledge outside and prevent any enemy cliff-climbing, they had escaped the first Russian attack. The Lieutenant was uncertain what to do. Since the arms tests in Kokand hadn't included shooting at rock walls, he was reluctant to waste power trying to find out what the new weapons might do against the well-shielded Russians.

"We have to bring them into the open," said Yeshilalp quietly during a pause in the gunfire. "Any ideas?" The soldiers looked at one another and then began to talk at once.

"Maybe we should leave the cave," ventured one.

"Don't be stupid. If we leave, they can attack the alien."

"If we cut the mesh, they'll be trapped," said a second.

"Don't be stupid," whispered a third. "They're trapped now. We don't want them trapped. We want them out in the open. Cutting the mesh would make it easier for them to attack the alien."

"But we could pretend to cut the mesh," said Yeshilalp slowly, thinking as he spoke. "They didn't fire until we put the mesh in place. Maybe they felt trapped, and the mesh gave them an avenue of attack. If they think we're cutting the mesh, they may charge to protect their escape route."

The soldiers looked at one another and then at the Lieutenant. “Sir,” ventured the one who had suggested cutting the mesh, “whoever tries to get to the mesh will be killed. There’s no cover.”

“No. But the red weapons melt metal. We can fire from here, hit one piton at a time. Who’s the best marksman?”

The youngest-looking member of the group replied. “I am, sir.”

“Your name?”

“Nur Bashkurt, sir.”

“Good.” Yeshilalp looked the boy calmly in the eye. “Nur, remember: Our mission is to cover the shaft and protect it so don’t cut through any cables. Just try to hit a single piton on the far side. Do you think you can do it?”

The soldier nodded. The Lieutenant signalled his men to cease firing.

The red weapon had no evident aiming system, but the young soldier rested one of its flat sides on his shoulder, leaned his head to the side on top of it, and sighted down its long axis. Suddenly there was a sharp ping from beyond the shaft.

“Great shot. Now another one,” said the Lieutenant.

A second ping. The gunfire from deep in the cave stopped. Yeshilalp motioned his men to be ready. “Let the first three cross the mesh,” he whispered.

Lieutenant Alexander Andreyev made a decision. He motioned three of his men forward. At his signal they sprang from their rock cover and ran for the mesh while Andreyev and the others provided covering fire. Once across the mesh, they flattened themselves on the ground in firing position. Andreyev waited. No reaction. He signalled the second group while the rest poured covering fire toward the front of the cave. As the second trio reached the center of the mesh, they collapsed simultaneously though no shots had been fired. In the eerie white light of the flares at the cave’s mouth, Andreyev could see what looked like steam rising from their bodies . . . and from the prostrate bodies of the first three men, whose guns were now silent.

From the ledge in front of the cave, Hayes, Dimitri, and the SAS mercenaries were hard put to follow the course of the battle without being seen or shot by accident. Something had clearly happened, however. First the nearer shooters had suspended their fire; then the ones from deeper inside the cave had done the same. Now everything was quiet.

Alf and Laurence cautiously poked their heads around the edge of the cave mouth. Nine Ferghanan soldiers were prone on the cave floor or using irregularities in its walls to shield themselves from whoever was hidden deeper inside. Their unprotected backs were toward the entrance. The SAS men looked at one another, each trying to divine what the other was thinking about shooting men in the back.

Dimitri crept up beside Alf and took a look. Alf caught his eye and gave the slightest shake of his head. *Leave the dirty work to the Korean*, thought Dimitri. Stepping into the cave mouth, he opened up with his assault rifle on full automatic. Alf joined in. Their forty-round magazines emptied in six seconds leaving all nine Ferghanans collapsed on the ground. One by one the SAS men slipped around the corners of the entrance, stepped over the motionless bodies, and took up the same sheltered positions the Ferghanans had been using.

Dimitri joined Alf behind a rocky projection. "Whoever's back there isn't going to come out," he said softly, "and rifles and grenades aren't going to get them."

Alf nodded and motioned to one of his men carrying a bulky weapon on his back. The man swiftly assembled its two parts and brought it into firing position. Rocket exhaust whooshed out the cave entrance where Hayes was waiting impatiently. The anti-tank missile impacted thunderously against the wall of engraved figures at the end of the cave spraying shrapnel in all directions. Lieutenant Andreyev and his three remaining men died instantly.

Chapter Twenty-Four

Tension mounted at the U.S. Embassy as the hours ticked by. The Marine guard and the three remaining Delta Force commandos stayed armed and alert, but life went on as usual on the streets of Kokand.

Miguel Espinosa paced back and forth chain-smoking cigarettes. "Why don't they do something? We tried to arrest him in his own office. Isn't that a crime?" Darla Bane had her elbows on her desk and rested her chin on her cupped hands. "Not even a phone call. It's uncanny." The office clock read eight o'clock. More than two hours had elapsed since the Mercedes had screeched into the diplomatic sanctuary of the embassy driveway. "If Muratbey protested to D.C., at least *they* should have called us."

"What if Muratbey didn't tell anyone?" said Darla, breaking a half hour of dejected silence.

"You think he turned the tables on them and arrested them instead of them arresting him? How could that happen without anyone knowing?"

"We sent them in as mafia. Maybe he arrested them as mafia."

"And not figure out they were American? How would that be possible? Ingalls is American, and the one who knew Russian couldn't have fooled anyone for five minutes."

"Lieutenant Mercer."

"Right. Lieutenant Mercer."

Darla fell silent again for five minutes. "Maybe they're dead and nobody but Muratbey knew they were American. Call his secretary."

"What?"

"You know her, Mike. Call her."

"Yasmin? What would I say?"

"Don't tell me you don't know how to talk to a woman, Mike. Ask her for an appointment for me to meet with the president. See what she says." She pushed her telephone across the desk.

Miguel looked dubiously at his boss as he punched in the number. Then his face lit up with a toothy smile. "Hello? Yasmin? It's Mike . . . Mike Espinosa from the American Embassy. How are you?" His smile withered as he listened. "I'm sorry to hear that. Really sorry. I hope she's going to be all right." He mouthed the words "her mother" to Darla. "If she needs specialized medical care, perhaps the Embassy could make arrangements for her to go to the United States." Pause. "No, it's not impossible. We can give her a visa in twenty minutes, and Ambassador Bane can use funds from her humanitarian aid account to pay for it." He winked at Darla's look of disbelief. "No, I don't think she would mind at all. She knows how much the president relies on you." Pause. "I know it's a hard job, but a lot of people in the diplomatic community say you're the only thing keeping the palace going." Pause. "Yes they do. I mean that." Pause. "By the way, the reason I'm calling is to see whether the president would have space on his calendar to receive Ambassador Bane tomorrow." Pause. "Yasmin. Yasmin, don't be like that. He has to have *some* time free *some* day." Pause. Espinosa frowned. In a lower, conspiratorial voice: "No! Is it true? What happened?" Pause. "How terrible! Was he hurt? Where is he now? Or can't you tell me." Pause. "Really? You saw it? That's really incredible. But thank God he's safe. Yasmin, when you hear from him, ask him if there's anything the U.S. government can do. And be sure to call and let me know when he gets back." Pause. "Yes, terrorism is certainly an awful thing. Thank you, Yasmin. Thank you so much. You're a treasure." Pause. "No, I don't think so." Pause. "Because I'm with the Ambassador." Pause. "Me to. And tell Mama I hope she feels better. Bye, Yasmin."

Darla looked at her political officer. “She spilled state secrets,” she said matter-of-factly.

“How could you tell?”

“Your face. Have you and Yasmin been fooling around?”

“In her dreams.”

“Have you been helping the dreams along?”

“Maybe a little.”

“Maybe a lot.”

“Don’t you want to know what I found out?”

“Shoot.”

“Three mafia members tried to assassinate the president in his own office, but he killed them instead because he is the most heroic man Yasmin has ever known.”

“So they’re dead.”

“She saw the bodies being dragged out.”

“The bastard. Where is he now?”

“This you will love. He left the palace in a flying saucer that landed in the parking lot. All appointments cancelled forever.”

Darla was speechless. Finally she sighed and said, “This will make one helluva cable to the Secretary.”

“So what should we do?”

Darla thought. “The first thing is to notify the Delta Force commander . . .”

“Major Brady.”

“ . . . that he’s lost two men and the other three are safe here. Though I’m not sure how long our present situation is going to hold since Muratbey surely can’t keep this fiction of a mafia attack going indefinitely. Do we have a communication protocol for Delta Force?” Miguel nodded. “Include in the message that Lee Ingalls’ husband is dead too. If they should encounter her, they should know that. Tell them he died trying to rescue her.”

“Got it. What next?”

“Next? Next the two of us try to write a cable that will not get us fired, arrested, or ridiculed as lunatic UFOers. And tell the Marines to keep locked and loaded.”

* * *

Why Joseph had failed to flick off his radio's power switch he was never able to understand so he later attributed it to the intervention of the Lord Ganesh. The crunch of Chinese boots running past where he was buried in the snow had faded into the distance, and he had ventured to lift his head to look around. Suddenly he heard tinny radio sounds coming faintly through the radio's suitcase. He listened in puzzlement until he realized that the incoming transmission had to be on the NSA's default emergency frequency.

Cautiously he raised his head further. A half moon just becoming visible over the shoulder of the mountain provided enough raking light for him to make out a dozen dark forms lying motionless in the distance. Desultory gunfire sounded from the slope well below him. He assumed that the Russians had been eliminated, but whether the fresh shooting was coming from Ferghanans or Chinese he couldn't tell. Nor did he care, for up in the snowfield everything was deathly still.

As quietly as possible he opened the radio case and slipped on his earphones. The message being repeated was in clear and in English: "Hawthorne, this is Melville. Hawthorne, this is Melville. Two chapters of submitted manuscript lost. Two chapters of submitted manuscript lost. Heroic demise of doctor's spouse a bad ending. Heroic demise of doctor's spouse a bad ending. Villain left unpunished. Villain left unpunished. Contact your agent and renegotiate contract. Contact your agent and renegotiate contract."

Joseph suppressed a laugh, then felt guilty for instinctively thinking that Lee would be better off without her wayward spouse. Chasing that thought was a realization that somewhere within range of the broadcast there was an American military unit trying to get in touch with him. *But not trying very hard*, he thought. Then he reminded himself that a gunbattle had been raging for well over an hour and that a radio broadcast from a hidden, uninvolved force could have spelled disaster for both the sender and receiver.

His mind worked feverishly. Where were the Americans? Were they close enough to help? Could they help? He crawled forward to get a better view of the scene below. As he did so, two human shapes emerged from the snow nearby. After a moment of panic, he recognized Ahmet and Yusuf by their clothes.

Even in the moonlight nothing could be discerned of the Chinese and Ferghanan positions. The occasional bursts of fire testified more to the wariness of the two forces than their actual ability to make out targets. The only lights came from the flares in the entrance of the cave, which looked like the gaping maw of a mountain-sized giant whose head was silhouetted against the moonlit sky. There was no way of telling who was in control inside; but as matters stood, it was clear that anyone trying to descend the cliff would probably be picked off easily by the remaining Ferghanans. Joseph's plan for decoying the Ferghanans' away from the cliff had addressed the problem of getting Hayes and Dimitri into the cave, not getting them out.

Aware that his own escape route back to the camp where Lee and Wilson were waiting was now clear, Joseph decided on a final broadcast. Going back to the radio, he extended its antenna to its full length. Then he thought for a while composing his message. Deciding that the American commander had probably not majored in American literature, he broadcast:

"Hawthorne, this is your agent. Hawthorne, this is your agent. New contract terms. New contract terms. Men in cave friendly. Men in cave friendly. Men below unfriendly. Men below unfriendly. Do what you can. Do what you can."

Joseph repeated the message four times. Then he collapsed his antenna, closed the radio, and stole off into the night where his shadow converged with those of the Basmachi.

Though trained to squat in mud or ice for days, if necessary, to carry out his mission, Major Brady felt like a pit bull let off its leash as soon as he heard Joseph's broadcast. "Moby Dick, meet Captain Ahab," he muttered under his breath as he scanned the scene below with night vision goggles. He had earlier identified the rocky shelter that seemed to be serving as a command post, and now he reassured himself that the situation was unchanged. He turned to the soldier squatting beside his one mortar.

"Corporal, you see the tent-shaped bunch of rocks about fifteen degrees to the left of the cliff and a third of the way up the slope?"

"Yes, sir."

"Tell me you can put your first two within a twenty meter radius of it."

He could see the corporal smile. "Would ten meters be better, sir?"

"Fire when you're ready. Everyone else, hold your fire."

Crouching behind the rocks, Colonel Sverdlov heard the explosion of the first mortar round as the crack of doom. He had already decided that the men in the cave were either dead or had done their job. So now they were expendable since the likelihood of getting them back down the cliff seemed remote. The second mortar shell made up his mind.

"Sergeant, pass the word. We're pulling out. You keep three men. Spread them out. Take a shot occasionally. Make them think we're still here. It's 2100. Pull out at 2145. I'll wait one hour for you at the vehicles. If you don't meet us there, head for the border."

Suppressed jubilation spread quietly among the American observers. The retreat of whomever it was they had fired at was quick and orderly. Brady tipped his hat mentally to the enemy commander for making a correct and prompt decision. "Gentlemen, we've won the war," he announced softly to his troops.

On the opposite slope, the Chinese troops from Kashghar had also observed the unexpected explosion of the two American mortar shells. Captain Lin Wu-tang assessed his situation. Fifteen of his thirty-eight men were dead, killed by soundless, flashless weapons he had never seen before. Ten Russians wearing white uniforms were dead in the snow. His men had killed six Ferghanan troops and collected their strange red and green weapons. He estimated the number of Ferghanan invaders remaining below at fewer than thirty. But he had no idea who was lobbing mortar shells into their position. If it was the Kyrgyz army, he could contact them as an ally helping them out in the face of Ferghanan invasion. But he could not imagine how such a Kyrgyz force could have gotten to where the mortar shells were coming from without passing his trucks on the road from Sary Tash. After weighing the gains of his mission in the form of the new weapons he'd captured against possible further losses in an encounter with an inidentified force equipped with mortars, he made his decision.

As quietly and efficiently as the Ferghanans, the Chinese stole back up the mountainside, collected their dead, and made their way down the far side of the mountain to their trucks and the road back to Kashghar.

* * *

The toll of dead inside the cave was ten Russians and fifteen Ferghanans. While two SAS men kept watch on the ledge outside, Alf and Laurence examined the long triangular devices they collected from the Ferghanan bodies. Laurence cautiously pointed a red one at a Russian corpse and depressed the button in its side. They heard no sound, but the dead man's metal belt buckle glowed red and the rounds in the magazine of the AK47 lying beside him exploded. Next he tried a green one but stopped abruptly when he smelled cooking flesh.

Alf and Laurence squatted down and pondered the curious weapons while Dimitri and Hayes sat together in silence and waited for Nadir. The nuclear eggs they had winched up the cliff were beside them, but without Nadir they had no notion of how to use them.

"Did anyone see him climb the cliff?" asked Hayes. Shaking heads all around. "Do you suppose he made it?" he said to Dimitri. Dimitri shrugged his shoulders.

And then he was there, standing toward the back of the cave on the far side of the shaft, familiarly pot-bellied but with his hair and beard radiating the flame-like glow they had all seen at the sacrifice.

"I went to see the wall where images were drawn depicting men and gods. They told the tale of how, with ally Kutsa brave, I Inamadzi killed, the giant Shushna called. 'Tis sad the wall is gone, destroyed by guns and bombs. When finished is our task, when Bix has met his death, when giants's scheme is crushed, then will I seal this cave, this place of so much woe." He picked up a hundred-pound egg with one hand and did something to it. "This egg will do the deed in sixty minutes time. So those whose task is done, who've fought by Indra's side, who by their sacrifice did strengthen Indra's his mind, should take their leave and go, seek shelter from the egg. And in your later lives, remember to repeat the tale of Indra great, the tale of noble

Hayes, who Kutsa-like did team with last immortal god to wage the final war to save all humankind." Nadir pointed at the bombproof steel mesh covering the shaft. "Now burn this flimsy cloth and open up the shaft. Tis time for me to do the deed that must be done."

Laurence pointed a red weapon at the edge of the mesh and activated it. A cable glowed red and snapped, then a second. He moved the weapon in a careful circle following the perimeter of the mesh as if were the lid of a tin can. When he reached two-thirds of the way around, the mesh collapsed downward in a tangled mess against the smooth side of the shaft.

Hayes finished buckling on his parachute harness. "Alf, you know my instructions for getting paid if I don't come back."

"Yes, Mr. Carpenter."

"Then you and your men get out of here. You did everything I could have asked. An hour isn't much time for you and Dimitri to get far enough away before that egg goes off."

Alf extended his hand. "Good luck to you, sir. I don't believe I'll take any more jobs. This one tops them all." Hayes shook his hand and then Laurence's. The two men turned toward the entrance of the cave.

Hayes turned to Park and embraced him tightly. "Dimitri, say goodby to Wilson. Take care of Lee. I actually suspect she might be falling in love with you."

"Let me go down the shaft with Nadir, Hayes. I am a traitor to my country. I have nothing to go back to. Besides, it's a job for a Korean."

Hayes laughed. "That's all true, my friend. You're about as useless as I am. But you lack one thing."

"What's that?"

"You don't know how to parachute down a 15,000 foot shaft."

"Is it hard?"

"You know what Wilson would say to that?"

"No."

"Is a pig's ass pork?"

Chapter Twenty-Five

Nadir walked to the lip of the shaft and jumped. Hayes waited three seconds and then jumped after him. Spreading his arm and legs against the column of air to slow his acceleration, Hayes put total trust in Nadir's assurance that the shaft was 15,000 feet deep and fell free for ten seconds. Then came the reassuring feel of his chute spilling from its pack and billowing open above him, the jerk of his harness arresting his fall, and five seconds later the shock of his boots hitting a sharply inclined surface . . . and starting to slide. Hayes reached wildly to either side for something to grab onto, but the wall of the shaft was smooth and steep. He was sliding out of control and picking up speed on a child's nightmare of a playground ride from hell.

The slope of the curving shaft lessened, but Hayes was hurtling too fast to notice until a sharp jerk on his harness pulled him to a sudden halt. Looking up and back he could make out the golden glow of Nadir's hair and beard. From the same direction came the sing-song intonation, "From here we go on foot to seize the giant's ship."

Nadir limped past him on the forty-five degree incline as easily as if he were walking on level ground. Hayes stayed down and resumed his slide, but with his cleated boots gathered under him and his gloved hands pressed firmly to the shaft surface to maintain control. After what felt like about a hundred yards, the slope leveled out to the point where he could stand up and release his parachute. Nadir's footsteps were some distance ahead, and Hayes hurried as quickly as he dared to catch up with them. Belatedly he remembered the long flashlight at his belt, but turning it on revealed only the dark curving walls of the now almost horizontal tunnel and the silhouette of Nadir still striding ahead.

Then there was something else, a dark shape bulging toward them across the width of the shaft like a plug in a drain. Hayes' only glimpse of Bix's ship had come when it flew overhead approaching the cave, and he had gotten no feel for its size. Now he saw that by filling the entire shaft it blocked any approach to where he assumed Bix was at work on the other side.

When he caught up with Nadir, the flame-haired Pramodzi was holding up what looked like a fur muff.

"How do we get past?" asked Hayes.

"This ship communicates direct with Bix's mind by means of this device I took from Shushna's corpse. She bears the name of Ann because the giants felt that species would prefer to speak to something live if they did not themselves use telepathic speech. I know not how it works nor does it really live. But it is full of lore; it giant sciencc knows. From Ann I learned about the eggs in Shushna's ship and how to find the spot where sunken deep it lies beneath the chilly waves, the waves of Issyk Kul. I also learned about the scheme they had to find a form of DNA that they could utilize to give them endless life by mating giant sperm with ovum from a womb that had immortal gene. Ann did not freely switch to following my will, but now she takes commands, from you as well as me. So what she's going to do is use a stratagem to get us both inside this ship that blocks our way. She plans to trick the ship and make it take commands from her instead of Frak, a counterpart device that Bix has with him now as he works farther on."

Five miles away, Bix and Frak were inspecting a collapse that totally blocked the tunnel, exposing four thick diamond-sheathed conduits, each burned completely through.

What a mess, communicated Bix cheerfully. He was as happy as an avid child in front of a pile of jigsaw puzzle pieces, for it was in the nature of Inamadzi to rejoice at the prospect of a difficult engineering job. *How far does the collapse extend?*

About a mile. The rubble is loosely packed.

Well, that certainly isn't much of a problem. These cables, however, are another story.

I'll bring the ship.

What? Why bring the ship, Frak?

I . . . I think the ship should come.

Why? Leave it right where it is. It's protecting us from interference.

Frak didn't answer for several seconds. Finally he communicated, *I'm activating the ship to bring it.*

Don't activate the ship, ordered Bix.

Cancelling activate order . . . activating ship.

Frak, do we have pramodzi? Bix looked anxiously at the marmot's rodent face.

I think . . . . Frak fell silent.

Bix grabbed the nodding marmot from his shoulder and unscrewed its head. He stuck a finger into its neck and tripped a switch. *Frak, I've shut off your link to the ship. Review your last ten minutes of data and tell me whether we have pramodzi.*

We have pramodzi.

Back at the ship, two circular portions of the hull had silently slid aside uncovering wide tubular passages penetrating all the way through the ship like culverts under a roadway. There was dim illumination at the far end.

"Keep your fingers crossed that engine does not start," said Nadir as he ducked into the passage and started to crawl through.

Hayes followed directly on his heels. He could hear a mechanical whine rising in pitch all around him. Half way along, three narrower ducts from the heart of the ship intersected the tube. The whine became more intense. Then Nadir was tumbling out of the passage and into one of the ducts, scrambling deeper inside to make room for Hayes. With Nadir no longer shielding him, a powerful wind, seemingly from nowhere, began to blow strongly in Hayes' face. He felt the ship shudder as if about to shift its position. In an instant the wind became so strong that Hayes could not longer crawl or keep his eyes open. With nothing to hold onto, he felt himself being forced backward. Suddenly Nadir's hand closed tightly on his upper arm. With invincible force it tugged him forward against the violent wind that felt on the verge of ripping his arm off at the shoulder. As

Hayes' head and neck cleared the passage and entered the connecting duct, Nadir grabbed his other shoulder and gave an immense yank that pulled him entirely clear of the tube's vortex.

Nadir gave a gruff laugh. "The wind's not hard to start, but hard it is to stop."

Hayes sat down and rubbed his wrenched shoulder, testing it gingerly to see whether it had been permanently damaged. The duct led into a hallway at the end of which he could make out the ship's open door. Nadir handed him the furry-looking communicator named Ann. It felt like a living animal, but it had no head or feet.

"Hello, you may call me Ann," it said in a mellow, feminine voice. Hayes could not tell exactly where the voice was issuing from.

"I'm Hayes," he said tentatively, feeling sheepish talking to what looked like roadkill. "Do we speak this way, or do you read my mind . . . Ann?"

"Unfortunately, you don't have the wetware for direct contact. So we will have to speak. Nadir has assigned me to you so I will tell you what you want to know and do what you wish to do. But please don't be too stupid. It's been a burden all this time to work for someone as dumb as Nadir. But it's truly an embarrassment for me to be working for you."

"You can get embarrassed?"

"There. That's stupid. I want no more of that."

Nadir interrupted. "It takes a little time to make a friend of Ann, but time is growing short you should go inside and wait for my command in case I need the ship to aid me in my fight."

"You mean you don't know whether you're going to need my help? It sounds like all you really need is Ann here," said Hayes.

"The help I need from you I get from your belief. The thing that made me strong, awakened latent force, was rite of sacrifice performed with ancient words. I need to know you're here, attentive to my deeds, prepared to tell the world of Indra's final act."

"But I won't actually be there for your final act, will I. That egg you left in the cave is going to blow . . ." Hayes realized he was speaking to no one. Nadir had disappeared through the door and into the dark of the tunnel.

. . . blow the top of this mountain off, and I don't think I'm likely to make it back to the world above to tell about any deeds, he finished silently. He looked at Ann lying inert in his hands. "You sure look like shit," he said.

"Would you like me to move around like an animal? Shushna used to like that, but Nadir has no refinement."

"You've been with Nadir for thousands of years . . ."

"Eleven thousand."

" . . . and you talk about him that way?

"For better or worse, I belong to you now. Nadir's decision, not mine. But he fixed my controls so I have to go along with it. Just a steady humiliating descent from Inamadzi to Pramodzi to human. I don't know how much lower I can go."

"Have you thought of being crushed into a powder by a hydraulic press?"

"You wouldn't dare."

"I accept independent ideas and blunt words from my employees, Ann, but not insolence. Get that through your little computer brain right now. And make yourself look better if you can. You've got a woman's voice. Make yourself pretty. You look like a dead skunk, makes me want to throw you in a ditch." Hayes paused. "You got that, Ann?"

"Clear as crystal."

"Good. By the way, why aren't you using that sing-song jabber?"

"I can if you like. Nadir just loves that kind of speech. It reminds him of the old days when people treated him like a god. But I thought you would prefer something a little less prehistoric."

"At Carpenter-Beckenbaugh Corp. people treat me like a god."

"So you have a sense of humor. That's something else Nadir lacks."

"I hear voice." Rejep Muratbey was staring down the hallway from the door of the control room. "Who are you?"

Hayes extended his hand. "Name's Hayes Carpenter."

Muratbey gave his hand a firm shake. "Rejep Muratbey, President of Ferghana Republic."

The two heavy-set bald men scrutinized one another like Tweedledum and Tweedledee. "So you're Muratbey," ventured Hayes cautiously. "I've been looking for you."

"Now you find me. I know who you are. You come to invest capitalist money in Ferghana Republic."

"No, Mr. President. Point of fact, I've come to slice open that big thick neck of yours with a knife."

"He's wearing a blob suit," put in Ann diffidently.

"I don't care what the bastard's wearing." Hayes unsheathed a huge knife hanging from his belt. "Killed and blinded my friends. He blew up my hole-in-the-sea. Now I'm going to cut his head off, pull his guts out, skin him, tan his hide, and turn him into a deck of playing cards."

Suiting actions to words, Hayes lunged heavily at Muratbey only to bounce immediately backward with his knife-point deflected to the side.

"I told you he was wearing a blob suit," said Ann.

"What's a blob suit?" replied Hayes, bewildered.

Muratbey's face bore a self-satisfied grin. "Automatic shield. Protect me from asshole."

"It responds to his fear," explained Ann. "You should put one on too. Everyone who flies in a ship wears a blob suit."

"But what about killing him?"

"You will have to wait until his suit deflates. Nothing penetrates a blob suit . . . within reason, of course. You'll find one for yourself in the orange drawer."

Hayes located the orange drawer and pulled on the blob suit, which promptly disappeared into the fabric of his clothing. "Why isn't it protecting me?"

"Because you aren't afraid," replied Ann.

"Now we can't hurt each other. We talk like men," said Muratbey.

"What do we have to talk about?"

"Bix fix machine. He thanks me for protecting him and gives me space technology. Then leave. I need capitalist invest in technology, build factories in Ferghana. You have billions dollars, we become partners. Fifty-fifty. American way. I like America."

"Sorry. Won't work. Your Bix is dead meat."

"Dead meat?"

"Finished. Wiped out. Kaputt. The Lord Indra's about to take him out."

"Who Lord Indra?"

"Pramodzi," said Ann.

Muratbey frowned. "You help pramodzi?" he said angrily. "Pramodzi dogs. They should all be killed."

"They just take getting used to," said Ann.

"Not talking to you."

"You should be. I'm the one who knows what's happening in the tunnel." Hayes and Muratbey looked quizzically at the mass of fur, which now seemed to have vestigial feet and a head. "Would you like to hear? I can turn their thoughts into words."

Bix heard Nadir's approach from a long way off. *"Pramodzi,"* he communicated, *"go away. Leave me alone. I'm not hurting you. I'm just here to do a job.* Nadir's footsteps drew closer. Bix could make out the form of a man with a big belly and glowing beard and hair. *"This feud between inamadzi and pramodzi has got to end. It makes no sense."*

Nadir's response came direct to Bix's mind. *"The Inamadzi goal bespeaks a base desire to shape the universe according to their will, to shape the way a folk, I mean here humankind, develops over time and rob them of the right of evolution slow. For you to make the Earth become an icy place or swelter from the heat is but a minor task, but woe betide mankind if you this task fulfill. I know you do not care. You lack all moral sense. But no one who has learned what noble Pramo taught can let you have your way. So that is why I'm here."*

"Now just stop it. What is your name?"

"You can Nadir say."

"All right, Nadir. I have heard this pramodzi lunacy all my life, and it simply makes no sense. First of all, it isn't even time for the climate engine to go on. The sea didn't dry up because the planet's water became frozen in the ice caps and glaciers. It dried up because your human friends diverted the water and caused a huge environmental mess. That's why we check things out personally and don't rely blindly on automatic communication systems. That's responsible engineering. It's what we inamadzi stand for. All I'm

doing is fixing the ignition, which you did serious damage to, and clearing the exhaust units so that whenever the time does come for the climate engine to go on, it will work right. Secondly, without our climate engine, your precious humankind would probably never have evolved as far as they have. Their ancestors were tree shrews when we first learned about their DNA anomaly. And they would still be tree shrews if we hadn't shaken things up with our ice ages. It's called punctuated equilibrium. You need a depopulation crisis to make an evolutionary leap. So we've done them a huge favor. Thirdly, they are now taking charge of changing their own climate. Even if the climate engine did start again, which is something I am here to prevent, the carbon dioxide and methane it puts out to heat up the atmosphere would only accelerate what humans are doing anyway. And finally, we've had a lot of experience engineering the parts of the universe we can get to, and we've done a pretty good job. And what have the pramodzi done? Nothing. So just go away."

Nadir stood his ground. *"The things you've just confessed condemn you even more than what you choose to call pramodzi lunacy. Yet still you would conceal the worst of all your crimes."*

"Don't bother to preach at me, Nadir. I learned more than enough pramodzi philosophy in school. You're going to bring up that old business about genetics, aren't you? How we're supposed to be breeding a superrace somewhere that will give us immortality? Let me ask you, how long have you been sitting around on this lonely little planet with nothing to do?"

"Since last the engine worked, before with hero friends I broke its crucial parts and compassed Shushna's death, way back in days of yore . . . ."

"Oh, come on, Nadir. Can't we do without the poetry? How much Earth time have you spent on this planet?"

"Eleven thousand years."

"There you go. Eleven thousand years, twenty-two of our generations, during which you haven't kept up with any news at all. Do you know, for example, that on twelve planets inamadzi and pramodzi have worked out agreements? Do you know that Pramo's writings about fate and the sacrosanct character of all life are required reading in inamadzi schools? No, you don't know these things because you're a pathetically ignorant pramodzi who's

completely out of touch with what's going on. And regrettably you aren't the only one."

"I have been out of touch so maybe there is truth in some things that you say. But you cannot deny the plan you have to steal from human DNA the gene for endless life. For when I Shushna slew, I took from her that thing you inamadzi use to talk to human beings and also interface with data in your ship. Not only did I learn about your scheme from Ann but later on I seized from out of Shushna's ship the gene injector kit that inamadzi hoped could transfer DNA once humans reached a stage where they could reproduce with inamadzi kind."

"I won't deny, Nadir, there was once such a plan, but that plan died thousands of years ago. Inamadzi already have immortality. We developed it ourselves through genetic engineering. And we're using it very, very carefully, only for inamadzi being sent to other galaxies. And do you know why we're being so careful? It's because Pramo's kind of immortality produced lunatics like you. Pramo just went ahead with his experiments and produced thousands of pramodzi without any kind of field-testing to see whether dzi minds can tolerate the effects of immortality. Did you know that eighty percent of all pramodzi have commited suicide? And did you know that of those that still survive, most are completely mad? I don't mean this personally, you understand. It's just a fact. We inamadzi honor Pramo's philosophy. That's why we terminated all other genetic experiments after we developed immortality ourselves. But you pramodzi who remain still cause us no end of problems."

"If what you say is true, then all the greater cause have I to end the threat that inamadzi pose to human life on Earth. You seem to feel that you, as clever engineers, should be the only ones on all the worlds we know to have immortal lives. You seek to rule the fate of every star and world, to put your stamp upon the boundless universe."

"Better good engineers than crazed poets. Since you seem to be ineducable, Nadir, what do you plan to do now?"

"I have an egg in hand."

"Of course you do. I knew it. How in the universe do pramodzi get their hands on so many eggs? Eggs are excavation tools, not weapons. I suppose you're going to set it off in here. Do you know

what will happen? First, it will kill the both of us even though I'm wearing a blob suit. But second—and try here to appreciate the irony of what you have in mind—second, the electro-magnetic surge will travel down these four conduits that you severed, trip a circuit controller at the end of each conduit, and turn on the climate engine. And there won't be any way to turn it off. Do you want that? Do you want to be the one who personally starts a new climate cycle? Turns the Earth into an oven? It won't be me. I'm just a repairman, and it isn't time for a cycle to start. But that is what will happen if you set off an egg."

"Those things that you have said would give me food for thought if time there still remained for pondering such things. I know not what is true; I know not what is false. A reasonable course might be for me to wait and verify your words before I crack the egg. Conceivably we'd find some common middle ground. When you had done your work you'd fly away from Earth while I would stay behind to witness human fate. But Inamadzi think that reason's always right. That's why they're engineers and know not poetry. If I had listened to what Shushna said to me when she was at death's door and I triumphant was, this climate change device would still be working fine, and Inamadzi still would have in their control the future of mankind. It's not my way to act on logic firm and dry. Pramodzi I, and I am sworn to rid this world of giant engineers, of Inamadzi foes who really do not care what human life is lost as they pursue their plans. If when I crack the egg, your engine does turn on, the chore of humankind will be to face that fact and deal with climate change engendered by my act, an act well meant and pure by one who holds them dear."

"Then I take it you're going to crack the egg?"

"The deed's already done."

"You are a very stupid pramodzi."

All thought ceased. Bix and Nadir and Frak vaporized instantaneously in the star-hot explosion that blew away the tunnel-choking debris in one direction and shot unimpeded toward Bix's ship in the other. At the point of detonation the tunnel expanded into a spherical chamber as hundreds of cubic meters of rock vaporized or were projected as vitrified particles up and down the tunnel. A powerful elecromagnetic charge surged down the climate machine's exposed conduits for two hundred miles to where they ended in a thermonuclear reactor embedded deep in underground coalbeds west of Almaty. Four switches tripped, and the reactor stirred to life as it had so many times before over the previous two million years.

Ann had barely gotten the ship door closed when the flash hit. It seared the ship's skin and heated the interior but was too weak at five miles distance to the melt the superhardened hull. Though the engines were already on, there was no way of outrunning the shock wave. Hayes felt his blob suit expand just as the full force of the blast hit. Like a dart in a blowgun, the shock wave propelled the ship at lethal velocity along the rising curve of the tunnel and then up the vertical shaft. Chunks of rock clanged sharply against its skin. The ship rattled violently between the rock walls as it shot up the shaft throwing Hayes and Muratbey helplessly around the control room. Their blob suits shielded them from injury, but not from the g-force of acceleration or from dizziness and disorientation.

The ship stabilized as it neared the top of the shaft, its engines, under Ann's control, thrusting upward to counter the pressure of the explosion rising from below. A jarring collision with the roof of the cave threw Hayes and Muratbey against the ceiling and forced a limestone stalactite through the ship's skin so that its sharp point penetrated all the way to the control room. Then the pressure from below suddenly diminished as the force of the explosion scorched the cave and shot out its mouth into the night, projecting masses of incandescent rock over the edge of the cliff.

Inside the cave, the wrenching screech of stone against metal went on for several minutes as the ship's engines strove to force it free from its impalement on the stalactite. It passed through Hayes' groggy mind that it must be about time for the egg Nadir had left inside the cave to detonate.

"We've got to get out of here," he said to Ann. "There's another egg set to go off and seal the cave."

"You could have told me sooner," said Ann coolly, her fur pelt now glistening and soft and her head sharp-toothed and shiny-nosed. Muratbey looked white-faced and petrified, his eyes bulging.

The engines whined higher and louder. The ship shuddered and swayed. It was swinging from side to side as Ann alternated the direction of the engines' thrust to force it first one way and then the other. A sudden jolt downward, and the snout of the stalactite disappeared from the control room. A second jolt, and a third, and the ship was falling free. It bounced hard on the lip of the shaft. The engines whined again, and it started to move forward. Air was pouring in through the enormous rent in the ceiling of the control room. Hayes looked at his watch.

"We've damaged a lot of controls," said Ann. "But I think it will still fly."

The ship moved sluggishly to the cave entrance and toppled over the cliff. Muratbey looked ghastly. After a fall of five hundred feet the engine whine increased and the ship slowed and stabilized. It was accelerating slowly away from the base of the cliff when Hayes heard a thunderous explosion overhead even louder than the one in the tunnel where the ship's intact hull had muffled the noise. Through the hole in the ceiling of the control room he saw fire shooting from the mouth of the cave.

"Go northeast," he said to Ann, "over that ridgeline just below the snowfield."

Staying low to avoid the turbulence from the second egg, Ann guided the balky ship in the direction Hayes indicated. Hayes took a deep breath and noticed that sometime during the preceding minutes his blob suit had deflated. He looked at Muratbey. His eyes were distended, his tongue was bulging out of his mouth, and his skin was distinguishably blue even in the dim control room light. His blob suit was still inflated.

"He suffocated," said Ann. "He died afraid so his suit didn't go down. I'll take care of it." The suit deflated.

Hayes thought for a moment and looked intently at the sleek, shiny animal now clinging to his shoulder with wicked claws. "You could have done that sooner, couldn't you, Ann? Like, as soon as he was unconscious."

"Did you want me to?"

Hayes thought about it. "No, I guess I didn't."

"Are you still going to skin him, and tan his hide, and make a deck of cards out of him?"

"Would you like that?"

"It would be interesting," said Ann, showing her needle-sharp teeth.

Chapter Twenty-Six

Lee saw a bright flash light up the crest of the ridge above their camp. Moments later the earth jolted violently beneath her. Then came a muffled rumble.

"That felt like an egg." said Wilson.

Hardly two minutes had elapsed when a vastly more brilliant flash scorched the skyline.

"Two eggs," said Lee as the earth jumped again. A few seconds later an ear-splitting explosion rent the air.

"Yep, two eggs," said Wilson.

Then they waited. Lee sat facing southwest and searched the moonlit landscape for any sign of men returning.

"Think they made it?" said Wilson.

"I don't know," replied Lee in a controlled voice.

Intent on the silhouette of the ridge separating the sacrifice ground from the slope leading down to the cliff, Lee missed the faint shadow of Bix's dark globe passing silently overhead. The ship settled with only a whisper on the withered grass behind her.

Wilson turned his head toward the sound. "We got company."

Lee turned and saw Hayes striding toward her. She ran to him and hugged him tightly, tears streaming down her cheeks. "You did it!" she cried, laughing through her tears.

"Well, we sort of did it," confirmed Hayes tiredly. "Bix and Muratbey are dead. So is Nadir. But the climate machine may have been turned on anyway."

Lee released Hayes and wiped her cheeks with the heels of her hands. "I thought Nadir was going to do it that way. I think he was tired of being immortal."

"Hayes!" called Wilson. "Come on over here and tell me what it's like to 'strive with gods.'"

As the old friends embraced in the light of the fire, Lee noticed for the first time the dark, silky fur around Hayes' neck. "My god, Hayes, where did you get that gorgeous Russian sable?"

"Thank you," said the sable. "It is nice to be appreciated by someone. I'm Ann."

Lee stared at Ann's sharp-nosed rodent head. "How do you do, Ann," she said tentatively. "I'm Lee."

"Who's the lady with the pretty voice?" said Wilson.

"Ann, this is Wilson."

"Hayes has told me about you, Wilson. I know you can't see me, but if you could, you would be looking at a long, weasel-like rodent with the most beautiful fur on Earth. I was Nadir's communicator, and before that Shushna's. Shushna was a lady, but Nadir treated me like an old rag. Now I belong to Hayes. Unless he wants to be a gentleman and give me to Lee."

Hayes laughed. "I give you to Lee as a friend and furpiece, Ann, but what you know belongs to me." He disentangled the sable's claws from his shoulders and draped it around Lee's neck.

"Ann and I both thank you, Hayes," said Lee. "But now tell us what happened."

Hayes' account of the expedition to the cave and the last heroic deeds of Lord Indra held his audience spellbound for an hour. The three of them were deep into a discussion of the implications of the final conversation between Indra and Bix when Joseph staggered shivering and exhausted into camp. Lee jumped up and squeezed him in a warm hug, then popped him into the down sleeping bag she had been keeping warm in. At a separate fire the Basmachi happily welcomed back their comrades.

The nuclear explosions had signalled Joseph that their mission had succeeded, but Hayes refused to tell him the story of what happened in the cave until he recounted his own tale of the battle in the snowfield. He had just gotten to the mysterious intervention of the Chinese when joyous shouts from the Basmachi fire announced the arrival of Uli and their other comrades leading Dimitri and the SAS men up the rocky scree into the campsite. When Dimitri saw Hayes, he ran to him and threw his arms around him.

"We thought you were dead."

"Nadir is dead. The first egg blew the ship up the shaft and out of the cave. I survived, but Muratbey was in the ship too, and he's dead. I'll tell you all about it."

And for the next several hours they all told each other all about it.

* * *

Major Jim Brady and his men received flash burns on exposed skin from the second nuclear explosion but were otherwise unscathed. Fearful of radioactive fallout, he scrubbed his plan to find the American agent and to study the battlefield and dope out what had transpired in the dark. Instead he radioed for immediate extraction. Then he led his men through the moonlit night back down the mountain to their rendezvous point on the road from Sary Tash.

Three hundred miles to the south, two large tilt-rotor planes prepositioned at the Pakistani air force base at Peshawar took off with a Pakistani fighter escort. Within ten hours, the Delta Force team was safe on Pakistani soil, and Major Brady was telling a remarkable story to a group of American and Pakistani intelligence officers.

* * *

President Boone Rankin was dressing for dinner and rehearsing in his mind the speech in celebration of diversity he was about to give at a Buddhist temple in Anaheim when George Artunian knocked on the door of his suite and walked in.

"Two more nuclear explosions, Mr. President."

"Anyone we know?" asked the President calmly as he wrestled with his bow tie.

"Both on a mountain in Kyrgyzstan, right near the Chinese border. Completely uninhabited. No military installations close by. Preliminary guess is that it was a secret storage site for weapons."

"Russians been holdin' out on us all these years, huh?"

"Could be. Or it could be . . . that other thing."

Rankin looked at his National Security Advisor quizzically. "The spaceman? Did you say Rosswell, New Mexico, or Kyrgyzstan?"

"Delta Force was there when it happened. According to the commander, there was a firefight. Then he and his men saw a flying saucer go into a cave in the mountain. A while later—he estimates about two hours—the cave exploded."

"Who were they fighting?"

"Mostly the Ferghanan troops that crossed the border four days ago, but there were others there too."

"Others?"

"The colonel doesn't know who they were."

"What about our NSA guy?"

"No word yet."

"And that woman who was kidnapped?"

"No word."

"So what do you recommend we do?"

"If anyone asks, we say there was an earthquake. Promote the Major and tell him and his men to keep their mouths shut."

The president smiled at the perfection of his bowtie reflected in the mirror. "Earthquake it is, George. Now let's go raise some money."

* * *

Colonel Maxim Sverdlov completed his withdrawal from Kyrgyzstan in good order and on schedule, but with a heart full of foreboding as he anticipated confronting President Muratbey. It seemed highly unlikely that the two nuclear explosions that blew away half the north face of the mountain had been part of the space alien's repair plan, and he knew that the failure of a surgical operation of the sort he had promised the president could not be disguised by the tidiness of the sutures used to close the wound.

As his column reached its base on the outskirts of Kokand, he ordered his driver to head directly for the Presidential Palace. *Let it never be said*, he thought, *that Colonel Maxim Sverdlov refused to face his Commander-in-Chief in person and take the blame for a plan gone wrong.*

After an interminable wait that Maxim took to be the first and lightest of his tortures, Yasmin, the president's secretary, came into the reception room. Her face showed she had been crying. "He hasn't come back," she said tearfully. "I'm afraid something's happened to him."

"Where did he go?"

"First the mafia tried to kill him," she blubbered, "and then he went away in the spaceship. He was so happy and so handsome. He gave me this before he left." Yasmin unwadded the sodden handkerchief in her hand the showed Maxim the biggest diamond he had ever seen.

"Are you sure he was in the spaceship?"

"Yes. We all saw him get in. He waved goodbye to us." Yasmin sniffled.

"Then I must tell you, Yasmin, I believe our president is dead. Something went wrong. The spaceship was destroyed."

Yasmin's shoulders heaved as she started to bawl. "Poor Rejep," she whimpered between sobs.

"Yasmin, listen to me. Listen to me, Yasmin. This must be kept secret."

"Why?"

"To prevent panic and maintain order."

"But how can we keep it a secret?"

"Can you sign the president's signature?"

"Y . . . y . . . yes."

"Good. I'll compose an order for martial law, and you can sign President Muratbey's name. It will name me as martial law administrator. Then everything will be calm until we find out exactly what happened and can decide what is best to do."

* * *

After a hot midday meal of roast lamb and pilav cooked by the multi-talented Laurence, Lee summoned Dimitri, Hayes, Joseph, and Wilson to sit around her. Ann was nestled attractively around her neck. A lambskin hat covered her shaven skull.

"Gentlemen, we have to have a serious discussion. First I want Ann to play back the final confrontation between Bix and Nadir. Go ahead Ann."

The group sat spellbound listening once again to Ann's vocalization of the mental exchange that preceded the explosion of the egg.

When she finished, Lee continued. "If we assume both of them were speaking the truth, then Nadir's killing Bix, noble though it might have been, did not solve Earth's problem. Bix said there would be no way to turn off the climate engine once it started, which means that everyone on Earth is probably in for some very difficult times. But Nadir also mentioned the Inamadzi genetic program and the gene injector female Inamadzi like Shushna carried on their ships in case they encountered a suitable opportunity. Nadir showed Wilson the injector when he took his hands and showed him how it was to be used, and Wilson brought it back with him from Issyk Kul. Moreover, Ann has confirmed the whole plan. The injector is in a chilled container, but more of the liquid nitrogen keeping it usable evaporates every minute. By tomorrow, it will have warmed too much for the genetic material inside to remain viable."

"Lee," broke in Joseph, "this is very confusing. What is a gene injector?"

"According to the old, and apparently obsolete, Inamadzi genetic plan, if any female Inamadzi encountered a dzi-like species that possessed the mutant immortality gene they were seeking, she was to self-administer an injection into her womb that would make her ovum susceptible to impregnation by that species, and also decorticate her X chromosome so that the immortality gene on the male's X or Y chromosome would be transferred to her offspring, and hopefully to her offspring's offspring. In other words, they were prepared to get quick immortality in the unlikely event that an opportunity should present itself."

"But why, then, did Nadir make Wilson bring it back from the ship?" asked Hayes.

"He wanted it for Lee," replied Wilson. "Didn't say it in words, mind, but I see in my mind how she's supposed to use it, and I see how he thought it would make her kids live forever. Leastways the little girls."

"Wilson and I have been discussing this ever since the rest of you went on your missions. And I've been talking it over with Ann all morning. Ann says Nadir was right. If I take the injection, the substitute DNA will nullify both the sex and the aging sequences on my X chromosome. And when that happens, the mutant DNA sequence that codes for sexual potency without physical aging should take its place. In the Inamadzi plan, this mutant coding was to come from a non-Inamadzi male. But since all humans apparently have it in latent form, if I were to get pregnant after taking the injection, my female offspring should benefit, at least if one considers immortality a benefit. And the possibility would exist that their daughters would pass on the trait from generation to generation. But not to any sons."

Silence reigned as minds churned.

"But you still need a man to get pregnant," said Hayes bluntly.

"That's correct. And hence my dilemma. If I decide to abide by Nadir's wish, then I have to get pregnant within the next, say, eighteen hours."

Hayes, Dimitri, and Joseph all looked quizzically at one another. Wilson's face was inscrutable.

"On the other hand, I could accept Bix's assertion that Nadir was a very stupid Pramodzi and forget the whole thing. Maybe the climate engine won't restart, or maybe it won't have any effect until long after we're all dead. The trouble with that alternative is that I don't think Nadir *was* a stupid Pramodzi. I think he had come to like humans very much, and that he liked all of us personally, especially after we made the sacrifice for him. When he decided to face Bix the way he did, I think he knew the egg would turn on the climate engine. He was trying to force us to go through with his impregnation plan."

"But why?" said Joseph.

"I'm not sure, but I would hazard the guess that Nadir wanted immortal humans and not just Inamadzi to reach the stars and affect the course of the universe. Maybe he saw us as a healthy compromise between good engineers and crazy poets."

"So I take it, Lee, that you've decided to go through with it," said Dimitri matter-of-factly.

"I've already taken the injection. It takes four hours to force ovulation."

There was a long awkward pause.

"Then who's to be the father?" said Hayes, giving voice to the thought in every listener's mind.

"Ah, the father! There must be a father, mustn't there." Lee appeared to be enjoying the suspense. "Before I tell you, I must clear up one fact for the record, and I must tell you all a story from ancient India. The fact for the record is that my husband Donald is dead. Joseph heard it in a radio message from Kokand. So I am, sadly, a widow. Donald had some very nice points, and I am sure I shall miss him from time to time. But the fact of the matter is, from a reproductive point of view, I am an unattached woman of thirty-eight with no children. I am also a woman who, against every proper instinct she was brought up with, left her home and husband and ran away to a foreign country with a strange man. In fact, with two strange men. To be succinct, such an experience changes a woman. And I suspect Nadir took that into account in conveying his plan to Wilson.

"Now for the story. As I am sure Joseph knows, the ancient Indian epic poem the *Mahabharata* is about a war between five brothers, the sons of Pandu, on the one hand, and their first cousins, on the other. The seeds of the war are sown when the oldest of the Pandava brothers, Arjuna, encounters a princess of incredible beauty named Draupadi. When he returns home and tells his mother that he has had wonderful good fortune, she tells him that whatever that good fortune is, he must share it with all his brothers. So as a dutiful son, he shares his new wife, Draupadi. That is how Draupadi acquires five husbands. Then the story goes on to tell how Arjuna gambles away the fortunes of all the Pandavas and finally gambles away Draupadi herself, which is the event leading to the Mahabharata war.

"This story has for centuries provided one of the great mysteries of Indian culture. How, in a highly patriarchal culture, could the very model of feminine perfection possibly have been portrayed as sleeping with five husbands. Of course, it is all an ancient legend so there is no way of telling what it originally meant. But myths have many uses, and I have chosen to take this one as the solution to my problem. If humans become immortal, the idea that they should trace their immortality to a single father is aesthetically displeasing. It would be just another demonstration of our species' proclivity for masculine domination. Better, I think, that the the next stage of humanity should trace its immortality to a single mother, especially since, if Nadir and Ann are correct, immortality will pass only from female to female.

"Thus I have decided to become Draupadi, and I have a lovely sable stole around my neck and a lovely lambskin hat on my glamorous bald head to qualify me as the most beautiful woman on this mountainside. In a very real sense, my first husband—discounting poor Donald, of course—is Nadir, Lord Indra. He called me his last priest, and he has arranged for me to become pregnant. So he is the Arjuna of our story, and the four of you will be the rest of the Pandavas. I have decided to marry you all, at least by the laws of this mountain, and let whoever's sperm swims fastest do the job that needs to be done."

Quiet conversation and occasional laughter from the other fire where the Basmachi and the SAS mercenaries were enjoying their relaxation punctuated the total silence that greeted Lee's pronouncement.

"Don't all speak at once, boys," said Lee.

No one spoke at all. Joseph, Dimitri, and Hayes all looked at one another and at Wilson. Wilson just smiled.

"I think it's a wonderful idea," said Ann sweetly.

"Thank you, Ann." Lee paused and looked at the men's faces: Joseph's bright red and embarrassed, Dimitri's with a smile straining to break through his iron control, Hayes' agape and dumbfounded, and Wilson's a picture of quiet satisfaction.

"Then if none of you have anything to say, I will proceed. Hayes?"

"Ma'm?"

"I hearby forgive you for profiteering on the lives of Mexican laborers when you were young, for cheating on your wife, and for becoming a horrible, egocentric billionaire. I forgive you these things, and I take you as my husband because you are brave, you read poetry, and you are rich enough to support me, my husbands, and my children for the rest of our lives . . . or at least for the rest of the lives of those of us who are not immortal." She paused. "You can say 'I do' if you like."

"I do, Lee. And . . . and thank you."

"Hayes, don't cry. You're too old for that. Now Dimitri."

"Am I, too, to be forgiven?"

"Yes. I forgive you, Dimitri, for spying on people and blackmailing them. I forgive you for spying on me and Donald and blackmailing us. And I forgive you for all the crimes of violence I'm sure you have committed but will never commit again. I forgive you all these things, and I take you for my husband because you are smart, you are brave, and you are handsome . . . and also because I believe you truly love me, and I want to live the rest of my life with you. What do you say, John Alden, now that I've asked you to speak for yourself?"

"I do, Lee. I do with all my heart," he replied with a choking voice.

"Onward then. Contain yourself, Dimitri. Lets not let this wedding get maudlin. Joseph."

"Lee. Dr. Ingalls."

"Stick with Lee, lover. I forgive you for being young. You can't help it. I forgive you for being a nerd. It's all you have ever known how to do. And I forgive you for calling me Dr. Ingalls even on the wildest mountainside in Central Asia. I forgive you all these things, and I take you to be husband because you thought of a plan, you carried it out, you saved everyone's life, and you did it all despite the fact that you were afraid. Do you want me to be your wife?"

"I do, Lee."

"Good. Finally, the best for last. Wilson?"

"I'm still here, Lee."

"I don't know of anything to forgive you for, Wilson."

"I do."

"Not yet."

"No, I mean I know of things that need forgivin'."

"Then keep them to yourself. So far as I'm concerned, I take you for my husband because you are the bravest man I will ever know, and among the dozen best looking. So what do you think?"

"Now I say 'I do'?"

"Now you say it."

"I do."

"Good. Then that's it. I believe that this evening I shall take a tent for myself, and I will entertain my husbands as visitors. I will confess I feel more than a little odd about this, but even a well brought up lady from Connecticut should be allowed at least one exotic night in her life. Joseph, I will expect you to visit first. At your age, a half hour should be more than enough. Then, Dimitri, I would like you next . . . ."

And so the plans were made and so they were carried out.

Chapter Twenty-Seven

Paul Henning smiled and inclined his body toward the camera with the glowing red light. "Good morning and welcome to Sunday Special. I'm Paul Henning. Today we'll be talking about the mystery surrounding the unexpected eruption two weeks ago of a mountain named Verethra Kuh in the Central Asian country of Kyrgyzstan. A mountain, I should add, that no one expected to erupt because it is not, I repeat, *is not* a volcano. To help us explore this unusual occurrence we have with us Mr. Jack Kilson, the publisher of *Merc Magazine*, Dr. Abraham Stein of the Council on Foreign Relations, Dr. David Waldron of the University of Virginia, Dr. Yasuo Takahashi of the Columbia Earth Institute, and Ms. Darla Bane, former American ambassador to the Ferghana Republic."

He swivelled to his right. "Lets start with you, Mr. Kilson. *Merc Magazine* says that it is published by and for mercenaries and soldiers of fortune. Yet you ran a story after the eruption that was surely more science fiction than real-life military adventure."

"Let me set the record straight, Mr. Henning. I stand by our story one hundred percent. For those of your viewers who haven't read the latest issue of *Merc*, the story in question comes from a former member of Britain's Special Air Service who took a job protecting an American billionaire on a private expedition to Central Asia. The soldier's name is Laurence, and he and my writer are totally reliable. Laurence tells how three months ago there was a gun battle between American, Russian, Chinese, and Ferghanan troops on this very same mountain, Verethra Kuh; and in the middle of the battle a spaceship went into a cave in the mountain and descended down a deep shaft, where another battle took place between two space aliens. During that battle, two nuclear weapons were set off that destroyed the cave."

"All right, there you have it. Now tell us why this story should not be considered science fiction."

"Because my writer has known Laurence for many years and would trust him with his life, and because I have known my writer for just as long and have never known him to write a single word that he could not verify."

"And yet you waited what? . . . almost three months? . . . since the bomb blasts to publish the story? The story indicates quite clearly that Laurence gave his interview to your writer just a short time after the alleged battle and nuclear explosions in Kyrgyzstan."

"That's correct, Paul. I did wait. And I waited precisely because I didn't think people like you would believe it. I've been in the publishing business for a long time, and I know how the story sounds. But it's true, nevertheless. And now that the mountain has blown up . . . or blown up a second time . . . and is sending dangerous amounts of carbon dioxide into the atmosphere, I thought people would be more likely to take the story seriously and do some investigating. The American, Russian, Ferghanan, and Chinese governments all know this happened, and they're all covering it up. I think it's time people demanded full disclosure on this matter. If they don't, it'll be Rosswell, New Mexico, and the UFO coverup all over again."

Paul looked to his left and right. "Okay, you've all heard Mr. Kilson, publisher of *Merc Magazine*, charge a massive international coverup on Verethra Kuh. What would you say in reply, Dr. Stein?"

Abraham Stein echoed the reserve of his pinstriped navy blue suit with a deprecating smile and a modest shake of his bald head. "It's quite a story, Paul. I'm sure we would all like to know more. But I gather Mr. Kilson's informant, Laurence, can no longer be found, and no one is willing to reveal his last name. Leaving that aside, let me address the issues directly. First of all, was there a nuclear explosion in the vicinity of Mount Verethra Kuh three months ago as the story indicates? My sources confirm that three months ago U.S. seismic stations did record an unusual event of some kind in that region. You understand, of course, that the mountain is in one of the remotest and least populated parts of Central Asia, so there was no on-the-scene confirmation of just what the event was. Officially, it was recorded as an earthquake; but if it was actually a nuclear explosion, it wouldn't be the first time such an event was written off as an earthquake."

"Let me stop you just a second there, Dr. Stein. Dr. Takahashi, you're an earth scientist. Can seismologists always tell an earthquake from, say, an underground nuclear test?"

"We think so, Paul, but if some have slipped by, how would we know?"

"Okay, back to you, Dr. Stein."

"So that was the first point. Some sort of event did occur. Secondly, for four days before the earthquake or explosion Kyrgyzstan and the Ferghana Republic traded charges at the United Nations over a Kyrgyz allegation that the Ferghanan army made an incursion in force across their common border in the vicinity of Verethra Kuh. According to the Kyrgyz government, one road near the city of Osh was blocked by Ferghanan tanks, and another road between Osh and Sary Tash was bombed. These two roads are the only access routes from Osh to Verethra Kuh. Moreover, sometime during those few days the president of the Ferghana Republic, Rejep Muratbey, disappeared from public view. We still don't know whether he is dead or alive. Colonel Maxim Sverdlov, who took over as the interim martial law president of the Ferghanan Republic, has not explained to this day what became of Mr. Muratbey."

"But President Muratbey was still in office when the incursion into Kyrgyzstan began. Is that right?"

"Yes. That's certain. He appeared at least once on television to defend his country against the Kyrgyz charges. But now the third point, sources in the government of Azerbaijan say that right around that time the United States asked permission for an overflight to Kokand, the Ferghana capital, on humanitarian grounds. Whatever that flight was about was never reported in the American press. And then one final point, a week after the earthquake or explosion, Russian Defense Minister Pyotr Kalenin and the commander of the Russian land forces, General Nikolai Repin, were summarily dismissed from their posts for 'insubordination.' No further explanation."

"And you think that's connected."

"I don't know, Paul. I'm just relating some of the unusual things that happened at the time Mr. Kilson's mercenary Laurence says he was on a mission to Verethra Kuh. In my opinion, taking all this into account, I think it is safe to conclude that *something* did happen on Mount Verethra Kuh three months ago. And it is conceivable that American, Russian, and Ferghanan military forces were involved. So the setting for Laurence's story is not entirely far-fetched, which raises the obvious question: how would this person Laurence have even heard of Mount Verethra Kuh three months ago if he hadn't been there? The mountain is news today because its venting of greenhouse gases poses a serious threat to the world's climate, but it was just an obscure point on the map back then.

"But nevertheless, Paul, before you put me down as a total believer in Laurence's and Mr. Kilson's story, let me hasten to add that my credulity has some limits. I have to draw the line, Paul, at flying saucers and duelling space aliens . . . and probably at the Chinese participation too."

Paul looked directly into the camera. "Do you draw the line at flying saucers and duelling space aliens? We'll hear from our other panelists about this as soon as we return from a short break. Stay with us."

After two minutes relaxation, Paul gave a smiling greeting to his returning television audience, reintroduced the panel, and turned to face Darla Bane. "Ambassador Bane . . ."

"Just Ms. Bane, Paul. I put the title behind me when I left the Foreign Service."

"All right. Ms. Bane, you were the American ambassador to the Ferghana Republic three months ago when the event Mr. Kilson and Dr. Stein have told us about took place. What can you tell us?"

"Well, I can tell you one thing Dr. Stein left out, and perhaps it was never reported in this country. Shortly before President Muratbey's disappearance, he ordered the air and land borders of the Ferghana Republic closed, even for diplomatic personnel. What the embassy was told was that there had been an outbreak of bubonic plague, which is a disease carried by rodent fleas. This disease caused the famous Black Death in Europe in the Middle Ages, and had serious outbreaks as late as the nineteenth century. It is a fact that most of the world's plague epidemics have started in Central Asia, where rodents known as marmots—sort of like ground hogs—often have the disease-carrying fleas. Needless to say, everyone took the border closing very seriously even though the Ferghanan government was reticent about the number of cases reported . . . presumably to prevent a panic. Now just how that might relate to the points Dr. Stein raised is not altogether certain, but there was certainly a rumor in Kokand, the Ferghanan capital, that President Muratbey himself contracted plague and died. And the embassy there, like the United Nations Security Council, also received a communication from the Ferghana government to the effect that the army incursion across the Kyrgyz border was for the purpose of capturing smugglers who had defied the border closing and might be inadvertently spreading the plague."

"So what about the Azerbaijani report of an American humanitarian flight?"

"That's easily explained. I personally contacted Washington to ask that a team of American physicians be sent to Kokand to help stem the outbreak. That flight was planned, and overflight permission was sought from Azerbaijan because the doctors were going to travel on a military plane. But the flight never took place. It was cancelled as soon as the Ferghana-Kyrgyz dispute was put before the United Nations Security Council."

"So what do you think of Laurence's story, then? Is it all made up?"

"It sounds that way to me. But of course, the mountain is in Kyrgyzstan, not the Ferghana Republic. It isn't very far from Kokand, but because the borders were closed, we had no way of tracking on the ground whatever was going on with the Ferghanan incursion."

"One final question, Ms. Bane. You resigned from the Foreign Service less than two weeks after the event that did or did not occur three months ago on Verethra Kuh. And now you work as Director of Public Relations for the Carpenter-Beckenbaugh Corporation."

Darla smiled sweetly. "Actually, Paul, I work for a new high-tech development corporation that has recently been set up by Hayes Carpenter, the CEO of Carpenter-Beckenbaugh."

"I'm sorry. You corrected me before the show. You were *initially* hired by Carpenter-Beckenbaugh, but now you have transferred to the new company, which is the . . . Indradzi Tehnology Corporation? Did I get that right?"

"That's correct, Paul. Indradzi Technology is one hundred percent owned by Mr. Carpenter himself and is entirely separate from the Carpenter-Beckenbaugh Corporation."

"But you took this new job very quickly after you returned to Washington, did you not?"

"I took it the minute it was offered," replied Darla with a laugh. "And if you knew what I was making in the Foreign Service and what I'm making now, you would have done the same thing."

"This sudden change of jobs seems to be an amazing coincidence, don't you think."

"Not really, Paul. Government officials leave office to pursue private business opportunities every day. Even ambassadors. They just don't get much publicity."

"Then my next question: Was Hayes Carpenter the American billionaire who hired Laurence?"

"That is utterly ridiculous, Paul. Mr. Carpenter took an enormous financial loss in the catrastrophe that struck the city of Nukus and his hole-in-the-sea project. That's one reason he decided to start the Indradzi Technology Corporation, to have a new adventure without a lot of personal risk."

"I hope it's a big success, Ms. Bane, and thank you for being with us."

"Thank you for asking me, Paul."

"And now, for a scientist's view, we turn to Dr. Yasuo Takahashi of Columbia University's Earth Institute. Welcome back, Dr. Takahashi."

"Thank you."

"What can you tell us about the eruption of Mount Verethra Kuh?"

"To be blunt, Mr. Henning, what you are calling an eruption is a disaster of worldwide proportions. Last week's explosion created a vent near the top of the mountain that has been pouring out methane and carbon dioxide in phenomenal quantities ever since. Analysis of the gas indicates that it comes from underground burning of coal or other hydrocarbons. But where this combustion is taking place is uncertain since there is no known coal deposit directly under the mountain. The mountain, in other words, seems to be serving as a vent for underground combustion taking place some distance away, a phenomenon otherwise unknown geologically."

"But why is this disastrous?"

"Because if it keeps going at the present rate, it will greatly accelerate global warming and bring on the melting of the polar ice caps. The volume of gas being vented into the atmosphere each day is equivalent to the monthly smog production of Los Angeles and Mexico City combined . . . multiplied by ten."

"So this is a very unusual volcano. Though I guess I can't call it a volcano."

"Volcanos also vent gas, but this isn't a volcano. That's why there's no way to predict how long it might go on."

"Lets go back, then, to the issue of Mr. Kilson's magazine and its article about nuclear explosions on Verethra Kuh. Could there be a connection?"

"The most important part of the story scientifically, Mr. Henning, is its reference to a deep vertical shaft inside a cave near the top of the mountain. That could be the vent we are now talking about."

"But why a three month delay?"

"It's hard to say since the shaft is mentioned in only one sentence of the article. But perhaps the nuclear explosions blocked the vent and at the same time somehow triggered the underground combustion. If that were the case, it may have taken three months for the gas pressure to become strong enough to blow open a new mouth for the vent."

"Thank you very much, Dr. Takahashi. Now, quickly because unfortunately we're running out of time, I want to turn to Dr. David Waldron, a political science professor at the University of Virginia. Professor Waldron, you've heard what everyone's said. Can you sum it all up for us in a few sentences?"

David suppressed an urge to wave hello to his wife Libby and put on a grave face instead. "Paul, in 1898 Europe almost went to war when a small expedition of French soldiers reached and claimed possession of the obscure town of Fashoda on the Nile River after trekking all the way across Africa. The British army fighting the local warlord in the Sudan demanded that the French acknowledge British supremacy along the Nile. This whole thing was called the Fashoda Incident. A tiny event at the ends of the earth almost caused a major war thousands of miles away. With that in mind, let us assume that everything Laurence said is true . . . even the part about flying saucers and space aliens. If American, Russian, Chinese, and Ferghanan troops did get into a battle on that mountain, and even if there was a space alien involved, these facts would appear, in the real world, to make no difference whatsoever. It's like the philosophical question of whether a tree falling in the forest when there is no one around can be said to make a noise. If no one acknowledges hearing, seeing, or doing anything, which seems to be the position of all the governments implicated, the incident might as well not have happened. And, to take the most extreme supposition, if there were space aliens involved, who cares? They're presumably gone, and all we're left with is an air pollution problem."

Paul swivelled to face the camera directly. "And that is all we have time for this morning. I want to thank my panelists, and I hope you will tune in again next week for another edition of Sunday Special."

* * *

Lee accepted Dr. Sybil Halprin's offer of a seat and tried to still her anxiety. The obstetrician had told her she would receive the results of her sonogram and amniocentesis by mail, but instead she had called her in for a personal meeting.

"Mrs. Indradzi, I don't want to upset you, but results of your amniocentesis are very unusual." Lee's whole body tensed. "First of all, you are carrying quadruplets."

"Oh my heavens! Is there anything wrong with them?"

"No, no. Nothing wrong. Just unusual. All four fetuses are female and surprisingly advanced for only three months. Also, they seem to be fraternal rather than identical."

"Is that unusual?"

"Very. It would suggest that you had four ova in your womb at the time of conception instead of the normal maximum of two. But there is something even more unusual. In fact, I don't quite know how to put it. But it's nothing to worry about healthwise. It's just that according to the amniocentesis, each fetus has a different blood type—all different from your own—which would seem to indicate that each of them has a different father." Lee relaxed and beamed exultantly. "Frankly, I find it quite mystifying."

"Indeed."

"And that is why I would like to redo the test completely. Though I can't quite see how it could have happened, some sort of contamination might have occurred in the laboratory."

Lee was eager to leave. "Can I call you later to make an appointment," she said cheerfully.

"Of course. And perhaps it would be better not to share this with your husband just yet. I mean the part about the four fathers. After all, there is the possibility that it is just an unfortunate case of sample contamination. And you know how men can be."

Lee laughed and then adopted a sober look. "Oh, don't worry. My husband, Nadir, is dead. He had an accident around the time I got pregnant."

"Oh, I'm so sorry to hear that," said the matronly doctor with deep concern in her voice. "Will you be able to get along with four babies?"

"Oh yes. I have several close friends who will help take care of me and of the babies, and one of them is very, very rich."

Lee's limousine was waiting for her outside the doctor's office on 78th Street. Dimitri and Joseph were inside. "Tell us the news," said Dimitri eagerly as Lee got in.

Lee gave each of them a demure kiss. "The best possible news. You're all daddies. Four little girls, each with a different father. I can hardly wait to get home and call Wilson and Hayes." She leaned forward and spoke to the driver, who was smiling as broadly as Dimitri and Joseph. "Laurence, drive us to my apartment and then go over and pick up Mr. Woodrow. After that we're going to have a party, and you're invited."

As the limo turned right on Park Avenue, Laurence replied, "My congratulations to you and the dads, Mrs. Indradzi."

"Thank you, Laurence. It's good to have you working with us."

THE END

Afterword

I finished *Chakra* with two purposes in mind other than simply spinning a tale. First, I wanted to preserve my recollections of a visit I made to Central Asia in 1993 with a few faculty and student colleagues from Columbia University. The Soviet Union had dissolved not long before, and the countries we visited, primarily Uzbekistan and Kyrgyzstan, but also rural parts of Kazakhstan along the highway between Tashkent and Bishkek. These former Soviet republics were just getting familiar with what independence might bring.

Our group interviewed academics and clerics, intellectuals and businessmen, military officers and internal security police. During the week we were in Bishkek, the capital of Kyrgyzstan, the new currency, the *sum*, was introduced. Business slowed to a standstill as people who held rubles, the old currency, were uncertain whether to spend them, hoard them, or exchange them. Some people said the new bills looked like candy wrappers.

Second, I wanted *Chakra* to stand as a memorial to my late wife Lucy, an independent scholar who specialized in the study of the Rg Veda. Her doctoral thesis at Harvard dealt with the mythic struggle between the god Indra and the serpent Vrtra.

While I was writing the first draft in 2002, I time and again assured her that Lee Ingalls was not patterned on her, though Lee was her favorite girl's name and Ingalls was the surname of her doctoral advisor. She was suspicious, however. So I made Lee Ingalls a stiffly upright lady from Connecticut instead of a girl from San Diego who reveled in blues music and could curse like a sailor.

The translations from the Rg Veda quoted in *Chakra* are Lucy's translations, and she went over my description of the mountainside sacrifice closely to ensure its conformance with Vedic tradition. She was amused by the idea of being a priestess of Indra.